Lost in Transition is a work of fiction. Names, characters, places and incidents either are the product of the author's imagination or are used fictitiously. Any resemblance to actual person's, living or dead, events, or locales is entirely coincidental.

Cover Photo by Malcolm Martinez-Wilcox

Cover Design by Maxwell Radford

All text, artwork and photography Copyright © 2014 by Maxwell Radford and Tales From Tha Town Inc.

I0633819

DON'T MISS OUT ON MAXWELL RADFORD'S
EXCITING DEBUT NOVEL ALSO AVALABLE ON
AMAZON.COM!!!

Lost In Transition

A Novel by Maxwell Radford

This book is dedicated to my little brother:

Miles Ward Radford
(He graduated college this year)!!!

A Message before Reading

Do you know who you really are? Your strengths, weaknesses, faults and desires? Are you the same person you were last year? Five years ago? Ten years? How have life's experience's shaped and altered your perception of the world around you? The amount of obstacles, perils and hostility that life can throw at you is limitless in possible events and scenarios.

This book was not written to glamorize any of the violence described within its pages. It is a merely a fictional story that could easily take place in the world we currently exist in. It is an exploration of the negative fallout resulting from a single bad decision and how easy it is to get caught up in the ensuing chaos . You know the feeling. Like your sinking into a black hole and can't stop your doesn't. No matter where you look it's just messed up things happening to you or someone you love. You see evil people run free while innocents suffer. It's the same all over the world. Many of us face the same question each day we walk out our front door; play by the rules or break them?

What would you do? What do you do? And what are the reasons that drive you to take your preferred course? I'm not judging anybody. I've made WAY to many mistakes in my life. Eventually several things happened that made me want to try and lessen the amount of BS I kept experiencing. It was a journey. Some things spiraled into others without warning and you couldn't do nothing about it but deal with it. Who knows why certain things happen. Do we cause then unconsciously with choices throughout our lifetime or are we just the recipients of good or bad luck?

I look at it like this; for every action there is a reaction. I try now to think about what I do before I do it. I think we all should. You never know where you'll end up.

We must not succumb to the ways of the devil. I know it can get and already is fucked up out here but it's still a mostly decent world to live in. It's really all about what you make it to be. We can't ever give up hope because to many already have. We owe it to those who paved the way before us and the ones who will continue to build it behind us. For those of you already enveloped in darkness's blanket, it's never too late to begin the journey back. I'm still on my own path out of corruption so at least you got someone to walk with. Let's do it for the ones who don't have a choice anymore.

Give me the strength to find light
in times of darkness –
Damien's Prayer

Chapter 1

It was a cool and breezy August evening in the Capitol Hill neighborhood of Seattle. Known for its popular, reasonably priced bars and diverse nightlife culture, it was a destination for the young and middle aged people of the city looking for a good time and the occasional fist fight. Hip-hop and rock and roll echoed out on to the streets and flocks of women in tight dresses and make up were everywhere. The street lights lit up the faces of the people passing between them in a yellow glow as the sunlight faded from the sky overhead.

Men in groups of two's or three's or sometimes even solo took their chances and approached the ladies with their pre mediated one liners and smooth music video walks. Other shadier groups of men walked the streets offering varying narcotics that would promise a night full of incredible adventures. For one of these men however the last thing on his mind now was money.

Small time drug dealer Roland Stone knew he was in deep shit. A dark skinned man of twenty-one who stood six feet two inches and weighed an impressive two hundred and thirty pounds with a bald head, he wasn't someone people readily started trouble with. A member of a local gang that operated mainly in Seattle's Central District, Roland hadn't graduated high school but had managed to scratch out a decent living selling weed and ecstasy to the bar hopping crowds that gathered on Capitol Hill. Every weekend night he was a regular amid the Capitol Hill bar scene and for the most part made a decent amount of money. Now however, his night had taken an unexpected turn for the worse.

Roland had been standing next to a hotdog stand wolfing down his food and eyeing a nice looking Asian girl with waist length black hair when all the whiskey and coke's he had been drinking earlier finally caught up with him. Saying goodbye to his friend, Roland had jogged down a couple blocks till he found a decent dark alley he wouldn't be seen in. Walking down to the most secluded part of the alley, he had unzipped his fly and let loose a golden shower down upon the garbage bags lining the wall. A noise alerted him to another presence in the alley and he had looked up just in time to spot two figures making their way quickly towards him with faces covered in ski masks and black gloves on their hands. *It's a fucking Robbery*, was Roland's first thought but there wasn't any time to keep guessing. The fight had started quickly and silently with Roland being evenly matched against his shorter, lighter opponents. But the effects of the alcohol were beginning to impair his motor skills and Roland knew if he didn't make his escape soon, he'd be eating concrete in less than a couple minutes.

Ducking a wild haymaker aimed at the right side of his face, Roland's left hand lashed out and caught his attacker square in the mouth knocking him back a few paces. A hard blow to his left cheekbone reminded Roland that he currently had to defend himself from not one but two masked men attempting to beat the shit out of him in a dark alley behind a popular bar. Faking a jab to the face, Roland caught the second attacker with a swift uppercut to the stomach. Doubling over, the man backed off slightly gasping for breath and clutching his stomach.

Roland took stock of his situation as he and his two assailants eyed each with no more than five feet of dirty concrete separating them.

"What the fuck do you niggas want man?" he yelled out at the top of his voice, hoping to attract attention. "I aint got nothing but some dollar bills on me so you shit out of luck!"

One of his attacker's heads turned towards the alley entrance, apparently looking to see if anyone had noticed Roland's yell. Seizing his chance, Roland leaped forward and dealt the young man vicious right-cross to the head. The masked youth fell back against the fence and collapsed on the pavement. Turning towards his remaining opponent, Roland rushed forward again and managed to sweep the startled youth into a brutal bear hug. The young man struggled and squirmed but was no match against the older man's brute strength.

Walking towards the opposite side of the alley, Roland threw the still struggling teenager head first into one of the many metal dumpsters lining the alley.

WHOOMP!

The dull thud from the impact of the youth's body onto steel frame vibrated through the alley. Aiming a kick at the stranger's midsection, Roland snarled down at his would be assailant.

"Bitch you aint so tough now is you! Tryna run up on me you must be crazy! Nigga I'm from…"

The dazed man on the ground never did get to hear where Roland was from, but it wouldn't have mattered anyways. At that precise moment the other masked attacker that Roland had thought he'd knocked out came back into the fight wielding a pair of brass knuckles on his right hand.

Whap!

A horrible pain exploded in Roland's mouth as the first punch landed. He instantly felt the warm taste of blood. Both of his lips were split wide open straight down the middle. The force of the blow had staggered him but hadn't knocked him out. He was however in no condition to defend himself against the next punch which had been perfectly aimed to land on the same spot as the first one even as Roland's hands flew up to protect his face.

Thud! Splat!

Nothing in Roland's twenty-five years; not the whooping's from mom when he was a kid, his gang initiation beating or the time he'd broken his ankle in a football game had prepared him for the pain that was now flashing through his brain and blotting out the rest of his senses. The second punch from the brass knuckled hand had split the front of his gums and knocked out three of his teeth.

3

Choking from the blood filling his mouth, he collapsed against the brick wall of the alley holding his mouth with both hands and slid down the wall into a sitting position. The man he had knocked to the ground struggled back to his feet.

Now both of his attackers stood over him. Roland's vision was so blurred from the pain and the tears streaming from his eyes that he couldn't make out much. As he wiped his eyes with one of his bloody hands, Roland saw that the man he had thrown against the metal trash can was now in possession of the brass knuckles. He watched in slow horror as the man slipped them onto his left hand and then stared down at him.

"Pleeb! I hab money! Dwugs! No more plebe!" he managed to gasp out despite having a mouth choked full of blood. The young man just shook his head and punched his knuckled left hand into the palm of his right hand. He leaned down closer to Roland and spoke into his ear.

""It aint even about the money homie! You been way past overdue. Now, it's just about the disrespect, and that's something you can't take back. You're lucky you're supposed to live through this. Oh and Money Mike says you can keep the fucking pills."

Roland closed his eyes relived at what he heard yet knowing the worst was still to come.

Cocking his arm back the young man hit Roland viciously in the face three more times. He collapsed unconscious onto the pavement, blood flowing freely from what was left of his ruined mouth, and his now broken nose. Bending down, the young man tossed the brass knuckles to his partner and began searching Roland's body as if he were patting him down for drugs. The other young man gazed down at the brass knuckles, now covered in blood and bits of tooth and his heart beat went up a couple notches. He looked around nervously as his friend stood back up holding a fat roll of bills.

"What the fuck Chris? I thought you said we were just going to come talk to this guy! Not fuck him up and rob him!"

The dark skinned young man called Chris only eyed his friend closely and held out half of the money to him. After a moment's hesitation the other youth slowly took the offered bills.

"Yeah we tried to talk to him and you see how that went. He swung first anyways so technically this was all just self-defense."

Chris glanced down at Roland's unconscious form and spit on his head.

"Stupid mothafucka should have paid up or stopped selling his shit here anyways. He's lucky Money Mike sent us down here to deal with him instead of coming to see about him personally."

Looking down at the beaten man with the shredded bloody mouth and badly bruised face, Chris's friend wasn't so sure lucky was the word. More like misfortune. Exiting the alley, the two friends quickly blended into the crown moving up and down Pike Street. Arriving at a nearby bus top the two friends sat down side by on one of the small benches inside of the rain shelter. Any random person passing buy them at that moment would have thought the two youngsters were brothers so similar in appearance that they were.

Covered head to toe in black clothes, the only notable difference was their difference in skin color. While one was dark chocolate brown the other had a light almost caramel hue to his skin. Both were of average height and build, something of which mattered little to them since neither boy was involved in sports of any kind.

Fishing a single cigarette that had been badly bent during the fight out of his hooded sweatshirt's big front pocket, Chris fired up the stogie with a black lighter his friend handed him and leaned back against the bus shelter wall. The two friends spent a quiet five minutes passing the Newport back and forth as they watched a couple buses pull up, off load passengers and acquire more then pull off back on their constant never ending journey through the city.

As the last of the burning tobacco reached the filter tip, Chris took the cigarette from his mouth and flicked it into the street. Standing up the two friends shook hands, Chris eyeing his partner closely.

"Don't get bent out of shape about this all right D? You helped me out so don't feel bad about that fool back there because he would of got it regardless and I would have been at least one of the people doing it either way so good looks on helping keep my black ass safe. I'm going tell Money Mike about this too so you can bet he'll be appreciative. Shit, he already likes you. Besides, Anthony would have been proud."

At the mention of their deceased friend's name, the caramel skinned youths face took on a more understanding look. Anthony had been the oldest member of their three man terror squad. Tall, muscular and an extremely talented boxer, he had been a ferocious street fighter and had taught D everything he knew about hand to hand combat but had been strangely quiet and shy when it came to dealing with people outside of his small circle.

He had been killed two months ago while attempting to break up a fight at a house party at his girlfriend's house. One of the young men involved in the fight had pulled out a gun and Anthony had the bad timing of running in between them at the exact moment the trigger was pulled. He had died instantly from a gunshot wound to the head.

The shooter, a hot headed youngster named Devontay had disappeared from sight after running from the party and hadn't been in months. But every member of Duce Trey was on the alert for any word about his whereabouts. There was little question of his fate once the gang got their hands on him but so far he was nowhere to be found. Anthony and Chris were members of the same gang but Anthony had always tried to keep D out of that life. Now he was gone.

His girlfriend was a petite but extremely curvaceous chocolate skinned young girl with long natural black hair named Latoya and she had been devastated. She now seemed a shell of her former fun loving jovial self, drifting from class to class like a robot not really paying attention to anything the teachers said. She was popular so she always had a crowd of females around her offering advice and counsel but the only people she really talked to were D and Chris. And that was outside of school away from prying eyes and itching ears. Anthony Jr. was a small mirror image of his father and had been born the previous year and it was in this baby that Latoya had thrown her life into now.

School was quickly fading in her rearview mirror as the situation she had been left in slowly began taking its toll on her. She worked a job as well as going to school to provide for her son but there still was never enough money. Damien made it a point to stop by regularly. He always gave her some of the money he hustled up and never asked for anything in return. He was fine with a plate of her incredible home cooking. Besides, she called on him for all her weed.

Looking at Chris, D couldn't help but feel a cold sense of menace about his friend. Quick to anger, easily dealing out violent acts with no remorse and a detached acceptance for the life he was getting sucked deeper into by the day were making him more and more dangerous to be around, But he was one of the only real friends D had left.

"You know I got you bruh," D said finally after a short pause.

The corners of Chris's mouth jumped slightly. He never really smiled, (unless he was laughing uncontrollably), his mouth stayed locked in an almost continuous frown but when he was amused by something you could see the corners of his mouth twitch. As if he was about to smile but caught himself just in time. Tapping his chest with his fist two times, Chis turned around and strolled off into the darkness of the night.

D whose full name was Damien Marvin Gram, looked after his friend for a minute then turned around and walked slowly off down Pike street. Reaching a popular pizza joint, D turned right off the main street and strolled up a dark residential street until he reached a secluded looking parking lot. Going to the far side of the parking lot furthest away from the street, D sank down against the back of a Jeep Cherokee, his entire body overcome by a violent shaking. It lasted all of thirty seconds then was gone as quick as it came.

Getting shakily to his feet, D wiped his sweaty forehead with the back of his hand then wobbled unsteadily off in the direction of his apartment building which was still a seven block walk from his current position on Yale and Olive. It had been a rough six months dealing with the death of one his closest friends. But unknown to D, Anthony's murder had only been the tip of the ice berg. In five days, D would begin his Senior year at Central High school and everything he thought he knew about himself was about to become ancient history. Life turns boys into men. It turns others into monsters!

Chapter 2

"...And so as you prepare for your fourth and final year here with us at Central High, we the staff will do our best to help see that all of you are fully prepared for the challenges awaiting you and the experiences you will undergo whether you decide to further your studies in school or join the ranks of the working people. Please, if you need advice we are all here to talk and provide counsel or give advice to you should you seek it. Thank you and congratulations seniors! Now let's make this a year to remember!"

A scattered halfhearted applause rang out through the auditorium as principal of Central High, a middle aged black woman with silver hair and a thin body named Helena Weathers stepped down off the podium and exited the stage of the auditorium. A firm believer in education, Ms. Weathers had been born and raised in Seattle and had decided to pursue a degree in education upon arriving at the University of Washington in the fall of 1980. After teaching History at several local high schools for the next twenty years, she became a qualified principal after completing her training.

Jobs were already scarce but determined to prove she was capable of running a school Ms. Weathers had taken the first job opening that became available. And so in 2000 she became the first female principal ever at Central High. The school was far from outstanding. A big two story building made primarily of brick; it had served as a middle school until its closure in the 1970's. After a heavy bit of remodeling inside it reopened five years later as a high school.

Located in between Capitol Hill and Chinatown, the schools primary purpose was to give lower income families from Seattle's South, West and central areas a place to send their kids that was outside of their neighborhood and therefore supposedly a chance for kids to get away from the various problems that plagued most of the areas they lived in mainly street gangs and drugs.

But the plan had backfired. Mixing in so many kids from different sides of the city, ethnicity's and backgrounds had come with its own set of problems. The first major problem to spring up had been violence before and after school and in the hallways between classes. Young gang members who would normally never cross paths with one another were now forced to see each other five days a week. While rules and regulations laid down by their respective leaders mostly prevented any new beef from being started, there was more than enough current and active rivalries, turf disputes, bad vibes, owed money and open hostility between different sets that any peace that was successfully avoided was cancelled out by what wasn't. Fights were becoming all too common at Central High and nobody knew what to do about it.

With the gangs of course came drugs. Weed, coke, mushrooms, acid and ecstasy were the most common. The surrounding campus had become no better than open air drug markets and kids who had avoided becoming involved in the gang disputes were finding themselves becoming hooked on various narcotics in their effort not to become a victim of the violence. But the drug world came with its own set of rules. Dealers who didn't belong to a gang were routinely subject to robbing's and beatings by anyone who thought they had found an easy target with no possible repercussions that would come. Unless the dealer was tough they usually got their shit took and couldn't do a thing about it.

Dealers that were part of gangs had it a little better but not by much. More known by the populace they had to deal with slightly more drama but were better equipped to handle it. Usually nobody messed with a dealer who was in a gang except other gang members looking to build their reputation. Those encounters usually ended a lot more bloody as weapons were twice as likely to be used.

Apart from gangs and drugs, school morale was probably the most damaging aspect of Central High. Poor performance on standardized tests, graduation rates and even in sports had led to a massive loss in funding over the past few years. The schools Soccer, baseball and track and field teams had all been gotten rid of. Basketball and football, being the only teams that actually preformed good and had high attendance ratings were saved and even then, a good half of the football games usually ended with students from Central High getting into massive brawls with students from the opposing school. In fact, apart from the school dances, which to this day remained miraculously violence free, engaging in riots for any reason seemed to be all of the student's favorite and most rewarding pastime regardless of race gender or gang affiliation.

It wasn't the worst school by district standards.

These problems were by no means just regulated to Central High. Almost every major high school in the Seattle had the same problems more or less. But in recent years, Central High had indeed made the headlines of local newspapers more than a few times and more often than not, it wasn't for anything good. Many in the district viewed it as a failed experiment but Ms. Weathers was determined to do what she could to turn the school's reputation around. She just hadn't know where to start. But she was trying.

So far, Ms. Weathers had been able to accomplish precious little against these outside forces besides hiring security guards and installing cameras in as many places as she could, which were precious few. In truth, those changes had done little besides help make the school feel more like a prison then an education facility. The graduation rate was at an all-time low of 60 percent.

Even as she had gave her enthusiastic and hopeful speech, Ms. Weathers couldn't help notice that thus years senior class had only about half of the students it had started with three years ago. It was all she could do to keep from crying. Arriving at her office, Ms. Weathers instructed her secretary not to bother her for a while as she had some important letters to write.

Closing the door and locking it behind her, Ms. Weathers sank into her soft black swivel chair, turned herself to face the wall and broke down crying and sobbing into her hands, tears of sadness and frustration for a generation that she apparently could do nothing for cascading down her face in an unstoppable rivers of pain and helplessness.

Chapter 3

Walking out of the auditorium after Principal Weathers had given her speech, D had already forgotten most of what she had said. Joining the mass of bodies flowing out into the schools hallways, D began making his way towards the school's gym. Truthfully, he had spent most of the assembly staring down at the handful of bills Chris had handed him after beating up that drug dealer last week. Drops of blood had dried onto the green paper and D had been strangely mesmerized by the bloodied bills. He would have thought he'd be disgusted by the thought of carrying around money with someone else's blood on it but he found himself actually sort of proud. He'd never punched anyone with brass knuckles before and the damage he'd inflicted because of them had been a terrifying but also exciting in a way. There was a savage pleasure in carrying out violent acts, a sort of calming reassurance in the power that lay inside of one's mind and body.

He was an average sized youth. Well, the doctor said he was average but it seemed to D like everyone else in the entire city was taller than him. His rigid workout regime kept him fit and muscular so he wasn't entirely outmatched by other taller youths. His dark hair was braided back into cornrows but because of the shortness of his hair his hang time was at an all-time low. The ends of his braids were basically tight against the back of his neck. Like most of his friends he was dressed almost entirely in black.

Black low top Nike's with black shoe laces covered his feet. A baggy pair of dark blue jeans hung low on his waist and an extra-large sized black tee shirt covered his frame. A black windbreaker covered his shirt and on his head sat a black Seattle Mariners hat with a White S symbol. His almond shaped eyes studied bodies moving casually through the halls ahead of him, no one on any apparent rush to get to the first class of the day. His dark heavy eyebrows gave him a serious look but anybody that knew him was well aware of his good humor.

"Yo D! Hey fool, wait up a second!"

Stopping in mid step and turning his body halfway around, D spotted a familiar big hulking form strolling towards him, a full head and shoulders above any other person in the hallway at that moment. Stopping just in front of him the big bodied young man stared down at D with a mixture of amusement and pity etched across his face. He extended a massive hand down and D shook it warmly.

"Sup Sumo? What you got that sad look on your face for? Too much sushi for breakfast? You got salmonella poising? I tried to tell yo ass bout eating all that raw fish!"

Sumo just shook his head and laughed at D's words. Half black and half Japanese, it was his tall, wide, and extremely round shape that had given rise to his nickname. His real name was Jarvis but nobody ever called him that anymore. Sumo and D had met while attending the same elementary school as kids and had reunited at Central High. They didn't leave in the same neighborhood or hang with the same crowds but they're mutual love of weed and money had guided them into an easy friendship mostly based on business but also out of respect. They'd done a lot of dirt together.

"Nigga if your little ass actually followed a healthy diet instead of eating all that fast food you stuff yourself with, you might actually grow some inches. You still the same height you was in freshman year that's just sad. Looking like Muhammad Ali's younger anorexic brother. You look sick bro! We need to get you on a weight gain plan!"

Damien frowned and acted as if he was going to walk past Sumo but instead turned around quick as lightning and took a wild swing at Sumo's face. A huge hand stopped his fist from doing any damage however. Grinning from ear to ear as he watched his smaller friend squirming in anger trying to unsuccessfully escape his bone crushing grip, Sumo gave D's wrist a quick jerk then released him. D stepped back rubbing his wrist and looking sourly up at Sumo.

"Not fair you big gorilla! Or should I say panda bear? Seriously though why are you so big when both your parents are midgets?"

Sumo shrugged and just continued grinning while D, snorting in fake disgust, motioned with his uninjured hand for Sumo to follow him. Together they navigated the crowded hallway filled with the loud unintelligible noise of teenage conversation filled their ears. Jokes, insults, stories of last night's adventure and tales of sexual conquests flew thick and fast through the air. Bodies of all shades of black brown and white gathered together and marveled at the changes that summer had brought upon each other. New curves and muscles were everywhere!

Reaching an empty classroom, D and Sumo ducked inside, D closing and locking the door behind them. Going to the back of the class room, they sat down in desks in the last row and turned to face each other. Sumo clapped his hands together excitedly.

"So, what's on the agenda for this year my nigga? I'm not even going to lie all that partying this summer done left ya boy a little low on funds."

"Nothing to worry about homie," said D taking a composition notebook out of his backpack, "I've been doing some research."

Flipping open his note book, D stopped at a page that had several different names of neighborhoods written down one below the other in a list that went down the whole page. Some names were crossed off while others had lines or circles around them. Still others had stars, checks, plus and or a minus sign next to them. It looked like a nonsense but it apparently made sense to D because he took one look at the page on got down to business speaking in a surprisingly serious and businesslike tone.

"So as you can see here, I've pretty much written down all the neighborhoods within a reasonable e distance from downtown since that's where all the buses from every side of town converge at. Now first, I'll tell you about these crossed off names. Since we hit up West Seattle a little too much last year, I'm thinking we need to stay away from that area for a while. What you think?"

Everything was always a democratic decision with the two friends. Each person made their point and the other was always given a chance to respond. There was no shot caller in their working relationship. Just two friends trying to make some money. After a short pause Sumo nodded his head signaling his agreement.

"I don't see any reason to be hot about shit. But if you're thinking that way, then the South End is out of the question too. Especially with all the other shit going on this year, I don't know if we want to get caught slipping in the dark homie!" Sumo's voice was surprisingly light for a young man of his size. Unknown to most, he had been in in the church choir as a young boy. He usually chose to withhold this information.

"And my neighborhood is really no bueno right now. It aint just us out there hitting licks at night. There's a hundred other fools running around trying to come up right now so the police are the least of our worries over there. "

D looked thoughtfully down at the names written on the page, frowned slightly, and then crossed several more out with his pen.

"Good idea Sumo. Aight well all is still not lost. I've been doing some bus riding and scoping out different areas over the summer and I've found a few potential jack pots!" D nudged Sumo with an elbow and pointed to the names with the circles around them.

"We've already done the West Side, the South End even Capitol Hill so what's the only side of town we aint been on?"

"Umm...the north?" offered Sumo, shrugging his giant shoulders. D slapped Sumo's arm in excitement.

"Yeah nigga, the North End! I've found some seriously low key neighborhoods where not much goes on and police presence is at a minimum. And some of these neighborhoods is pretty big. Big and quiet! And full of fancy ass cars!"

16

At the mention of the cars, Sumo's eyes lit up in anticipation of the possible fortune to come.

"You know, China Sam done updated his car list. It might be worth getting in touch with his nephew to see what models he's after now."

"Aww, nigga!" exclaimed D excitedly, "that's what I was just finna tell you about! Now I've already patrolled some of these streets in Queen Anne, Ballard and Magnolia and boy, you can see cars fresh from the lot with the stickers still in the windows parked right on the street! No license plate or nothing. I'm talking the fresh newly released models!

"But besides that, there's hella regular cars too so I know well have some easy scores if nothing else. Comfortable ass white folks probably leave their car doors unlocked every night! So if we have to, getting a stoley will be the last thing we'll have to worry about."

Sumo was now rubbing his hands together, his eyes squinted so tight they were almost shut. It was at these times that D would say Sumo's Asian side was taking control and he was about to transform into some kind of Mega Robot Nigga Gundam Wing Super Decepdacon. Sumo usually put D in a head lock for those kinds of comments.

"So where to first?" asked Sumo as D closed the book and put it away in his backpack. Zipping it shut, D slung his bag over his shoulder as the two youngsters got up and prepared to leave the empty class room.

"I was thinking we'd hit up the West Side of Queen Anne first. It's more spread out then the rest of the hill and there's more house's then apartment buildings so more cars out on the street. Less dead end streets too so less chance of getting cornered by the police if we have to run."
Sumo nodded his head in agreement.

"Sound's good. What night you tryna do the first run?"

D only had to think for a few seconds.

"How about tonight?"

Sumo grinned widely.

"That's what the fuck I'm talking about. I aint tryna waste no time either."

The two shook hands then headed towards the class room door. D stopped to erase the chalkboard. Walking out into the hallway they looked up as the bell signaling the start of classes rang its shrill tones throughout the school. Digging into one his jeans pockets, Sumo withdrew a crumpled piece of paper and opened it up. Frowning, he stuffed the paper back into his pocket.

"Shit bro, they gave me Mrs. Peterson!"

D shook his head in sympathy.

"Math in the morning huh? Sorry dawg. On the bright side I heard she's about to have a baby soon so you might only have to put up with her for a little bit. That sexy Latina girl that was always coming last year might even come back again."

Sumo looked dreamily into the air as he remembered the brown haired golden skin beauty that had captured every male student's imagination last year. Bumping fists with D, he headed off towards his classroom. Taking out his own schedule, D glanced down at the paper and saw that his first class was Senior Language Arts. From prior knowledge, D knew that this meant they would be studying Shakespeare plays and the art of the written word. A perfect class to go to after smoking a blunt. D turned the opposite direction that Sumo had walked in and headed for a secluded stairway he had found as a sophomore that was devoid of security patrols. He had ten minutes before the teacher would mark him as absent. Plenty of time for a quick smoke!

Later that night…

Everything was still and quiet on Queen Anne that night. It was strangely warm for September, the temperature hovering around 65 degrees Fahrenheit. Whether it was Mother Nature in a good mood or just global warming doing its dirty was a debate that nobody's mind was currently involved in. As long as it wasn't raining the general population was happy. Tonight, a light jacket or sweatshirt was all one needed to keep the wind chill away.

On the west side of Queen Anne, two dark figures dressed in matching black Dickie suits and black beanie's moved silently down 8th avenue, each on a different side of the street. Each time they passed a vehicle they would stop and do a quick survey of the car or truck. Usually they would stop for a second, do a quick look over and move on down the street to the next target.

Sometimes however it seemed as one of the figures would find what they were looking for. They would stop and signal their partner over and set about breaking into the car. Usually a slim piece of metal called a "jimmy" or one of several homemade "keys" had to be implemented in order to open the doors but more often than not on this night, the two thieves were finding an abundance of doors that hadn't even been locked. While one man searched the car for valuables, the other would stand watch for police or watchful civilians. Once all valuables were stuffed into one of the two duffel bags they had hanging from the shoulders, the door was quietly closed and they were off to the next target. Having started together as sophomores, D and Sumo had found there to be a lucrative trade in raiding people's cars at night.

Electronics were the usual haul but drugs and money and other valuables also came up frequently. And sometimes if a car happened to be wanted by one of the many chop shop owners, a real score could be found in actually stealing a vehicle. But since that put neighborhoods on the cops radar faster than simple break in's, they chose to keep actual Grand Theft Auto to a minimum. D's motto was; if it wasn't worth five hundred dollars or more on anybody's list, it wasn't worth their time.

It was approaching four in the morning when the two accomplices ducked into an alley and crouched down beside two large garbage cans. Panting slightly, D pushed his beanie up high and wiped sweat off of his forehead. Sumo pulled a pack of Newport's out of his hoody pocket and took one out. He offered the pack to D but he declined. Reaching up to his right ear, D pulled half of a blunt that he'd been smoking on earlier out from behind his ear and stuck it in his mouth. Sumo looked from the blunt in D's hand to the cigarette in his and decided to put it back in the box.

As D sparked up the blunt, Sumo set about rummaging through his bag looking at some of the merchandise they had acquired so far. It had been a decent night: two iPods, a subwoofer, some amps, a giant bag of quarters, four radios, and a sleek looking black laptop that looked brand new. All of which they would most likely sell before the week was over. Central High was a black marketers dream.

Looking over at his smaller friend, Sumo took the blunt that D was holding out to him and took a long slow hit off the strong weed. As his lungs tightened up from the harsh THC packed smoke, Sumo breathed out a fat cloud in a heavy sigh of relief.

"Thank god you brought a swisher with you D. I aint seen a store since that one we passed three hours ago. And that one was closed! How do people get snacks around here without any corner stores?"

D shrugged. He wasn't really too concerned with the problem. Looking up in the sky, he searched for and located Orion's Belt just down and to the left of the North Star. D sometimes wondered what it would be like to smoke a blunt on the moon with nothing but the stars for company.

A solitary person by nature, D imagined it be a welcome experience. A tap on the shoulder reminded D that now probably wasn't the best time to wander off into fantasy land. His mind always did that, randomly going off into some other dimension whenever he got bored with what was going on in front of him.

Taking the blunt back from Sumo's outstretched fingers he took a long pull on the blunt and looked over at Sumo's face which was half hidden by shadows.

"Did you say something?" he asked.

"Yeah," said Sumo, "I was asking how come you stopped me from going in that Escalade that was parked outside of that big corner house back there. There could have been some good shit in there!"

"Umm no real reason," said D, "I just didn't get a good vide from that truck. It looked real nice but in a straight-from-the-factory kind of way. I bet you the owner likes to be on top of his shit. He's probably super anal about food in his ride so he'd obviously be concerned with its safety. He probably got the most up to date car alarm system, money can buy!"

Sumo didn't look entirely convinced but he didn't look like he cared that much either.

"Your call," he said, still checking out the nights haul "I'm not tripping at all. There's probably at least four hundred dollars' worth of stuff here plus the bag of quarters. There's got to be another fifty or so dollars in there alone. And I can't believe you found that bag of powder in that fucking minivan!"

D grinned.

"Damn soccer moms right? She gonna be itching tomorrow!"

Sumo bellowed out a quick laugh.

"You know anybody who's gonna want that yayo?" he asked D

D thought for a second. He didn't usually deal with cocaine. But he knew somebody that did.

"Naw I don't got a buyer right now but I will by tomorrow. I'm gonna go see somebody that can help me out"

Sumo nodded still looking through his duffel bag.

"Not bad for the first night. Where to next D ?"

Damien glanced up at the night sky again and noticed the eastern edge was getting a brighter hue to it.

"We should probably call it a night fam. Don't want to press it too much. Besides we've barely hit one fourth of this area so we still got plenty opportunities to come up over here." Finishing the blunt, D stubbed it out with his heel and stood up. Zipping his bag closed, Sumo stood up as well.

"What keys did you bring out tonight?"

D checked his key ring.

"I got one for any 1990's Honda and one for 1980's style Toyota Camry's. That's if you not tryna use the tools."

Sumo snapped his fingers.

"I saw an old Camry about five blocks back outside this old brick house on 11th avenue. It's in the driveway but I know that thing don't got an alarm on it. We just gotta be in and out real quick!"

Damien sighed in relief. His legs were tired from they're all night trek and he was looking forward to getting at least a few hours of sleep before school in the morning. He patted Sumo on the shoulder and gestured for him to start walking.

"Lead the way bro."

Chapter 4

D's eyes snapped open a split second before the alarm on his bedside clock went off. Slamming his hand down on the cancel button, D rolled over in his bed and began rubbing the crust out of his eyes. Throwing his heavy quilt to the side, D swung his legs over the side of the bed and sat up yawning heavily. It had been a long walk home last night and he'd only managed to get about an hour and a half of sleep.

Getting unsteadily to his feet, D stumbled across his room to the closet door. He'd already chosen his outfit the previous night before sneaking out to meet Sumo. Black Dickie pants, a pair of black Chuck Taylor shoes, extra-large white tee, a plain black hooded sweatshirt and his favorite black Mariners hat with the white S on the front. Glancing in the mirror at his sleepy eyed face, D shook his head slightly. He needed a new occupation. This all night creeping shit never did sit well with him. It was low risk true but it was also low pay. True enough there were sometimes big finds that led to serious cash but the time in between those big scores was growing. He was glad he almost had enough to re up with his weed connect.

Being a speedy dresser, it only took D ten minutes and he was fully clothed swinging his backpack onto his shoulders. Standing in front of his mirror, he made a few final adjustments and he was ready to hit the streets. Quietly, he inched open the door to his room and stepped out into the hallway.

D resided in a ground floor two bedroom apartment with his parents, a black couple in their early forties named Marcus and Stacey. Both were born and raised in Seattle and had been long time residents of the Central District and Capitol Hill areas.

They had been on the move a lot during D's younger days due to his father's tendency to slip in and out of alcoholism. He had made some improvements over the last five years and his training as a cook meant he always had a job. He currently worked as a prep cook at a popular seafood place on the waterfront. Seattle was a huge restaurant town.

D's mom Stacey was a nurse at Harborview Medical Center and made decent money but spent long hours away from home at work. His home wasn't an awful place, just cold and empty at times. His dad wasn't the best at communicating or expressing feelings and it was a trait that D seemed to have inherited. The two men mostly avoided one another. Previously that week, Marcus had informed D that at the end of the year he would have to start looking for his own place. And a job.

Closing his bedroom door behind him, D glanced down the narrow hallway towards the living room. He could just see the end of one of his dad's feet sticking out over the arm of the couch closest to him. Whenever his dad slept on the couch it meant one of two things; either his mom had kicked him out of their room for being too drunk or she hadn't come home and he passed out watching the television. Today it was obvious what had happened.

Creeping down the hallway until he stood directly beside his sleeping father, D reached down and scooped the remote off of the ground. Switching the power off on the TV, he placed the remote on the coffee table directly in front of his Dad's snoring face. Straightening up, D stared down at the man who had brought him into this world. Tall and muscular but with a sizable stomach, Marcus Gram looked like a football player who'd been out of the game for more than a few years. At forty two , he was far from frail but by no means was he in shape. When he wasn't drunk he was kind enough. But lately that was a rare occurrence.

His mother Stacey was piece of work. She was a slightly chubby but very attractive forty one year old with black hair that stopped at her shoulders and big brown eyes that gave her a friendly appearance to people who were just meeting her. Kind and outgoing at work, all that changed when she was at home. The long hours were taking a toll on here and she was often rude and irritable when she got home. D had quickly learned to occupy his time elsewhere when she came home in one of her moods.

Turning away from the sleeping form of his dad, D walked quickly towards the front door. Unlocking and opening the door with the stealth of a professional robber, D exited his house without making a sound, carefully closing the door behind him.

Central High School...

"Yo wassup D! Good looks on the speakers for my car essay I was outside banging those shits this morning in the parking lot!"

"You already know Hector, no problem! Don't get go getting your shit impounded this year man I'ma need some rides to the house parties!"

"D! Wassup bro damn I been looking for you all day! Where the Kush at?"

"Sorry homie it's all bad right now. I'm getting some tonight though so tomorrow I got you for sure. Come find me at lunchtime I'll be by the benches out in front of the school."

"Hey Damien!"

"Oh shit what's up Courtney? How was your summer?"

"Good. Listen, you still got that pink IPod you were telling me about this morning?"

"Yup. I was saving it for you."

"Shut up boy you just saying that."

"Naw for real!"

"Whatever. Meet me by girl's bathroom on the second floor at the start of lunch. Gotta get some money my friend owes me first."

"I'll be there"

Flashing him a bright smile, Courtney, tall, black and beautiful Courtney, turned away from D and walked away down the hall, shapely hips switching from side to side causing more than a few heads to turn and even inviting a few cat calls. D watched her go, wishing he had the courage to ask her out. She was real popular and from the crowd of guys she usually went

25

after, D figured she was out of his league. No one said he couldn't look though!

Turning from her retreating coke bottle shaped figure, D turned and walked slowly towards his fourth period Science class located in the second floor. It had been a productive morning. Old friends had been shouting at him all day and it had been good to reunite with people he hadn't seen in the last couple months. As soon as he had stepped foot in Central High's hallways D had begun advertising all of last night's merchandise to his fellow returning students. As he was already know as a possessor of wanted materials, other kids would seek him out half the time just to see if he had anything worth buying. And he usually did.

So far, he'd managed to sell everything but an IPod and two of the car radios and it sounded like Courtney was set on buying the IPod. So that just left the radios. D had cashed in the quarters at a Safeway while on his way to School that morning. It had totaled fifty dollars in all, ten more than Sumo's original guess. After the fee, D walked out with exactly forty five dollars. Combining that with the money he had already made so far and D had around three hundred dollars in his pocket!

He'd figured he'd make another thirty to fifty dollars on the remaining IPod depending on how much he could squeeze out of Courtney. The coke he had plans for elsewhere and had stashed in a bush off school property. Deciding to throw the two radios in his locker, D turned around and headed towards the building s North wing and the senior's locker hall.

Opening a door into one of the main stairwells, D was about to jog up the stairs when his nose caught the sweet dank smell of burning marijuana wafting up from the bottom level coupled with the sound of harsh coughs. Peering over the railing, D saw a group of about five black male teenagers gathered together at the foot of the stairs passing a blunt around in a circle. D stared quietly for a second.

They were all rough looking individuals in big oversized coats and hoody's and baggy jeans with hats pulled low over their eyes. One of them, a tall chocolate skinned young man with a heavy hooded eyes that made him look half asleep happened to look up as if sensing D's gaze and looked him directly I the eyes. D nodded to him and then hastily made his way up the stairs towards his locker. He might have had a reputation as a hustler and money getter, but it was the gangsters and shooters that really ran Central High.

While most young people in high school definitely had an understanding and deep love of money, it was rare to find those who actually appreciated it. What this meant was that while plenty of young people could get their hands on money, it was extremely unlikely that they would have any left within a couple of days. There was therefore an expectation that while one might have a pocket full of loot one day it was a general understanding they would be back dead broke the next. That's why the only money getters that actually got respect where the ones that continually had money in their pockets.

Gangsters and Shooters however operated on different principals entirely. Their main focus was not the accumulation of money but receiving and maintaining respect through fear and intimidation. If they wanted something they took it. If a person said anything they didn't like, a fight was sure to start within the next few seconds. They were even more respected then the drug dealers and because of the sheer number of gangs at the school, and their conflicting relationships with other it was impossible to be cool with one group and not be labeled an enemy by another. D just tried his best to stay on cool terms with as many people as he could. And avoid those he couldn't.

"…one hundred thirty, one hundred forty and one hundred and fifty!"
Finishing counting out Sumo's half of the money, D handed the cash to his big friend. It was lunchtime and they two were outside at a bus stop right across the street from the high school. It was a guaranteed way to keep unwanted eyes from spying on their transaction. D watched as Sumo counted out the bills in his hand again and then slipped them into his front right pants pocket. Extending his hand he shook D's offered hand warmly.

"Damn homie not too bad for the first run of the year. I still can't believe you sold all that shit already."

"Hey, it's all supply and demand. Supply what they want and they will demand more. Shit after all that work we put in last year I had people coming up to me expecting me to have shit for them. At this rate we'll be rich before December."

"Ha, I'm cool with that. Ya boy seriously needs a car this year. 1986 box Chevy on 22's nigga! I'll be the freshest thing driving through the CD!"

D smiled softly at his friend's ambition.

"I aint mad at ya Sumo. I think I'm just gonna stack my bread this year. I'm trying to get the fuck out my house mane my parents keep tripping over little shit and we don't even see each other like that."

Standing up together, the two friends shook hands and prepared to head back to school. D was having second thoughts about returning to school. He hadn't made as much as he had thought he would from the night's activities. Even with the money Chris had given him for his part in Roland's punishment, he was still a good three hundred dollars short of his goal of eight hundred. But all was not lost. He knew of a way he could easily make up the difference. But if he expected to get his weed before the sun dropped, he had to go now.

"What class you got next?" asked Sumo.

D shook his head.

"I got a weak ass art class and I can't even draw. I think I'm going to call it a day right now. I got some business to attend to downtown. I'm trying to re-up tonight and I'm still short some dollars."

"What, you finna hit some cars up in broad daylight?" Sumo looked surprised that D would be willing to risk getting caught in such an obviously bad time of day.

"Hell naw Sumo why would I be downtown breaking into cars? My Patna downtown deals with that white so I'm taking that lil package down to him to see what he can do with it. If I'm not back before schools over I'll call you about our next mission night. I'll have your share of cash from the yayo tomorrow. "

Sumo nodded, then he got a slightly uncomfortable look on his face.

28

"Sorry about Anthony D. He was a good guy. He's missed by a lot of us and just so you know, it wasn't any of my niggaz that shot him."

D looked up at his big friend and saw genuine regret in his small black eyes. He nodded at Sumo in gratitude.

"Thanks Sumo. Keep your eyes open out here homie. I'll hit you up tomorrow."

"Cool. Be safe Dame."

"You know it. Happy studies!"

As Sumo jogged across the street heading back towards Central High, D turned and began walking down 13th avenue. He knew Chris usually hung out around downtown at this time of day and he wasn't down there trying to look good. His cousin Money Mike's main source of income came from pushing drugs, primarily dope and weed. And one of the main hotspots for dope was a grimy neighborhood south of downtown called Pioneer Square. Because of the high concentration of homeless shelters, work release programs and probation offices, a large number of ex-convicts, drug addicts, prostitutes and other vagrants stalked the area day and night. This made it an ideal spot for drug dealers to come peddle their merchandise. Wherever you could find drugs being sold you could usually find Money Mike. And wherever Mike was, Chris was sure to be close by.

Chapter 5

Stepping off the number 12 bus at the Union Station stop in the International District, D immediately spotted the group of people he was looking for. Standing directly under the stop sign across the street was a tall black man with his long nappy hair pulled back in a bushy ponytail. He was extremely light skinned; almost white except for the black features of his face and the way he talked.

He was extremely skinny and the scar running down the left side of his face gave his otherwise handsome features a sort of wolfish quality about them. As a result of attempt on his life in Walla Walla prison, a knife had sliced his face open and cut a little bit of the upper lip off. It had healed but now his canine teeth were more visible when his mouth opened. His smile now resembled a snarl more than anything.

Despite his rough physical features, he was dressed smartly in a white Polo shirt, form fitting creased blue jeans, some white and Black Jordan 12's with an unscratched pair of aviators perched on his nose. A fresh appearance that hid a young man with no morals and an incredibly volatile personality underneath! It was Money Mike!

Gathered around him were four other young blacks. While Money Mike was in his early twenties, the rest were all in their teens. All of them were dressed in black or various other dark colors and three of the youth all had their hair in cornrows. The fourth a dark skinned had a short fade. Waiting until the light turned, D crossed the busy intersection and approached the youngster with the fade.

The boy turned and threw a crooked grin in D's direction.

"Aww shit look who it is? Wassup nigga?"

D nodded his head at the other four and shook the outstretched hand.

"Wassup Chris? How you doing it out here?"

Chris shrugged.

"Same shit, different toilet! But it's still stinking, you know? Taking a break right now but I think some of the homies bout to get it back to the hood though. You remember Justin and Elbow?"

D nodded and shook hands with two of the other youths standing around the bus stop. Justin was a short brown skinned kid with a backwards black hat and glasses and Elbow was a tall muscular teenager with a round face whose family had come to Seattle from Ethiopia almost ten years ago. They called him Elbow because of the way he liked to fight.

Turning to Money Mike, they took turns shaking his hand and everyone else that was present then headed side by side back up Jackson Street in the direction the Central District. Now it was just D, Money Mike, Chris and a brown chubby youngster with dreadlocks and mean eyes that D had met last year named Whop. He was two grades below D and Chris but was no less capable when it came to putting in work,

"Wassup D?"

Money Mike's voice, a smooth mixture of deep baritone dripping with honey came floating over the noise of car horns loud shouts and the movement of the many large buses passing by in the street on their way to various parts of the city. D glanced up into the eyes of one of the most influential people he'd ever known in his short time on this planet.

Second in Command next to their leader who was currently serving life on a first degree murder charge, he was the man everyone on the street took their orders from. Everywhere Money Mike went he projected an aura of confidence and underlying hostility that women found enchanting and other men found intimidating, which of course meant most of them wanted to be like him. But few could. He had a way with words that could talk down the most stubborn resistance in minutes and form alliances with hated enemies. But you definitely didn't want to get on his bad side. And he always had money.

31

Mike's skill at making and holding on to money was legendary among the group. He never had anything less than a couple thousand dollars on him at all times. And having money meant that was able to get things that most of the young boys could only dream about. He had a 1994 all black Ford Thunderbird with tinted windows, a house right on 23rd avenue, a closet full of expensive clothes and women that looked like they had just came from a music video shoot. D was in awe of Money Mike but he didn't want to show it. He wanted to be cool and collected at all times too. Choking back the excitement he felt at being recognized by him, D extended his hand.

"W'sup Money, how you been?"

Money Mike shrugged his thin shoulders.

"It's all gravy baby. How bout you? Staying safe out here?"

"More or less," replied D. Money Mike nodded his head.

"True all we can do is try." Suddenly from the sound of his jeans pocket came the sound of birds chirping. Pulling out a black flip phone, Money Mike glanced at a message he had just received. Putting his phone away he clapped his hands and looked around at the teenagers gathered in front of him.

"Aight ya'll, I gotta be outta here in ten minutes. Chris, you and Whop can either post up out here longer or call it quits for the day I'm not really tripping at this point. I got business up north for the rest of the day."

Chris and Whop looked at each other.

"Shit I need the money," said Whop, "I'll stay out longer, I aint got nowhere else to be."

"Well if Whop kicking it then I'm out here to," said Chris.

"Aight cool. You got stones or you need some more?" Both Chris and Whop said they needed more. Telling them he'd be right back, Money Mike prepared to stroll off in the direction of his car. D, seeing his window of opportunity closing, quickly spoke up.

"Yo Money, could I talk to you for a second. I just wanna holla at you about a proposition I was thinking about."

Money Mike raised his left eyebrow at D.

32

"Aight D, you know I fuck's with you. Walk with me to the car."

Crossing the street with Money Mike, D followed him up 5th avenue to a secluded parking lot behind a rundown apartment building. Money Mike's dark green Thunderbird was parked near the back. As they crossed the parking lot, Money Mike turned his head towards D.

"So waddup lil homie? Everything straight? You aint still tripping bout Anthony is you? I know it sucks believe me he was a soldier in my set so I feel his loss too you know. But we gotta keep going. We'll find out who pulled that trigger eventually don't you trip about that!"

D nodded understandingly. Anthony's death had been weighing on him but Money Mike was right. Feeling sad wasn't going to bring him back. He had been a solid person to stand beside but now that he was gone it was time for the crew to make up for what they had lost. It was soldier time. D often wondered if he could do the things that he had heard Anthony had. Now that he was gone, D had a strange feeling he would soon find out. But D hadn't come to Money Mike for advice.

"Yeah I know you guys gonna handle it, I'm not worried about that. I'm just kind of in need of some cash. I could make it by next week but I really need it today. I came up on a bag of some powder last night but no one I know wants any. I figured I could sell it to you or something. Also I was thinking that if you needed some runs taken care of like we use to do last year then I'm ready right now and any day after."

Money Mike glanced down at D's young but determined face and chuckled softly shaking his head. He loved to see the youngsters with ambition and thirst on their path up the criminal ladder. It was how he had come up and how his older brothers and cousins had too. D in particular had his attention because of his skill at saving and investing the money he made. At least, he was better than a lot of the other guys he usually hung with. Besides, anything that he had one his younger protégés do made him more money than he paid them for actually carrying the deed out.

There was just one small problem when it came to D. No matter how useful he proved, he still wasn't an official member of the gang until he had gone through something referred to as "Death Row"! It was essentially a twenty three second beat down by fellow members. He knew Anthony hadn't wanted D to get to involved with the gangs dealings but as far as Money Mike was concerned, he halfway a member already. It was just a matter of time till he had D's talent firmly under his control. As they arrived at his car, Money Mike turned and leaned against the hood of his car staring D in the face.

"Let me see the shit," he asked.

D rummaged in his pockets and passed the bag over. Money mike opened the bag and stuck a little taste in his mouth. He nodded looking satisfied.

"That's some good shit young D where you get this?"

D shrugged.

"Put some work in this week and came up. So you want it?"

Money Mike laughed. Taking out a roll of money, he peeled off two hundred dollar bills and handed them to D.

"You got a solid few grams worth here. Take that and get your shit lil nigga." He was about to leave when D stopped him.

"Yo Money. I still need a little more bread. How about I make some runs for you? I still know all the routes!"

Money Mike sighed deeply.

"Look D, you were a good ass runner and I really would put you back on the routes since I know you know them by heart, but already got some reliable runners right now and since they're actually from Deuce-Trey I gotta give them priority. A lot of people need money out here D, not just you."

D couldn't help but find it amusing every time Money Mike said the word "money". It always sounded as if he were referring to himself. Suppressing a smile, D looked around him as if gathering strength from an invisible hype man.

"Well is there something, anything you need done that I could do for you to earn a little bread? I can do more than just sell drugs. Just ask Chris!"

34

Money Mike snarled, a sight that would have made D nervous if hadn't gotten used to seeing it already. Persistence was something he liked. He beckoned for D to come sit next to him and D shuffled forward and leaned against the car hood next to his mentor.

"Look D, you know I fucks with you the long way. Chris told me how you helped him handle Roland. I appreciate that. You helped me as well as helping Chris that night. That fool was taking money out my pockets every night he was out there. But If I remember right you already got some payment for that. Now I know you're a solid nigga D but the fact is you're not from my set and I can't keep letting you come and go as you please making money off of our connections.

"Now, Anthony vouched for you and so does Chris and I know for a fact you're far from a punk, but we just lost Anthony and he was a good person as well as a good money maker for us. We need to make up for his loss right now so in order for me to be able to spare and money to pay you, you're going to have to start taking a bigger role in providing funds not just for me but all of Deuce-Trey. But bigger jobs mean a bigger payout for you!"

D stood his ground. He had only came down here trying to make a quick eighty dollars but this transaction was taking on a much more serious tone than D had been prepared for. But it looked like it was either admit he was serious or go back to staying out all night wandering unknown streets and breaking into cars for his money again. D narrowed his eyes.

"I'm serious Money. You can count on me."

Money stared seriously at D for a few seconds longer than clapped his little partner on the back.

"Good for you D, I knew I could." Getting up off the hood, Money Mike went to the passenger side door of his Thunderbird and opened the door. Leaning down, he took a grey backpack from where it lay crumpled on the seat and put it on one shoulder. Closing the door, Money Mike came back to stand beside D and handed him the back pack.

"Aight D, I got something you can do today to earn some money. You'll be working with Chris and Whop but just go to

Chris if you got any questions. He'll show you how we do things. You might have to move around a little if the traffic gets slow or cops show up but it shouldn't take you more than a couple more hours to get rid of the rest of this stuff. As for the jobs, I'll be in touch when I need you."

Shaking D's hand, Money Mike unlocked the driver side door and hopped inside his car. Slamming the door he started up the engine, the slow sounds of The Isley Brother's floating out of his expensive speaker system. Throwing up the deuces to D, Money Mike threw the car in reverse and backed quickly out if his parking space. Turning the car around, he gunned the engine and flew across the empty parking lot. Turning left out onto 5th avenue, he was gone in a loud screech of tires. D watched him go, chest swollen with pride at the responsibility's he was about to receive. He headed back to his friends.

Chapter 6

"Chris on my mama you're trippin! You could never in your life pull more bitches then me!"

"Well shit nigga, you're gonna have to put your mom on the line because me getting more females then you aint a possibility homie, it's a muthafuckin fact!"

"Naw bro look at you! Wanna be P. Diddy but no J. LO just bucket hoes in cornrows! Your game is wack! Who have you even smashed? Yo ass aint even in school to get bitches! You old everyday I'm hustling ass nigga but never fuckin ass nigga!"

Arriving back at the bus stop, D found Chris and Wop in the middle of a heated debate. The unique thing about this debate however, was that it was probably the fourth time that Chris and Wop had engaged in this same debate this week. And it was only Thursday. D personally felt like he'd heard this argument one hundred times over and still didn't see what the huge deal was. But then again, D wasn't particularly fond of girls right now. A bad breakup last year had shattered his youthful idealism of what love was.

Bitter towards the entire female race, all D's young mind believed in now was the accumulation of cash money. But because watching these arguments play out provided endless entertainment, D suppressed the urge to break it up and instead stood a couple of feet back and continued to watch. Chris had a slightly irritated look on his face and D assumed it was because Whop had just called him a "midget". Chris had always been sensitive about his height even though Whop was only a couple inches taller.

"At least I ain't an oversized wanna be Too Short! You look like you never took a gym class in your life. That shit was mandatory in middle school nigga how'd your big ass avoid being seen? You could've used some of those Mile Runs!"

Whop's eyes narrowed as Chris began targeting his weight but Chris took no notice. Turning to D, Chris didn't see Whop clench his right hand into a fist.

"Hey D, do you know how Whop got his name?"

"Shut the fuck up Chris I'm warning you!" snarled Whop. Chris turned to look at him, laughed at the look on Whops face and turned right back to D.

"This fool's full name is Whopper because he don't eat shit but fast food. Wondering why his stomach won't shrink and…"

WHAP!

Before Chris could say another word, Whop rushed forward and threw a wide haymaker that caught Chris right on the right side of his head just behind his ear. Caught off guard, Chris lurched to the left and turned to face Whop. Dodging two more punches with cat like quickness Chris put his fists up in front of his face and shuffled quickly towards his taller, heavier opponent with the light of combat in his eyes. People walking past on foot moved quickly out of the way of the fighting boys or stopped to watch curiously.

Circling each other like cage fighters, Chris and Whop went into a kind of violent dance routine. Jabs, haymakers, uppercuts and crosses were alternately being thrown and defended against with the occasional punch landing on target. Their arms were like intertwining whirlwinds intent on bringing pain and destruction on everything they touched. It was scary and fascinating to the people watching the two fighters.

D also had to admit that there was something strangely hypnotizing about the way Chris and Whop fought. Neither giving nor taking any ground but instead moved with deliberate concentration. Each foot was perfectly placed as if the entire thing had been choreographed for weeks before hand. The droplets of blood flying through the air and landing on the ground were like the confetti thrown from an appreciative audience.

As suddenly as it began it was over. Side stepping a poorly timed haymaker from Whop, Chris threw two solid punched into Whop's soft pudgy stomach and the youth doubled over clutching his gut with one hand and waving his hand in a "no more" gesture at Chris. Besides clutching his gut, Whops nose was leaking red all over his shirt. Chris meanwhile was spitting mouthfuls of blood down on the pavement. The crowd of onlookers quietly resumed walking wherever it was they were headed to and the corner of Jackson and 5th avenue was quiet once more. Well, as quiet as it would ever be.

Panting hard, Whop straightened up massaging his stomach with his left hand and glaring angrily at Chris.

"You'ze a punk for that nigga," he gasped out. Chris just smirked at him, still sucking on his cut lip.

"That's what you get for sucker punching me fool!"

Whop held his nose and tilted his head back.

"Nigga that's what you get! I told you to shut the fuck up."

Chris stared at Whop for a few still seconds then, seeming to come to an inner personal decision, casually shrugged his shoulders. He stuck his right hand out.

"Aight, you right. My bad nigga," he said to Whop, no trace of a joke anywhere in his voice. Whop, head still tilted back to prevent the blood flow, shook Chris's hand. D decided it was time to intervene.

"Aight, now that you guys are homies again can we please get to work? I'm trying to make some money for some shit I'm trying to do later this week. I can't hang out on the corner while you muthafuckas fight all damn day!"

Whop, his nose leak stopped, nodded his head in agreement.

"True enough," added Chris, "let's dip before any police show up."

"Where we going?" asked Whop. Chris thought for a second then turned and starting walking towards the waterfront. He put on a southern accent.

"C'mon y'all! We bout to hit the slow stroll!"

The "Slow stroll" as Chris called it, was really nothing more than the three teens walking slowly throughout the Pioneer Square neighborhood of downtown Seattle selling drugs. Although D had some previous experience helping Chris and Anthony last year, it was still a nerve racking experience every time he did it and according to Chris, that paranoid feeling of imminent danger never left no matter how long you'd been a street dealer. The combined threats from police, hostile encounters with potential buyers and rival gang members that lurked just beneath the surface of every transaction was enough to play tricks on the most disciplined of minds. And the fact that each of these potential threats had at one point in time all become real only added to the seriousness of the situation.

To counter each of these threats, Anthony had come up with a decent solution. Instead of standing or walking around in a group, which only made them a bigger target, they would stay twenty to thirty feet away from each other at all times in an extended line so if one person got caught. The person at the front of the line was responsible for talking to potential buyers and determining whether they were ok to deal with. They were called the Lead. Taking the money, he would then direct the customer to the person walking behind him. The middle person in the line (called the Bag Boy) held on to the product and at a sign from the Lead would pinpoint the customer, walk towards them and slip the customer their designated amount. The person in the very back of the line was the Enforcer and was there as security. They kept their eyes peeled for any signs of potential trouble and if anything went down would quickly make their presence known.

Anthony had designed it so that no one man would be more at risk than another. The Lead, while not having any drugs on him, was the face of the operation and the cash holder and therefore the first in line if anything went down. The Bag Boy of course had all the drugs and the Enforcer generally carried a weapon (more often than not a stolen pistol) in case of a robbery or other confrontation occurred.

Usually things tended to go smoothly but trouble was far from uncommon. Some of the things D had seen down here had been seared into his brain and it would a while before he forgot them. The randomness and quickness with which violent acts were dealt out had unnerved him at first. D tended to use violence as a last resort but over the course of a few months last year spent hustling with Chris and Anthony among drug addicts, ex-cons, homeless beggars and dangerous gangsters, he had learned that the majority of people around him used violence as their first and only means of settling disagreements.

Now the only thing that really bothered D was the appearances of the people that they primarily dealt with. The smell of unwashed private parts and hair always made him feel queasy. He also hated the sick ones. The addicts with snot running down their nose and scars from poorly treated wounds all over their faces. Toothless mouths, discolored skin and skinny underfed bodies gave one the feeling of being stuck in a zombie horror movie. Some couldn't even talk, they just muttered unintelligible words and held out hands clenching old wrinkly bills. D called them the walking dead but the promise of money always overshadowed his distaste for this occupation.

Today there was no change in the set up. Chris, as the most experienced was the Lead. Since was already carrying the bag he was the Bag Boy and whop brought up the rear as the Enforcer. That had been no argument about this which had made D wonder what kind of weapon Whop had on him. Nothing had fallen out of his pockets during his fight with Chris so D assumed there was a gun stuck in his waist. Better for all of them. Crack heads could get unreasonable some times.

Spreading out in their line, D said a quick prayer asking Anthony's spirit to watch over them. The people walking past never looked twice at him as he tried to assume his role as an innocent teenager on his way to or from somewhere that involved an educational agenda. Despite his outwardly nonchalant appearance, D was as tense as a rattle snake on the inside as he felt the old nervousness return. Everybody was a potential threat and he was determined not to take a fall. All he needed was another two hundred dollars and he could get another quarter pound of homegrown Granddaddy Kush from his special connect and be done with crack rock business. He'd stay out all night if he had to.

Up ahead, D saw Chris talking to an old man. As Chris shook the man's hand, D's trained eye noted the exchange of bills. As the man headed slowly towards him through the crowd of people walking up and down the street he saw Chris flash him his left hand with four fingers held straight out. A forty sack. Good first sale. As he prepared the order, D looked quickly back at Whop, confirmed his presence and looked back straight ahead. The hand came out, the product went in and D continued walking like nothing had happened. One down. D breathed a sigh of relief and clenched his jaw. It was going to be a long night.

Chapter 7

Turning off the water that was cascading down onto his head, D pushed back the shower curtains and stepped out onto to the heavy floor mat. Pulling a brown towel off of the towel rack, he set about drying his body vigorously. A glance at the numbers on the small digital radio by the sink told him he had about ten minutes to get out of the house if he wanted to catch the bus. Otherwise he'd be walking to school which, while not actually that far away, it was far enough that jogging the distance would result in an incredibly sweaty back which would then make for a very uncomfortable morning. And D hated having a sweaty back.

Opening the bathroom door, D quickly crossed the hall to his room and shut the door behind him. Thinking quickly, He threw on a pair of blue jeans, a tall white tee, his favorite black hoody and a black beanie. Slipping into his white air force ones, D shouldered his backpack and looked around his room to see if he missed anything. Thinking quickly, he crouched down next to his bed and reached into a slit in the mattress and withdrew a crumpled up brown sandwich bag. Opening it, he reached in and took out the wad of cash that was inside.

Everything had gone down smooth yesterday. D, Chris and Whop has stayed downtown for around seven hours after Money Mike had left. It had been close to eight thirty in the evening when they called it quits and began the long trek up Jackson Street back to 23rd avenue. Halfway there Money Mike had pulled up on them and ordered them inside the car. After checking the amount, he had broken off one hundred dollars in mixed bills for each of them. He had offered to take them out for something to eat but D had declined in favor of going straight home and passing out in his bed.

In all, he had exactly six hundred and thirty two dollars. Not enough for the quarter pound of weed he had planned on purchasing but at least he could get a couple ounces and still have some pocket money left over. A sudden realization made him grit his teeth. His dad was expecting him to have some money to contribute to the house today. D wondered for a brief second why his dad had taking to asking for odd amounts of cash at random times of the month but after a minutes thought just brushed it aside.

It wasn't strange that his parents needed help around the house. They weren't exactly billionaires. Still, D wondered whether or not something had happened at his dads work. He'd been home a lot lately and D's mom was spending even more time away from home working at the hospital. D hoped nothing bad was going on. He hadn't set eyes on her in at least a week. Even now his dad was passed out on the living room couch just as he had been now for the last two weeks in a row. Did his mom and dad ever sleep together anymore?

Stepping out into the hall, D quietly placed one hundred dollars on the kitchen table. Staring at his father's disheveled snoring form, D hoped to god he wasn't drinking again. Turning around he hurried out of the apartment, closing the door quietly behind him. He seemed to leave the house like that a lot these days.

Walking down the side walk on his way to the bus stop, D took out his cellphone and a half smoked Newport from his jeans pocket. Sticking the cigarette in his mouth and lighting it with a cheap plastic lighter, he dialed a number in his phone and put it to his ear. It rang six times before switching over to an automated response informing him that the person he was trying to reach is unavailable and at the tone to please leave a message.

"Yo waddup GT this is Damien. I was just calling to see if you wanted to shoot some hoops later. I got a few guys with me already all we need is two more and we got a game. Let me know if you're free. Aight, peace."

Not seeming too disturbed that the person he had been calling hadn't picked up, D slipped the phone back into his pocket and continued puffing contentedly on his cigarette. Reaching his bus stop, D leaned against the bus sign pole and waited to be transported all the way down Broadway to Central High. A buzzing in his pocket indicated he had received a text message. Flipping open his phone, D glanced down at the message.

It's all good. Busy after 8pm. N E time before is cool.
Smiling to himself, D closed his phone. It was go time.

Later at school…
"Hey Damien!"
Halfway through the combination to his locker, D looked up to see Courtney walking down the hall towards him. She was looking immaculate dressed in red and white Air Jordan's, tight blue jeans, a red tube top with a small white coat and a white headband holding back her long dark hair. Two massive hoop earrings hung on her ears and a silver necklace with a heart on it glittered brilliantly around her neck.

D couldn't help but be captivated every time he saw her. As mad as he still was about his ex-girlfriend's dirty doings, one look at Courtney was enough to wipe all thoughts of her or any other girl straight out of his mind. The only problem was, every time they talked it was always business related. Even now as he watched her approach with that dazzling smile stretching across her beautiful face, he had the sinking feeling that this wasn't a social call. She needed something.

"Wassup Courtney? How you doing?" D asked as she came to a stop in front of him.

"I'm all right thanks. Wassup with you?"

Her voice was like the sound of spring flowing across the land bringing renewed life to everything it touched. D had to catch himself from staring in open mouthed fascination at this young woman who could make professional models look like drug addicts.

"Oh um, nothing. Just putting some shit away real quick before class. How's that iPod working for you?"

Courtney reached in her purse and waved it at D, showing him that she still had it. He noticed that she had outfitted it with some pink headphones. *Must be her favorite color,* he thought to himself. He tucked that piece of information in the back of his brain.

"That shit is dope thanks again for hooking me up," Courtney told him, real appreciation in her voice. If D had had a tail, it would've been wagging right now.

Looking around briefly as if searching for eves droppers, Courtney leaned in a little closer to D. D felt his heart rate go up and hoped she couldn't hear it beating through his chest. The scent wafting into his nose was the right mixture of strength and softness so that it didn't overwhelm the senses but instead, provided a perfect stage on which to enjoy them.

"Are you still on deck with some of that Kush that you and Anthony were selling at the end of last year? I'm throwing a back to school party this weekend at my cousin's house and I wanted to get him some weed to show my appreciation. But most of these dealers out here are hella shiesty and I'm not tryna spend my money just to get bopped. You were always hooking it up so I figured I'd spend my money with someone who I actually like."

D felt his chest swell up a little upon hearing Courtney's words. Now he really needed to re up ASAP! Opening his locker he emptied out his backpack into the bottom of his locker and closed it again. School had just lost its interest for the day.

"Well you in luck Courtney. I'm getting some more later today. I had to give my dad a bunch of money over the summer so I been kinda down. But I'm right again so I can definitely set you right later."

"Thank god," said Courtney, "What time you thinking?"

D shrugged.

"Probably around five or six. How much was you looking for?"

Courtney did some quick mental calculations.

"I guess like a half ounce would be cool. I don't want my cousin coming out of his room tripping so I got to make sure he's good for the whole night."

46

D grinned.

"I can dig it. Well where do you want me to bring it when I got it?"

"Oh shit," said Courtney slapping a hand to her forehead, "good question. Hang on!"

Taking a pen out of her backpack, Courtney grabbed D's hand and wrote a number down on his arm in small but very nice handwriting. D felt himself blushing slightly at the feel of Courtney's hand on his skin and hoped it went away before she noticed.

"There we go," she said, straitening up, "just like in middle school. That's my cell number. Do you know where the Food Depot is?"

"The one on MLK and East Union?"

"Yup, exactly."

"Hell yeah that's the same area I'm about to be in later." Courtney smiled.

"Good, well that all works out then. Call me when you're headed towards the Food Depot. I'm literally right across the street."

"Aight cool. See you later."

Still smiling brightly, Courtney squeezed D's hand briefly and walked away down the hall. Looking back over her shoulder she winked at him then turned back around and disappeared into one of the stairwells. D closed his locker slowly. That girl had a strange power over him. Her entire personality was seductive and D was quickly finding he was unable to ignore the feelings that went rushing through him every time he saw her in the hallway. This was their last year of high school and then who knows what would happen? If he didn't make his move this year he might never get another chance. Maybe he'd try when he saw her later tonight. Start the New Year off with a bang! Yeah, he liked the sound of that.

Throwing his backpack over his shoulder, D once again made for one of the broken emergency exits. Why wait another second? He decided to make the pick up now. Walking out of the busted fire exit doors, D took out his phone, dialed a number and put the phone to his ear. It rang twice before it was picked up.

"Yo it's Chris! Speak on it!"

D shook his head at his friend's lack of manners.

"Is that how your mama taught you to answer the phone?"

"Oh shit waddup D. Shut up nigga you aint no goddamn saint either muthafucka! Sup though?"

"Where you at? I gotta make a run to 30th and Union you tryna roll with me?"

"Let's do it! Meet me in the town!"

"Yup."

Hanging up, D made a bee line for the bus stop.

Chapter 8

D and Chris were sitting down on a large brown sofa across from a brown skinned man who would have been Bob Marley's twin except that instead of long nappy dreads he was sporting a large but equally nappy afro. His eyes were so low they looked shut and every time he grinned row a yellow teeth were revealed. This was GT. GT stood for Green Thumb. Apparently, GT was originally from Jamaica but had moved to United States as a little boy with his mom but he'd been selling weed in the Capitol Hill/Central District areas for as long as D could remember.

He didn't speak with a typical Jamaican accent and didn't dress like an islander either. In fact he looked like an average African American teenager with his baggy jeans and long shirts. His heavily bearded face gave him away as being slightly older. In fact he had just turned twenty seven a couple months ago during the summer. He wasn't a part of Deuce-Trey but he was close friends with Money Mike and the two commonly did business with each other. After all, GT had some of the best weed in town.

And he grew it himself! GT was a master marijuana grower and had been since he'd been a teenager. It was a skill he'd picked up while working on the big outdoor marijuana fields in North California. Here in Seattle due to lack of open land, he had moved his operation indoors. Now, with the help of Money Mike and a few other investors, he had secured a two story house in a neighborhood just behind the Central District called Madrona. Inside he had filled every available room that had a door with plants inside individual five gallon buckets with huge 1000watt lights attached to the ceilings above.

Currently his crop numbered over one hundred plants and he was rewarded with a yield of several pounds every two weeks as long as kept his production rate at full speed. It was a science requiring hours of painstaking observation and careful application of the different nutrients required for the different stages of growth. It was pure biological science and something not a lot of people could honestly say they were experts in. But GT had figured it out.

D had been introduced to GT by Anthony almost two years ago when Anthony had started selling weed in his sophomore year. He'd eventually showed D how to successfully make a profit on his investment and soon enough the two were running a small but successful operation (sponsored of course by Money Mike) in the halls of Central High. Opting to move on to bigger money making opportunities after Latoya had gotten pregnant, he had left D solely in charge of the business. Unable to keep up with the demand, D's customer base shrank considerably but he was able to keep enough people happy to keep him busy and his pockets full whenever he had product to move. And because GT kept the circle that he sold to small, D was always guaranteed to be one of the few people in the city with this specific strand. Thanks to this, his customer base was loyal and dependable, waiting anxiously for a text telling them he was back in possession of his magical strand.

D liked GT for the most part. He was an easy going man who loved reggae and smoking oversized joints that usually put D to sleep for several hours. But d had heard stories from Money Mike about GT's legendary temper that flared up at the slightest sign of disrespect. It was rumored that he was wanted dead or alive back on Jamaica but nobody could prove it true or false. Whatever the case, GT always gave D the cheapest prices for weed that D had ever heard of and D wasn't about to let rumors of a hazy past and psychotic violence get in the way of meeting up with Courtney later.

At the moment GT was hunched over a small coffee table halfway through rolling another one if his monster sized joints. Putting the finishing touches on the perfectly rolled joint, GT placed it up in his ear and walked into his kitchen and opened his refrigerator. The sound of glass bottles clinking together snuck its way into D's ears.

"Hey, y'all little niggaz want a beer?" GT's voice called from behind the fridge door. D and Chris exchanged brief smirks. At their age, they one thing they were always in pursuit of besides money and girls was a strong buzz.

"Yup please. Good looks GT!" D called back.

Returning to the room with three dark bottles, GT passed one each to D and Chris and sat down on the couch facing them. Reaching into a backpack that was underneath the coffee table, GT withdrew a large bulging plastic bag filled with marijuana. The entire room immediately was engulfed by the potent sweet aroma of the weed within. Placing it on the table in front of D, GT sat back and opened his beer, took a huge gulp and burped loudly with content when everything finally went down.

D withdrew the small roll of money from his pocket and placed it on the table besides the bag looking slightly confused. Even using just his eyes D could tell that the contents of that bag was way over the amount he was paying for. He looked up at GT for an explanation. GT simply looked back at him evenly. D decided to break the silence.

"Umm, that's a lot of trees in that bag GT."

"Yeah I know. That's a half pound right there, as you ordered."

D was baffled. He had spoken the right code words he was sure of it.

"Naw GT, I said I only wanted two ounces nigga. That's only four hundred bucks there that aint enough for all this and you know I don't like being fronted an amount like this. I don't like owing people."

Chris was looking at the bag of weed with mild interest. He was used to seeing drugs in amounts larger than this but was interested in the way the deal seemed to be playing out. Four hundred dollars for a half pound! This was unheard of! D could make a lot of money off of this deal and Chris was confused as why D was arguing the present. GT seemed to like it though because he a wide grin on his face even as D had a serious one on his.

51

GT finally stopped smiling and shaking his head and held up a hand to silence D's indignant outburst.

"Look lil homie, I'm giving you this shit as a present. We've done a lot of business together since Anthony introduced you to me and you've been one of the most consistent people that come to me and actually have straight money every time. I've seen Chris since Anthony's murder but this I the first time I've seen you. This is my way of saying thanks for all the work you've put in at his side and all that you will continue to do in the future. You're a good money maker D I'm glad to be doing business with you. It shows how strong you are that you came back even though the one who put you in this is gone. We do this for him. The least I can do is show you some love seeing as how cool you was with him."

D was stunned at GT's words. Few people in his life at ever spoke to him with affection and appreciation in the same breath as well as provide him with a way to make a decent amount of cash. It also made him think about Anthony and how much he'd do anything to preserve his memory. D was determined to be as much of a soldier as his friend had been. The combined words from Money Mike and GT were beginning to infest his thoughts and he wanted nothing more than to make them proud. Even if it meant doing what Anthony had fought so hard to prevent and begin following in his friends footsteps. He turned to look at Chris who just nodded his head as if approving the authenticity of the transaction.

GT held out a dark heavily muscled hand and D shook it without hesitation.

"Now you know who coming back and spending that money with right?" asked GT seriously. D looked into the man's eyes and saw no trace of amusement in the dark pupils. The faintly uneasy feeling D had gotten after shaking Money Mike's hand in the parking lot a few days ago returned. The feeling that he'd just signed his life away on some unseen contract without reading the fine print. But he remained cool on the outside.

"Oh you already know GT! Those people are going to want more after this shit gone so you already know I'm hitting you soon as I need it."

52

GT released his hand and sat back on the couch. Pulling another decent sized bag out from behind one of the couch cushions, GT broke it open and began pulling out several small nuggets of the green crystal covered weed and placing them on the table. He pointed at Chris and tossed him a swisher sweet.

"Roll up nigga. Business is done, I'm tryna get faded!"

D didn't waste any more time in grabbing the package and putting it inside his backpack.

Almost two hours later as D and Chris were walking slowly down Union Street towards MLK Boulevard, D was on his phone busily texting every one of his and Anthony's old customers and letting them know he was back on deck. Almost immediately his inbox was flooded with responses naming various quantities that were needed and where. By the time they walked the next three blocks to Union Street and MLK he already had twenty different orders lined up. As excited as he was about the money to come, he was more excited at the prospect of seeing three of his favorite customers whom he happened to actually be close with.

Well, he was close with two of them. Courtney of course was the one he was hoping to get close too and she had already texted him back. It was to her house that he was headed now. Latoya, Anthony's girl, had replied instantly as well and he would be stopping through her house immediately after leaving Courtney's house.

The third person hadn't hit him back yet but he wasn't bothered. They had their own hectic schedule but D knew they would call at the first available opportunity. The rest were just customers that he would get to as quick as possible. He hadn't been selling weed for months but the fact that his customer base was still there said something about the way he did business. You had to reward that kind of dedication.

Chapter 9

As they passed the Food Depot, D stole a glance at Chris. Chris, busy texting somebody on his phone, didn't look over. D was on his way to Courtney's house just to drop off some weed sure, but D had hoped to maybe engage her in conversation and maybe even get to know her a little better. Already shy as he already was though, D wasn't sure he could pull it off with Chris standing by hearing every word that he said. On the other hand, he was walking around with a half-pound of weed on him and having somebody with him seemed like a good idea at least until he was headed home on the bus.

"Yo Chris?"

Chris stopped texting long enough to look up for a second.

"Waddup D?"

"How you bout to do it right now?"

Chris smirked slightly and held his phone up.

"This girl wants me to come over for a little bit before her mom gets off work. I don't know though. I was over there all last week and really this bitch is hella annoying. She talks way too much and won't shut up for shit. But she is a little freak you know what I'm saying? But there is this girl who works at Red Apple I been meaning to get at for a while now. Decisions, decisions."

"You feel like making a couple stops with me right quick?"

"Where?"

D nodded across the street.

"This girl from school wants some weed and she lives right across the street. Then I was gonna slide through Latoya's house for a little bit."

Chris thought to himself for a moment.

"You tryna holla at this girl or what?" he asked.

Chris was famous for wasting no time when it came to girls and it was a trait that D both hated and envied. It was the same reason d had been hesitant to invite Chris along in the first place. He'd watched many girls that he'd had crushes on but just never had the nerve to talk to get snatched up by Chris only to be discarded like a useless playing card some weeks later. Sometime the turnaround was less than a week. D had an unwritten rule never to date a girl that any of his friends had been with and he didn't want Courtney joining that list.

"Yeah bro. Well, I mean I aint said nothing yet but I'm about to. I just don't know her that well really so I'm tryna you know, break the ice or whatever before I do something."

Chris held up his hands.

"Hey, say no more homie she's all yours. But if I could give you one word of advice?"

"What's that?"

"Don't do that D shit where you get all nervous and start pussy footing around with the conversation. You're horrible with girl's bro. Just open your mouth and say what you got to say and be done with it. You aint scared of no nigga how you going to be scared of a girl?"

D looked up into the sky, annoyed but unable to deny the truth of Chris's words.

"I know, I know nigga don't remind me. It's not going to happen this time."

Chris raised an eyebrow. D just shook his head. Feeling his phone vibrate he took it out of his pocket and checked the message.

"All right she said to meet her in the alley by the garage with the red graffiti on it."

Crossing over MLK, D and Chris walked through an abandoned overgrown parking lot and squeezed through a hole in the fence at the back of it. In the alley running parallel to the street they strolled down until they arrived at the designated meeting spot. It was an old grey garage whose paint matched that of the two story house in front of it. Old and dirty, it was clearly not used much by the people that lived in the house. As Chris leaned against the garage door with a foot kicked up behind him for support, D dialed Courtney's number.

"Hello?"

D's nerves jumped a little at the sound of Courtney's voice.

"Waddup Courtney its D. I'm out in the alley."

"Oh what's up D? I'll be right out in two seconds."

"Yup."

Hanging up the phone, D set about checking himself to make sure he looked presentable. No sooner had he nervously wiped a hand across his tired eyes then he heard the sound of footsteps and Courtney came walking around the side of the garage. D felt like he would never get tired of seeing her walk into his presence. Coke bottle figure, long straight hair and more developed than half of the girls at the school, D wouldn't be surprised if she became a fucking model later in life. Catching sight of D, Courtney's face broke out into a smile. Walking up to him, she gave him a big hug the feeling of her breasts against his chest sending D's blood rushing through his body at 1000 degree temperatures. He let go before he broke out in a cold sweat.

"Thanks for coming through D. Sorry but we should make this fast I got a friend coming by to pick me up in a second. I gotta go pick up food and drink supplies for the party."

"No problem," said D feeling slightly disappointed, "I already got it weighed out for you."

"All right my nigga damn you on point! That's why I fuck with you. Here come around the side of the garage so were not all out in the open."

"Yup, oh and real quick this is my Patna Chris. Chris this is Courtney."

Courtney, who hadn't even seen Chris standing on her garage door looked over at him and jumped slightly. Chris was staring at Courtney with something like amusement on his face. He was shaking his head slowly from side to side and chuckling softly.

"Well, well, well. Wassup Courtney? I aint seen you in a minute."   Courtney smiled back at Chris and walked over and gave him a quick hug. D was surprised they already knew each other and got a sinking feeling in his gut.

"I know right. I went to Cali for the summer to stay with my cousin in Oakland. It was cool them Oakland fools are crazy though. How you been?"

"Cool," replied Chris.

Turning back to D, Courtney looked at him with curious expression on her face.

"I didn't know you knew Chris."

D looked at his friend briefly before answering.

"Man, I been friends with this guy for a minute now. He and Anthony have been like the brothers I never had."

At the mention of Anthony's name, Courtney's face took on a somber expression.

"RIP Anthony. That's right you guys were always hanging out in school. I'm sorry he's gone. And they didn't catch the guy that did it?"

"Naw," Chris angrily, "but he'll turn up and when he does it's a green light on his cranium. Don't doubt that he'll get his when we find out who did it!"

Courtney looked at Chris and D could tell that she was impressed with Chris's words from the faint smile that was playing around her lips as she looked at him.

"Yo," interrupted D, getting slightly annoyed and deciding to add some base in his voice, "not tryna be pushy but let's handle this business though I got some other stops to make."

This time Courtney looked at D with that interested look in her eyes and a faint smile on her lips. Turning around, she motioned for the two boys to follow her. Stepping around the side of the garage, D reached into his bag and withdrew a half ounce he had weighed up before leaving GT's house.

"How much I owe you?" asked Courtney.

D thought for a second.

"A hundred bucks is cool. And you won't find anything like that anywhere else in the city that's a fucking fact."

He passed the bag over to Courtney and she took a wad of cash out of her pocket. Peeling off five twenties she handed them over. Cracking open the bag, she stuck her nose inside and inhaled.

"Damn D this some strong smelling shit! I know my brother is gonna be happy. Is it cool if I give him your number?"

"I guess so," said D counting the money, "I stay in Capitol Hill but I can be over here within thirty minutes."

Courtney closed the bag and rolled it up. Running to the back door of her house she opened it and placed the bag inside a drawer. Closing the door, she jogged back to the two young men. Just then her phone began ringing. Picking it up, she cocked her head to the side and pressed the phone to her ear with her shoulder.

"Hello? Oh wassup Smoke. Yeah just come down the alley I'm out there with some homies right now."

She hung up the phone and looked at Chris and D.

"Aight you guys I'm bout to be out. My friend is taking me to the Costco by the stadiums for the food then to this cheap ass liquor store in Lake City. The party is Saturday night and starts at ten. Come on through!"

"You already know!" said Chris.

As they turned around a black Cadillac Escalade came barreling down the alley and came to a quick stop right in front of them. Waving goodbye to Chris and D, Courtney ran and climbed into the passenger side door. Chris seemed to recognize the driver and nodded at him. The man was dark skinned with a black headband around his forehead and large round ears nodded back. The big truck lurched off without a moment's hesitation as soon as Courtney's door closed and D watched the vehicle fly off down the alley.

Turning around, D and Chris headed the opposite way up the alley. D was first to break the silence.

"Damn Chris, so you already know her huh?"

"You damn right I know her," said Chris, "I've known that girl for a while now. I've never done anything with her," he said quickly seeing the look of irritation that was creeping into D's eyes, "but she is definitely not a stranger."

"How do you know her then?" D asked.

Chris looked at his friend evenly and tried to figure out how to best let D down easily. He could tell he obviously liked the girl. But the truth was the truth.

"Look D," began Chris as they walked slowly through the connecting alleyways, "Courtney is the type of girl we call a team player. She knows she looks good and she uses that shit. But she aint a pimp. Far from it. But she has been known to get what she wants."

D looked at Chris with a slight frown.

"Nigga what the fuck are you talking about?" he demanded.

Chris sighed and shook his head trying to put his thoughts into words that D could understand.

"Look man, Courtney is no stranger to Deuce Trey. Most girls out here love to be known and popular and admired and all that shit by guys. Courtney is the type of girl that loves to be admired by gangsters. She loves that feeling of being wanted by a bunch of hard ass rough ass niggaz that most people wouldn't think of fucking with. I think she gets off on it. She loves being able to say she fucks with Deuce Trey niggaz and just being able to say that makes her feel special. And she aint the only one. Every gang or clique out here got groupies just like any famous R&B group or rock band. Everyone wants to be part of a movement in some way. You wasn't thinking of getting at her was you?"

D had just heard the very thing he hadn't wanted to hear. Now he didn't know what he was thinking.

"So you saying everybody in Deuce Trey has fucked her then?" he asked.

Chris shook his head slowly.

"Naw definitely not everybody but yes some have. I haven't personally but I can guarantee you that Money Mike has been in there a few times. And that nigga Smoke that just came through in that Escalade, he's from Deuce Trey too. And you better believe he aint giving her that ride for free. "

D's hopes rose and fell at the same time. Chris hadn't been with her but his cousin and possibly others had. It didn't

really seem that bad when he thought about it. After all every girl was ran through as far as he was concerned.
But if all she fucked with was money getting gangsters then what chance did he have?

As the two friends walked in silence, D felt his phone vibrate in his pocket. Taking it out he saw a message from the last person he had been waiting for earlier ad finally responded.

Sorry was out of town! Glad your back come by 2morow ASAP! Yay! TTYL!

Now that's what he had been waiting for! A chance to clear his head and relax far away from any forms of chaos. He had hoped everything was all right. He knew the woman's alcoholic husband had to be on another one of his frequent business trips since tomorrow was Friday and she was telling him to come by. No one knew about his friendly relationship with this woman and he preferred to keep it that way. Besides, it was really for her protection more than anything else. That husband of hers was no good when he when he got his hands on that bottle. Opening up a new text message D typed:

B there round 3pm.

Sending the message, D tried to clear his mind of Courtney for the night. He'd discuss his issues tomorrow at a more appropriate time with a more appropriate person. If only she was in high school, D found himself wishing for the hundredth time.

Chapter 10

"Damn that shit stank D! You wasn't lying!"

"C'mon bruh you know I stand by my products whether electrical or pharmaceutical! What you needed?"

"Lemme get a eighth."

"Yup. Forty bucks."

Money and drugs rapidly exchanged hands. The white kid who had just made the purchase stuffed the bag of weed into his pants and jogged away to meet his group of friends who were waiting for him a few feet away. D watched them go as he folded the two twenties he had just received and placed them in his wallet. He was very familiar with this group. Young hippies on their way to smoke some early morning joints before school.

Turning around, D began a slowly walking in the direction of the McDonalds directly across the street from Central High's front entrance. He still had about a half hour before school started and didn't feel like going inside just yet. Besides, his mind was still working to process the information he had learned from Chris last night about Courtney.

D had long been aware of good Courtney looked but he had always assumed that the closest he'd ever get to her was during a business transaction where he was selling her stolen goods or drugs. But apparently she was just as familiar with Duce Trey and the people involved as he was. They basically ran in the same circle! Chris had told him that she apparently was obsessed with Duce Trey and anybody involved in it but also according to Chris, the only people that Courtney involved herself with on a sexual level seemed to be either the top money getters or the violent psychopaths that got respect simply because others were scared of them. So what chance did he have when he wasn't even an official part of the gang?

Dismissing these thoughts from his head, D arrived at the edge of the parking lot of the McDonalds. Looking down at the ground to make sure he didn't step in any shit, D was about to push his way through some waist high bushes when a burst of loud conversation entered his ears. Out of the main doors a group of seven teens emerged. All of them were black and dressed in baggy jeans and oversized hooded sweatshirts. Gangsters!

Not recognizing any of them right away, D thought about turning around and avoiding a possible confrontation when a familiar voice called out to him.

"Oh shit waddup D! How you doing it right now?"

D peered closer at the group of teens who were now staring him down and saw Whop emerge from the middle of the crowd. On seeing Whop's grinning face, D's mood relaxed slightly. Only slightly. Just because he knew Whop didn't guarantee his safety if the other six youths he was with decided to turn hostile. Walking over to the group, D shook Whop's hand and nodded in greeting to his friends. He received a few in return. Used to hostility from people he didn't know, D ignored the stares and turned back to Whop.

"Sup Whop, what's going on with you?"

Looking around at his friends standing around him, the chubby youngster produced a swisher from his pocket and held it up.

"Oh you already know what's up D, were tryna find something to fill this up with. We would've been smoking but Chaz over here lost the fucking weed we put up on yesterday."

Chaz, a skinny young man with cornrows and thick eyebrows scowled as Whop pointed him out.

"I told you nigga two times already I swear I don't know what happened. It was in my pants pocket last night but..."

Whop waved away any more of Chaz's excuses.

"Like I said this nigga lost the fucking weed so now we aint got shit to smoke on before class. I'm bout to be pissed off in first period."

D thought to himself for a second. It was always a good idea to stay cool with the younger crowd because they were the ones who were thirsty for reputations and willing to do anything to get them. No respect and a willingness to do anything made them dangerous. And it was always best to have danger directed away from one's self. GT's generous blessing of extra weed was going to come in handy in more than one way.

"Shit Whop if tree's is what you need then you talking with the right man. I be smoking at that bus stop back there every morning. You already got the swisher so we aint got to waste no more time in this damn parking lot."

Whop's face split into a wide grin.

"My nigga, let's do this! My fault let me introduce you to the homies. Eh y'all this nigga D, he's friends with Chris and Money Mike. He hustles with us in the town sometimes."

"Aw I knew I recognized you," said a tall youth with an afro and East African facial features, "you was like best friends with Anthony huh?"

D looked the teen in his eyes.

"Was and I still am! He taught me a lot and I'll never forget him. Nice to meet y'all though. Now you niggas tryna smoke or not?"

"Hell yeah!" came the reply.

As the group walked down the streets and introductions were made all around, the initial hostility that D had felt emanating from the young teens faded and was replaced by respect and curiosity. Chris and Money Mike were like legends to them and to suddenly find themselves talking to someone that was best friends with those legends brought out nothing but admiration. As soon as they knew that D was pretty much one of their own, scowls disappeared and conversations started flowing. D in turn found out from Whop that all of the young men were active members of Duce Trey that had joined within the last year of so. A mixed group of freshmen and sophomores, none of them were over the age of sixteen. They were foot soldiers whose main tasks were patrolling their neighborhood watching for enemies and police or being sent to other rival gang territories to disrupt activity and disrespect them in any way

63

possible. They were the backbone of the gang, the unsung heroes and D had nothing but respect for them.

Reaching the bus stop, D and Whop sat on the bench while the rest of the teens gathered around them. As D began breaking weed buds down on a creased dollar bill, Whop took a pint of cheap vodka out of his pocket and after taking a huge gulp began passing it around the circle. Taking the swisher from Whop's hands, D split the cigar in half and emptied it of the dry tobacco leaves. As D stuffed the wrapper with weed, Chaz, whom Whop had cussed out earlier began free styling as the boy next to him began laying down a beat with his mouth.

> *Yeah nigga what it do its ya boy Chaz Cool*
> *Before school with the homies drinking puffin a few*
> *Shit aint new fuck a square life I'm heavy in the street*
> *Every day with a banger shoot at strangers I settle beef*
> *So young but out here life fast and furious*
> *No movie I satisfy young girls that's curious*
> *It's Duce Trey on mines them other niggaz is lame*
> *Really we run central high them other niggaz is tame*
> *We run through and wreck shit like we a crime mob convention*
> *They knuck so we buck knocking out teeth and teaching lessons*
> *I aint no bitch boy I'll whoop that ass like you was stealing*
> *Triple threat punched kicked and stabbed now you bleeding*
> *Deuce Trey waddup though! My FAM till the death*
> *Roll a swisher of that bomb every time that I'm stressed*
> *No less than five bitches on my dick at all times*
> *I run my city like marathons causing crime*
> *Fuck doing time I'll hold court in the street*
> *I was raised by Eazy and Cube so Fuck the Police*

D was impressed. This kid Chaz actually had some good rhythm. He might be forgetful but he clearly was quick on his feet when it came to thinking up rhymes out of nowhere. As the blunt and bottle were passed around different youngsters all took their turn at rhyming. While not all of them sounded as good as Chaz, they each went at with a furious determination.

All but two of them. Whop was more concentrated on the bottle then the rap session going on around him and D was quietly observing the skills being displayed by the young Duce Trey members. They had rhythm but only Chaz had any real concept of rhyme. As the rhymes stopped and an argument began to erupt   about whose flow was better, Whop looked over at D.

"Yo D. Can I holla at you bout something right quick?"

D looked back at his red eyed friend but saw, through the haze of weed and liquor, a sincere request. D nodded. He and Whop stood up and walked through the crowd of bickering teens to stand about five feet further down the street. As they came to a stop, D noticed that Whop was looking unusually agitated. He was taking frequent large gulps of the alcohol and it appeared as if he couldn't stand in one spot without shifting his body weight from foot to foot and looking around as if he was expecting someone to jump out from behind a tree.

"Whop wassup bro you feeling aight? You look like you got something on your mind."

Whop nodded his head.

"Yeah I guess you could say that. Look D, some shit went down in the neighborhood last night that you need to know about. Chris told me to mention it to you when I saw you in school."

D suddenly began to feel uneasy. Something about Whops tone of voice and the way he was drinking out of that pint were suddenly taking his thoughts down a very sinister path. Whatever had gone down the previous night clearly didn't belong in the good news department.

"Well damn Whop don't tell me everything at once. Just spit it out this aint no damn suspense movie."

Whop took a deep breath.

"Remember that nigga who shot Anthony? Devontay?"

D's eyes narrowed dangerously.

Whop shrugged.

"Yeah never mind dumb question. Anyways, you know how we aint been able to find him?"

"Yeah so what, fuck that nigga."

"Yeah I know. Anyways, he's back."

D's entire body froze in place. He saw but stopped hearing the words coming out of Whop's mouth. Images of the night Anthony died danced through his brain. The fight between Devontay and Duce Trey member. The harsh yells and sounds of knuckles on flesh. Anthony trying to break up the fight. The loud bang as Devontay pulled his gun and fired. Blood squirted out of the huge ragged hole in Anthony's chest as he sank to the ground, body shaking and convulsing from the pain. It had been months but all of a sudden it felt like it had happened yesterday. Devontay being found meant that revenge could finally be taken by Chris and the rest of Duce Trey. D was no killer but Chris and Money Mike had vowed vengeance and it looked like they'd finally get their chance. Why then did Whop seem so upset?

"Sorry Whop I didn't hear what you just said my mind is kind of fucked up right now. What's wrong with him being found?"

Whop looked up at D with a slightly annoyed expression but proceeded to tell the short version of his story.

"Like I said man, apparently this nigga been locked up this whole time in county. Some probation violation. Nobody knew though so it seemed like he just disappeared. Anyways something's going on now because the word is that he had to join up inside and it aint with some friendly's. But there's a truce so touching him would start up a war again. Money Mike is pissed. There's a meeting happening on Sunday between him and the leader of the gang Devontay joined. I don't know what's going to happen though. We're not supposed to touch him until then."

Whop took another sip from his bottle. Back at the bus stop two young boys were participating in a heated rap battle to settle the dispute once and for all. D's mind was struggling to make sense of what he was hearing.

"So who's Devontay with that's able to tell Money Mike to stand down? I've never known him to take orders from anybody?"

Whop took another sip.

"Nigga I don't know yet, I wasn't there but fuck whoever it is. We'll find out soon enough. Chris will probably call you when he gets a moment."

D was about to ask another question when he felt his phone vibrating in his pocket. He checked the text message.

Umm, where r u mister?

D shook his head. He had completely forgotten about his waiting customer! Checking his watch, D saw that he was supposed to have called her a half hour ago. He had been looking forward to this visit all week but now he found himself fighting back the urge to go find Chris, grab a baseball bat and go on a man hunt for Devontay so that he could beat his head until his skull bust open!

He had almost assumed that they would never find Anthony's killer and all thoughts of revenge had slowly melted from his brain to be replaced with eventual acceptance. Now, with the knowledge that any retaliation that could've been enacted was now forbidden was causing D's brain to do somersaults in his skull. Whop was right though. Chris wouldn't hesitate to call once he had solid information. Until then, D was done with school for the day.

Looking up at Whop, D extended his arm and shook his young friend's hand.

"Good looks on the update my nigga. I think I'm gonna cut out for the day."

"Where you going D?"

"Just some runs I got to go make up north. I might be back before the end of the day. Shit, before I forget, take these."

Looking up and down the street to make sure no one was watching, D shook Whops hand one more time using it as a cover to pass several plump weed bags into his possession.

Whop looked down at his hand and then up at D. D answered the question in Whops eyes with a light punch to the shoulder.

"Don't trip you don't owe me nothing. That's all you. Good looks on keeping me informed."

Whop pocketed the weed bags.

"Well like I said you aint exactly a stranger. Preciate the trees."

"Yup. Stay safe out here Whop. I'll probably be through the hood later if this business up north don't take too long."

"Yup, hit me."

"Yup."

Turning around, Whop slouched slowly off back in the direction of his friends. D watched him go for a few seconds before setting off at an easy walk up 12th avenue towards Jefferson Street. From there he could catch the number 4 bus all the way to Queen Anne neighborhood.

As he walked, D found himself shaking slightly as the realization of what Whop had told him continued to sink in. Devontay was back! The boy who had murdered his best friend. The news that he was now a gang member was a little unsettling to D but not because he was scared of Devontay but because D was aware of just how much harder it was going to be to get to him now that he had protection.

He wondered what Money Mike's plan of action would be. He also wondered why it was he was leaving the responsibility solely in Money Mike's hands. Didn't he owe it Anthony to seek revenge for his killing?

Quickening his steps, D shoved his hands in his pockets. He wasn't a killer. Sure he'd beat people up but he'd never even come close to taking somebody's life. D viewed violence as an unfortunate part of life but didn't see the need to use it unnecessarily. Up until Anthony's murder guns hadn't been a part of his routine. Money Mike and Chris however were another breed entirely. D knew them well enough to know that whatever retribution they were planning against Devontay was sure to be unforgivingly brutal. And D had an uneasy feeling that he might be expected to participate in carrying out the punishment. But the more he thought about it, the more he realized that's exactly what he wanted.

Chapter 11

D both liked and hated the upper middle class neighborhood of Queen Anne. Unlike the other places he usually hung out in, Downtown, Capitol Hill and the Central District where the streets were heavy with activity, Queen Anne was a relatively quiet and secluded section of the city. A haven for rich young couples with kids and the elderly looking for a place to escape the danger's that plagued the poorer sections of the city, Queen Anne was practically devoid of street crime and therefore its police presence was relatively low.

Queen Anne Avenue, a major street that ran directly through the neighborhood and separated its east and west sides was the lifeline of the area. The street was a mile long but only half of it was commercial venues. Banks, a grocery store, several pubs, restaurants and other small stores lined the sidewalks. Everywhere there were young women pushing strollers, couples jogging and middle aged women hopping out of mini vans and expensive luxury trucks on errands for their families. And everybody was White. The rest of Queen Anne Avenue and the whole neighborhood for that matter was houses and parks on quiet residential streets.

Getting off the bus at the corner of Queen Anne Avenue and Boston Street, D passed a Starbucks on his left and headed west into the neighborhood. As he walked down the litter free streets lined with green lawns and old Victorian style two story houses, D was amused how differently this neighborhood was compared to Capitol Hill which was a little more than ten minutes away by car.

Sending a text on his phone, D looked up and saw a middle aged white woman walking towards him pulling along a little girl by the arm and looking severely irritated. At around thirty feet, she happened to look up and spotted D. Her eyes widened with shock and another emotion that D identified as something along the lines of outrage. Quickly however, she plastered on a huge fake smile and sped her pace. She passed D with a stiff nod and a puff of wind. She was walking so fast she was almost speed walking, her young daughter damn near flying up in the air behind her. On a hunch, D glanced behind him. The lady was still walking at her quickened pace. She turned and looked over her shoulder but turned around quickly when she saw that D was looking at her. She turned her head around several more times until D got tired of his game and resumed his walk. It was funny how people treated Racism. Almost like it didn't really exist. D knew it did. All you had to do was be a person of color and it would become apparent almost immediately how little difference the change in times had on people's minds.

The neighborhoods blocks were about twice as long as the downtown blocks. Almost ten minutes later as D was crossing over 8th avenue West, a brand new solid black Cadillac Escalade with limousine tints on all the windows pulled up beside him. D kept walking but eyed the big truck warily out the corner of his eyes. The front passenger window rolled down.

"Excuse me! Excuuuusssee me! Hey there, are you lost?"

D stopped dead in his tracks. The sweet, youthful sounding voice belonged to a sweet, youthful looking white woman with long blond hair. She was leaning across the seat as far as her small frame would allow and was gazing at D in an innocent expression on her face. D fought back a retort that was dancing around his lips and instead focused on the generous amount of cleavage his eyes were being treated to. White people were funny acting. Some were scared others were overly friendly to complete strangers. This lady looked like one of those young soccer moms; Blond, attractive and driving a truck that was entirely too big for her. Her blue eyes sparkled in the morning light and as D's gaze moved up from her chest to

71

connect with their hypnotizing embrace he found himself imagining many ways this situation could play out. *If only*, he thought.

"No I'm not lost thanks. I'm visiting a friend who lives just up the street from here." He pointed in the direction he was already walking.

The woman nodded. Then she looked at her watch.

" Shouldn't you be in school young man?"

"On no ma'am I already graduated and I don't have work today. I'm older then I look trust me. Good genes I guess. That or all the Ezelles fried chicken I eat!"

The attractive blond laughed. A sound that seemed to brighten the colors around them and bring the world a little more into focus. It was as if D eyes had just turned into twin high definition cameras. Damn she looked good when she laughed!

"You're funny. I've been to Ezelles before. Great chicken. I'm Breanna by the way." She stuck her small hand out of the window. D shook it softly. Her skin was smooth and delicate to the touch.

"I'm Damien. But everybody I know calls me D for short."

"Oh ok. Well nice to meet you D."

"Nice to meet you Breanna."

Breanna eyed D up and down quickly like a jeweler would appraise a diamond.

"Would you like a ride the rest of the way to your friend's house?"

D tried to conceal his surprise and delight. He looked up and down the street but saw nobody paying any attention to the interaction taking place between him and the lady in the escalade. He grinned at her. The doors unlocked and less than a second later the big luxury truck peeled away from the corner. Relaxing in the passenger seat, D enjoyed the feeling of the breeze on his face as they continued through the neighborhood. He snuck a quick glance at Breanna out of the corner of his eye. She was dressed casual in a tight grey shirt with hip hugging black jeans and grey boots in her feet. Her straight but thick blond hair cascaded down her back and a pair of pink sunglasses were perched on her forehead. She was fine!

The woman kept driving for another five minutes, well past the spot D had indicated he was headed but he didn't appear to be worried. As they reached a particularly affluent block which was dotted with big three story houses that resembled miniature mansions, Breanna rolled all the windows up and turned off the radio. Arriving halfway down the bloc in front of a two story brick house with a large two car garage in front, Breanna pressed a button on her trucks dashboard and the garage door began to slowly open, When the door was all the way up Breanna drove inside. D reached for the door handle in preparation to exit the vehicle but Breanna grabbed his hand.

"Not yet. Wait until the door is closed all the way."

Less than thirty seconds later the door to the garage was back down and Breanna and D were exiting the vehicle. Following Breanna through a door in the back of the garage and down a long low hallway that opened up into the basement level of the house, D found himself in a long low ceilinged room. It was a complete man cave! A huge 72inch plasma screen hung on the left side wall with a huge plush leather couch with a lazy boy chair on either side directly in front of it. A bar occupied the back wall space with genuine bar stools all in front of the counter. A full sized pool table was set up behind the couch and behind that was the staircase leading to the main floor.

Throwing her keys onto a nearby table, Breanna turned around and gave D a big hug which he returned with equal enthusiasm.

The little show they had put on before had just been a stunt they had come up with to fool anybody who might be passing by or paying too much attention to them. In reality the two knew each other extremely well.

Apart from being Breanna's weed man, D also happened to go to school with her little sister. An equally pretty white girl named Samantha who was a senior like D. D had met Samantha years ago when he had first started selling weed. Samantha's boyfriend had been a regular customer which is how they first crossed paths. Samantha then started calling D whenever she or any of her friends needed some and eventually had asked him if it was cool if she gave his number to her older sister who was married but still an avid pot smoker. The two had formed an instant friendship due to Breanna's free spirited nature and D's laid back attitude towards life and everything in it.

Letting go of D, Breanna turned around and sat down on the couch. Shrugging off his backpack D placed himself in one of the lazy boy chairs.

"D how have you been and what took you so fucking long? I thought you were going to be here yesterday?"

"Sorry about that I was busy in other parts of the city yesterday. I would have been here sooner today but I saw some friends on the way up here and stopped to talk for a second. It was kind of important. Came as quick as I could though. How was your trip?"

Grabbing her bag, Breanna took out a pink digital camera and powered it on. Accessing the image library, she tossed the camera to D.

"Here check it out. If you haven't been San Francisco is the most beautiful city you will ever step foot in. At least to me. The Bay Area is like Seattle multiplied a dozen times over. Hills, water, the views and the people, it's just an amazing experience."

As D perused the pictures he could see exactly what Breanna was talking about. Images of huge glittering expanses of open water, immense redwood trees, and huge hills dotted with majestic multiple story homes, it looked like a world the likes of which he'd never seen. Up until now D had spent his entire life in the Capitol Hill neighborhood of Seattle. It wasn't the super ghetto but it wasn't the nicest place in the world either. He'd often wondered what life was like outside of Seattle. He just wasn't sure of how he'd ever get a chance to experience it. Passing Breanna's camera back to her, D picked his backpack up off the floor and placed it in his back. Unzipping the main pocket he withdrew a sizable sandwich bag filled with weed and tossed it to Breanna. Opening it, Breanna took a huge whiff of the weed inside and a wide smile extended itself across her face.

"Thank god! Just what I needed. This is an ounce right?"

74

D nodded.

"Yup it's the same price as always. I even brought you a complimentary package of swishers."

"Tell then let's not waste any more time. I'll go grab the money from upstairs and you mister, how about you start rolling that blunt up."

"Yes ma'am!"

Together, the odd pair of friends spent an enjoyable couple of hours talking, playing pool and smoking blunt after blunt of D's excellent herb. Breanna went in to detail about her trip to San Francisco, telling about all the places outside of the city that she and one of her old girlfriends had visited.

D mostly listened and asked questions. When they were finally too high to concentrate on anything but sitting down, D and Breanna collapsed on the couch. After a few moments of silence Breanna turned towards D.

"So D, you've been asking me all these questions about my life I haven't been able to see how you're doing. How's school going for you? Isn't this your last year?"

"Yup." When he proceeded to tell Brenna that he had left school to come see her she was horrified. D calmed her down by explaining that he didn't really need the classes he was missing today and besides he needed the money more than the schooling.

"I know it might not seem so right now but D, I promise you an education will pay off more in the long run than a few dollars right now. I'm glad you say you're going to graduate but have you thought about what you're going to do after high school? "

Sitting back in his chair, D was too distracted by thoughts of what was going on now with Chris and Money Mike regarding Anthony's killer to answer the question. He'd had nothing but bad vibes since he had encountered Whop and his friends earlier that morning. He checked his watch. It was coming up on Four pm. He'd spent almost the entire day getting high and drunk while serious shit was probably going down as he sat here.

Standing up, D began gathering all his belongings.

"I don't really know. What about you?" he asked Breanna repacking his backpack. "Did you leave high school with a plan? And if you did, are you still following it? Because honestly, I haven't really been able to focus on nothing lately. Life don't exactly make sense to me right now if you can understand where I'm coming from."

Noting the seriousness of D's tone, Breanna placed her half-finished glass of wine on the table and stood up. Coming around the table, she gave D a light hug.

"I know Damien. I'm very sorry about your friend. I don't really understand what goes on in other parts of the city but I wish it didn't involve kids like you. As far as my plans went, well…" Breanna looked around the den at the pool table, the huge plasma screen TV, the complete bar on the back wall and frowned. "Looks deceived me. I was blinded by my dreams and wanted to get them the fastest way I could."

Breanna turned to look at D and the teen could see the depths of sorrow emanating from her soul to mass just behind the pupils of her eyes so that blue orbs became almost black for a moment. D knew the reason. Breanna had told him about her high paid executive husband who was almost ten years older than her. He was nice enough when he was sober, which was rare. His job constantly had him traveling across the world and the constant separation had created a rift in their relationship. When he was home he held on to the bottle like it contained the secrets of like within in its silvery depths.

He began to think she was cheating on him and instead of simply ask a question, he had turned bitter and angry and one night had badly beaten her in a drunken rage. He had apologized profusely and cried and promised to get help and she had eventually forgiven him and refused to press charges.

They had since made up but things were forever different from that moment on. Their love felt forced at times.

Damien looked down at the small blond woman who had become his friend. He felt oddly protective of her and wished he could do more than hook her up with good weed and provide her an ear and good company when she needed it. But D understood. She was like his therapy too.

Walking past him, Breanna picked her keys up off the counter and drained the last sip of whisky out of her glass. D couldn't help but stare at her shapely figure in her tight clothes. He would've sworn she had some black genes somewhere in her family tree.

Turning around, Breanna caught D staring and waited patiently with a smile on her face until his gaze traveled back up to her face and they locked eyes. D jumped.

"Uh my bad I was just uh…" he hastened to come with a reasonable excuse, failed and just shrugged his shoulders.

"What can I say? You're fine as hell and you know it. Sorry."

Breanna's face turned bright red and she covered her mouth with a small hand.

"All right you little charmer where would you like me to drop you off at?"

D grinned. He knew she liked his compliments.

"Back at school is fine. I got some people to meet."

Chapter 12

"It's all bad bro."

From the look he saw on Chris's face, D wasn't finding it hard to believe him. It was late Friday evening and D had just met up with Chris before the two of them headed to Courtney's party. They were currently sitting on the porch of Chris's house watching the traffic flow lazily by on 23rd avenue. After Breanna had dropped him off, D hadn't bothered going back to class and instead had headed straight for the Central District to see Chris and Money Mike.

He hadn't liked what he'd been told.

Money Mike had been so furious that after walking around the living room screaming insults punching walls he had grabbed his car keys and stormed out of the house slamming the door behind him. With the house quiet, Chris had rolled up a blunt, suggested that they go out and smoke on the porch and proceeded to explain how the previous night's events unfolded.

A meeting had occurred that previous morning at the break of dawn in the middle of the Judkin's Park field between Money Mike and the leader of FEB, a big but slightly chubby dark skinned man by the name of Trouble.

Chris along with twenty other members of Deuce Trey stood a little ways apart from the meeting directly behind Money Mike. Around the same number of FEB members did the same behind Trouble. The tension in the air had been thick with possibility of violence behind every still second. Devontay was nowhere in sight.

Trouble was just that; trouble. A bully for the short time he actually attended school, Trouble got into the early habit of forcefully taking what he wanted through fear and intimidation.

78

Sneering at the Seattle teens that joined up with California based gangs like the Bloods and Crips, Trouble wanted something from Seattle he could represent. This eventually led him to form a small five member gang called FEB (Fuck EveryBody) which was aimed at police, rival California gangs and other homegrown Seattle gangs.

After dropping out of high school at the age of sixteen, Trouble soon found himself coming into constant contact with "Everybody" and his unofficial gang began to officially take shape. FEB didn't own any particular territory but instead let its criminal activity take it all across Seattle to wherever they could make money at. Most of its members were from the Central District but Trouble recruited anyone with a knack for criminal talent. In his early thirties now with multiple bids to the penitentiary under his belt for drug trafficking and assaults, he showed no signs of giving up his criminal career. And it just so happened that Devontay was his cousin.

Under no circumstances was Trouble going to allow anything to happen to Devontay without a swift and violent retaliation being delivered. Money Mike argued that since it was an FEB member who spilled the first blood, retribution was not only necessary but allowed. Trouble had said that since Devontay hadn't been a part of the gang at the time of the killing it had nothing to do with FEB. Money Mike said since FEB took Devontay in they also took on his baggage. At this, Trouble had flatly refused any kind of deal. Any strike against FEB by Deuce Trey would be a declaration of war and an open invitation for FEB to take matters into its own hands.

This statement had only pissed Money Mike off more and the meeting had dissolved into shit talking with threats and jeers being thrown out by either side. Hands began forming gang signs in the air but before any violence could break out a passing cop car flashing its lights had sent both sides scattering into the darkness leaving nothing but bad blood in the air.

Technically everything came down to whether Money Mike chose to move against FEB in revenge for Anthony's death, which was really a beef directed entirely and solely at Devontay. But if Devontay was hit then that would mean war

79

with FEB because of his blood relationship with their leader Trouble.

The way Chris saw things, there was so much hostility now between the two groups that it was only a matter of time before a chance encounter between rival gang members would result in some serious bloodshed.

"It all comes down to whose gonna trip first," said Chris through a mouthful of smoke. "Either one of us is gonna get so mad about Anthony being killed they're going say fuck it and just blast the first FEB cat they catch slipping or FEB is gonna think we've gone soft if we don't do shit and come through tryna take our shit over. It aint even the older fools we gotta worry about. It's the young niggaz trying to make a name for themselves that are going to take advantage of this situation and flex their little muscles."

Chris looked over at D seriously as he passed him the blunt.

"It's bout to go down at Central bro. Just so you know, you might wanna walk a little more careful in these coming days. That school is full of FEB niggaz! Deuce Trey is in there tough too but that's exactly why it's going to go down. You should start bringing a knife with you." After D had grabbed the blunt, Chris broke eye contact with him and went back to staring out at the street.

Taking a strong hit of thick smoke, D inhaled deeply and held it for as long as he could until he had to breathe out again. The buzz usually hit him stronger when he did that. The information Chris had shared with him had sent several emotions running through his head in the same way as when Whop had told him the initial situation. Only now, things had gotten more serious.

Duce Trey and FEB's numbers combined easily numbered over a hundred. To contain that many different individual feelings of hatred wasn't going to be any small task. Chris insisted that both sides would obey they word of their respected leaders but there was no telling what the word would be. Nothing had been decided at the meeting and it was clear that

80

had there not been any interference from the police then the two sides would have already come to blows or worse.

"The thing is," said Chris seriously taking the blunt D was holding out to him, "we came off the worse in this situation. They technically are getting away with murdering one of ours on a technicality and that isn't going to sit well with anybody. Anthony wasn't just your best friend he was considered family to everybody in Duce Trey. His loss is being felt by hundreds of people besides you. They all want payback but are now being told not to do anything when we all know exactly who did it! This shit is fucking ridiculous and Money Mike knows it! Trouble knows it too but he also knows Money Mike isn't going to start a war if it can be avoided."

D thought quietly to himself for a moment. It felt weird having the inner politics of Chris's gang life explained to him in such a matter of fact way. Like a teacher explain to a student why two countries were at war with one another and the history relating to how the conflict began in the first place. Everything was so structured yet the underlying threat of pure chaos was always on the horizon. Anthony had used to explain certain things like territory and rules of engagement to D but had always told him never to repeat anything he learned during their conversations.

Anthony had told D he was trustworthy enough and because their movements frequently brought them into dangerous areas, he had thought it best for D to know what was going on around him that he normally wouldn't have been aware of. It looked like Chris was the new teacher and D knew better than to is or piss him off. He looked and learned.

"Why you saying I need a knife though?" he asked Chris.

"Because D, you never know whose looking at you at any given moment. Someone from FEB might see you with us one day and make the assumption that you're down with Duce Trey. That makes you a potential target should all this tension explode one day and we really have to go to war with these fools. Also, these niggaz are sneaky. They don't have any real territory so they're just spread out all across the CD and the rest of Seattle for that matter. We gotta go looking for them but they know exactly where we be at all day!"

Chris raised both his hands in the air; pointer finger, thumb and pinky all pointing straight out and spaced apart and his middle and ring finger pressed together and folded down towards his palm. It was one of Duce Treys various hand signals. The pointer finger and folded down middle and ring fingers formed the slight image of a number two and the pointer, pinky and thumb resembled a sideways view of the number three.

"DUCE TREY YOU PUNK ASS NIGGAZ!" he shouted out towards the street, "TWENTY THIRD AVENUE AINT GOIN OUT LIKE THAT!"

There was no response. All remained quiet. The cars kept driving past. A few passing pedestrians offered quick glances but nothing more. Chris lapsed into silence with a heavy look of concentration plastered across his face. After a few moments, he stood up beckoning for D to do the same.

"Yo D, you're like a brother to me bro foreal, that's on everything I love. But in saying that, you know I got to keep it real with you. You might not want to come to this party tonight."

D looked confused,

"Why the fuck not nigga? You know I can look after myself!"

Chris shook his head.

"You not hearing me D. The shit is about to go down. I can feel it in the air. My gut is telling me something is about to go down tonight but I don't know what. It could be a fight, a jumping, a stabbing, or even a killing! I'm going because I'm in this shit ya feel me but you shouldn't put yourself in harm's way like that if you don't have too.

"You already know you're going to be around nothing but Duce Trey niggaz and if another muthufucka come around and start shooting he's not gonna stop to ask you whether you bang or not. Death walks amongst us homie."

D nodded fully aware of what the possible outcome of going to a party like this under such dire circumstances could be like. But the memory of Anthony and everything they had been through only fueled D's desire to be there for his only remaining

82

friend. He had already pledged his services to Money Mike and something told him that his card was going to get pulled much sooner than later. This would be like a training session. D squared his shoulders.

"Fuck it! Let's go!"

A rare crooked smile spread itself slowly across his friends face. Bending down, Chris withdrew a Highpoint 9 millimeter pistol from under the couch cushions and shoved it into his jeans waistline. He fumbled with his shirt for a moment until he was sure it covered the slight bulge in his crouch area. Satisfied, he looked up at D.

"Aight, we out!'

Chapter 13

Several hours later…

"…yeah man can you believe that shit? So then the nigga wanna tell me 'c'mon bro this is a neutral zone I'm not even up here beefing I'm just tryna get some new clothes.' I was like nigga fuck you, fuck this neutral zone and fuck your clothes! Smack! Had to beat this niggaz ass right in front of the Macy's! Then I just ran across the street and hopped on the bus."

As Chris finished telling his story, D and the rest of the young men that had been listening laughed as they pictured the event play out in their minds. Draining the last of the beer from his plastic cup, D signaled to Chris he was going to go get another refill. Nodding his head in acknowledgment, Chris went back to telling his story. Turning away from the group, D weaved his way between other groups of chatting teens and made his way towards the back door of Courtney's house whose backyard they were all congregating in.

Contrary to Chris's predictions the party was actually going pretty smooth. There hadn't been any incidents so far and considering the amount of people that had shown up it was actually surprising there had been any fights yet. The party was really about five different parties in one with people gathering mainly in the front yard, the kitchen, the basement, the living room and the back yard. The people in the front yard were mostly older gang members acting as security for the party and the girls they had come with. The kitchen was the booze center. The counter tops were loaded down with beer, liquor bottles, chip bags and plastic cups. Intoxicated young men and women stood around in easy reach of a refill and were drunkenly engaging in loud conversations with one another. The floor had turned sticky had turned sticky with the access of spilled drinks but no one seemed to care.

The basement and living room had been converted to mini dance floors and each was packed with a congregation of gyrating bodies. The young men and women were glued together at the hips moving in ways that would have earned them a week's suspension had they been caught doing them at a school dance. The backyard had been labeled "the smoking section" which of course meant that anybody who had something to light up was out here. Whether cigarette or swisher, Courtney wasn't allowing none of it inside. That was the reason Chris and D had stepped out but the smoking had made D thirsty again.

Stepping through the back door, D entered the kitchen. It had emptied out a little since last time he had been in here. There were only five people left. Two boys in baggy dark clothing that D recognized were nodding their heads and taking turns rapping over an instrumental that was blasting from a set of portable speakers plugged up to a cd player. Their names were Skully and Jovan. Skully was currently rapping while Jovan listened. Skully, true to his name, had on a black skullcap to match his entirely black outfit. Jovan, a little on the chubby side, had on a large white tee and dark blue jeans. Three extremely attractive girls stood around them dancing and clapping their hands in time with the music. With a jolt to his stomach, D realized that Courtney was one of the girls in the group!

Moving her hips to the rhythm of the bouncy southern beat that was playing, D felt himself becoming mesmerized by her body. Dressed in a loose white tee that was tied in a knot in the back with black tights and black heels, it was almost as if she was stealing the air right out of D's lungs. Pouring himself a large cup of Hennessey, D was about to go back outside and rejoin Chris when he was distracted by Jovan beckoning him to jump in the session. He was about to decline but Courtney turned around and seeing that it was D smiled and gestured with her hand for him to come over. That did it. *It's a damn shame she has this spell on me*, D thought to himself. The chance to possibly impress could not be missed. Taking a big gulp of liquid courage, D made his way across the kitchen. Jovan and

Skully parted to make room and just like that it was on with Jovan taking over without missing a beat:

Aint a damn thing handed down I did all from scratch
Lost my mind in the Central District I'll never get it back
I mix intricate wordplay with a passion for stayin true
Twistin delicate herbs laced with some hash that was made to use
Gotta stay true to my vision to many homies in prison
Still aint impressed with my living that's why I feed my ambition
Don't take no for shit I just acquire and upgrade
Whoop ass and take names fuck what a nerd say
A past full of baggies filled with felony products
Today the same need money called the man and I stocked up
Money, money, money I'm from Duce Trey eastside
The honeys always love me I been fucking since knee high
Born into chaos another fetus gets drafted
Introduced to a cold world it won't be long for he's active
We all got problems it's just the way that you face em
My niggaz turning out bitches your niggaz turning out basic

As he came to the last line, Jovan nodded at D, signaling it was his turn to jump in the spotlight. D was not a novice when it came to free styling and actually was considered to be pretty good by those around him. The alcohol and weed in his system boosted his confidence as well. Taking a breath he opened his mouth and stopped thinking, letting the words come out of his mouth without pre meditation. Rapping was easy to D. And fun.

I use Ill-gotten gains to buy beer and Mary Jane
Chase intoxication homie I aint changing in my ways
No path to Bill Gates cash I'm stuck on this petty shit
House licks and stolen cars aint nothing I won't hit

86

Don't play street fighter but I've fought in the street
though
The boxing skills will knock a nigga out of his steel toes
Not really a gangsta just as broke as the next man
Rob someone sell something then it's on to the next plan
Lost a few friends due to struggle and violence
Some died driving drunk some got shot between the
eyelids
So I continue to pursue the prize of life
While most folks continue to misuse god given rights
Dark clouds and grey skies this Seattle for life
Bark loud with no bite you getting beat up tonight
My nigga Anthony, A1 as he known in the street
You'll always be remembered don't trip just rest in peace

"NIGGA YOUR FILTHY," screamed Skully, pounding D on the back with his hand.

"Hell yeah bro that was sick," agreed Jovan. D smiled and shook Jovan's outstretched hand.

"Thanks bro, y'all was sick too. I remember hearing y'all rapping in the cafeteria before you guys dropped out."

"Yeah," said Skully, taking a huge gulp of beer from his cup, "the good old days."

"Fuck school," added Jovan patting his bulging pockets, "get paper nigga!"

"Trying bro," said D shaking his head, "you know how it goes."

Both Jovan and Skully nodded in understanding. Life was hard enough to get through as it was. Add being black to the equation, it only got harder.

Courtney and her friends were looking on the three young men with interest sparkling in all three of their eyes. Skully was talking but D's attention had focused entirely on Courtney. She was staring at him with a curious expression on her face. The kind of way a jeweler would examine a newly made diamond ring that was to be delivered to a king or queen. D knew that look. He'd seen it before in girls faces. He was being appraised.

As Skully and Jovan resumed rapping, D, deciding he needed a refill, went back over to the fridge for some more beer. Hennessey was easily his favorite drink but right now he needed a chaser. As he poured another can of high life into his cup, Courtney came over and stood next to him.

"Nice rhymes, she said nodding towards D's cup. "Mind hooking me up with one of those?"

D nodded

"Yeah no problem."

Taking another can out of the refrigerator, D snatched up one of the few remaining clean plastic cups and cracking the beer can, carefully poured out the liquid at an angle so that it didn't leave a thick layer of foam. He handed Courtney her full cup.

"I didn't know you be rapping," said Courtney, taking a small sip from her cup. D took huge gulp from his and shrugged.

"Well, I don't really rap like that. I mean, I don't have any songs recorded or nothing like that. I do it mostly because I like the idea of telling stories through rhyme and rhythm. It's fun too. I would never want to be a rapper though. Too much politics involved."

Courtney nodded her head slightly.

"You wouldn't want to be famous though? Music videos, commercials, award shows, all of that glamorous lifestyle shit. You don't ever imagine yourself up on stage being applauded and appreciated for what you do with thousands of people all screaming your name?"

It was a good image. There was only one problem. D didn't know what he'd be famous for. Almost everybody he knew wanted to be a rapper or a singer or a movie star. Not wanting to be another one of many, D was trying to find something he could do well enough that would enable to him to make a life for himself while avoiding the mass rush to microphones and recording booth's that most of his friends were getting caught up in.

"I guess I could see myself being famous," D agreed. "But it wouldn't be for rapping."

"What then?" asked Courtney, taking another sip.

Before D could answer the sound of loud angry voices became audible over the music bumping in the background. Everybody in the kitchen instantly stopped what they were doing and rushed out the door into the backyard.

A good amount of people were still outside but the majority of them were quickly backing up from a confrontation taking place between two groups of teenage boys in the middle of the yard. One group was sizable. Around ten angry youths throwing hand signs and jeers while one of them in front was busy shouting angrily. Opposite them were three young dark skinned teens looking equally angry but making no move to engage the larger group.

One look and D instantly recognized Chris as the one doing the shouting. Currently he was arguing with what looked like the spokesperson for the outnumbered group a cocky looking cornrowed youngster in a white tee and baggy beige khakis. Skully and Jovan were already pushing their way through the on looking crowd and D without a second thought, followed them. As they got nearer they were able to hear what was being said.

Chris's face looked like it was turning purple with rage.

"I'M ONLY GONNA TEL YOU NIGGAZ ONE MORE TIME! GET THE FUCK OUT OF THIS PARTY RIGHT NOW!!! I DON'T KNOW HOW THE FUCK YOU GOT IN HERE BUT YOU DAMN SHO AINT WELCOME! FEB AINT GOT NO FRIENDS HERE!"

"NIGGA YOU NOT GON DO NOTHING!" Cornrows yelled back, "WE GOT A TREATY AND YOU AINT GON BREAK THIS SHIT OVER SOME WEAK ASS PARTY SO FUCK YOU! WE LEAVIN ANYWAYS Y'ALL AINT SHIT BUT FAKE ASS NIGGAS AND UGLY ASS HOES!!!"

Chris's hands were balled into fists and clenched so tightly that his hand was turning white from the blood loss. His face didn't look human anymore. But as angry as he was Chris made no hostile movements. Even he wasn't dumb enough to go against Money Mike's orders unless specifically told too by Money Mike himself. A catch 22.

As D watched the proceedings a hot wave of anger washed over him. Here were three members of the gang that had taken in his best friend's killer and were now prevented from retaliating against all because of some half assed gang peace treaty! The combination of alcohol and anger reached a boiling point as he saw the three boys preparing to leave and realized that if he didn't something, they were going to get away free as birds even with the disrespect they had showed just by coming to the party.

Glancing to his side, he saw Courtney cussing out the group as they walked past for disrespecting her party. They only waved her away with their hands spitting on the ground.

"Shut the fuck up bitch!" said Cornrows spitting at Courtney's feet. It was then that D knew what he had to do. Breaking through the crowd, D ran up to stand beside Chris.

"Hey you, bitch boy with the braids," he called after the retreating FEB members. The dark sinned boy he was talking to spun around instantly, eyes searching furiously for the person who had called to him. D raised his hands in the air to identify himself. Cornrows scowled.

"Nigga what did you say?"

"You heard me," replied D, nervous but refusing to back down. "You aint shit for coming here when you knew nothing would happen. Well. They might not be able to touch you, but I can!"

Chris looked at D in surprise, but only for a second. Immediately his face split into a wide grin.

"You damn right get on out there D! Fuck this nigga up for the hood!"

Cornrows was looking slightly nervous.

"Nigga what the fuck you mean Duce Trey can't make any moves and we can't either so back up before we both catch violations."

"Nigga this nigga aint Duce Trey so he can do whatever he wants," said Chris with an evil smile dancing around his face, "wassup are you a bitch boy like he saying you is?"

90

"I don't bang bruh I swear," said D, "But one of yours killed my best friend and tonight I'm getting some payback anyway I can take it. So fuck this talking!"

Throwing his cup on the ground and pulling up his pants, D took several steps away from the crowd and assumed a boxer stance. An instant roar went up from Chris and all the Duce Trey members gathered behind him. Moving quickly they formed a circle around the three FEB members and D preventing anybody from getting out of the coming fight.

"You two niggas get the fuck back!" demanded Chris pointing a finger viciously at Cornrow's two friends. "This is going be a fair fight or fuck a violation somebody getting stomped the fuck out tonight!" No argument came.

Cornrows saw there was no escape so he squared his shoulders and put his hands up.

"Let's go then nigga!"

Cornrows came in fast and began swinging immediately for D's head. He ducked the first few but caught a glancing blow to the side of the head and another to the jaw at the end. D countered with a set of straights and felt one connect. The attacking arms stopped swimming for just a second and D used the moment to back away and straighten up. Coming back in quick he caught Cornrows just as he was repositioning himself and landed two solid haymakers, making Cornrow's head bounce like a speed bag.

Not stopping his momentum, D hurled a hard punch right into Cornrows stomach. As the youth gasped and doubled over, D grabbed his shoulders and kneed Cornrows brutally in the face. A horrible *CRACK* rang out through the air and the Cornrows collapsed onto the ground holding his face and sobbing as blood gushed like a fountain out between his fingers.

WHAP! WHAP! WHAP!

D staggered to the side as he was hit repeatedly in the face by the two remaining FEB members. Another punch caught him directly in his right eye and he went temporarily blind. Suddenly, as quick as it had begun, the attack stopped.

THUD!

Blinking through the fog of tears and pain, D saw that Whop had just blasted one of the other FEB members in the face had put him in a chokehold and was now busy calling him a bitch over and over while punching him in the ribs. The other had met a much more unfortunate fate and had disappeared underneath a mob of Duce Trey members kicking and punching him all trying to cause as much bodily harm as they could.

Girls were screaming and guys were yelling. D felt himself grabbed being dragged through the yard and the mass of bodies towards the alley. It was Chris. As they reached the alley, Chris spun him around and pointed in the direction of his house. D was expecting to get yelled at but the look of joy in Chris's face told another story.

"Look go to my crib and wait for me. I gotta stay here and clear this shit up then I'm gonna have some explaining to do. But don't trip, you aint do nothing wrong tonight nigga. If anything you proved yourself once again."

D heard the praise, but as the adrenaline began to wear off he began thinking about what had just happened and what he might have caused. His body started to shake uncontrollably. He was shocked by the sudden explosion of violence that taken over him. He looked down at his battered and bloody hands. His face was throbbing and he could already feel his eye swelling up. The sounds of screaming and fighting were still ringing out from Courtney's yard.

"Chris, I think I fucked up. What about the treaty?"

Chris shook his head angrily.

"Fuck that treaty D. it was going to break anyways. You see the type of shit they tried to pull. Sooner or later it would have gone done just like this just in someone else's backyard. Better we just get this shit out in the open anyways. Money Mike won't be mad I guarantee you. Now get to the crib before the cops or some more niggaz show up. We got it from here."

Turning around, Chris ran back towards the brawl. Looking after him, D suddenly noticed Courtney standing by her back gate. It looked she had been there watching D and Chris talking the entire time. She was looking at D with the same expression from earlier. As if she was judging the worth of his quality. Only now, it looked like she was more than happy with what she saw. She half smiled at him then shut the gate as the last of the stragglers ran out past her.

Turning around, D rubbed his face where he had gotten hit. Damn Cornrows punched hard. It was good the fight didn't last too long. D honestly felt like he'd gotten lucky. He had been scared shitless but wasn't about to admit that to anybody. He didn't usually instigate fights like that. He looked up at the sky as he walked through the dark Central District streets. If only it had been Devontay. Did this mean it was a hollow victory?

"That was for you Anthony," he said quietly, "Hopefully they got the message. At least nobody died."

Still, what was Money Mike going to think?

Chapter 14

"Well D, Trouble wants your head on a plate," said Money Mike in a strangely cheerful tone.

D looked up at him in shock. This didn't sound like the type of thing that would put someone in a good mood yet Money Mike, who didn't normally didn't look happy about anything, was walking around his house smiling like a teenage boy who'd just lost his virginity. D wondered if there was something he wasn't entirely understanding about the situation. Money Mike, saw the look on D's face patted him on the back reassuringly.

"Don't worry D, Trouble aint getting shit! He wanted me to hand you over so his soldiers could beat the hell out of you. I told him the only way that was going to happen was if he let Devontay get what's coming to him for killing Anthony. Of course Trouble said no deal so now it's open season on anybody from FEB that gets caught slipping. This fucker has been taking business away from me for years and now I can finally take his ass out! Now, I gotta get out of here and go make sure all the trap houses got extra security and that everybody knows to be extra aware of their surroundings. When Chris wakes up tell him to call me."

Grabbing his jacket off the coat rack by the door, Money Mike had just out his hand on the door knob when D spoke up.

"Yo, Money."

Money Mike turned half way around.

"Sup lil nigga?"

D shrugged. A whole list of emotions had gone parading through his head since the fight and as the understanding of what he had helped set into motion began to dawn on him, D found himself beginning to regret jumping into the middle of the confrontation. People were in danger because of him now. Blood was already on his hands.

"Sorry for starting all of this, I wasn't thinking. I just wanted to do something, anything. I felt like I was going to let Anthony down if I didn't do shut that fool up from talking all that shit and fucking up the party."

Money Mike grinned. He came over and put a hand on D's shoulder looking down at him the way a proud father would do at his son.

"D, you made me proud the way you handled that. You weren't even part of the confrontation but you jumped in to help support your friends both living and dead. That's the qualities of a real man right there; unafraid of danger and refusing to let an unjust act go without punishment.

"We need more like you D, that's the honest truth about it. Be safe out here aight lil homie? I'll scream at you guys later tonight. I need you and Chris to go on a mission this weekend okay?"

D nodded his head, his entire body flushed with an immense filling of loyalty and appreciation towards this man who was really no more than a few years older than him. All the guilt he had been feeling seemed to melt away in the face of such praise. He now felt like he hadn't done enough. As Money Mike closed the door behind him, D sank back on the couch feeling like he'd just won a lifetime achievement award.

He didn't necessarily like violence, but for Money Mike, D was pretty sure he'd beat up anybody if asked too. Lying back down on the couch, D turned the TV on. It was Monday but school wasn't even on his radar today. His face still ached from the previous night's encounter and besides, he hadn't done any of his homework.

Two hours later, Chris was up. He didn't seem surprised when D repeated Money Mike's words to him and actually patted D on the back in an eerily similar way. He called Mike as D had said and after a short conversation where Chris glanced at D out of the corner of eyes and nodded quickly and hung up the phone.

95

"We got to make a stop real quick then its mission time tonight boy! Let's go."

"Aight. What we gotta do for Money Mike?"

"Aww don't trip just make a couple pickups. Some easy shit."

The two friends headed out of Chris house and began walking down 23rd avenue heading north towards East Union Street. Chris was rocking an all brown Dickies suit with the pants tightly creased and black chucks and a large brown fitted hat sat on an angle on his head. D was in a long white tee and baggy black jeans with white Air Force Ones on his feet.

It was a normal grey fall day with a sky that was entirely blocked by clouds. As always the four street lanes of 23rd avenue were filled with cars travelling north and south taking their drivers through their daily routines of navigating the Seattle streets to their various destinations.

Catching the number 48 bus on the southbound side of the street the two friends rode the bus down 23rd avenue getting off five minutes later in the south side of the Central District. Walking up Judkin's street, they passed 24th avenue and took a right into the alley in the middle of the block. Stopping in front of a shabby looking brown garage, Chris walked up to the door on the side and knocked three times. The door opened and Chris motioned for D to go in.

Walking up beside Chris, D peered cautiously in to the darkened interior. It resembled something like an entrance to a tomb. He caught a brief glimpse of several shadowy figures standing just on the other side but before he could say anything he felt a hard shove to his back and catapulted forward into the garage. He landed hard on the ground.

A door slammed behind him and he looked over his shoulder to see Chris locking the door behind him. Standing up, D looked around the people surrounding him. There were about a dozen other teenagers in the garage besides him and Chris. All were tough looking black teens of various height and builds. They were all dressed in black and all of them looked ready for a fight.

96

Turning to Chris, D looked for an explanation.

"Chris, what the fuck is this nigga? Why you got me trapped and surrounded like some kind of fucked up gangster movie? Does Mike know about this?"

Chris only grinned.

"Yeah of course he knows D don't trip! Aint nothing bad going on here. If anything this has been years in the making. Sorry you a lil beat up already but that can't be helped. Besides, it aint that bad anyways."

D had no idea what Chris was talking about and was starting to get a little nervous. He had noticed that some of the thuggish looking youngsters around him had started massaging and cracking their knuckles. Something was about to happen and then, with a freighting wave of clarity, he realized something was about to happen to him that he was not about to enjoy.

Chris, noticing his apprehension laughed.

"D, c'mon man you aint dumb. You think you're safe out here in these streets now? Trouble is looking to fuck you up and the whole FEB has a green light to get on your head the moment they see you. Now, the only way Money Mike can legitimately protect you without seeming like he's just getting involved in something that isn't his business, is if you actually belong to his organization.

"Otherwise it seems like he's just being nosy. Aint nobody round here going for that. Since anyone of us would have been found guilty of violating the agreement and would have had to stand punishment, that means you do too. Don't trip though, after this your officially one of us now and Money Mike says your forgiven."

Taking off his fitted hat, Chris dropped it on the floor and, throwing his hands up in front of his face, crouched down into a fighter's stance and began moving in the light of combat igniting his otherwise emotionless eyes. All around D, he heard the shuffling footsteps as the rest of the group moved in ready to attack at any second. This was going to hurt. A lot.

Turning around suddenly, D launched himself at the man behind him catching him with a hard straight directly into his mouth. The force of the impact split both of the kid's lips and blood flew up into the air. It was a good hit, and it was his last. Immediately pain exploded all over his head torso and legs as twelve other pairs of legs and arms joined in the fight punching and kicking every part of D's body with freighting brutality. A ferocious blow to the head stunned him and he felt his legs get kicked out from under him. As D saw the cement floor rushing towards him he found himself hoping they didn't accidentally stomp him to death.

Chapter 15

"D, you are one stupid ass nigga!"

A hard backhand to the side of his head reiterated that fact. D winced in pain. He noticed she had taken care to slap him directly on of the many swellings that covered his head. Using his one good eye, his left was swollen shut, D gazed up from where he lay on a huge soft tan colored couch at the young woman who had helped bandage him up after the beating. It was Latoya!

Apparently it had been her garage that everything that had gone down in. As Chris had helped D up the back steps and into the living room, he had mentioned that a friend of his requested that it happen here. After getting D to the couch, Chris had left. Then Latoya had come down the stairs and played doctor.

It had been a vicious beating. Twelve on one for twenty three seconds sound like it felt. That was forty-eight fists and feet that were constantly hitting him as hard as they could.

D's nose was busted and one eye was swollen shut. His lips were cut and bruised and his whole face was a mass of bruising. His whole body was an aching mass and his arms were cut and bloody. He was lying lengthwise on an extremely soft couch in Latoya's living room.

The room was heavily furnished with a big comfy brown couch and two equally comfy sofa chairs. On the wall opposite the couch was an immense flat screen with two low shelves full to bursting with DVD cases. It looked like she had every movie that had been made since the year 2000. A big mahogany wood table was next to the couch with four chairs around it.

Every inch of open space on the walls had been covered with pictures of Anthony and the brief moments they'd been together as a family. It was eerie and yet refreshing to see picture of his deceased friend staring down at him from every angle.

Tearing his one good eye away from the wall of memories, D's gaze settled on the young woman standing over him. Beautiful, dark skinned and petite with the fiery spark of a born rebel burning in her eyes, Latoya was the kind of girl who never let the fact that she was a female stop her from doing what she wanted. In fact, she and Anthony had met because she had tried out for the boys basketball team her freshman year. Most of the boys had laughed until she had crossed one boy so bad he fell over.

She had been fun loving with a vicious sense of humor at one point. Now her eyes held the haunted look of someone who had been through too much too fast. And despite the care she had taken while looking after D's battered body, she did not look happy. And D was oddly surprised.

As Latoya finished putting away the first aid kit and came and sat next to him on the couch, D turned and looked her right in the face.

"Thanks,' he said simply. The beating had caught him completely by surprise. He hadn't known Moncy Mike was setting something like that up for him at the same time he was congratulating him on beating up the cornrowed FEB member.

The brutality of it had frightened him. And yet, they had all undergone similar beatings when they joined the group. It was a rite of passage. And even though Anthony had been against it, D liked the feeling that was slowly flooding through his veins. The sense that he a part of something big, a movement of people just like him or similar enough that would have his back through thick and thin. Something that Anthony himself had been a part of. So why was Latoya scowling?

"It's nothing D, but I'm going to ask this again; are you fucking stupid?"

"No."

"Nigga you doing a pretty good job at seeming like you are! Look at you!"

D winced. Latoya's shouting wasn't exactly helping his already aching head. She didn't look sympathetic.

"To be honest, I didn't know this was going to happen. Chris didn't say nothing and neither did Money Mike."

"Well, what did you think was going to happen after that shit you pulled at the party?"

D sighed heavily.

"So you heard about that?"

Latoya's raised eyebrow was all the confirmation D needed. He settled back into the couch. After looking at him with a serious expression on her face for a few silent minutes, Latoya's features softened into something more like concern. Reaching beneath her couch, she pulled out a fairly new black shoe box and opened it up. Inside were all manner of blunt wraps, flavored cigars, and several bags of marijuana. D watched as she set about rolling up a blunt using a blueberry flavored swisher. They didn't say another word to each other until Latoya had lit the blunt and the sweet sharp smell of burning OG Kush filled the room.

"I mean, I was drunk too," D said halfheartedly after a few moments. Latoya did not look convinced.

"D, you expect me to believe you involved yourself in a gang confrontation at a house party because you were drunk? You don't drink like that. Even after my baby died you didn't run to the bottle. You've always preferred weed over liquor. Anthony was the same way. So what was different?

Her tone was no longer harsh but soft and probing. D looked up with his one good eye and saw a face full of worry and concern on Latoya's otherwise tough features. She laid a soft hand on D's right leg as she leaned over and passed him the blunt. Settling back, her gaze fell on a wide angle photo hanging directly over the TV set. It was of her and Anthony lying intertwined together on a grassy hill at a nearby park.

"I think I know why you did it." D's good eye followed Latoya's gaze and saw the picture she was staring at. He missed his friend so much but he knew he wasn't even a fraction of the loss that she felt.

"It's just, I don't really know who I'm supposed to be," said D. "Anthony showed me everything I know and now he's gone. Yeah he tried to keep me out of this shit but now he's gone! He was such a factor to so many people that I feel like as his friend I'm responsible for keeping up his image. This guy was bad mouthing Deuce Trey but nobody could do anything to shut him up. This wasn't even the nigga that killed him but I just felt like I had to do something." D chose not to mention the fact that he had thought it would make him look good in front of Courtney.

Latoya sighed heavily.

"I feel you D, I really do and it's completely understandable but don't you see what's happened? Beating up the living won't bring back those that are already gone. Now you're a part of what killed Anthony! Does that make any sense to you! It doesn't matter whether he was fighting or not, just being in that kind of function is the kind of place this thing goes down at! It's not a game D. You think you've seen the worst but you haven't. By the time this thing is over, Anthony won't be the only one that's dead. And if you think you're going to turn around and kindly ask to not be involved you got a sorry reality check coming your way. "

Latoya's words were sobering but true. If anything the beating he had just endured was just the first dark cloud of a much bigger storm emerging on the horizon. He was confused and distraught. Subconsciously he had always longed to a part of something, to have numerous friends and girls that wanted to be around him. To be somebody that mattered. And despite realizing he might have put his foot into a deeper hole then he bargained for, a new feeling was stealing through his veins.

D had just been beat up by twelve gang members all with many years' worth of fights under their belts and he was still talking with no broken bones or other major injuries. He was obviously tougher then he'd ever imagined himself to be and he found himself wanting to listen to Latoya but also to show her that he wasn't some scared little boy. That he could handle business just as good as Anthony used to.

"I might be moving to Texas at the end of this summer," said Latoya after a few moments of silence. D looked around in surprise.

"Texas? What for?"

Latoya waved a hand towards the pictures lining the wall.

"I don't have any good memories of being here anymore. There's too much hostility and how can I ever hope for little Anthony to grow up in the same neighborhood his dad was killed in and not get drawn into this insane mess of violence? I have a kid to think about. It's time to switch it up. I have family down in Dallas so I won't be alone. I just think it's the best thing to do for me and Anthony Jr. I just need the money."

D didn't know what to say. Anthony was already gone now Latoya and the baby were leaving. His entire support structure was breaking down.

"Damn Latoya now it's just going to be me and Chris out here. I'm going to be real sorry to see you two go. Can't you just move into a different neighborhood? The north end of Seattle aint as crazy as it is over here. "

Latoya shook her head in a firm no.

"I'm sick of people talking to me about Anthony and saying how sorry they were and what a tragedy and what they would have done. It's all some bullshit anyways. Have the people that promised to come by and help with Anthony junior haven't done a damn thing. Sure Money Mike and Chris help but I don't want their money. Oh, and while we're talking about them, you need to watch out for Chris.

"I know he might seem like a cool nigga to you but you don't know him like I know him. Anthony used to tell me stories about Chris that made me wonder why that fool aint already locked up for life. He don't give a fuck about nothing or nobody and if you keep hanging around him like you're doing now then your safety is going to be in some serious jeopardy. "

D looked surprised but not shocked. It wasn't the stories she was referring too but the fact that it seemed like Latoya thought Chris might try to hurt him one day.

"Are you saying that Chris aint trustworthy? You think he'd do something to fuck me over?"

Latoya's face was deadly serious as she responded.

"D, all I'm saying is that this world you've been living on the edge off is Chris entire life. He lives for nothing more than to represent Deuce Trey to the fullest in any situation. He doesn't know how to back down or when to say no and he doesn't care who he takes with him. The more chaos he causes the better is how he and all his little friend's minds work. One day he's going to get into a situation he can't get out of and when that happens I just hope you're not with him and I'm too far away to even hear about it! His aspirations lie far away from the world of 401K plans and respectable communities. Sooner or later you're going to have to think about want for yourself before this shit is all you have left."

D didn't have a response.

Chapter 16

Ms. Weathers sat in her chair like a queen about to pass judgment. Her arms were folded across her chest with her silver hair pulled back into a tight bun, and was dressed simply in a dark blue suit. She stared disapprovingly over the glasses perched on the edge of her nose at the self-important looking funeral dressed man seated directly across from her. She nodded to the secretary waiting by her door and motioned for her to leave. The secretary bowed her head and shut the door behind her with great care.

Ms. Weathers once again focused all her attention on the man opposite her.

"Okay Mr. Stross your office called me about some sort of 'special program' last week. I'm assuming your hear to explain what exactly you downtown people are talking about now?"

The man called Stross coughed quietly into his hand.

"Well uh, Ms. Weathers," he began. His voice was full of the pompous attitude that radiated from his pointed face, brown greasy combed back hair and expensive black suit all radiated. "It seems that your school and a few others in the district have come under the watchful eye of the people in DC."

Ms. Weathers frowned. This sounded like it could be good news for the school district. They might finally get the funding they deserve. But if that was the case then why did Stross look so unhappy?

"Why are people in DC be interested in a few schools in Seattle?"

"Well," said Stross, "it's not that they are now but that they could be in the future. And not in a good way."

Ms. Weathers frown deepened.

"Could you do a little better job of explaining please?"

Stross coughed into his hand again before going on.

"Well you see Ms. Weathers, the latest numbers have shown a significant decrease of the performance of your school over the last few years. Both in Standardized Testing and in graduation rates. We're not sure if the problem is the students or the teachers or the curriculum. We've tried attacking this from every angle and have come up short every time."

"So where does D.C. come into all this?" Ms. Weathers asked.

"Well, it has come to our attention that a current debate is taking place on what school districts funding are to be cut. Yes, again!" Stross added as Ms. Weathers rolled her eyes in exasperation, "so it's time to put our last card into play."

Reaching down beside him, Stross withdrew a medium sized folder from his black suitcase and placed it on the table in front of Ms. Weathers. She eyed it skeptically. Picking it up, she flipped back the cover and began skimming the pages. Her eyes narrowed as the meaning of what was written on the pages began to dawn on her.

She looked up at Stross in disbelief and dropped the envelope back onto her desk. Anger was creeping into the corner of her eyes and her feet began tapping on the ground in irritation. It took her a moment to find her words.

"Are you serious?" Ms. Weathers gestured at the folder as if were a pile of human shit on her desk. "This is your solution? A take home test for seniors that will allow them to miss class but still graduate? So instead of keeping kids in school you're purposely taking them out of it? What is a take home test going to teach them? They're just going to look the answer's up on Wikipedia! Do you just want to hand out diplomas without making sure these kids actually understand the material?"

Stross was strangely quiet. Ms. Weathers sat back in her chair in disbelief as she realized that she had just hit the nail on the head. The School Districts grand scheme for improving graduation rates was nothing more than an extreme lowering of

106

standards. She repeated this to Stross. After hearing her out, he leaned forward.

"Look, this isn't exactly a freebie diploma. It will be on their record that they opted to take the take home package equivalent of their senior year and as such does not carry the same weight as an actual high school diploma. Technical Schools of course would take them no problem. Four year Universities however would most likely pass over an applicant with that on their record. Community college is always open though. There is also the hope that this will help weed out those students who have no real ambition towards graduating high school in the first place."

Stross ended his statement and sat back in his chair looking completely drained. Ms. Weathers was speechless. She couldn't comprehend how the school district could possibly get behind something like this. They were sacrificing education and standards to fill a government quota. She herself had no real knowledge of the entirety of the problem the deficit in the School Districts budget was causing but it couldn't be that bad. Could it?

But to intentionally weed out "bad" students rom good by putting their own futures in their hands without really knowing the true purpose of the test? It was all she could do to keep herself from diving over her desk and strangling Stross to death.

"Look," said Stross in a much softer voice, "I like this about as much as you do, but this is coming from above me. The decision has been made. All I can do is simply tell you the message. You think I'd want my kids taking the easy way out? But were in serious trouble here and we cannot afford to lose any more federal funding then we already have."

Ms. Weathers appreciated that Stross was trying to explain that this wasn't what he wanted to happen either. But he was missing a key point. It wasn't kids like his son that were going to be affected by this.

"Mr. Stross," she said slowly, "I'm sure you're aware that the students that will most likely view this as a positive substitute for another year in school and who will most likely require this as an only option will fall under the 'minority' label."

"Uncomfortably aware," was his reply.

"And what do you intend to do if that turns out to be true?"

"We will cross that bridge when the time comes to it. Right now that's not the issue. If and when it becomes a concern it will be given the proper attention. Now, my apologies but I have to be going now. I have two other schools that I must notify of this before the day is through."

Ms. Weathers nodded stiffly. Getting to her feet, she shook hands with Stross and walked him out of the office. When he had gone, she closed the door softly and collapsed back into her chair. This job was physically and mentally draining her. All her life she had fought to improve the educational system and now he they were about to give handouts to students who needed anything but that if they were to ever have a chance in the real world. And it all came down to money. As if the big wigs downtown weren't taking home fat enough checks already. But what could she do?

She gained a little comfort from knowing that kids who might not have otherwise graduated might get the chance to actually get handed a diploma. For some it could possibly be a lifetime achievement. But what did it mean if they're record would be forever be tainted? Futures might actually get stunted because of this. But then again, futures might also be born out of this.

Heaving a great sigh at the failure of education, Ms. Weathers picked up her phone and dialed her secretary. She answered immediately.

"Yes Ms. Weathers?"

"Margaret, can you please get me a list of all the seniors that appear to be in jeopardy of not reaching the required number of credits for graduation? After you have done that arrange a meeting in the auditorium that they will all attend. I will be speaking to them."

"Yes Ms. Weathers. Anything else?"

"No."

She hung up the phone feeling mentally exhausted.

Chapter 17

The doors to the auditorium opened and the fifty or so students who had been called to Ms. Weathers meeting left under a cloud of confusion and speculation. Various people were all talking at once.

"Is she serious?"

"I'm saying though homie, a take home test?"

"This is a joke y'all I'm telling you. Aint no way they really that dumb!"

"I don't know Trey, she looked pretty serious. She said to stop by the office for the permission slips if we want to go that route."

"Hmm…fuck it! I'm on my way!"

"Hold up Trey I'm coming too!"

Lead by Trey, a light skin boy who resembled Will Smith from his early TV days, a group of twelve curious seniors headed off towards the principal's office. D was last to leave the auditorium. He watched the group go with mild interest but dismissed thoughts of tagging along. He liked school. It was where some of his friends were and where he made his money at. There was no way he wanted to give that up for an easier chance at graduating.

Setting off down the hall in the opposite direction, D's thoughts were interrupted by a group of white skateboarders looking for some weed. Walking into a nearby men's bathroom, D sold them two eighths and shook hands with them all before they turned and walked out.

Standing over one of the sinks without washing his hands, D stared into the dirt stained mirror at himself. His face wasn't entirely healed but looked ten times better than it had two weeks ago. The cocky attitude he had been feeling at Latoya's house hadn't gone away.

He felt like a badass for getting through his beating without more serious damage being done. Maybe he was just as tough as Anthony. *I bet if I beat up a couple more of them FEB dudes, Latoya might stop thinking of me as soft,* D thought to himself. He didn't even think Latoya thought of him as soft. Just not as tough as Anthony. Courtney was already texting him asking him when they were going to hang out again. She clearly had been turned on by what she witnessed at the party. D didn't really what no what felt better at the moment. Courtney giving him the attention he wanted from her; the fact that all of Deuce Trey had opened up their arms to him since the beating or the fact that he had taken on a gang member in a one on one showdown and hadn't got his ass whooped!

Now they were offering a get out of jail free card with this test Ms. Weathers had just informed them of. The more he thought about it, the more D was becoming intrigued with the idea. She hadn't mentioned too many specifics that much he figured was in the packet she had said they could get from her office. Somehow, something about this was seeming too good to be true. It might be worth looking after all.

Pausing to gaze at himself a second longer, D had just made up his mind to head to Ms. Weathers office when the door to the bathroom banged open and Sumo's huge form came striding in. D caught a brief glimpse of a group of angry looking teens outside in the hall before the door swung shut.

"Sumo what the fu…"

Before he could finish his sentence, Sumo had reached out and grabbed a hold of D's shirt with both of his hands. Picking D up off the ground, Sumo slammed him into the wall as hard as he could!

THUD!

D felt the air blasted out of his lungs from the impact! His backpack held nothing more than a couple composition notebooks and various sized pens and did nothing to soften the blow. D struggled to break Sumo's grip on his shirt but Sumo only slammed into the wall again. His right arm exploded with an odd tingling sensation as his elbow hit the wall hard directly on his funny bone. Instead of slamming him in the wall again, Sumo released his grip and D landed in a heap on the floor. D glanced up angrily at Sumo as he massaged his elbow breathing hard.

"Sumo…what the fuck bro…the hell you tripping about?" D gasped out.

Sumo glared down at D.

"What the fuck is this I hear about you joining Deuce Trey?" he demanded.

D looked surprised. How did he know about that? It had literally just happened and D still wasn't completely one hundred percent sure he was an official member of Deuce Trey. He had pictured something much more ceremonial then a brutal beat down in a garage. But that was beside the point. What was Sumo tripping about?

Eyeing his big friend warily, D slowly stood up still massaging his elbow. Sumo backed away a couple feet but remained glaring at D with hate and something like betrayal in his eyes.

"Well? Speak nigga!" Sumo barked out.

D found himself becoming angry. What was the attitude? And what did it matter to Sumo anyways? He could feel his elbow getting better and began readying himself for an altercation.

"Look bro some shit went down at a party and I got involved. The only way to stay alive apparently was to get up with the homie's who I was there with. It really happened without me knowing but what's done is done. So what the fuck is your problem anyways?"

Sumo took a deep breath.

"Look D, this never came up between us because it was never was an issue until now. Me and damn near all my cousins are from FEB!"

D felt like he had been slapped in the face! All these years and he hadn't thought to ask exactly what gang Sumo was from! Of course it had never been a topic of discussion between them but it was only dawning on D now how serious a situation he might be in right now. He also took note of the group he had seen before the door closed. He assumed they were still there waiting to see what happened. Sumo was obviously high on the respect level.

The two friends stood a mere few feet apart staring at each other. Mixed feelings were floating through the air and so far had failed to result in either words or punches. It was D who broke the silence.

"Look Sumo, you should know I don't got any kind of beef with you. But that fool Devontay killed my best friend. I shouldn't have took it out on that dude at the party but I been real frustrated lately. If anything, I'm only in this to pay Devontay back for taking away someone close to me. I aint looking to hurt you or anyone related to you. But if you would have seen the disrespect that nigga was showing, you would have done the same thing."

D waited. He felt his explanation was true and honest and it was up to Sumo what would happen next. To his relief, D saw of the tension go out of Sumo's posture.

"Yeah, I'm sorry about Anthony. RIP. I got two homies that's under the ground so I know how you feel. I honestly wasn't cool with Devontay until he joined up but then again we really aint that tight now. I guess you right about joining up too because niggaz is sure on your head."

D looked over Sumo's shoulder towards the bathroom door again.

"Oh don't worry about them," said Sumo. "They aint coming unless I call em. But that's only because I'm here. It's a green light on you bruh. You about to see niggaz popping out the woodwork to come fuck with you over this. You can't control who you see and when you see them."

D took in Sumo's words with a sobering clarity. The angry mob outside in the hallway was a freighting glimpse into what lay ahead. If the only way out of this was to take care of Devontay then he was better off doing it sooner than later. Sumo seemed to be off the same mind.

"My advice to you, D would be to cancel out Devontay as quickly as you can and hope that settles the dispute.

Otherwise you're asking for all kinds of trouble. If you do that niggaz will at least know why you did it. Even Trouble couldn't deny that. If you get away with it that is." Sumo looked knowingly at D and winked. "You know about stealth nigga. So do what you do."

D was grateful, surprised and suspicious. Sumo was giving him tips on how to assassinate a member of his own gang! Not only that, but he was basically saying he'd turn a blind eye to the whole thing as long as none of his family were harmed. D was more than aware that this situation could have gotten a lot worse. And owning to Sumo's considerable size, this was not a fight he had been looking forward to.

Sumo seemed to be reading his mind.

"I'm only doing this because of Anthony," he reminded D, "Devontay wasn't in FEB when he killed him and he shouldn't be protected from repercussions. That's the Law of Retaliation." His tone suddenly got a lot more serious. "But you touch anyone of my family members or if we meet on the battlefield, there won't be any love lost between us. I'm going to beat you to the ground the first chance I get! Today you get a pass. Tomorrow is another story. Sorry bro, but we're enemies from here on out. Nice working with you though. We made a nice little bit of cash together."

With that Sumo stuck out his hand. D shook it. Sumo then turned and exited the bathroom shouting for the angry crowd of hooligans to follow him outside. D waited a few minutes before exiting the bathroom himself. The hallway was empty. He hurried off towards his next class confusion and surprise running through his mind. But there was another feeling creeping through his veins. Anger! Who the fuck was Sumo to threaten him? D was Deuce Trey now and not afraid, or as Chris would say not allowed to be afraid of anyone!

If they were enemies now, D was determined to make Chris, Money Mike and everybody from Deuce Trey proud. He thought back to the beat down he and Chris had given that drug dealer on Capitol Hill. A pair of brass knuckles would even things up nicely when it came to dealing with Sumo's oversized ass!

Chapter 18

"Boy, what the hell is going on with you?"

D turned from looking out the window to stare at his dad. He was dressed in a red collared shirt and tan slacks with business looking black shoes. At first glance he appeared to be clean cut but a closer look revealed the frayed appearance of the clothes and the unshaven face of the man. He looked like someone life was deciding to pick on. D could also smell the scent of beer on his father's breath. It was faint like he had just brushed his teeth or rinsed his mouth out. But it was there.

They were driving away from Central High heading towards the IHOP on Capitol Hill in his dads 1987 Chevrolet Caprice. D had just been sent home from school and suspended for the rest of the week for his involvement in a brawl earlier that day in the cafeteria.

In actuality a small group of FEB juniors had ambushed D as he was leaving the cafeteria. However, Whop and several of his homies had been nearby and rushed in to help D. Security had come and most everybody involved had been rounded up and suspended too.

It had been a little over a month since D and Sumo's last meeting in the bathroom and since then the number of violent incidents at the school had almost tripled. Even though Sumo hadn't been openly hostile, D was certain that he had told his fellow FEB members where D usually hung out or did business. Ever where he went now it seemed like a crowd of angry black teens were waiting for him. Hallway riots were becoming a regular thing as well. All it took was for the wrong people to walk buy each other and fists would start flying. But the drama at school was the least of his worries.

Chris was stuck in the Central District. There had been several shootings during the last few weeks owing to the increased presence of gang members on the street. Chris lived for times like these and would have been out flashing gang signs and shooting bullets at any FEB member he came across if hadn't been for Money Mike. He had been working on something that he said he would need Chris and D's help with eventually. He was vague on the topic but just reminded them to keep their heads down as much as possible. It was an order Chris was not pleased with.

D scowled and rubbed the back of his lead where a decent sized bump had sprouted up. That and a split lip had been the battle wounds of the day.

"Well?" his dad asked him again as they stopped at a red light. "What the hell is going on with you? How come all you do now is get into fights?"

D contemplated whether to tell the truth or to lie. He knew his dad wasn't ignorant to the ways of the street but times had changed since he had been out there doing his dirt. Youth violence had been just a big of a problem for D's dad as it was for D but the difference was in the type of violence that occurred. Instead of fists and knives and the occasional shooting like the old days, shootings had increased to a level almost unheard of. Fights happened any and everywhere over the smallest offense and usually led to something much worse. It wasn't entirely safe for a male or female to walk the streets alone night or day.

It had been hard enough for D to avoid problems when he hadn't been as involved with Duce Trey but now it was proving almost impossible. He knew his dad would be furious if he knew what was really going on. But what else could he say? D stared angrily out the window as his dad navigated the big vehicle through the heart of Capitol Hill. Apartment buildings, trendy looking shops and restaurants lined the busier sidewalks. People all of all shades were out walking in the cool November weather wrapped in scarves or wearing various types of light jackets. It was an average grey day in the city and the local population was loving it.

Despite feelings that he should do otherwise, D decided to tell his dad the truth. As much as he needed to know at least. He took a deep breath.

"Honestly pops it's not my fault, well, not entirely. Things got out of control at a party I was at and now this group of guys is after me because I beat up one of their friends. And it just so happens that this is the same group of guys that the guy who killed Anthony hangs out with. Come to find out one of my other homies that I've known for a while now is also part of the same group. Now I got enemies that were friends two months ago. They know all the spots that I hang out so now there's nowhere for me to go without possibly getting into a fight."

His dad frowned as he kept his focus on the road ahead of him. Ever since his son's friend had been murdered at that house party, he had lived in secret fear that D had become involved with a street gang. You didn't go through something like that and come out the other side the same. Pulling into the IHOP parking lot, Marcus Gram chose a spot in a corner away from the main cluster of vehicles. Killing the engine, he looked across at his only son with concern and anger in his eyes.

"So tell me, Damien what made you beat up this guy at the party? And what kind of party was it that you were around all these kids in gangs anyways?"

"It was a party for Anthony," replied D looking furiously at the floor. "Everything was cool until all of a sudden these three guys came through talking shit and being disrespectful to everybody at the party. I was already feeling a certain type of way from just thinking about Anthony so when these guys started in with their bullshit I just snapped and ran at the one doing all the talking." D fell silent. It was a true enough explanation. Things were already bad enough without adding in the factor that he had thought it would make him look good in front of Courtney.

"This just don't make no damn sense," his dad said.

"Why it don't make sense dad? Just because you don't understand it? You always said you used to get down back in the day so why is this so hard for you to understand?"

117

"That was different. Things aint the same any more. You young thugs out here these days don't play by what little rules there used to be. Killing each other over stupid shit all the time and now you done went and got yourself mixed up in this damn mess. Why? Do you think your friends going to mysteriously come back from the dead because you went and joined his gang?"

The last words his dad spoke resonated loudly inside D's conscious and halted his comeback. It was true of course. Anthony wasn't coming back simply because of an allegiance. But there were also extenuating circumstances surrounding D's assimilation into Deuce Trey. He hadn't known e was going to get put on when he entered that garage. He really hadn't wanted to. But none of that mattered now. Silence fell inside the car.

Marcus sat quietly next to his son thinking hard. He honestly couldn't blame is son for what how he had reacted. Anthony had been D's closest friend besides that dark skinned trouble maker named Chris and to lose him in such a violent way was something no one should ever have to go through. But by all accounts, Anthony hadn't been the intended target. It seemed like these boys were going out of their way to come after D.

The worst part of it all for Marcus was that he felt entirely responsible for the situations his son had ended up in. It wasn't like he was about to win the Father of the Year Award anytime soon. He knew he'd been a mess most of life but he'd been trying to get it together. Part of that meant trying to get back into his sons life. Now that he was it seemed as if it was already too late. If only he would have just paid attention to what was going on with those around him instead of drowning in his own sorrow. This made the news he had to tell D even harder. What kind of example was he setting?

It had taken Marcus a long time to emerge from the darkness he had sunk down into and to realize the error of his ways. Now he was determined to save his marriage and his kid. He had already come around too late to save one. His only hope now was in preventing his son from following in his footsteps.

"C'mon D lets go eat. I got something important to tell you."

118

Several hours later…

"They got divorced?" Breanna asked breathlessly for the third time. D looked up from his current sitting position on the couch where he was busy rolling a blunt and glared at her.

"Yes Breanna they got fucking divorced. Now how many times you gonna ask me the same damn question?"

D was at Breanna's house. Already having taken three shots from a fancy looking Tequila bottle that was in the liquor cabinet, he was busy rolling up the second blunt of the evening as he tried to digest and make sense of the bomb his dad had dropped on him a little less than three hours before.

His dad and mom were getting a divorce. After eighteen years of marriage another beautiful union of two people came to a bitter and ugly end. For an entire hour D had listened to his dad attempt to explain how it had come down to this while seemingly living a comfortable existence beside each other. But in actuality it had been anything but comfortable.

Over by the pool table, Breanna was trying unsuccessfully to knock the eight ball into a corner pocket but was missing every time. The fifth time she watched the white cue ball drop lazily into the hole instead of the black one, she threw her stick on the table and came to sit next to D. Breanna was dressed simply in a black and blue gym outfit and white running shoes. Out of place were the big pair of Gucci sunglasses on her face but D didn't question a rich white woman's style. He didn't even own a pair of sunglasses.

"C'mon D, you can tell me what you're thinking. Remember me and my lil sister's parents are divorced so don't think I don't know what you're talking about brother man. This white girl aint that lame!" She snapped her fingers in front of her face in imitation of the hundreds of black girls D had seen repeat the same motion. A flicker of a smile passed across his lips.

"You might wanna leave that to the black girls B," said D ducking a fake slap from Breanna. As they both settled back on the couch, D in a heavy slouch and Breanna with her legs crossed under her, D lit the blunt and related the bombshell his dad had dropped in him earlier at the IHOP.

"Pretty much, my mom has been having an affair for a while now. My dad figured something was up but never could prove anything because she works crazy hours in the first place. Besides that, he aint really been the best dad for most of my life. But he was doing good. Anyways, my mom's is leaving him for the dude she been sleeping with who by the way is the doctor she works for! Oh, and she said that his drinking was a serious problem for her and that he's never really truly stopped and some other shit" D shook his head and took in a heavy cloud of smoke.

Breanna stared at her unique young friend. She was sure none of her girlfriends would believe her if she told them that she bought weed and hung out with a black teenager in her basement! It was weird how their relationship had evolved over time. She was older than him by almost six years but at times it felt like she was standing beside someone much older than herself.

She learned things from him about a culture she had only ever seen the tip of and she in turn tried to give him the best advice she could whenever he had a question. Now she saw a time where she could be off some comfort. D liked to hide his emotions but Breanna could tell by the stiff way he held his body that he was fighting back the urge to truly express himself. She decided to let him think about it in his head before she offered an opinion.

Apparently whatever D was thinking was too much to keep in because not two minutes later he posed a question.

"I mean, why draw the thing out? Why wouldn't she just tell him what the deal was?"

"You mean your mom?" asked Breanna.

"Yeah. I don't understand how you could be with somebody else and go back smiling to your family. That's gross don't kiss me with those lips! I can't believe she really did this shit! Why?"

Breanna could see that D was angry. He wasn't jumping out of his seat angry but he definitely had some strong feelings about what was going on between his parents. Breanna's parents had been through a similar situation involving a house maid but at least then it wasn't so much of a phantom menace. And it had been their dad who had been the perpetrator not the mom and had happened over the course of a summer.

Passing the blunt back to D, Breanna got up from the couch and made her way to the bar. Pouring out two glasses of Sapphire Gin she mixed them with a little tonic water and lemon. Tasting one to make sure it was ok, she nodded in satisfaction then took the drinks back to the couch.

D ranted and raved until the blunt was gone and his drink was getting low but eventually ran out of steam. He stayed slumped dejectedly in the corner of the couch. He stared silently at the pool table for several minutes then sighed heavily. Turning to Breanna he looked at her causally.

"Why you still got your sunglasses on inside? This aint no music video!"

The question was innocent enough but it caused Breanna to freeze in the act of taking a sip from her drink. She had hoped D wouldn't ask. Breanna set her drink down on the coffee table slowly. It wasn't like D didn't know what was going on between her and her husband Todd and he always told her what was going on his life. Reaching up with one hand, she slowly removed the sunglasses from her face. D's eyebrows arched quickly in shock.

"Breanna, what the fuck happened to your face?"

While Breanna's left side of her face was perfectly normal, her right eye was a gigantic blue and black bruise. It was almost closed it was so swollen and looked fresh. As soon as he had asked the question, D already knew the answer. It had to be that coward ass husband of hers. It looked like he had punched her with a closed fist as if she was another man!

Breanna stared down at the floor. Her head hung low in shame and embarrassment as her long blonde hair fell across her face covering her features like golden drapes hiding a dark secret within a beautifully painted house.

"We got into a fight over the fact that he's always drinking or already drunk when he comes home and he when he tried to walk away I tried to stop him from leaving and this is what I got." The story came out rushed and breathless.

121

Putting the blunt down in the ashtray, D peered closely at the woman beside him. Feelings of pity and sympathy briefly flared up inside him but were tempered down by a blanket of anger that had fallen across his senses. Was Breanna really a victim of an abusive husband or just suffering the consequence of some previous offense? What drove this man to constantly put his hands on her in this kind of way?

D's mind began to have some very unpleasant thoughts. Women were hard to control and even harder to trust. How did he know if Breanna was the victim or aggressor in these fights she had with her husband? Women were good at manipulation and deceit until they got caught. And even when that happened their ability to mind fuck their way out of blame was remarkable. At least, that's the way it seemed to D in his limited experience dealing with relationships and women.

Leaning back against the couch, D looked at Breanna out of the corner of his eyes.

"Can I ask you something B?"

Breanna, who was looking thoroughly miserable next to him, nodded her head. Brushing some loose strands of blonde hair out of her face she turned her head towards towards her teenage friend.

"Yes D, what is it?"

D paused for a few seconds to get his words together. Something wasn't making sense to him and he wanted to get to the bottom of it. He realized Breanna might get offended at him for what he was about to say but if it was true, then she really didn't have a reason to be.

"Well I'm curious, how come you're still messing with this guy Todd even though it seems like all he does is beat you up and fly out of the country on trips and never takes you with him? That doesn't seem like the kind of existence a married couple is supposed to have. But then again, I don't know how you white people operate so this might be completely normal. But you don't seem very happy. My mom dipped because she wanted something different obviously. How come you don't do the same?"

122

Breanna slowly turned her head and stared curiously at D. Her eyes had a wary look in them like a deer who knew it was being stalked.

"What do you mean?"

D knew he probably shouldn't voice the opinions floating around in his head but the combination of anger, weed and whiskey had filled his blood with fire and the filter button between his brain and his mouth seemed to have disappeared.

"What I'm saying is that when women want to leave a situation they do. So what could possibly make you stay with a man that beats on you? Then I think about it. You don't work do you? So that means that this house and that fancy truck you drive are all paid for by him. Aint this man like ten years older than you? How come you aint with somebody in your age group? The only common denominator I see is money. You like the feel and smell of that paper too much to leave a man that's whooping yo ass over stupid shit! I don't know man that sounds like hooker tendencies to me."

Smack!

D's head pitched to the side from the force of the slap that hit him. Ear stinging, he looked up at Breanna who was holding her hands in front of her mouth in an expression of shock and hurt. Slowly she stood up and walked towards the staircase that lead up to the main floor. At the base of the stairs she turned around to face D. She spoke softly.

"Thanks for the weed and the company D. You can finish your drink. When you're done please let yourself out of the bottom door. I'm going to California to visit my mom so I won't be contacting you for a while."

With that said, she turned around and disappeared up the stairs.

D sat quietly for a couple seconds scolding himself for being so careless with his words. Breanna had never done anything to hurt him so why was he saying nasty things to her! Gulping down the rest of his drink, D set the glass on the table grabbed his backpack from the floor and left.

Chapter 19

Rob Jenkins was an ordinary man on an ordinary mission. At fifty two he was graying but not balding. Even though he was dressed in a white collar get up, suit and tie, briefcase dark polished shoes sitting behind the wheel of a new but slightly used 2003 Camry LX. Seeing as how it was 2005, he didn't consider himself too far behind the pack. It was the day before Thanksgiving and he was on a last minute run to the store for ingredients to a cranberry sauce his wife was making.

Driving along Broadway, Jenkins pulled into the popular Dick's drive in burger joint. His stomach was growling he was so hungry. When his wife was in the kitchen she turned into something resembling an overly territorial badger and no one in their right mind tried to interfere. Snacks were out of the question unless bought beforehand and stashed out of sight!

Locking the car doors behind him, Rob Jenkins joined the always present line of people waiting to get a taste of the Seattle staple for fast food. Bouncing slightly on his heels in anticipation, Jenkins eyes scanned the extremely limited but superbly delicious menu for what must have been the millionth time in his life. He already knew what he wanted. It was the same every time; a deluxe, a cheese burger, an order of fries and a chocolate milkshake.

Suddenly a loud burst of harsh language and laughter echoed in his earlobes. Turning half way around and looking over his shoulder, Jenkins felt himself stiffen as a large group of black teenagers came strolling into view down the side walk. It was a large group, about fifteen young people. It was mostly boys but there were a scattering of young girls among the crowd.

They were all rough looking youngsters and everybody's was dressed in a variety of wind breakers, hoodies and baggy jeans. Cigarettes were being passed around like candy even though Jenkins doubted any of them were eighteen.

The strong smell of burning marijuana crept into his nose and his nostrils flared involuntary. He hadn't smoked weed since his college days which were now long behind him. He kept a wary eye on the group. One boy was out in front now and clearly the ringleader of them all. From the rhythm of his voice it appeared as if he was rapping.

Rob Jenkins turned around and tried to ignore the teens. Not that he was racist even though most people considered old white men to be racist no matter what. Really, he hated all teenagers equally. But he was always uneasy around blacks. They made him think of that show, the one about the drug dealers in Baltimore. Murderous bunch of fuckers! Jenkins bounced on his heels some more. He hoped the fat slob in front of him would hurry his wide ass up!

He groaned loudly as behind him one of the young men began doing that thing known as a "free styling".

They thought I'd never be shit but a spectator fighting for respect
Players puffin out they chest these haters wanna see me stressed
But I'm floating, ozone destroying
The fumes from my swisher tip dense as hell and potent
Kanye West boastin, I think I'm in the biggest movie ever
Lead actor and Director always shoot in any weather
Recline in some shiny leather habitual line stepper
A black Ruger and a chrome Beretta
I do it aint no one better
A blunt means a good day, a bottle means a bad night
Both his lips split and eyes still black from our last fight
Bitch niggaz fold but in the district boy we boss up
Burn rubber gun thunder homie let yo Glock bust
Don't listen bitch I'm ignant to used to ballin off break in's

So my current car is stolen when I took it I wasn't
shaking
Crime easy like my ex was sticky green and fresh blunts
So CD the king of 23rd and Marion
Never seen the struggle so authentically portrayed
So that's why it's Belly over every other movie made
East side Boy that's what I'm screaming every evening
after drinking
Get to creeping start swinging on some weaklings
Savage life so bopper bring that ass so I can stab it right
I'm outro this weed is outdo and I'ma wrap it tight

"It's KILLA!" Chris finished off his freestyle rhyme by yelling out the name he had gotten by the older homies of Deuce Trey. It was more out of respect to Money Mike that he had gotten the name. Chris hadn't actually killed anybody. Yet. But that sure as hell didn't stop him from repping his name proudly.

The crowd around him burst into loud shouts and cries.

"THAT WAS FILTHY!"

"Aww shit my nigga Killa got bars!"

"Nice bro, you definitely clean with it!"

Those were just some of the phrases being tossed at him from among the large group of excited teens. Directly nest to him, D was walking beside him with an odd look on his face. But it didn't have anything to do with what Kevin was rapping about.

D was experiencing an odd sensation. Surrounded by a large group of dangerous teens that he wasn't really too familiar with, D could never remember feeling more comfortable and at ease with himself. A couple bottles of Jose Cuervo several cigarettes and two blunts were currently being passed around the group and nobody got passed up. There was plenty for everyone. Conversations about several different topics were taking place all around him besides the rapping going on in the front of the group. Despite the fact that D wasn't familiar with some of the other youths that were present, as soon as it was established that D was part of Deuce Trey everyone had welcomed him with open arms. Now it was if they had known each other for years.

The other boys all congratulated him on beating up the guy at the party and the girls all offered him cigarettes and sips from the various bottles they held. Also, when it was discovered that D had been Anthony's best friend it only served to further cement his status. Now he was here, mobbing down one of the best known streets in Seattle forcing people to move out of their way drinking and smoking in public, cursing loudly and moving side by side with the kind of people who wouldn't hesitate to beat you over the head with a baseball bat. It hadn't been long ago that he avoided groups like these.

D, Whop and Chris had formed a rap group they had decided to call The Sidewalk Gang. It wasn't so much a rap group as it was three friends who spit rhymes together while selling drugs downtown. When it was slow they circled up and began either reciting the latest bit they had come up with or making up new material on the spot. But it wasn't just disconnected raps that had nothing to do with one another. They actually took the time to come up with songs. They all worked together to come up with the hook to express the main point of the song then would each come up with a verse on their own time. When they were all done they would come back and share what they had and if it sounded good they wrote it down in a composition notebook they had nicknamed "The Rap Bible" which held all of their finished works and works in progress. All in all, things hadn't gotten to out of control. Yet.

Suddenly, D realized that people in the group were looking at him now with something like expectation shining in their eyes. Chris spoke what was apparently on everybody's mind.

"C'mon D, snap out of that day dream and spit something! Whop already rapped we're just waiting on you to seal the deal!"

D looked around at the eager young faces surrounding him. Courtney was there two. She and a couple of her friends had joined the group on Broadway and they had been exchanging looks the entire time without saying a word to each other. D had constantly been called on by Chris to back up or confirm that he a statement he was making was true. Now that

127

all eyes were on him, it was his moment to shine. Somebody started beat boxing. It only took a second for D to catch the beat:

Check it, its D boy that shady lil nigga in the black hat
That's what the police say, I just laugh back
I do it all and they never stop this
And that's for everyone I know just look around, you think the boys can stop this
Weed bags, crack sacks, thizz pills, molly caps
Shroom stems, graffiti pens, stolen cars and stolen straps
Look at how we think and act different state same trap
I don't even wanna hear your rhymes boy there probably wack
Jobs? Nope every nigga on some gangsta shit
That's what happens when these money hungry homies try n make it with
No boss, time cards or write ups included
Just us and our movements who needs your two cents
The bankrolls lookin like a tank when it can't fold
Hand to hand how I serve products to the hobo's
Hell no I could never stay away
New faces made of paper everyday digi scales for the weight
This is trill shit boy I throw slugs like a gardener
The bitch acting shady don't trip you know I'm on to her
But laid back living how I want it
No tension just ounces of the chronic and a beauty on my arm its
Life shit the way the cookie crumbles
Pack mentality's rule these jungles its jump or get jumped fool
Find me on the sidewalk two middle fingers and an iPod
Bumping old B.I.G. and 2pac
I guess I got a message to spread
I'm really tryna get this money I don't care about niggaz or feds
I got a picture in my head of foreign lands

Leave the concrete behind and drag my feet on long
beaches in the sand
Sidewalk gang that's the squad
I do this shit for A1 I always pour out my licka for my
dog
RIP ANTHONY BROWN NIGGA!

As soon as he had finished the group around him exploded into yells of admiration. People waiting in line to order food all looked around in surprise. Several appeared to get nervous and left the line to walk quickly away from the rowdy teenagers.

"Aww shit this nigga D is filthy!"

"Damn bro! Where'd you learn to spit that?"

"Chris what the fuck? Where you been hiding this fool at?"

Compliments poured in and D was finding it hard to keep from smiling. People were slapping his back, giving him pounds and trying to recite lines that he had just said. Just months before they wouldn't have even paid any attention to him if he had tried to join in a rap session. As the group began heading off down Broadway, D looked around and noticed an older white man with two large Dick's burger bags in his hands staring at them with a disgusted expression on his face. He was shaking his head slowly as if unable to accurately describe the disgust he was feeling at the moment.

D and the white man locked eyes and D, without a moment of hesitation, flipped both of his middle fingers up and mouthed "fuck you!" Caught completely off guard and unprepared for the sudden hostile gesture he was receiving, the man jerked so hard he dropped his bags on the ground. Burgers and fries spilled out across the dirty pavement and a cloud of pigeons instantly descended onto the newly found treasure.

D laughed ruthlessly and then turned and rejoined the group as the small army of teens marched their way down Broadway; laughing, arguing, play fighting and generally enjoying the freedom of not being in school. Most of them were now paying attention to an impromptu rap battle broke out between two boys. While most were nodding their heads and listening to the words being said, D's focus was somewhere different entirely.

Courtney and her posse of sexy girlfriends were here as well. She and D had been trading glances all afternoon but so far hadn't spoken. D was confused. Here he was, damn near a career criminal and he didn't even have the guts to walk up and talk to a fine girl who was obviously interested in him. He was weird like that. However the praise he had received after his freestyle had momentarily boosted his ego beyond its usual limit. Once they got to the park he'd figure he could try and get her off to one side so he could talk to her without other ears listening in. Somebody passed him a Crown Royal bottle and D took it gratefully. There was nothing wrong with a little extra liquid courage. The higher the alcohols content the better!

One hour later…
"Sooo, you might as well stop with the games and just be my girl right now!"

Sitting next to D on the edge of a shallow reservoir at the north end of Kyle Anderson Park, Courtney looked over at him with a raised eyebrow and a smile dancing around her lips.

"And why would I want to do that?" She asked. D was ready with his response.

"Cuz you aint never had a guy like me before that's why!" Courtney rolled her eyes and sucked her teeth at him.

"D that old basic ass line is not going to work on me boy. 'I've seen the way you've been looking at me all day. I don't know why y'all niggaz try and always run game when there aint no need to. Wassup with that? Just talk with me is that so hard."

This threw D's cool demeanor way off! There were times when he envisioned himself as a younger version of Money Mike. Brutal in the street and smooth between the sheets! Able to get any girl e wanted with a catchy phrase and a wink and a smile. The reality was that he was far from the young Mac he thought he was. Girls still made her nervous. Even now with all the weed and alcohol in his system, he was still having a hard

130

time keeping his composure when he was this close to a girl as fine as Courtney.

"Well?" Courtney asked.

D looked around, stalling for time. The group of teens were loosely spread out around the small reservoir in small groups. The trees scattered throughout the park were all various shades of yellow, red and orange, the last of nature's efforts to bless the world with color before the cold grey of winter set in. there wasn't a break in the clouds above, just a thick blanket of grey as far as the eye could see. The buzz of several different conversations filled the air and D was grateful they couldn't be overheard.

"Look Courtney, I know you aint starving for attention. I see niggaz tryna holla at you all day long at school. I even see niggaz you be kicking it with outside of school. But yet you still here talking to me."

"Yeah, so what that mean?"

"It means that you ain't really with any of them niggaz you talking to right now. That means you're available. Your ass ain't tied down to nobody."

"So?"

D almost lost his mind with frustration.

"So why not finally find a place to park that car? Your fine as hell Courtney! I mean you are for real beautiful! But you out here fucking around with niggaz that don't even give a fuck. Why? Because they getting money? I aint broke if that's what you worried about!" He finished talking and looked away from Courtney. The words had just erupted from his mouth before he could stop them. God damn alcohol!

Beside him, Courtney laughed softly as a happy smile spread across her face. She nudged d with her shoulder and he looked over at her, surprised to see the happy expression on her face. He extended his hands out to the side, palms up, and hunched his shoulders in an "I don't know" gesture. This made her smile again. Taking one of D's hands in her own, she gave it a small squeeze.

"Your funny D. Funny and cute as hell. You're also different. Even though you're around all these crazies all the

131

time, I can tell there's something else going on in your mind. How about you call me this weekend? You already got my number right?"

"Oh shit, I do! I hella forgot! That was last year though."

"So why didn't you ever use it?"

"I don't know. That was business. You just wanted me to keep you updated whenever I had the super fire Kush or something else you might wanna buy. I didn't want to bother you or nothing like that."

Courtney glanced over at D with a half amused half confused look on her face.

"Yeah, you are different," she said. From the tone of her voice it sounded like a good thing. About fifteen feet away a shout from one of her friends caught Courtney's attention. Three of her friends were sitting on a bench having what looked like a girl's only meeting. Courtney nodded in her friend's direction.

"All right then we got action. Call me this weekend boo," she told D. Giving his hand a brief tight squeeze, Courtney got up and headed over to join her friends. D watched her go hypnotized by her thick and inviting hips and ass.

After a moment, D's heart rate returned to normal. He couldn't believe it! He'd finally gotten up the nerve to approach her and instead of a "hell no" she had told him to call her this weekend! He felt pretty fucking good about himself! Pulling a swisher out of his pocket, D was contemplating rolling up a blunt when Chris returned.

He had strolled off earlier in search of a homeless man to go to the liquor store for them and was now back. He didn't have a bottle or a bum with him but the look on his face brought D's entire good mood crashing down around him. He knew that look. Someone was about to get hurt. Chris cupped his hands around his mouth.

"Treys Up!" he yelled out. Instantly all conversation stopped and every boy that was there immediately surrounded Chris waiting for orders.

"What's going down?" called out Whop.

Chris nodded over his shoulder in the direction he had just come from.

"So check it out, when I was down there taking a piss behind some bushes I got a better look at these dudes that's hooping on the court and I recognized some of them niggaz. They're FEB. At least five of them is for sure. I don't know about the rest but right now I'm assuming they are. So fuck em! Their status don't matter anyways it's time to put some work in!"

Looking around him, Chris picked up a half-finished bottle of beer. Pouring out the rest of the liquid, he hefted it in his hands feeling the weight. A small smile indicated he was pleased with the result. Looking around he did a quick head count. Thirteen boys and seven girls. Even without the girls they still outnumbered the players on the court. It was time!

"Aight lets do this!" said Chris.

As they group moved off through the park, D felt the atmosphere around him change. Smiles had disappeared and laughter had dissolved into low murmurs. Serious faced young men were cracking their knuckles and pulling up their pants and tightening belts while bad mouthing and naming FEB niggaz that they hoped were there. The girls were being loud and D saw Courtney look over at him with an excited expression on her face. Like the thought of impending violence was something to welcome instead of be scared of.

D looked around at the other boys faces. Some looked excited. Others appeared pissed off. A couple even looked fearful. D was feeling nervous. Mass brawls were new to him but surrounded as he was by his new street family, he refused to let it show.

As the group passed a low electrical building and came into view of the basketball courts, D's stomach jumped slightly as the situation suddenly became real. There was the game, in full swing. Dark and light bodies were running up and down the court dribbling and passing the basketball and occasionally someone would take a shot. D's insides felt a little like that ball; bouncing all over the place. The fights he had been in before were nothing like what he was walking into mow. If this thing played out like it seemed it would, there was about to be around thirty people duking it out in the middle of a public basketball court.

A shout rang out from the courts as several players noticed the approaching mob and the game stopped instantly. Hands went up and fingers began forming intricate symbols, letters and numbers in the air. Chis held up his right hand, pointer finger, pinky and thumb held straight out and the middle and ring finger pressed up against his palm. If viewed a certain way it looked just like the number 23 and it stood for 23rd Ave. At the same time he slipped the beer bottle in his hand into his back pocket out of sight from the boys on the court.

On seeing the hand sign a loud angry outburst erupted from the court as the boys came together, unified against the threat now facing them. Chris looked back at the teens arrayed behind him.

"Aight y'all, you see they ready. So let's fuck these niggaz up! DEUCE TREY!"

Walking on to the court, Chris stopped less than ten feet away from the opposing group with D and the rest right at his back. Adrenaline pounding through his veins, D searched the faces of the FEB members but couldn't find Devontay's face. But there was another person he recognized. Dark skin, cornrows and two eyes that were filled with white hot rage and focused directly back at him. It was the kid D had fought at the house party almost two months ago. Cornrows began pointing and yelling.

"Eh y'all that's the bitch ass nigga who jumped me at that party. He's the one who started all this shit!" A couple heads turned and began staring at D too but amid the general loud noise going on around them, Cornrows statement went unnoticed by the larger group.

Both sides began spreading out into lines. Gang signs were going up everywhere and taunts and insults were being hurled back and forth like verbal bullets. Chris held up his hands for silence among the Deuce Trey niggaz then pointed across at the FEB members across the court.

"Tell you what, y'all strip down butt ass naked and walk off this court right now then wont nobody get cut today."

From out of the ranks of FEB members stepped a tall light skin boy dressed in baggy jeans and red hoody. D's heart suddenly sank as he recognized the tall boy as one of Sumo's cousins. But there was no time to worry about what was going to happen. Sumo's cousin was already pointing and yelling back at Chris.

"Wassup Chris why don't you quit all that show boating and step on over here and let your fists do the talking? You aint crazy nigga you just retarded! You all talk bitch!"

At this Chris eyes went wild! Before anyone could blink Chris had closed his hand around the handle of the beer bottle in his pocket and was running towards Sumo's cousin. Whipping the bottle out of his pocket Chris swung it as hard as he could against the side of the boys head.

SMASH!

"AAAAAAGGGGHHHHHHH!"

As the bottle shattered into about a hundred pieces the boy let out a scream like a banshee as Chris began attacking his face with the jagged broken bottle. Immediately there was a stampede of feet as both sides ran towards the two struggling teens. Instantly all was mass confusion of swinging arms and wild yells.

Chris disappeared under a swarm of attackers as D got caught up in the charge. Immediately fists were flying through the air. D found himself trading punches with a short kid with dreads when he was suddenly tackled from behind and taken to the ground. Amid the wild spinning of the world, D could just make out the dark cornrowed head of the boy he'd fought at the party.

Unable to stop his momentum, they hit the pavement hard. He and his attacker rolled across the ground away from the main brawl. They came to a stop several feet away and D found himself on the bottom. The boy immediately unleashed a flurry of punches aimed at D's face.

Struggling with all his might to protect his face, D began frantically twisting his body to try and escape the punches raining down in him.

"This is what you get nigga," screamed the dark skinned boy on top of him as he continued trying to punch D as hard as he could. Not all of his punches were connecting though and eventually, D got his body halfway turned around. Finally with a huge burst of strength D was able to turn himself completely over so that he was on his stomach. Getting his arms under him, D pushed himself upwards with all his might. The boy was dislodged from his position on top of D's back and fell back on to the pavement. Getting up, D turned around and kicked the boy in the face as he was trying to get up. The boy fell back to the ground holding his mouth as D began kicking him repeatedly.

Whoop! Whoop! Whoop! Whoop! Whoop!

Suddenly the sound of sirens came roaring into D's ear. Looking up, he saw about three police cars tearing their way down the street on the dark side of the park. It was time to go. Glancing around, D saw that everybody else was already running for their lives in separate directions as they all sought to escape the incoming police. There were still a few teens fighting but not seeing Chris anywhere in sight, D decided to call it a day.

Looking down at the boy he had kicked clutching his face, D spat a huge glob of spit on to him and turned around preparing to run. That's when he saw him. The boy Chris had hit with the bottle was lying on the ground holding his face and moaning loudly as a pool of blood was forming around him. It was leaking between his fingers like a broken faucet.

The skin beneath looked an absolute horrible mess, shredded as if someone had taken a cheese grater and decided to make a pizza with human skin instead of cheese. There was a lot of blood. Feeling sick, D struggled to keep control of his churning stomach and ran full speed out of the court as the police cars came speeding down the street toward him.

Several hours later...

D was on his apartment rooftop staring down at the downtown Seattle skyline. The Space Needle was off to one side looking like a rocket waiting to be launched into the endless world that existed just beyond the blanket of thick grey clouds covering the sky. The majestic scenery was lost on D as he stared unseeingly out at the city beneath him.

He hadn't been unable to locate Chris in the mad dash out of the basketball court and through the park as everybody struggled to evade the cops arriving on the scene. D had seen a couple boys get grabbed but hadn't stopped to watch. Pumping his arms and legs wildly he had managed to break off from the main group and make his way through the familiar streets of Capitol Hill to eventually end up at the top floor of a house that was nearly finished being built. He had stayed there panting and nervous until the sirens had all stopped screaming. Only then had he dared venture back out. It had been an extremely nervous walk home.

Every ten seconds, D had stopped to anxiously scan the streets for cop cars or listening intently for the sound of approaching sirens. His dad had been absent when he got home. After pacing up and down the apartment multiple times, D rolled a blunt and headed to a short flight of stairs a couple blocks away on the corner of Yale Avenue and Olive Street.

He and Anthony had spent many nights here smoking weed and getting drunk off of cheap beer. Olive Street didn't actually connect with Yale Avenue. The road simply ended and a thin strip of sloping undeveloped land led the rest of the way to Yale Ave. There were two apartment buildings on either side of the street, a trash dumpster and a flight of six stairs connecting the two streets. Since the highway entrance was just off to the left the corner was mostly uninhabited and noisy but at night it made for an ideal smoking and thinking spot. And that's exactly what D needed it for now.

Antony had told him numerous times that being in a gang seemed to bring about more drama rather than keep you safe from it. But he had been loyal to the end. Deuce Trey really felt like a dysfunctional family but a family none-the less. But Anthony had died because of his affiliation. And now here d was sinker deeper by the minute. That boy had been fucked up! D didn't need to be a genius to figure out there would be major repercussions for their actions at the basketball court. And D was nervous.

D had seen some pretty brutal fights but none as bad as today. The cuts on that boy's face had almost made D throw up as he pictured the ripped bloody skin and pulsing muscle tissue raveled beneath. Fist fights had kind of been the norm but now... Shots had been fired but were few and between at this point. Beef hadn't taken priority over money making yet. Staring out at what little stars he could see dotted throughout the dark sky, D sighed heavily, his hands shaking slightly in anticipation of the coming week of school. He was willing to place a good bet that priorities were about to make a major switch!

Chapter 20

"Well done young soldiers well done!"

Money Mike stared with approval at the two teens sitting on the couch in front of him. Like a proud parent he eyed both of them up and down head nodding and mouth twisted into a sly grin.

It was the Sunday after thanksgiving and D and Chris sat side by side on the couch in Chris house listening to the praise they were receiving with mixed feelings. While Chris was so swollen with pride his head actually looked two sizes bigger, D was sitting in silence with a number of different emotions running through him. While it felt good to be congratulated about anything, D was just beginning to realize the degree of danger he had put himself in.

Gang altercations weren't the same as regular teenage fights where somebody just got beat up with nothing more than fists and that was that. In this arena something as simple as fight could quickly lead to much worse in a matter of seconds. If more incidents like the one at the basketball courts lay in the future, D was beginning to wonder what could happen to him if he was ever on the wrong end of a bottle. Or a knife. Or worse.

Money Mike disappeared into the kitchen for a few minutes and returned with a bottle of whisky and three shot glasses. Filling each glass to the brim he gestured at the boys to grab one each. Taking the glasses, D and Chris looked at each other and held them up in the air like Money Mike's was doing with his. Money mike looked directly into D and Chris eyes while he said his toast.

"To family, to Deuce Trey and to you lil niggaz! I love y'all from the bottom of my heart"!

All three quickly swallowed their drinks and slammed the glasses on the table. Taking out a bag of weed, Money Mike tossed the bag across to Chris and then took a seat one of the big comfy looking chairs facing the couch. Chris picked up the bag and looked at Money Mike with a raised eyebrow.

"What in supposed to do with this Mike? I ain't got no swisher. I told you we were out yesterday."

Money Mike looked at D who just shrugged and looked at the wall. Money mike stated at D for a brief second longer before turning back to Chris.

"Alright here go to the store and get a pack. And some beer too. Make sure you go to the union store. Tell the clerk it's for me he'll be cool about it."

Fishing out a twenty from his pocket, Money Mike handed it to Chris who took it and left the house throwing a huge black puffy coat over his shoulders. When he had gone, Money Mike turned back towards D who was shifting uncomfortably in the couch and looking everywhere but back at him. Something was bothering the teen that much was clear.

"D look at me!" The command was soft but firm. D stopped following the fly he had spotted and looked at Money Mike. The older man stared back at him, not judging but exploring. It was like he was scanning him and D had the strange feeling that he had just had his mind read. But he held the gaze. Money Mike nodded and smiled faintly.

"Fight got you shook up huh?"

D was shocked and couldn't hide it. He looked down at his shoes for a second. It was useless to lie.

"How did you know?" he asked looking back up at Money Mike.

"Its obvious lil' homie. Besides what you been doing for me with Chris, you just really getting involved in this life. I know you been homies with these guys but that's still outside looking in. That shit you see on the news, that's what you involved in now.

"You ain't no coward D, that's why I fuck with you and you can hustle with the beat of the them. But at the end of the day out world is largely ran on violence. That is what equals

140

power. You can have money and people will respect you too but they respect and fear a man that will physically hurt them. That's how we hold out territories that's how we keep others from messing with us. That and some bullshit politics but that shit barely works anyways."

D nodded his head slowly. He understood what Money Mike was saying but that wasn't exactly what was bothering him. He didn't want to seem weak but he also felt like he could tell money mike the truth.

"I guess what I'm tryna say is, I mean remember that dude we beat up for you a few months ago?"

Money Mike nodded.

"Yeah Roland's bitch ass. What about him?"

D shrugged. The memory of the damage the brass knuckles had down still lurked in the back of his mind.

"It's like we ain't fighting the same no more. People getting they teeth punched out and their faces cut up. I guess I didn't know it was gonna be like this. I guess in wondering when something fucked up is gonna happen to me."

Money Mike gazed thoughtfully over at D. Getting up he came and sat by him with his harsh glittering eyes fixed on D's face.

"I know it's a harsh place out there D. But understand that we didn't make it this way. Not one of us asked to be put on this earth but we're here so we have to deal with the circumstances. Understand that this ain't just your regular little kid bullshit. Fair fights and one on ones ain't the norm anymore. These boys HATE each other. And whenever they see you they will not think two seconds about fucking you up whatever the circumstance. If one of them had had a bottle or knife or a gun you better believe they would have used it on you. All Chris did was get there first.

"You think that little initiation beating you went through was something? Me and Chris been through way worse than that. Especially Chris! He's been jumped numerous times cause he crazy and don't give a fuck. And they've messed him up for it. He don't care what happens as long as he gets his licks in. And you right to be concerned. But there ain't nothing you can do but except stay on point and don't get caught slippin.

"I got plans for you niggaz so you keep following Chris and you'll be good. I wouldn't steer you wrong D and I'm glad you finally stepped up to the plate. We're family and these FEB niggas are tryna kill our family. We didn't fire first remember?"

D remembered. He would never forget the sights sounds and smells of that horrible night. The blur of movement all around him. The screams, cries and music still playing in the background. The acrid stench of gunpowder with the deep metallic smell of blood. Anthony's wide eyes almost bulging out of their sockets as he gasped and coughed as D tried desperately to stop the flow of blood. Oddly enough however, his heart hadn't been filled with hate. Mostly he just missed his friend. If anything the anger that he did feel was directed at Devontay alone. Not every single member of FEB.

He looked up at Money Mike. The feeling of calm reassurance and pride that he felt from Money Mike's advice and praise began to outweigh the nervous feeling he's had since the stabbing incident. He wouldn't let him down.

"I remember. I won't ever forget. All I'm saying is I just want to deal with Devontay. I don't care about running around starting fights with these dudes I don't give a fuck about and potentially getting fucked up before I can even deal with the guy I'm really after! That don't make a lot of sense to me Money that's all I'm saying."

Money Mike sat back on the couch and stared at d with an amused but satisfied look on his face. He like determination and focus in his solders but what he really liked to see was brutality.

"Ok young gunna. Let's say you do devote your time to finding Devontay. What you gone do when you catch him?"

D sat slumped in the couch. Not for the first time he realized that he hadn't really thought about what would happen if he and Devontay were to ever cross paths. Devontay had taken his best friends life. Granted, Devontay hadn't been aiming at Anthony but the deed was done. Did he really have the heart to...
BANG BANG BANG BANG BANG!!!

Out of nowhere the sound of loud gunshots broke through the afternoon stillness followed by the screeching of car tires on pavement! Money mike moved like a cat first grabbing D by the shoulder and forcibly throwing him to the floor then leaping across the room he snatched a big black pistol from a table drawer and rushed to the front door.

Peering out of the window, D was just in time to spot a grey late eighties model Chevrolet Caprice speed off down 23rd in the direction of Garfield high school. Yanking open the front door Money Mike looked cautiously outside then let out a strangled yell and disappeared. Getting slowly to his feet, D went to the front door and peered out to see what was going on.

There on the pavement in front of the house Money Mike was on the ground holding onto Chris. There was red everywhere. A crowd was beginning to gather as pointing and screaming. Turning to look at D, Money Mike screamed out but his words fell on deaf ears. D was staring down at the scene beneath him, the horror of the night Anthony died playing over and over in his head. Chris normally dark face was turning ashy grey as he cried out in pain. Eventually with great effort, D tore his eyes away from Chris blood soaked shirt and focused on money mike. His hearing came rushing back in one great wave of commotion and yelling.

"D! D! C'mon mane snap the fuck out of it and go call the fucking ambulance! He ain't dead yet so hurry the fuck up!!!"

Nodding his head dumbly, D turned and ran back inside the house to where the phone sat in its charger on the kitchen counter. Praying that he didn't just lose another friend, D picked up the phone and began forcing his shaking hands to dial 911.

The next day at Central High...

"Damn D that's fucked up! Is Chris going to be okay?"

"Yeah I think so. The ambulance got their pretty quick and even though there was hella blood, he only got shot in the arm. He was pale but the guys driving the ambulance said nothing vital had been hit. Hopefully he gets out the hospital soon. Money Mike is pissed."

With thanksgiving break over, D was back at central high. He was currently replaying the events of the day before to Courtney. It was lunchtime and they were sitting in the bleachers of the football stadium sharing a cigarette.

Chris was in the hospital with a gunshot wound to the arm money mike was on the warpath. Later that day three more shootings had occurred as roving groups of Deuce Trey and FEB members encountered each other up and down 23rd avenue and on surrounding streets. The news had picked up the story and now were running reports about the rise of gang violence in the city and what government officials were doing to combat the problem.

Exhaling a large cloud of the toxic smoke, D stared out over the field in silence rubbing his temples with his thumbs. A dull pounding had been going on in his head ever since Chris had been shot and wouldn't go away no matter how much Tylenol he took. Money Mikes words were repeated themselves over and over in his head.

"These boys HATE each other. And whenever they see you they will not think two seconds about fucking you up whatever the circumstance."

It was becoming real faster than D would have liked. Shoot outs and drive buys in broad daylight!! Nowhere was safe. D was having a hard time remembering the last time an entire day had gone by without a fight or a stabbing or shooting.

You couldn't go to a party, a gathering at a park or even just walk down the street without worrying about whether or not the day would explode into violence during the next few minutes. D was becoming suspicious of strangers and beginning to actively despise any and everybody who belonged to or was affiliated with FEB.

After a several incidents he had been involved in including the shooting D had arrived at several conclusions that only seemed to fuel his anger. FEB niggaz liked to do a lot of shooting. Numerous confrontations had occurred on corners throughout the central district and always seemed to go the same. A group of Duce Trey members would encounter a group of FEB. Taunts and insults would be hurled out gang signs would get thrown up and eventually a fight would break out. Someone from FEB would call out somebody from Duce Trey and it was on.

The problem was as soon as somebody stared losing tempers began to flare more insults would get thrown and eventually everything would dissolve into a rumble. It was at this point that the boys who didn't like to fight usually pulled out knives or guns and lately it always seemed Ike it was the FEB members who were first to pull weapons rather than duke it out with fists. This revelation had led to more tension between the groups because now instead of fighting with their hands first everybody would automatically pull out weapons. To D anybody from FEB was a certified pussy.

Brushing some hair out of her face, Courtney flicked the shrinking cigarette off to the side and looked over at D. She watched him for a second, tracing his outline with her eyes, admiring his tightly clenched jaw and eyes glittering with hostility. She had her eyes set on someone a lot more powerful and well known then D but she had to admit there was something about him that set him apart from the rest of the guys she went after.

While he didn't have a lot of money a car or house, she had noticed he was extremely observant and analytical of everything that went on around him. Instead of judging the world like most, he seemed to be trying to figure it out. Even as she carefully avoided becoming exclusive with him she had made a mental note to keep him close. And keep him interested.

Leaning against his arm, Courtney laid her head on his shoulder. D looked down at her briefly then back out across the field. For his part he had a hard time trying to understand Courtney. He only really saw her at school and noticed she avoided answering him anytime he brought up the subject of them being an item. But she hadn't stopped kicking it with him yet. He had decided to just go with the flow.

"Chris's will be aight. That nigga been through more shot then anybody I know. If anything he's gonna pumped he got another scar to show people," said Courtney.

D didn't doubt that at all. From across the field the sound of the school bell signaling the end of lunch rang out across the grounds. Picking up their backpacks d and Courtney began strolling toward the main building. As they neared the rear entrance doors, Courtney stopped and grabbed D's shoulder. Pulling him away from the door she led him around the corner to secluded spot out of sight from the doors. D looked down at her not understanding what was going on.

"You still on deck with that bomb ass Kush you been having?" she asked. D nodded.

"Hell yeah! Why, you tryna get a bag? You can just have one shit it's all good." He went to open his backpack but Courtney grabbed his hand. She looked up in his eyes with a sneaky look on her beautiful face.

"Well actually I was trying to get a little more than that. Like a quarter. But I don't need nothing for free. But since I'm kind of short on cash, I was thinking more like making a trade."

D looked slightly amused.

"Oh we bout to get on some old-school Barter system shit huh? What's the offer?"

Looking around, Courtney moved closer and her hands fastened around D's belt buckle.

"Something I been wanting to do for a minute now!" She licked her lips and before D knew what was happening she had knelt down in front of him unzipped his pants and found what she was looking for.

D had no words. His brain had just melted.

Hours later…

It had been a strangely good day. Central highs normally volatile hallways had been strangely inactive except for the usual congregations of students hanging out between classes. D had been ready for an all-out war as soon as first period had ended but nothing happened. D guessed the shootings from the day before had everybody laying low. No one had died but three drive buys in broad daylight was nothing to sneer at. Now here he was surrounded by FEB members and no moves had been made. It was like the calm before the storm.

The encounter with Courtney had blown his mind. Literally and figuratively. She decently knew what she was doing down there. And yet they still weren't anything exclusive. His good mood began to vanish as he realized he might not be the only one she'd made this trade with. Walking down a flight of stairs he checked his watch.

It was 1:15pm. *Only one more class to go*. Caught up thinking about Courtney and whether or not their little encounter had meant something, D failed to register the movement behind him until it was too late. All he felt was a big hand grab the collar of his short and another one on his backpack. Suddenly, he was moving rapidly towards the wall. Looking over his shoulder D had just enough time to see that it was Sumo who had grabbed him before his head collided with the lockers.

Stars exploded in his vision. Stumbling to the side, he felt himself pulled upright and his mouth exploded with pain as a giant fist crashed into it. His head flew back into the lockers and he tasted blood on his tongue. Through the fog of pain D could see he was surrounded by at least eight people. Sumo was the one who had his hands on him but the rest were shouting and jeering at him.

"I told you not to touch my cousin D," Sumo roared out and punched D in the face again. That one hurt. A lot. D was spotting blood now and his jaw defiantly was starting to hurt. A few more punches from sumo and it would probably break. Suddenly from down the hall came a loud angry shout. Whop, along who about twelve other boys were running full speed down the hall towards sumo and the rest.

"LET MY NIGGA GO FUCK BOY!" yelled out Whop brandishing a pair of brass knuckles. The group around Sumo moved to confront Whop and the hall immediately broke out into an immense racket of yells screams and the dull violent sound of bone connecting with flesh.

D found himself slammed against the locker again and punched hard right in his left eye. There was an angry shout and

147

someone collided with sumo and d was dropped. He fell to the floor but immediately was surrounded by a sumo and two other FEB members who all began kicking him in the body and head as hard as they could. The last thing D heard before he lost consciousness was a loud WHAP and a heavy grunt and then all went dark.

Chapter 21

"Is this all you fucking do? Are you fucking kidding me? Are you trying to get yourself fucking killed!"

Lying on the couch in the living room, D stared with his one good eye up at his dad's angry silhouette. The big man was standing over him attacking the air in all directions with his arms and screaming his head off at the fact that D had come home from school beat up again. Only now, D hadn't been able to explain it away as simply being bullied for having the wrong friends.

His dad has had enough of being played for a fool. He knew his son was no saint and was convinced that the beatings d was receiving were all the result of something D had done to deserve it. He was distraught at the fact he didn't seem able to connect with his son but also filled with rage and resentment towards his wife for having left him. She was apparently in Hawaii now win the doctor and never seemed concerned enough to ask about her son. Frigid bitch!

Gazing down at his battered son, Marcus felt himself losing control of the world around him. What would happen next?

"D, you have to understand, when you leave for school in the morning I spend the whole day wondering whether or not you're going to come home with all your teeth! I thought you and this young man you got into a fight with were friends. He almost killed you with his bare hands!!! What the hell did you do to piss this young man off so bad?"

"You don't want to know," was D's reply. It was muffled slightly by his swollen lips.

"Oh yes I do! What the hell do you do when you walk out of this house that has people you used to be friends with trying to punch your head off?!"

"I was in a fight with a bunch of guys and his cousin was there and got stabbed with a broken bottle by someone else. But Sumo's taking it out on me cuz he thinks i was the one who did it."

His dad looked up at the ceiling as if appealing to god for help.

"Did you? Jesus fucking Christ "

"Nope!"

His dad looked at him closely.

"I really didn't that's on everything!" D repeated stubbornly. He didn't have the patience for this conversation when he was still coming to terms with the way recent events had unfolded.

He and Sumo were now official enemies but as of right now Sumo was in the hospital. He was in a coma from being bashed repeatedly in the head with a pair of brass knuckles. Whop had saved D from getting kicked to a pulp but was now in County jail awaiting trial for his assault. Sumo would no doubt be on the war path when he got out of the hospital but D didn't care. His mind was filled with the grisly images of the boy sliced open on the basketball court and the feeling of Sumo's giant fist repeatedly smashing into his face.

More than anything, D was becoming increasingly scared at the amount of violent incidents that continued to happen everywhere he went. But beneath the fear laid a deeper more complex emotion. His life had never been filled with so much excitement! Each violent encounter he came away from only served to make him feel tougher and stronger than before. Somewhere under the nervousness and fear a new emotion had begun to slowly invade his soul; arrogance! He headed to the bus stop.

Thirty minutes later…

The rear doors of the bus opened and a pair of black low top Air Force ones carried their owner from the last step to the pavement with a short hop. Looking up and down the street in both directions, D began a slow walk towards the school. He had gotten off the bus about three stops to soon so he could smoke a blunt on his way to school. Reaching in his pocket, he took out the blunt, slightly crooked from being bent during the bus ride and a black lighter.

He lit the blunt inhaling the smoke deeply with his closed so as to savor every moment. Exhaling very slowly, D heaved a great sigh of relief as he felt the burn of the smoke in his lungs. His face had half healed in the week that he had been absent except for a right eye that was still a little sore.

As he smoked his blunt and walked towards the school, D wondered what would happen today. Retaliation violence was always to be expected after a confrontation occurred. Today however D was expecting things to go a little different. In his back pocket was a black and silver switchblade he had borrowed from Chris. With a 4 inch retractable blade it was a dangerous weapon. D had vowed never to be jumped again and he would prevent it by any means ness scary. He had never stabbed anybody before and didn't want to start now. But what he wanted to do and what he had to do were two different things.

"Hey look its D! Waddup nigga hey we over here!"

Making his way through the morning crowds surrounding the front entrance of the school, D heard a familiar voice calling to him. Looking over the heads of a group of small Asian girls, D saw the young rapper Chaz and a group of his friends congregating around a group of blue colored benches. All were Duce Trey members and most had been involved in the rumble the week before. D nodded and headed over. He was greeted by handshakes and hugs from all the boys while the two girls that were off to one side of the group shot him sly glances.

"Waddup y'all? Treys up!"

"Treys up!" The group responded all throwing up the hand sign. A few passing boys glanced over but kept walking. One of the boys passed D a lit cigarette and he took it inhaling deeply.

"What's it been looking like up in here this last week?" He asked Chaz.

Chaz just shook his head.

"Crazy. Ms. Weathers been kicking people out like she trying out for the soccer team or something. All Duce Trey or FEB dudes. The hallways were a battle field after that rumble with you and sumo. Did you really attack that nigga all by yourself?"

D paused halfway through a healthy sized inhale on the cigarette. Did he really attack sumo? Sumo had definitely been the one to attack him but apparently these boys has heard something different.

"I mean I really didn't have a choice bro that nigga came at me so fast it was on before I even knew what was going down. You don't think in situations like that ya feel me"?

The youngsters in front of him all nodded their heads. None of them were strangers to violence. Chaz spoke up again.

"Well shit niggaz ran down as soon as we heard the noise. Sorry we reached you too late. How's your helmet?" He was referring to D's head.

"I'm cool now. That shit hurt though. Good looks on the backup. It ain't your fault they jumped the hell out of me. He thought I was the one who stabbed his cousin at that basketball Court brawl."

"Damn at least you aight though. You shouldn't have been walking alone anyways D that's why we stay deep. You should come through the sophomore floor more often we run that shit down there."

The sincerity in Chaz voice almost made D pause in curiosity. For some reason he had never expected to receive so much love from people involved in so much crime and violence. It was intoxicating. And he wanted more.

"Yeah it wasn't me but fuck it I'm here in he's in the hospital. Fuck sumo!"

He said the last sentence loudly and it rang out across the small courtyard. On the opposite side a small group of teenagers jumped up and began making their way across the concrete towards the Duce Trey members. Immediately, D Chaz and everyone around them hopped up and began cracking knuckles and punching their hands into their fists.

152

"What you say nigga!" A tall light skinned teen dressed in a red hoody and baggy jeans yelled out at d as the group approached.

"You heard me nigga!" D yelled back. "Fuck sumo and anybody affiliated with him. Since you getting mad that obviously means you got something to do with him. So FUCK YOU TOO!"

D was ready. Surrounded by His young dangerous friends all yelling and baring their teeth like rabid animals about to attack he felt invincible. Shrugging off his backpack he faced off against his tall opponent. The words his father had told him earlier that morning meant nothing in the heat of the moment. The kids behind him and at his sides were becoming a better family then the one he'd ever had at home. Putting his fists up, D crouched low and began shuffling towards the talker light skinned teen.

Seconds before the two sides collided a sharp whistle rang out across the courtyard and several security guards came bursting out of the main school doors accompanied by what looked any nearby faculty that could be mustered. Ignoring the incoming police the two sides of teenagers immediately rushed at each other attempting to get as many punches and kicks in before the fight was broken up.

D's short arms were a disadvantage but he ducked a wild swing from his tall opponent and sank his right fist into his stomach. The kid doubles over but before, D could do any more damage he found himself in a strong headlock and couldn't escape. Eventually he went limp and was dragged off to one side and dumped like a rag doll onto the pavement. The fight was already over. Several kids were caught by the arm or in headlocks like D had been. It took a while to regain complete control of the courtyard amid all the screaming and general chaos but things eventually quieted down.

D was taken along with Chaz and three others to an empty classroom and told to wait quietly. A single security guard stayed watch over them. After almost an hour the door opened and another security guard followed by the principal Ms. Weathers entered. All the boys straightened up the sight of the

153

ultimate authority figure. Walking purposefully towards the front of the class she leaned up against the desk and beckoned for the security guards to leave. At first both men looks hesitant to leave their boss in a room with suspected gang members but a second gesture and a stern look finally sent them walking out the door.

After the door closed behind them, Ms. Weathers looked around sternly at the kids seated before her. Gradually her eyes softened and she put her hand to her face and shook her head slowly sighing deeply.

"So please help me understand gentlemen," she said and there was a pleading to her voice that was shocking, "please help me understand what all this recent drama and violence about? I know the streets are always going to have that stuff going on but c'mon y'all!! I don't even have to read the news to see that something serious is going on. Shootings in the neighborhoods fights at school! Please tell me is there anything I can do to stop this?" She was really appealing to the young men with all her night. Most of them were looking at each other with surprise shock and confusion plastered across their faces.

Ms. Weather's eyes were wide and expectant as if the tiniest bit of information would feed her for a month. Then slowly the light of understanding came into her eyes and she peered intently into each boy's eyes in turn.

"Is this about that boy that was killed over the summer? Anthony Brown?"

By the stiffing of body postures and suddenly deathly quiet that fell across the room, Ms. Weathers felt like she had the nail on the head. It was what she had feared ever since seeing the report on her television all those months ago. She knew he had belonged to a gang and that there were gangs present at her school and the return of school would bring rivals back in close contact with each other. But she had hoped it wouldn't have infected her hallways. But it had. And if she didn't do something about it now then somebody was going to lose their life in Central high and there had never been a death on the property as of yet. She wanted to keep it that way.

D was looking at Ms. Weathers with an intent gaze on his face. Ms. Weathers caught his eyes and she looked right at him. She spoke to him.

"I know you and Anthony were close Damien. I was so saddened by his death believe me. But fighting amongst each other is only going to bring about more tears. Look at what's it's doing to this school!"

"They started it," blurted out Chaz.

"Who is *they*?"

Chaz shut his mouth and refused to say more. She looked back towards D.

"Damien you're a smart individual. You've had your run in's with my security before but never anything as bad as this year. I know you must miss your friend but is this how he would want you to remember him?"

"I don't know. He's not here so I can't ask him?"

Ms. Weathers looked helplessly on. It was like she powerless against the forces these kids faced outside of her walls. What good was education if they wouldn't be around to use it? Maybe they had already figured this out long before she had. As far as her next moves she had little choice when it came to D. He had been in to many violent incidents already this year. The rest would all get long term suspensions since they were young and with less infractions under their belts. She gazed down at Damien and felt shame and remorse at the fact that he had almost made it past the BS to actually graduate. He's only had a year left. She had failed yet another of her pupils in the never ending battle of the hallways vs. the alleyways.

Thirty minutes later…

"Damien I'm sorry to say this but I'm left with little choice but to suspend you for the remainder of the school year. You will no longer be allowed on the premises and a guard will escort you off of it. This breaks my heart child but you've made it so this is my only option. "

The works echoed around his head again and again as D stumbled up the street away from his former high school. He was kicked out. Ms. Weathers had basically expelled him except with a catch.

"This packet that I'm giving you is a take home test that the state has deemed good enough to replace an official high school diploma. Now you've got until the end of the year to do the work assigned within and send it to the school district building downtown before the last week of school. If you pass you can still walk but you won't get a diploma. It will be more like a certificate."

D had been confused.

"Why are you giving me this?" He has asked.

"Because the things that you young people have to go through these days are horrible and I can't imagine what I would do if I was in your position. But I hope you do the right thing. You're not too far behind that you couldn't catch up if you start now. I'm sorry about your friend."

At least she had seemed genuine. But it hardly mattered now. He thought about the thick packet inside his backpack. Could he finish it time with everything else that was going on? Should he do as she said and try and graduate for Anthony? He was lost and scared. D had no idea what his next move would be. He'd never imagined he'd actually get kicked out of school for his behavior. Another bad lack of judgment on his part. He looked up at the wall of grey covering the sky and tried to imagine what the world looked like on the other side if the clouds. He needed something anything to take his mind off of what his dad was going to say when he found out. He opened his phone.

An hour later…

Now why in the hell had he called Chris of all people?

"Get that nigga D!"

Running flat out D was in hot pursuit of one of two FEB members that had been spotted at a bus stop on 23 and union. Chris, his arm still in a sling, was slightly behind trying his best to catch up. The other one had already been caught by a group of Chris friends and was getting a brutal beating right in the street somewhere on 22nd. Chris and D had chased the remaining FEB member up the street and around the corner.

He hasn't known what else to do. He was suspended indefinitely from school. His dad wouldn't speak to him. His mom was somewhere in Hawaii with her new man. Latoya was with her family. Chris had been the only one who picked up. He had been looking to ease the tension in his brain but now not thirty minutes after leaving his apartment he was running down some kid he didn't even know. And what's worse was he didn't even care.

Putting on an extra burst of speed, D urged his legs to go faster and the distance between him and his target began to shrink. The youth risked a quick look over his shoulder saw he wasn't going to get away and turned around preparing to fight. But he wasn't fast enough. D cannoned into him in mid turn in a tackle that would've earned him a scholarship had anybody college scout had seen it. The two teens hit the ground hard and D felt skin being scrapped from his elbows as they rolled across the concrete. Quickly struggling to the top position, D began swinging with all his might at the kids head. Some connected and some didn't. But D had the upper hand and it began to show. Cuts began to open and blood began to flow. A hard punch right to mouth opened up a gash on D's middle knuckle as it connected with the front teeth.

Chris arrived on the scene and sent a heavy kick thudding into the young man's rib cage then tripped over him as he lost his balance. D thought he heard something snap. It must have been one of his ribs. The boy immediately curled up and began screaming. D got up quickly and as Chris steadied himself and grabbed D by the arm.

"Time for us to go nigga! He got his though. Good work!"

And somehow as they ran through the backstreets cutting through alleyways and side yards as sirens began blazing back where they had come from, D felt proud if himself. And grateful for the compliment.

Chapter 22

"You look different."

"What you mean I look different? Different like how?"

"I don't know, you just look different. You look mean."

"Mean?"

"Yeah D you look mean. Ever since you first walked up you've had this big old scowl on your face like somebody just took your lunch money. Look you doing it right now! What's up with you?"

D struggled to adjust his expression. The result was Latoya shaking her head at him.

"Now you look like you caught between a sneeze and a heart attack! You look crazy! C'mon D what's going on you can tell me. I know something's up you forget I've known you just as long as Anthony did. God bless my baby's heart he wouldn't want to see you like this d I know he wouldn't."

The mention of his deceased friend did indeed bring a softening to his face. D looked up at the grey skies above him. Somewhere up there Anthony was looking down on all the shit that was happening and it made D wonder if Anthony would approve of his recent actions. He was willing to bet the answer would be no.

It was a Thursday afternoon. Not that it really mattered to D anymore. It wasn't like he had anywhere specific to be. It was cloudy and chilly as usual. D had met up with Latoya and one of her girlfriends at Judkin's Park. It was a large park and many people came here to take walks through its landscaped paths. He had originally met up with Latoya only to sell her a quarter ounce of weed but had stayed to talk for a little bit. Her friend was up ahead pushing the stroller and talking to Anthony Jr.

about her latest crush while D and Latoya strolled about ten feet behind them.

"Well it's not like I'm out here trying to look mean. I just don't feel very positive about a lot of shit right now. My life's a little fucked up if you haven't noticed. Lost my best friend got kicked out of school and can't go a week without some crazy shit happening!"

"Well let's think who wanted to get involved in the first place? I'm sorry shit is happening to you the way it is but that's how that life goes. And no matter how fucked your life is right now it ain't Nowhere near as close to as fucked up as mine has been D. I've been living in a nightmare since summer! My man is gone and now my baby is going to grow up without his dad. One of the two people I loved more than myself was ripped from my hands and now I've got nobody."

D felt a little resentment at Latoya's words.

"That shit ain't true Latoya you got me!"

They stopped moving. Latoya looked over at D with a skeptical expression on her face.

"Yeah I bet that whit sounds good coming out your mouth. Where you been at then D? I've barely seen you since school started. You said you were going to come to the park with us hella times and never once showed up! The only time you actually show up is if I call you for some weed like today. What happened to the guy who used to come check on us every other day just to see how we're doing? You barely even call anymore! I need you D! I need someone to talk to sometimes other than my home girls. I don't know a lot of them other guys because Anthony always tried to keep me away from them. Except for you. He trusted you like nobody else and told me I could too.

"You said once that if I ever needed anything to just ask. Well D I'm asking you; please just keep in touch like you said you would. I feel his spirit in you D and I just, I like to be around you because of that. But with you never around anymore, it's like i lost another piece of the man who's already gone. "

D was shocked. He had no idea that his visits had meant so much to Latoya. But then again, he hadn't really taken the time to really think about how life must have changed for her

159

after Anthony's death. He had been selfish in thinking that no one else could possibly understand his grief. His expression softened as he looked over at Latoya. Guilt began to take hold of his conscious.

"Damn Latoya. I, well," D shifted from foot to foot unable to find words to express the unfamiliar feelings swirling around through him. Latoya held up a hand to stop his attempted explanation.

"Really though D, I'm not tryna hear any of your reasons or excuses. I'm just tryna let you know where I'm coming from. You think I don't hear what's been going on with you? All this shit you been involved in? If you not careful you're gonna end up just like Anthony. In the wrong place at the wrong time around the wrong people! I care about you d and whether you realize it or not you do a lot to help keep me going in this world. I need that right now. So if you're not gonna be here for me then just let me know so I can stop depending on you right now."

D was lost for words. A vibrating phone provided a brief distraction and he retrieved it from his pocket. It was a text message from Breanna!

HEY D WHERE U AT? I THOUGHT WE HAD A STUDY SESSION?

D was confused but happy to see a text from the older blond woman. Last time they had parted ways it hadn't been on the best of terms. But here indeed was the code they had established that meant she wanted to buy some weed from him. He sent a quick reply saying he'd be there within the hour and put the phone back in his pocket. He looked over at Latoya who had crossed her arms over her chest and was looking at D with a cold expression on her face. D felt helpless. On one hand he felt bad for not living up to his promise of constant drop ins and phone calls but on the other hand it wasn't like he was absent for no reason. But he owed it to her. And to Anthony.

"Look Latoya, I know i fucked up by not being around like I said I would. It's just shit has gotten so out of hand I don't even nowhere to begin. I've never felt this much stress on my

160

brain or been so tense all the time like I am now. It's made me lose track of a lot of things."

He looked her deep in her eyes.

"I promise I will do better at coming by and checking in with you."

Latoya continued to stare at him but eventually her gaze softened. She gently brushed D's arm with her hand.

"I hope so D," she said softly. "I need you right now."

Thirty minutes later…

"So if you can't help me just let me know so I can stop depending on u right now!"

Latoya's words were still doing laps around D's head even though it had been almost a half hour since they had parted ways. Walking down 25th avenue he had just passed over Jackson Street down from the Walgreens. After a quick scan of the people on the street, he crossed and continued his journey through the neighborhood.

His mood had changed slightly from guilt to annoyance. Here he was going to war with the people responsible for her man's death and she wasn't showing the least bit of gratitude. If she understood the life so bad then why was she tripping on him like this? She should know what is!

Reaching the Corner of 25th and Washington, D was about to cross the street when a noise to his left made him turn his head to discover its source. He froze. About 20 feet away gathered in front of a derelict looking white house were around a dozen young men all in large black Hoody's or windbreakers and baggy jeans. All conversation stopped as soon as they saw D.

Immediately, D felt a wave of hostility wash over him. He knew he should get moving as fast as possible but something inside of him refused to let act as if he was scared. He was Duce Trey! But it appeared as if he wouldn't have to say anything.

"Hey I know that nigga," came a loud voice from the middle of the group. From behind two larger boys a short dark skinned teen with braids emerged with his right hand shoved into his waist. It was the boy D had nicknamed Cornrows from the house party and the basket basketball court fight that he kept beating up! D crossed his arms and sneered at him but all the time he was ready to run at a moment's notice. This was not an ideal situation to be in.

"Waddup bitch nigga you looking to get that ass beat again?" D called out.

"Fuck you nigga the only one getting beat up today bout to be yo ass! You on the wrong street boy where the rest of your weak ass squad at?"

"Never mind that come on and see me one on one and we see whose weak."

Cornrows looked around at the group standing behind him then back at D. The look in his eyes was wild and suddenly d began to wonder why he still had his hand shoved in his waist. D's stomach churned suddenly as he realized what Cornrows must be holding onto and the machismo that been pumping through his veins seemed to evaporate instantly. Cornrows was staring at him with an intense hatred pouring out of his eyes like water from a broken damn.

D knew what was going to happen a split second before it actually did. Cornrows whipped his hand out of his waist gripping a black pistol while at the same time D spun around on his heels and took off back the way he had come! The quiet evening erupted with the sounds of violence.

BANGBANGBANGBANG!!!

Bullets went whiz zing by D smacking into cars and tearing through bushes as he made his escape back down 25th avenue. Loud shouts and curses followed him as he pumped his arms and legs as fast as they would go. He hadn't thought cornrows would actually shoot at him! He's been an idiot not to realize why cornrows had kept his hand in his pants the whole time. Not bothering to look behind him as he ran, D prayed no bullets had been made with his name on them yet!

Two hours later…

D felt a little strange being back in Breanna's basement after their less than friendly parting weeks before. As he sat at the basement bar and watched her pouring out a couple of

162

tequila shots he played with some words that were bouncing around in his head as he tried to construct an apology for his behavior. She turned around and placed a shot glass full of deep golden liquid in front of him.

"Thank god for Jose," exclaimed Breanna holding her glass in the air expectantly. D grabbed his glass and gently tapped it against Breanna's. They both drank their shots quickly and cleanly. The anxiety D had been feeling since being shot at not an hour before lessened a little as he felt the liquor hit his stomach spreading its comforting warmth across his body. As Breanna went to refill the glasses, D cleared his throat loudly.

"Um Breanna? I just wanted to say I'm sorry for the way I behaved last time I was here. I shouldn't have said those things to you and I'm sorry. You didn't deserve that."

Breanna paused in refilling their glasses and looked across the counter at D.

"Don't worry about it D. It's ok."

D shook his head.

"No it's really not though! I was angry about some other shit that had happened that day and I took it out on you. You don't deserve to have those type of things said to you. You get fifty percent off your purchase today. I wish I could do more to show you how sorry I am. How bout I mow your lawn for a year?"

Breanna smiled softly and slowly shook her head from side to side.

"You don't have to do anything D. It's all right honestly. I've actually been doing a lot thinking since then. Everything you said to me even though it hurt to hear it really made me question this position I got myself into. Plus these little kick it sessions we have down here do more for me then you'll ever know. So let's start off on a clean slate ok?"

D looked a little uncomfortable but Breanna waved his concern. She came around the counter bringing the bottle and her glass with her and sat down next to D. He was still looking guilty.

"I'm serious D. If anything I'm sorry for slapping you. I shouldn't have lost control of myself like that. You just hit a nerve. But it's fucking stupid because really I have only myself to blame for how I'm feeling. I haven't been happy in so long I think in forgetting how it feels. And the fact that somebody else can see the truth of my situation better then myself only proved how much denial I've been living in.

"Now I'm thinking who else has seen through me? I know my mom always has because all she does is tell me to leave Todd. But I never do. I thought he had everything I wanted and that we would be able to start a life together. But the reality is he's in love with his job not me. He's always out of town or the country on business and when he gets home he's always drunk or out with his buddies. I even think he's cheating on me but I'm not sure. And I put up with it all because it feels good to wake up in a big house and drive a nice truck and have money all the time.

"But what is it all really worth? This isn't a real home. This isn't even a real marriage and if it is then I don't think married life is for me. Half the time I'm too scared to say anything to him because he'll get angry and go into one of his crazy tantrums. Ugh! What have I become? Sorry for rambling?""

Breanna paused to pour herself another shot. She downed it quickly and immediately poured another. Picking up the glass she held it up to her face as she examined the liquid inside.

"They say the truth will set you free. Here's to hoping it will," She downed the last shot shaking her head vigorously as the alcohol spread its warmth threw her body. Not wanting to appear awkward, D tossed back his shot as well. Breanna rested her head on one hand and looked over at D while tapping her nails on the counter top. Her long blond hair flowed across her shoulders and down her arms as she wiped a few tears out of her hazel colored eyes.

As usual D was almost struck dumb by her beauty and confused that a woman so beautiful could be in a situation so fucked up. Breanna looked like a super model and D used to think that women that pretty never had any problems in life. He was learning a lot from Breanna and Todd's troubles whether they knew it or not. How could two people who had everything going for them be dealing with issues like domestic violence and infidelity?

"So what are you going to do?" D asked. Breanna shook her head.

"I honestly couldn't tell you D. I have to do something that much I do know. I can't believe I'm so vain that after all I've been through I still don't want to leave all this fancy crap behind. Anyways you got my medicine?"

"Sure do," said D happy to change the subject. Reaching into his backpack, he dug around inside until he felt the package he was looking for. He took it out and placed it on the counter in front of Breanna.

"Half ounce of granddaddy Kush just for you! Fresh and sticky and can you smell that aroma?" Breanna laughed.

"Sweet! Still $150 right"

"All day every day! But for you today its $75."

"That's why I love you!" Breanna handed D a wad of rolled up bills. While D put the money in his pocket Breanna opened the big bag of weed and took out a few buds. She took a glass pipe out of a drawer but just before she was about to light it snapped her fingers and placed the pipe on the counter.

"Damn I completely forgot! I have something for you D."

Walking to the other side of the room, D saw her grab something up from the floor and return to the bar. In her arms was a box with a picture of a pretty nice looking camcorder on it. She places the package next to D and sat back down next to him. D wasn't sure what to think. He glanced at the small box then back at Breanna.

"Soooooo..."

Breanna shook her head smiling and nodded at the camera box.

"I told you I had something for you. Go ahead check it out."

D slowly opened the box. Inside was a collection of different black cables, a wall charger, an instruction book and a sleek black camcorder. Taking it out, D looked it over from every angle. He flipped open the viewfinder and stared at screen as the room came swimming into focus. He pointed the camera

165

at Breanna and she waved smiling widely and flashing her incredibly white teeth!

"Damn this is a nice ass camera! Thanks Breanna! But I gotta ask; why are you giving this to me?"

Breanna's face fell a little and she purée herself another shot.

"It was Todd's birthday last week. He was always talking about getting a camera to film his golf games with so I bought him one. He threw a fit when he unwrapped it though. I guess one of his friends had the same one and he said he had to get the newer model so it would be better than his friends camera and I didn't pay attention to his wants because I didn't care and he got up and walked out in the middle of dinner.

"He hasn't apologized or asked for it back so fuck it. I'm so over it! I was going to throw it away since I can't stand looking at it but I don't want my money going to waste. I'm sure you can find some uses for this thing. I just, I don't want it in this house anymore."

D was hypnotized by the camera. He had never owned anything as nice as this in his entire life. And to just be given one for free? He was struck dumb by Breanna's generosity and surprised she hadn't tried to facilitate a trade. But he reasoned she obviously wasn't hurting for money. He looked over at Breanna and nudged her with his knee. She looked over at him.

"Thanks Breanna. Really. No one's ever giving me something like this. I don't know to repay you. You're like the best woman I've ever met! There has to be something I can do for you!"

Breanna smiled softly. She had never expected that she would grow so close and come to love and respect a black teenage drug dealer but it had turned out to be one of the best things that had happened to her. She honestly didn't know what she'd do without him.

"Just keep yourself safe young man ok? Watch your back and please, please always treat women the way you'd want them to treat you! They're enough asshole men in this world already. A woman will do anything for her man D. Even swim through lava if that's what it takes. And that's even when their man is a complete pig. Imagine what she'd do for you if you actually gave her the love she needs?"

From the tortured look on Breanna's face, D could sense that this question was more for her husband then him but he still saw where Breanna was going. He put a gentle hand on her shoulder.

"Don't trip Breanna. You ain't got to worry about me. I got this girl I like right now and I think she likes me too. I'll make sure to treat her right and show her I'm serious."

Breanna cracked a small smile.

"That's all we want D. That's all we want."

Five hours later...

The red light was blinking, indicating that the camera was now filming. D stared into the lens, which looked like a huge lidless black eye. He had placed the camera on top of a stack of books so it would be at eye level. He was quiet, hands together as if he were praying fingers gently tapping against each other as he were going to say "excellent" In that classic way that only Mr. Burns from the Simpsons can say it. D spent fine more minutes staring at the camera while it filmed him in silence.

Then he spoke.

"Hello Devontay. I don't think you remember me. We've never officially met anyways. My name is D. I'm the best friend of that boy you killed this summer at that house party. Now I know you were arguing with somebody else at the time and probably didn't mean to shoot my nigga Anthony. But you did. And that shit hurt deep. You've affected a lot of people just cuz you wanted a quick solution to a little problem. You should've just fought the guy and left it at that. Nobody would be dead. Nobody would be grieving and a little boy would get to grow up with his dad. But that isn't possible now is it? All because of you! Well since you started it I'm going to end it. I'm coming for you Devontay. You're not safe and neither are any of your punk ass homies!

"To bad your nigga can't shoot and missed me today. Now I know how deal with y'all. No mercy. You don't know

167

how I can get down. One of these days I'mma creep up on you when you least expect it and then, you better pray to god you die fast! Duce Trey nigga! Your fate is in my hands Devontay, and I'm about to dump this shit down the toilet! That goes for you too Cornrow's! Bitch ass nigga i got something special in store for yo ass!"

Message delivered, D got up and turned the camera off.

Chapter 23

The door to D's bedroom opened slowly. The creaks of the floor boards signaled that someone was walking across his room towards his bed. A shadow fell across his face as the person standing over him stared down at D for a few still moments. It would have made a touching scene for a commercial if hadn't been for what happened not two seconds later.

"Damien! Damien! Wake up right now nigga I ain't playing with you I know you hear me! Get up now because you need to hear some real shit and know just how serious your situation is! "

D's eyes didn't immediately open. He heard his dad's voice booming through his councious but it sounded faint at first. A rough shake of his shoulders brought him crashing back into reality. He opened his eyes to see the hulking form of his father Marcus leaning over him yelling almost directly in his face

"Get up boy ain't no more time for this sleep shit! Get up right now we got some things to talk about"

D struggled to wipe the crust out of his eyes and sit up in bed. His dad wasn't even giving him any space to work with so D tried to give him the hint by pushing his dads body with an outstretched hand.

"C'mon dad back up a lil bit damn I'm barely waking up over here!"

POW!

The side of D's face exploded with pain as his dad backhanded him dead in his temple a split second after the words had left D's mouth. D's entire body lurched to the side from the force of the impact. Eyes stinging from the pain, D looked up at his dad in anger and confusion.

"Oww what the fuck dad?"

"Shut up Damien!"

POW!

The second slap definitely shut D up. He sat silently in bed holding his stinging face and staring up at his dad's anger filled expression.

"That's better. Now stay like that while I'm talking to you!" He demanded.

D glared up at his dad with hate dancing in his eyes but didn't dare open his mouth. After a few seconds of silence, Marcus sat down on the edge of his bed. The enraged expression that had been on his face softened a little as he attempted to reason with his only child.

"Look here son, I know that life hasn't been the easiest for you. Especially this last year what with losing your friend. But I'm worried your letting this street shit get to your head. You know what I think?"

D stayed quiet. His only movement was to lower his hand from his face. He could tell he wasn't going to like whatever it was that was about to be said. His dad continued talking.

"I think that you're on some sort of revenge fantasy charade. Yeah I said it a FANTASY CHARADE!" Marcus yelled as D eyes flashed angrily.

"I'm sorry about your friend but the reason he's dead is because that's what happens when you hang around the wrong crowd. Now look at you! Coming home beat up all the time looking like you tried to fight Mayweather! It looks more like someone's taking revenge on you for even thinking about trying something. I respect that you had the heart to do what you thought was best but wake up fool! You're not cut out for this life. It's clear as day only one can't see it is you!"

Marcus paused in his rant breathing hard like he just ran a mile. D was silent. Thoughts that had been playing around his head had just been giving a voice by his dad but were at the same time being rebuked by another feeling he had inside.

It was true. D was plagued by the idea that he really wasn't as tough as he perceived himself to be. He could fight but beyond fists and the incident with brass knuckles he had never used a weapon against another person. But he knew that wouldn't last for long and he was worried about how he would hold his own when it happened. However the desire to prove himself and the euphoric feeling of finally being accepted were over riding his caution circuits. There was still time to prove both himself and his dad wrong!

Marcus could see the battle going on inside his sons mind and sighed deeply. Heaving himself off the bed he made his way towards the hallway. Stopping as he reached the bedroom door, Marcus turned around and stared at his son quietly for a few seconds.

"All I know is, you ain't about to keep living here and not be in school or working. Keep up with this nonsense you gone find yourself without a place to call home."

"What you gone kick me out?" D asked indignantly. His dad stared right back at him with no emotion in his face.

"Try me." was his only response. Then he walked out the room closing the door roughly behind him and leaving D with one question burning into his brain; how far was he willing to take this?

Later that evening...

"Haaappy birthday to yaa! Haaappy birthday to yaa! Haaappy biiirrrthdaaayyy! Haaappy birthday to ya! Happy birthday Tasha!!!"

As Courtney and five of her girlfriends finished singing a loud soulful vodka fueled birthday song the large crowd around the table clapped and cheered! Tasha, a long legged brown skinned and very attractive girl who ran on the Central High track team waved shyly at the girls as she took a giant sip from a red plastic cup.

"Thanks, you bitches are the best I fucking love y'all! She yelled across the table.

"We love you too boo!" Courtney called back. Out of nowhere, Chris appeared right next to Tasha holding shot glasses and a bottle of whiskey.

"All right, all right enough of this kid shit it's time to turn this party into a FUNCTION!!!"

Lining up the shot glasses on the table, Chris filled each one to the brim. Then he looked up at the person directly across from him holding on to a small camcorder and purposely filming the action going on around him. He lifted a finger and pointed right at the camera lens.

"Hey Spike Lee, why don't you put that damn camera down for two seconds so you can come and celebrate with us? Ain't nobody paying you to do that shit so you definitely can afford to take a quick break!"

Taking his eye away from the viewfinder, D looked up at Chris with slightly annoyed expression on his face.

"Damn Chris that whole scene was looking good until you looked at the camera! I was trying to capture the moment!" Chris laughed loudly.

"Nigga bring your Hustle and Film ass over here and take a damn shot! It's like you not even part of the festivities! You can go back to filming shit after we celebrate this beautiful young woman's 18th year on this earth."

Tasha smiled coyly over at Chris and he winked back at her. D knew what was going on. Chris had his eyes on a prize! He hated when his friend was pursuing a lady. The complete 180 degree flip in his attitude was always amazing to watch. No more was he a rage filled psychopath seconds away from committing brutal acts of violence for no reason. Now he was all smiles and laughs and jokes. But it would only last as long as it took to get what he wanted. Then it was back to business as usual. But D had to admit it. He liked this Chris better than the regular Chris.

Spotting a chance to have some real fun for once, D switched off the camera and headed to the far side of the table where Chris, Tasha, Courtney and her friends were standing. As he squeezed in beside Courtney and one of her friends, Courtney looked over at him and smiled seductively. D returned the smile feeling his insides melt a little. He turned to look at Chris.

"My nigga," said Chris approvingly. He passed out the shot glasses to the group.

"To Tasha, beauty and brains in the same package!"

Tasha blushed and everybody held their glass up then emptied them into their mouths in swift fluid motions. Some of the girls coughed and made screw faces because of the strong taste of the whiskey. D and Chris exchanged quick smirks then Chris was at Tasha's side talking quietly into her ear while she laughed and moved closer to him. Not wanting to be around Chris and Tasha, D turned and strolled towards the coolers where the drinks were kept.

He was in the bottom of a house in the Central Districts Madrona neighborhood. The house belonged to an older female friend of Money mikes and she had allowed them to celebrate their friend Tasha's birthday in her basement. It was a long low ceiling room that had no separate rooms so it was basically a large rectangle. Half had been made into a dance floor complete with small DJ booth and the other half was a "bar". The "bar" section was really just several tables about two feet apart from each other and coolers filled with beer and liquor against the wall. They had There were upwards of fifty people at the party right now. All the boys were Duce Trey and the girls all either lived in the neighborhood or were friends from school. Hip hop music was blasting out of several speakers hanging on the wall and already the floor was full of gyrating bodies.

Opening up the cooler, D leaned over and picked out a can of Rainier from the ice. All of a sudden he felt two hands grab his ass cheeks from behind and a soft voice whispered into his ear;

"Wanna grab me one too?"

D relaxed as he recognized the soft melodious voice. Snatching another beer from the cooler, he turned around and held it out.

"Sup Courtney? Wassup with the prison grab while I'm all bent over and shit? I almost swung on you! Damn you looking good girl."

Courtney smiled back and put her hands on her hips as she poised in front of D. She was looking good with her hair done up in fancy braids and dressed in a red and white striped button up tied off above her stomach with tight blue jeans and red and white Air Jordan's on her feet and big hoop earrings dangling from her ears. They both opened their beers at the same time.

"Thanks D. You don't look to bad yourself."
D looked down at himself. White Nikes, black jeans, a long white tee and black hoody with a black beanie on his head. Honestly, he looked like almost every other young man in the house but a compliment was a compliment. Courtney nodded at the camera in D's hand.

"You been walking around filming the whole party the entire time you been here. Are they paying you or something?"
D shook his head.

"Not even but that would have been cool though. Naw, somebody traded me this for some weed. It's pretty dope honestly. Now I just walk around recording. I got some crazy shit on here you wanna see? I got fights, niggaz rapping, niggaz slanging. I hope the police don't get a hold of this otherwise we're all going to jail."

"So why record it then?" asked Courtney. D looked at her as if the answer was obvious.

"Memories girl. Who knows what could happen out here? At least now whether it be jail or death people can always live through this film."

"That sounds kind of dark. Why you planning on people dying?" asked Courtney sipping from her beer.

"I'm not planning on people dying I'm just saying, they do die. So why not catch every moment while they're alive?"
Courtney nodded.

"I guess nigga, but um about you trading some weed for that camera."
D cocked an eyebrow.

"What? It was a good deal. I do t never turn down good deals."

174

Courtney smiled that sexy mischievous smile that she had flashed him that day she had taken him behind the school. She moved closer and whispered into D's ear.

"You want another good deal?"

D looked at her and immediately knew what she meant. Before he could answer her, Chris appeared out of nowhere and grabbed D by the arm hauling him towards the middle of the dance floor. Courtney, looking interested, followed close behind. The space had cleared and four microphones had been set up. Chaz and another one his friends were already standing behind two of them and Chris steered D towards the other two.

"What the fuck Chris?" asked D, "do you know what the fuck was about to happen? She was feeling me!"

"Yeah Right," responded Chris, "c'mon nigga the sidewalk gang is bought to perform for Tasha for her birthday."

"You ain't tell me!"

"Nigga it's been in the plans my bad but don't trip. We gonna do 'get high with me' ok? We got Chaz replacing whop so we're gonna be aight on the middle verse and DroCain is in here to sing the hook! It's all for the broads remember that! Courtney gonna love you for this!"

D looked over at Courtney with skepticism written all over his face. Courtney however looked excited.

"Yeah I love to see the homies do their thing." She agreed. "And your good D go on! I know Tasha is about to scream her head off! And you guys get to perform with DroCain? He's filthy and his new mix tape just came out!"

D looked around at the crowd of people surrounding him. Then down at his camera.

"Who gonna film the show though?" He asked not wanting to miss recording his own performance. Courtney held up her hand.

"I will. I can be camerawoman for a little bit. Just show me how to work it."

D quickly explained how to operate the camera to Courtney then turned and followed Chris into the cleared area around the microphones.

175

As he placed himself in front of the remaining microphone stand, D glanced over to where the DroCain was standing surrounded by his entourage and a crowd of admirers. D felt a brief spasm of jealously run through his body as he gazed on. DroCain was a singer in his mid-twenties who was born and raised in the Central District and making a name for himself in the local music scene. Tall muscular and dark skinned, he had long dreads and work a large sparkling chain with a cross hanging down his chest. Friends with Money Mike, he had agreed to make a special appearance at the party for a small fee.

Suddenly the lights flickered and Chris grabbed his microphone and began to take control of the crowd.

"Waddup waddup y'all!" Chris's voice boomed out over the speaker system. People around the basement looked over and began gathering in front of the four performers.

"That's more like it muthafuckas! Now first off you already know who we are! It's the sidewalk Gang niggaz Duce Trey represent with Chaz Money standing in for Whop. Hope you get out soon nigga!"

A loud cheer rang out from the crowd! Chris grinned and continued the introduction.

"All right all right that's wassup! You already know who our guest performer is! He hardly need me to say anything, the CD's very own DroCain!"

Again cheers and applause erupted from the crowd at a tremendous level. DroCain nodded at the crowd lifting his plastic cup up in salute.

"Aight so we not gonna waste any more time let's get right into it. This a track called Get high with me! We jacked that pretty Ricky beat "grind with me" and did something way better with it. So DJ play that fucking track bitch!!"

As the first sounds of the beat came on D took a moment to calm his nerves. He was first up and was determined to come correct. Opening his eyes, he searched the crowd until he found Courtney. She had the camera pointed directly at him and when she saw him looking smiled and waved! Confidence found D took a breath and waited for it to begin.

176

Right on cue, DroCain entered with the hook:

(DroCain)
Oooooooo yeahhhhhhhhh
Come get high with me
Relax your mind break up this pine with me
Twist up this swisher filled with nice fine leaves
Forget your problems here's the light to your relief
Its slow burning
Baby try this weed
Let down your walls put me inside your dreams
Say she want pleasure here's the right remedy
I let this candle spark the blunt for you and me
It's slow burning babe

(Damien)
When she met me she was used to beef
Fuck boys kept her losing sleep
Up all night like 'where the fuck he be"
Just the same old lames till she fuck with D
Walk with me slow talk to see where our minds just chill
and relax
Want a white man cuz she through with blacks
Too much pain in the past it's a proven fact
But wait, I ain't cool with that
I don't blame you for my past few encounters
Same old hood brand new bar counter
Sippin all alone that's the way I found her
So much on her mind cuz life done took her heart to trial
Wanna call love no number to dial
Hmm I gotta idea of what could make you smile
Just

(DroCain)
Come get high with me
 Relax your mind break up this pine with me

177

Twist up this swisher filled with nice fine leaves
Forget your problems here's the light to your relief
Its slow burning
Baby try this weed
Let down your walls put me inside your dreams
Say she want pleasure here's the right remedy
I let this candle spark the blunt for you and me
It's slow burning babe

(Chris)
Man the shit gets deeper all the thanks to the creeper
purple passion
I'm a firm believer in the reefer long as this shit long
lasting
Fuck with the saints but that Reggie bush ain't enough
for me I need Purp or Kush
Frosty leaves off a big old bush blow smoke in the mirror
just to see how it looks
She feeling good loosened up responds to the questions I
ask
Been too long since she had a good laugh
Now she wanna tell the wrongs that she did in her past
damn
She know she bad for some things she did
Never said she was an angel she just tired of sin
Now she wants a new life to live
First thing I gotta teach you how to roll up a swish

(DroCain)
Step one
Break the swisher down the middle with them thumbs
Step two
Take the buds and crush them nuggets into crumbs
Step 3
You got the wrap dump it out then fill it uuuup
Step 4
Lick it shut light it up take a puff and

178

Come get high with me
Relax your mind break up this pine with me
Twist up this swisher filled with nice fine leaves
Forget your problems here's the light to your relief
Its slow burning
Baby try this weed
Let down your walls put me inside your dreams
Say she want pleasure here's the right remedy
I let this candle spark the blunt for you and me
It's slow burning babe

(Chaz)
It's been 2 hours 3 pills and 4 blunts since we linked up
No place to go we just walk and smoke take an easy
stroll through these city clubs
Yeah we danced a bit I broke her off
Then she broke me off had me gripping the walls
Took it low to the floor she was killing em all
I see them other girls hating but I don't feel them at all
Now the mood changed the pied piper singing
She hear his words and slow wind for me
Not Bruce Wayne no car or cape but she still wanna
spend more time with me
Said it's just my looks my clothes my slang and she love
to smell the smoke in the air
Make her feel like she's actually there I got what you
need girl I'm always prepared!

One hour later…
"My niggas, can you believe that shit back there? It's like
they thought we were fucking superstars! Well, DroCain is a
superstar but damn I ain't never been a part of some shit like that
ever in life! Females crying and niggas all wanting to shake your
hand and be cool and shit. Damn life as a rapper wouldn't be too
bad. Foreal though man I'm over here shaking and shit! Damn!"

In the backseat of a late eighties model Cadillac
Fleetwood, Chaz was talking nonstop about the crowd's reaction
to the song he had just preformed with Chris D and DroCain. D

was sitting next to Chaz and Chris was in the front passenger seat. A light skinned older teen named Dryvah was behind the steering wheel. It was dark out now and the street lights bathed the sidewalks in pools of orange and yellow.

Chris turned around to look at Chaz.

"It be like that homie! As soon as people see that you got a little bit of importance about you they can't wait to be your best friend. Just watch how many females are gonna be on your dick now that they've seen you with a microphone in your hand."

Chaz looked excited at the idea of countless teenage girls all scrambling to be the first to touch his hand after a concert. D was looking out of the window not really paying attention to the conversation between Chris and Chaz. The only thing his mind was focused on was the way Courtney had been looking at him when the song had ended.

When D had come over to retrieve the camera from her, she had grabbed him around the neck and pulled him close kissing him sexually in the lips. Other girls around them had looked at Courtney with anger and jealousy in their eyes but she clearly hadn't cared.

In honor of the song they had just preformed, Chris had come over and suggested they make a store run for more Swishers and beer. D hadn't wanted to go but at Chris urging finally agreed and left with Chris Chaz and Dryvah. Leaving the house which was on 21st and Valley Street, the teens had piled in the car and took off headed for the AmPm on 23rd and Cherry Street. As they passed the gas station on 23rd and Union, D happened to glance out of the window towards the entrance doors. Several young black teens had just exited the store and were heading up Union Street in the direction of 22nd avenue. Quickly, D leaned forward and tapped Chris on the shoulder.

"Waddup nigga?" said Chris.

D pointed at the group walking up 22nd. Chris instantly sat up straight and stared hard at the group as the car rolled thru the intersection. Looking out from the back seat, D thought he recognized a familiar figure but before he could say anything, Chris was already talking.

"Oh shit niggaz you know who them fools is right?" Chaz immediately bounced upright and began peering out of the back window while Dryvah looked over at Chris.

"What niggaz? I don't see anybody?" said Dryvah.

"Nigga you didn't see nobody because your too busy driving! D pointed them out leaving the gas station back there." said Chris

"So what you tryna do?" asked Chaz. Chris thought about it briefly.

"Bust a U-turn Dryvah! It's on sight with these niggaz right now and they've just been sighted! Go back to union and take a left. They was walking towards 22nd so of they ain't already at the place they heading to then they should still be walking. We can creep up right behind them."

Dryvah nodded to show he understood. After looking both ways for any police cars, Dryvah quickly turned the car around in the middle of the street and headed back towards Union. Reaching underneath his seat, Chris took out two pistols and began checking their ammunition level. Satisfied they were all fully loaded, Chris turned in his seat and held one out to D.

"Here D, take this shit."

D hesitated for a brief second before taking the pistol from Chris outstretched hand. The weight and feel of the metal gun in his palm was unnerving and reassuring at the same time. The power to take someone's life was now in his hands.

"That's a 1911 colt my nigga," said Chris from the front seat. "You only got seven shots so make em count."

D was quiet.

"Oh shit, there they go up the block!" Said Dryvah. Sure enough visible in the fading light of the day was a small group of teens still walking up union about three blocks in front of them. Chris cocked his gun back baring his teeth like a wolf with an almost maniacal glint in his eyes.

"All right here we go niggaz." He whispered softly.

From the back seat, D decided it was time to speak up.

"Yo Chris man, maybe we should chill out and just go back to the party. I'm not a shooter like that anyways I'm a hustler. I ain't scared to fight a niggaz but this is something

181

different. We was supposed to just be going to the store anyways."

Chris mood switched instantly. Instantly, he turned around glaring at D with an intense savagery that would have been better suited for an angry lion.

"Nigga what the fuck you mean this something different? There ain't nothing you don't do for the cause D you better hear this shit I'm telling you. If you a shooter your also a hustler and the shit goes the other way too! You're whatever niggaz say you are homie and tonight you're a fucking shooter!"

"Shit if D don't wanna do it let me get at these niggaz!" offered Chaz. Chris shook his head.

"We about to pass them," said Dryvah quickly.

"Pull over," directed Chris. As Dryvah pulled the car to the side, Chris turned and put the barrel of his gun directly on D's kneecap.

"Chris with the fuck?"

"Nigga this is what the fuck! You ain't running around no more just being cool not getting your hands dirty. Time to put in some real fucking work and earn your keep! When we drive by these fools you better empty that clip or I'm popping you in the kneecap for disobedience bitch!"

The car was deathly silent. Chaz and Dryvah were looking on but saying nothing and D could tell from the look in Chris eyes that he was serious about his threat. D looked over at Chaz for help but Chaz shrugged and looked out of his window. Chris took the gun off of D's knee but continued to look him I the eyes.

"Pull up on them niggaz Dryvah." He directed.

As the car pulled away from the curve, D thought briefly about hopping out and running. But the thought of Chris sending a bullet into his back kept him sitting where he was. Adrenaline was flowing through his body as the car drew nearer to the group. Beads of sweat began making their way down his face and his foot began tapping uncontrollably. He rolled his window down as the car crept closer to the unsuspecting teens.

His mind began playing tricks on him. He thought he heard sirens coming towards them. Images of jail cells, blue uniforms, bad food and violent stabbings began playing themselves in front of eyes but before he knew it they were right behind the boys and Chris was pressing the barrel of his gun into D's knee so hard it was hurting. Could he shoot Chris? As quick as the thought came it vanished.

And then time was out.

"Aaaahhhhhhh"

BANG BANG BANG BANG BANG CLICK CLICK!!!

The sound of the gun going off was incredible inside the car. It was as if the world was ending around them. Screams and shouts erupted from the group on the side walk. D saw bodies throwing themselves to the ground and diving behind cars but didn't know if he'd actually hit anyone. The increasing darkness made it hard to tell. Just as they pulled off, D thought he recognized a familiar face but then they were gone, speeding up Union Street in attempt to make good their escape.

The party didn't feel the same now. Standing in a corner holding on to an unopened corona bottle, D felt alienated from the rest of the happy intoxicated people around him.

He'd just shot somebody if not more than one person while leaning halfway out the window of a car. In other words he's just commuted a drive by. Five shots. The gun had jammed on the last two and D had felt a deep surge of disappointment wash over him as he continued to pull the trigger. For about two second he had felt such a strong sense of complete power and invincibility it had boiled out in an animal like yell that had exploded out of his throat as he was shooting. The heavy recoil had felt good in his untrained hands and the smell of gunpowder still lingered about his clothes. He felt different but it was more bad then good. A question had been burning itself into his mind ever since they had got back to the party; would Chris really have shot him in the leg?

Too distracted to mingle and not in the mood to dance, D decided to get some air in the back yard. Walking upstairs, he passed a few older teens drinking in the kitchen and walked outside to the small backyard. Breathing in the crisp night air, D sat still and looked up at the dark sky. For the thousandth time he found himself wishing that Anthony would suddenly appear out of nowhere say it was all a joke and he hadn't been dead just somewhere taking a long break from it all.

But he wouldn't. D had learned that. Somehow, even with all the people that he had around him admiring him wanting to get to know him and hang out with him, D had never felt lonelier. These people only cared about him because he had joined their gang. Anthony had been cool with him regardless.

A noise from around the corner of the house made D jump slightly. It sounded like an animal or was eating something messy with loud slurps happening every few seconds followed by what sounded like moans or grunts. D couldn't help it. His curious side had taken hold. Walking slowly so as not to startle whatever was in the bushes, D crept up to side of the house and peered around the corner. He froze. Time stopped and for second D was literally stuck to the ground as he gazed on the scene in front of him.

Courtney was down on her knees in the garden and standing over her was an older twenty something man that D recognized as one of money mikes associates named trigger. His pants were down around his ankles and his head was leaning against the house eyes shut and loud moans coming out of his mouth. Courtney had both her hands up one holding his dick the other cupping his balls as she worked her mouth up and down his member.

D's world dropped out from under his feet. Years' worth of feelings that he had stored up inside began swirling and bubbling inside his stomach to the point that he started to feel sick. He staggered away from the wall and the noise made both trigger and Courtney look over in surprise.

"Nigga get the fuck outta here lil homie can't you see I'm busy!" Trigger screamed out. But D was looking at Courtney who was gazing back at d with a mixture of guilt shock on her face even as she slid triggers dick out of her mouth. That sight broke the spell and before a word could be spoken, D had turned around and walked away as fast as his feet could carry him.

Walking past a couple younger kids hanging on the front porch, D began walking up the sidewalk away from the party.

All at once he couldn't hold it in anymore. Leaning against a nearby jeep Cherokee, D proceeded to throw up in the street. It took three times to clear everything out of his stomach and when he was done he remained crouched over a few seconds longer just to center himself.

"Hey nigga what the fuck you doing over here?" came a familiar voice. D looked over his shoulder to see Chris walking up with a plastic cup in his hand smiling like he'd just found out the secret to life.

"The fuck it look like I'm doing?"

"Shit nigga fucking up that man's tires is what it looks like. You good?"

D straightened up.

"Yeah fuck this shit though I'm about to slide man. I'm done with this party."

"Why fool? This shit is still active downstairs I don't know what the hell you doing out here. Besides throwing up all over people cars. Come back inside nigga we bout to twist up some blunts and just chill for a minute."

"Naw Chris I'm good I'm bout to dip."

Chris eyes narrowed and he a look of irritation flashed across his face.

"Nigga what the fuck is your deal bro? Why you wanna leave all of a sudden? What, you gonna be all antisocial after what went down or some shit? That's your job nigga! And it's my job to make sure you do your job! Now quit trippin and come back inside!"

D looked at Chris for a long moment. Then told him about what he had just seen. The corner of Chris mouth moved and a second later he broke out laughing. Now it was D's turn to look annoyed.

"Nigga I'm sorry but I told you," said Chris when he had calmed down.

"It's not funny," replied D.

"It kind of is. She's a jump off homie and I don't know why you wasn't trying to hear that shit. Just cuz you different don't mean she is nigga now quit acting like a bitch over a bitch and come back..."

185

WHAP!

D's hard punch interrupted Chris in mid-sentence and knocked the youth flat on his back. His cup went flying sending the clear liquid inside everywhere. Chris looked up at D with anger in his eyes as his hand flew up to his mouth. He spit blood out on the ground but before he could get up, D was standing over him fists clenched and a look of pure fury on his face.

"Nigga I ain't a bitch and you better quit talking to me like I am one! Fuck you and that ratchet ass female! Don't think I didn't see you up in there tryna front for that one broad! You ain't special nigga! And if you ever point a gun at me again you better pull that fucking trigger cuz I will sure as fuck pull mine! I ain't scared of you Chris."

Without waiting for a reply, D turned and walked away into the night. From his position on the ground, Chris stated after D for a long moment. Wiping the blood off of his lips he spit on the ground then got slowly to his feet. Surprisingly there wasn't a trace of anger about him now. Brushing himself off, he took out his phone and dialed up Money Mike.

"Hello?" he heard his cousin say.

"Waddup money it's Chris."

"I know who it is nigga. Waddup you still at the party?"

"Yeah. Hey I got something for you though. It's about D."

Money mike paused.

"Wassup?"

Chris grinned before answering.

"It's D. He's ready."

There was a few seconds pause before Money Mike responded.

"Aight cool. Make sure you and him are ready to move by next week. I'll call when I got everything set up. Till then keep ya heads down and out of trouble. aight?"

"Aight gotcha!"

The line went dead.

Chapter 24

Eight thousand dollars. Well seven thousand eight hundred and fifty six dollars to be exact. It lay piled across the top of D's bed in all matter of denominations from one to one hundred dollar bills. D sat in a chair in front of his bed. Elbows resting on his knees with his hands together in front of his face as if he were praying. His pointer fingers were pressed against his lips and his nose and chin rested on his outstretched thumbs as he stared down at the earnings he had acquired since the start of the year.

Stolen cars. Drug transactions. Property theft. A couple strong arm robberies. D had long ago stopped referring to the things he did for money by their crime name. He simply called it 'hustling'.

"Cash rules everything around me," D muttered to himself. That's how the world worked wasn't it? After all no one really cared about how you got the money you have, just that you have it. It helped ease his mind from thinking too much about the people that suffered behind all his illicit doings. It had been rare that he had to physically hurt somebody.

But the things that were happening in this war between Deuce Trey and FEB were bringing out a savagery he hadn't know existed within him. And he was finding it hard to get the images of bloody faces and mangled bodies out of his head.

The sudden sound of footsteps in the hallway caused D to causally look over his shoulder towards his bedroom door. Even with the sound of footsteps walking up and down the hall passing back and forth in front of his room, D made no moves to hide the money covering his bed. It was the everyday sound of his dad Marcus getting ready for work.

D knew he wouldn't come in his room let alone knock on the door to say goodbye. He and his dad hadn't spoken in weeks. Finally the sound of the front door closing signaled his father's exit from the apartment. D stared at the door a couple seconds more then turned back to the money pile. Picking up his backpack, he opened it up and began shoving all the money rolls inside. Getting dressed was easy. Grey baggy sweats a large black long sleeved shirt with a black beanie sitting crooked on his head. Throwing on a large bubbly black coat, he shouldered his backpack stepped into some black Adidas and headed out stopping to leave an envelope and a folded letter on the dining room table. Then he was gone.

Later that day...

"Wait a fucking second! You gotta go where and do what for who?"

Latoya was standing in her living room arms folded with a vicious glare in her eyes. D stood opposite her leaning with his back against the door face completely expressionless even though he was currently being cussed out by a close friend.

"I told you, I'm going up north for a little bit. Money Mike wants me and Chris to do something up there for him. I'm not sure what it is he ain't really saying too much right now but he said were going to be taking on a big responsibility."

Latoya laughed scornfully.

"Oh a big responsibility huh? Like what? Standing on some corner in the north end instead of downtown? Or maybe you gotta go collect money from someone that Money Mike should be going to see his damn self? When are you gonna stop being that niggaz errand boy?"

"Man look it ain't even like that," said D, "Money Mike says we gonna be taking a serious step up. And since I'm not in school no more I gotta start thinking how in going to provide for myself. My dad don't even talk to me no more. It's complete silence at my house except for the TV. I might as well get out. And if working for Money Mike will get me the money to do that then fuck it. It's just how it's going to be."

Latoya looked at him. The anger from her eyes faded to be replaced by a look of pity.

"He got Anthony the same way he's getting to you D," she said quietly. "I know your family is fucked up just like most people out here but why you guys go running to people like Money Mike, I'll never know. He's poison D."

D shook his head.

"Naw Latoya he ain't poison. He's the only person I know that bothered to really look out for me all these years. Him and Anthony and Chris, they're the reason I even have a life. I didn't know anybody before I met them. No friends, no girls. Shit, I couldn't even get an ugly girl to go to a dance with me. These niggas made me into somebody. And Money Mike ain't never stopped looking out for me. I owe him. So whatever I can do to help him out I'm gonna do it.

"Your right my family sucks. But what sucks worse is having no family at all. So I'll take what I can get. Deuce Trey is a fucked up family but it's better than the one I got at home."

Shrugging off his backpack, D tossed it on to the couch.

"Look Latoya don't worry about me. Whatever this shit we bout to go do is it probably won't even take that long. I'll call you when were done. In the meantime that's for you and Anthony Jr."

Latoya looked over at the back pack then slowly looked back at D.

"What's in there D?" she asked slowly.

D looked at Latoya staring directly into her eyes so she knew he wasn't playing a joke.

"There's about eight thousand dollars in there. Like I said it's for you and Anthony Jr. All I ask is that you keep one grand of that stashed for me in case some crazy shit happens and I got to get out of town. Money Mike cool enough but I think Chris is actually crazy. Ain't no telling what might happen with him around so I just wanna be ready."

Looking at D suspiciously, Latoya walked over and picked up the backpack. She unzipped it and looked inside. Her entire body went still as her eyes took in the numerous rolls of money.

"D...I can't take this."

"Yes you can," said D forcefully, "you can and you will Latoya I told Anthony I'd look out for you of anything happened and I'm not breaking that promise. I won't let you make me. You're the only one that money is safe with anyways. I can't keep it at my house and I don't know if it will be safe where I'm going."

Latoya stared at D for a long moment. Then coming over to him she wrapped her arms around his waist and have him the tightest hug he's ever had. He could feel her body shaking with emotion as fresh tears from her eyes soaked his shirt. At first, D didn't know what else to do but pat her shoulder awkwardly but eventually his arms extended and he returned Latoya's hug with equal force. They stayed like that for a while embracing each other as if to let go would mean the end of the very existence of life.

Finally, D untangled himself from their hug. Kissing Latoya on the forehead, D let himself out the front door and closed it behind him.

Chapter 25

"D, stop looking all depressed in the back seat man. I told you I ain't mad about that shit the other night. You could learn to punch a little harder though," said Chris.

In the backseat of an old-school bubble Chevrolet Caprice, D chose to ignore the remark and glanced out the window instead. He had been woken up earlier this morning by a phone call from Money Mike telling him to get dressed and be ready in twenty minutes. He had hesitated for a second when he saw Chris In the passenger seat but Chris had smiled at him told him don't trip and to get in the car.

Currently they were driving north on I-5 having just entered the freeway near downtown. Staring out the window, D's eyes took in the glittering blue water that was south lake unions surface as they passed it by on the right hand side. For a few seconds, D imagined what it would be like to sink into the dark blue depths and never come back up. Not that he was suicidal. But at the moment, he just didn't feel like dealing with anything or anyone.

Money Mike looked in the rear view mirror at D's gloomy expression and frowned.

"Waddup young soldier?" he asked. "Chris told me about what happened at the party last week. Sounds like you put in some good work. I'm proud of you. And don't let whatever lil scuffle y'all got into fuck with your mind state. Chris ain't trippin so I hope you ain't either. A busted lip ain't nothing to get mad about."

D locked stares with Money Mike's eyes in the rear view mirror.

"Oh is that all he told you? Shit I guess he didn't mention the fact that he tried to make his pistol be my kneecaps new best friend!"

Money Mike glanced across at Chris who shrugged and chose to look out his window at the passing traffic. Money Mike looked back at D.

"Yeah he told me about that lil situation. But he also told me you were disobeying a direct order. I already told there's rules to this shit D it's not all fun and games. You were told that you're gonna be expected to do certain things. Chris is your big homie you gotta listen to him."

D shifted around in his seat looking slightly uncomfortable.

"Yeah but Money, we was supposed to just be going to the store to get some fucking swishers. I wasn't thinking about blasting nobody. I was fresh off the microphone thinking about a chick I was trying to get with."

Money Mike looked hard at D through the mirror for a few silent seconds before returning his gaze to the road.

"There ain't no such thing as the right time D," he explained. "Were at war with these niggaz and to give someone a pass one day is giving him an opportunity to kill you the next. You see someone from FEB no matter who it is you better get on his ass with whatever you got at that current time. We ain't doing this 'run home and grab the homies' or 'it's to many police out" shit! Fuck em! You got me?"

"Yeah I hear you," said D.

Silence returned to the car for a moment. Chris looked over at his older cousin and grinned evilly tossing up the Deuce Trey hand sign in the air with his right hand. In the back seat, D went back to staring out of the window lost in thought.

Truthfully it wasn't the shooting that was messing with his mind this morning. All week long he had been beating himself over the head about Courtney and wishing he had just listened to Chris in the first place.

The image of her going down on that guy on the side of the house kept repaying itself in his head.

She'd done the same thing with him a number of times at school but he had been dumb enough to think he was the only one she was doing it with. If he would have been on point with his senses he would have seen she was foul when she started offering him blow jobs for weed. Clearly this type of behavior was a practiced art for her.

In the front passenger seat, Chris finished rolling a blunt and looked over at his older cousin.

"So Money, you gonna tell us where we going finally? You been talking shit for weeks now about how were about to move up in the world but you ain't said what we about to be doing. How bout a hint nigga damn!"

In the backseat, D turned from looking out of the window. He too had been curious about this secret mission that Money Mike had been talking about. Money mike looked over at Chris then back at D.

"You light that blunt lil nigga and I'll tell you."

As Chris took a lighter out of his pocket and lit the blunt, money mike cracked the car windows.

"Aight look this is what's going down. I got about four different houses all across the city. The South End, the Westside, of course here in the Central District, a couple apartments in Capitol Hill but nothing in the north end. Now, I use this bitch I fuck from time to time to get these places. She puts her name down so my face stays out the situation and I set up shop. Well, I've been trying to get a spot up north for a minute now and three months ago she got approved to rent a two story house out in the lake city neighborhood."

Money Mike paused to hit the blunt Chris passed him. In the backseat, D's mind was connecting the dots and he believed he already knew what was happening. But he decided to stay quiet and let Money Mike finish his explanation.

Money Mike passed the blunt back to D and continued talking.

"Anyways let me explain why I got the house in the first place. The streets used to be where all the hustling was done but we live in different times. There's too many police and surveillance systems are everywhere. Posting up on the block

193

don't work and the only reason y'all have been getting away with shit downtown is because you guys got a nice little system.

"The trap house is the future but you can't have just one because if it gets busted then you're fucked. You need several spread out across the city so you can avoid detection and make it harder for people to pinpoint your activity. If a bunch of niggaz all post up in one spot hustling all it takes is one bust and everything's gone. This is the solution. Multiple places where transactions can take place away from watching eyes! But I can't be everywhere at once. I need stand up guys, niggaz I can trust to run these places. That's where you two come in."

"Are you bout to say what I think you're gonna say?" asked Chris sounding excited.

"What do you think I'm bout to say?"

"That you're putting us in charge of running your operations!"

Money Mike laughed ruthlessly.

"What! Fuck no you ain't bout to run my shit! At least not all of it and not until I've moved on to bigger and better things. Naw but I am putting you guys in charge of this new spot. That means you get a cut of all the money made there and believe me, it's gonna be a lot more then stealing cars and selling crack sacks on the corner would get you!"

Blowing a thick cloud of smoke out of the side of his mouth, D couldn't help but be intrigued by the idea of being in charge if one of money mikes house operations. Only thing was, he had no idea what went on inside the houses to even make the money come.

"So what we gonna be doing up this spot anyways?" D asked.

Money Mike looked at D in the rear view mirror again with a mischievous almost sadistic look in his face.

"You'll see."

Twenty minutes later…

They came to a stop in front of a brown two story house on 132nd Avenue North a couple blocks off of Lake City Way. The paint was chipping and the grass needed cutting but it didn't look like a complete dump. The windows were covered with dark blinds but all in all it was like every other house on the block.

Killing the engine, Money Mike turned to look at both of his young prodigies with a serious expression.

"Aight you two listen up! When we walk inside these doors that's it. Ain't no backing out of this shit. But trust me, you follow the rules and do as you're told and we'll all be paid men." He looked at the house the back to D and Chris.

"Aight now I got a lot of different hustles. You have to if you wanna make any real money. Drugs hoes guns whatever you can think of I guarantee you I got finger in it somewhere.

"This house specifically I got set up for tricks and drugs. I got two girls already and if everything goes the way I think it will then I'mma see about getting some more up in here. Now they don't walk the streets. I got other girls for that in other places. These are call girls. Literally. Their tricks call em come through to handle business then leave. All you gotta do is be here to make sure the boys don't get rough. Aside from that , I sell drugs out of the back of the house.

"Now the good thing about his area is that they ain't as ghetto as they are in the CD. Grimy yes but nothing you two ain't used to. There's other gangs up here though so don't go walking around here tripping. Just because they ain't known for shooting up here don't mean it never happens ya dig? The last thing we need is war with another set. So, y'all ready to go inside?"

D and Chris glanced at each other. Chris looked excited. D was confused. This was the last thing be had expected to hear but the even more unnerving thing was that he too felt excitement coursing through his veins. He had already given hope of ever getting out of his current lifestyle and had decided that if he was supposed to be a gangster then he would be the best one he could. But a pimp? He was already horrible with girls as it was. But what other choice did he have?

D nodded back at money mike.

"Let's do this shit."

Despite its shabby exterior the inside of the house was decently clean. Walking through the front door that Money Mike unlocked, Chris and D found themselves in a spacious living room furnished by two big comfortable looking couches with a big screen TV up against the wall. A fancy glass table had been placed between the TV and the couch with nothing on it. A staircase to the immediate left led upstairs but Money Mike directed them down a hallway with several doors lining the walls and into a small kitchen and dining room.

D's head was swirling with thoughts and ideas now that he was actually in the house he was going to be working in. The place looked better then he could've imagined. It wasn't a damn penthouse but it wasn't a shack either. Just as he was beginning to wonder where the girls were at Money Mike's voice accompanied with a smack to the head jolted him out of his daydream.

"D! Eh nigga you even paying attention?"

"Yeah my fault Money damn! It's just a lot to take in right now my head was thinking of all the possibilities!"

Money Mike shook his head but looked pleased still the same.

"Well good for your ambition but right now listen the fuck up this ain't game time this is your ducking orientation to some serious next level shit!" His face went deadly serious and D felt the sense of danger creep back into the room. That feeling never went far whenever he was around Money Mike or Chris.

"Ok last run through. D, you ready?" D nodded.

"Aight cool. Now you see the downstairs layout. The tricks are gonna knock on the front door and whoever they seeing is gonna come down and escort them to one of the two rooms down here. All you have to do there is make sure they see you when they come in the house and look mean. That way they know not to try anything. And if they do then fuck em up take their shit and toss em out. You know, like bouncers.

"Don't cripple em though. I don't wanna make the block hot. Just let em know that they're lucky we don't press charges or some bullshit like that. Keep their ID just in case. As far as that

196

shit goes that's it. Now I figure Chris can be in charge of that since he's already a violent type."

Chris grinned evilly. D felt resentment building inside him but said nothing. Money Mike nodded at Chris but then turned to D.

"Aight now this is what I need you doing D. This door on the back wall leads to backyard. Now aside from these girls, I got some work up on here. This the North so fuck the crack shit. I got powder and pills all day. Specifically oxycotin's and morphine. That should do it. If niggaz out here keep asking bout ex then I'll get that too. But I'm gonna try and just send people that want yay or pills specifically."

D was interested when he heard pills. He managed to get his hands on some ecstasy pills over the years but oxycotins and morphine were something he hadn't previously messed around with. Money Mike pointed to two separate drawers in the kitchen.

"The bottom drawer is pills. The one above that is the yay. Put the money from each deal in the corresponding drawer. Don't let them niggaz see you take the shit out. Serve em right there behind the door then let em out. Easier then breathing. The yay is separated into $50 bags and the pills are $20 each. Don't get inventive. Stick to those prices.

Money Mike looked at D and Chris with long hard stares.

"Always stay strapped. That is not negotiable. You already know how things can get out here and I've picked you exactly because of that. Under the couch opposite the TV is two pistols and a Mossberg. Under no circumstances do you pull them out unless you're ready to shoot that motherfucker dead. Otherwise grab that Louisville slugger over by the front door and bash some heads in."

Hearing his phone ring, Money Mike pulled it out of his pocket and answered it instantly breaking out into a heated argument with whoever was on the line. D felt an odd energy running through his body and he was so tense he felt like a statue. This shit was really ducking happening! Guns prostitutes packs of drugs! He was almost ready for a team of FBI Agents to

197

come storming through the front door and arrest then all on the spot! But the busy never came.

Money kept arguing on the phone and Chris was leaning on the kitchen counter looking like a dream had come true. And in a way, hadn't it? Five minutes later when Money Mike hung up the phone D was feeling pretty relaxed.

"All right niggaz," Money Mike declared, "I gotta go the tours over. Time for you to meet the girls."

Money Mike turned and walked down the hallway headed for the front door and living room.

"Jamie! Ashley! Come on down my beauties i got some people that I want you to meet!" He called out.

Chris and D exchanged looks of excitement and quickly followed Money towards the front of the house.

"Upstairs is the girl's private bedrooms and one that you guys will share. No customers go up there!" Money Mike ordered.

Above the group the floor boards creaked and suddenly two people came walking down the stairs yawning and stretching. D and Chris couldn't help but stare. Even with the head wraps loose shirts and sweats that they were dressed in it was obvious that these were two fine young women. Pretty faces sat on top of curvy bodies that reeked of sexuality. One had dark skin the other was a light brown complexion. Coming down the stairs the two girls walked up to Money Mike and put theirs arms around his waist. They were pretty much the same height.

"D and Chris meet Jamie and Ashley. Girls these are your new caretakers."

They were young. That much D was sure of. Ashley was dark skinned and thick. A nose ring was in her left nostril and D could make out what looked like a tattoo of a heart on her shoulder. Jamie had a lighter complexion was about a half inch taller and skinnier then Ashley was but somehow had come away with bigger breasts and a bigger butt then Ashley had.

Despite their attractiveness however it was the eyes of both girls that made D pause. They were cold. Ice like and emotionless in the way they looked out on the world. Dark portals that spoke volumes about the type of lives the girls had lived up to this point. D wondered how two girls could look so good but so mean at the same time.

"Hey," said Ashley. Jamie smiled or at least her mouth smiled. Her eyes kept the same steely emotionless glare.

"Now y'all do ya thing and introduce y'all selves to each other. Girls finish showing them where y'all do your business down here. I got some business to handle in the Westside but I'll be back later."

Money Mike kissed both girls on the cheek nodded at D and Chris then disappeared out the front door closing it behind them.

Silence descended on the house. The four young people stood eyeing each other up and down. Finally, Jamie broke the silence.

"So if Money Mike got y'all up here that must mean he fucks with y'all the long way. How long have you two been with deuce Trey?"

Chris puffed his chest up at the question and shot a brief superior look in D's direction.

"Man, I've been a soldier in this shit since I was 11 years old. Money Mike is my cousin."

Jamie raised an eyebrow.

"He's your cousin huh? That's wassup. So what about you?" She asked looking at D. D hesitated for a second before answering.

"Uh me?"

"Uh yeah you! Who else?"

"Uh really I only been down like four months."

"Why only four months? You was scared to get jumped in huh?" asked Ashley rudely. D immediately fixed her with an evil stare that made her step back. Who the fuck was this bitch to say some shot like that? Didn't she know the shit he'd done out in the streets even before he'd been put on to Deuce Trey.

Suddenly the nervousness that D had felt at being around two hard looking sexy females vanished. Everybody always thought they were better than him. Somebody always had something to say about the way he lived his life. Well it was time people realized just what the fuck he was capable of!

199

"Aight bitch why don't you watch your fucking mouth when you talk to me! No I wasn't scared. My Patna Anthony RIP was down for hella long but always tried to keep me out of it. He got killed this summer. Shot right in front of me. I held him while he bled out all over my shirt and pants. It was the worst fucking moment of my life. Now I'm here to get the muthafucka that did it. That's why I'm just now down.

"How bout you ask yourself how long you been a hoe! Now next time to try and downplay my commitment to this shit I'm gonna backhand the fuck outta you! All you dumb bitches are the same. Fuck how long I've been at this I'm here to kill a muthafucka n it seems like your job is sucking dick! Now ain't you supposed to be showing us some shit or you just gonna stand there in your busted ass pajamas making stupid ass comments all day?"

Ashley was speechless. D looked from one to the other breathing hard. He was so sick of females and their stupid attitudes and mind games he would've have really liked to actually slap Ashley just to let some steam off. But he would never do anything to either of them without having first cleared it with him. But it sure didn't hurt to let the threat hang over their heads. Chris looked like a thunderbolt had just struck him in the chest.

Everything changed after that. Ashley's attitude switched completely and she immediately went about showing them the two bedrooms downstairs where she and Jamie took their customers. She and Jamie both took them upstairs and showed them their room which had beds on both walls and a dresser with a small TV on it.

Halfway through an explanation of their work hours the sounds of Keisha Cole came floating out of Jamie's bedroom. As she ran to pick it up Ashley looked at both boys with respect

"Well let me get ready for the night cuz the shit is about to start going in a second."

D and Chris nodded and Ashley ran off to her room. The two boys walked downstairs and stood for a moment in the living room. Not really knowing what to do next, d's eyes roamed around the living room and settled on the couch directly

200

opposite the TV. He looked over at Chris and saw that Chris was staring at him. He nodded.

Instantly they both went to the couch and lifted up the cushions. A black pistol a short chunky revolver and a shotgun greeted their eyes. They leaned in for closer looks. Chris identified the brands.

"Oh shit we got a snub nose 357 Taurus Magnum, a 9mm Springfield XD and a moss berg 500 12gauge of course! Money got us stocked up here." Chris looked over at D then back down to the guns.

"I'ma take this here Magnum my nigga I gots to have this shit." he said quickly scooping up the gun and hefting it on his hand.

D leaned down and picked up the 9mm. He liked the reassuring weight of the pistol in his hand. He ejected the magazine. Sixteen bullets. Not too bad. Looking down at his pants d stuck the gun in between his pants and his shorts on his right hand side. It fit perfectly. Chris shoved his gun into the front of his waist.

"There's bout to be a knock on the door!" Jamie called down. "Just let him in!" This was what they had been waiting for. The knock came almost immediately. D stood back by the hallway as Chris walked up to the door and opened it. A middle aged white man entered wearing a shabby grey suit and looking like he'd had a very bad day. He hesitated a little when he saw D standing still and silent but Chris ushered him in and closed the door behind him.

"Um hey fellas how are you tonight?" the man asked nervously. Chris stared him down before answering.

"Oh we good my guy. Just keep things cool tonight and we'll stay that way ya feel me?"

"Umm...I think I understand. I'll definitely keep things cool. They might get sweaty though you know what I mean?" He ended with a small laugh and looked back and forth between D and Chris seeking approval. He got silence. He was saved by the arrival of Jamie walking down the staircase. She was looking extra sensual in a loose pink bathrobe. All the eyes in the room immediately went to her toned brown legs.

"Oh Dennis sorry to keep you waiting baby I just had to freshen up right quick. I hope these boys weren't disturbing you their new."

"Oh no, no problem," replied Dennis who seemed to have been hypnotized by the sight of Jamie and apparently had forgotten the incident.

Taking the white man's hands Jamie shot D and Chris nasty looks then led Dennis back to one of the empty bedrooms. After the door had closed, Ashley came down the stairs in a sexy black dress that showed off all her curves amazingly.

"Hey you two, come here." She said. D and Chris who had been eyeing her up and down went over to her.

"Wassup?" asked Chris.

"What's up is you need to lay off the customers. They know not to get rough with us. Besides you threatening folks ain't gone do nothing but ruin business. You can be present but let us handle the transaction. Just chill out and watch TV. And you don't gotta post up looking like you back up for the door man, D. People gonna think you about to rob em. Just relax. If we ain't down they'll sit on the couch."

Chris held up his hands in the surrender gesture. Ashley rolled her eyes and walked back up the stairs.

"And stop looking at my booty," she called over her shoulder. D and Chris both kept looking until she was gone. A second knock came this one from the back door. Chris nodded at D.

"That's for you homie. Handle that!"

Adjusting the gun in his pants, D with a surge of machismo walked with an exaggerated limp in his stroll down the hallway to the back door. He pulled it open with one hand on his gun handle to see a an elderly black man a dark sweat suit shifting from foot to foot.

"Sup homie! What you need?"

Chapter 26

A youngish looking white man dressed in shabby and dirty clothes knocked twice on the back door of the house he had come to know so well in the last several months. It was immediately answered by a young but tough looking black teenager with a scowl on his face and his right hand hovering about his waistline.

"Wassup what you need white boy?"

The voice was low but menacing. The boy's face was shrouded in darkness from the hood he was wearing but his eyes glinted back at the man with such intensity that any thoughts of an attempted funny business flew right out the window.

"Wassup D its Nate!"

The boy seemed to relax. Just a little.

"Oh shit wassup Nate? My bad I didn't recognize you. That's a new coat?"

"Yeah thanks for noticing. I'm tryna get two bags."

"All right hold up."

The door closed but only for a few seconds. D was back in the blink of an eye opening the door and looking around to check for any suspicious activity. There was none. Time to finish the deal.

Quickly, D passed Nate two bags of coke and took the hundred dollars that the man offered him.

"Damn, Nate this shit dirty as fuck and smell twice as bad. Where the hell you get these bills from?"

"Sorry D you know how it goes. They won't let me in the real banks. I do all my business with the UBOA credit union."

"UBOA?"

"Yeah. United Bums of America."

D flashed a brief smile. It wasn't reflected in his eyes.

"United bums of America? You crazy Nate. Aight man I gotta get back to it."

"All right. Thanks D."

"B safe out here."

"Yeah you too man," Nate called over his shoulder as he shuffled off into the darkness.

D closed the back door and locked it. Walking into the kitchen he opened a drawer and dropped the money into it. The two bills fell on top of a pile of other bills crammed into the same drawer. Everything from 1 to 100 were there in numerous amounts but d, used to such sights merely closed the drawer and leaned against the counter top.

Taking a blunt that he had tucked up in his ear, D stuck it in his mouth and roasted the tip with a lighter until the end burned hot and orange. He inhaled held the smoke in for several seconds then exhaled long and slow.

It had been several months since the day Money Mike had first brought him and Chris to the house in Lake City. That had been back in December which was now considers last year. Currently it was March 13, 2006 and even though it had only been about three and a half months since they had first arrived in Lake City it might as well have been a lifetime to D.

He was changed. Constant contact with drug addicts, pussy starved men reeking of alcohol and bad decisions, two hard ass prostitutes (he knew that's basically what they were) and Chris and money mikes crazy ass had altered his point of view on life. The relationship between him and Chris was at a tipping angle. D didn't fear Chris anymore and almost looked at him with contempt. Watching over the girls really was just making sure they had what they wanted and Chris ended up spending most of his time on the couch.

D was always in the kitchen answering the door conducting sales and counting money. Money Mike had even praised him for his organizing skills. In short, he did more work than Chris and was starting to take it as a sign of weakness on Chris part.

He had had to get pretty rough with a couple customers and had cracked at least three heads with the baseball bat but lately hadn't had any problems. It was now known to the buyers that frequented the house that the young man who answered the back door was not to be messed with. People came usually sent by Money Mike but only after they'd been approved. And it worked like a charm.

D had lost respect for humanity after seeing the vast multitudes of men who came to see either Ashley or Jamie. Young and old. Shaved and bearded. Some entered the door still taking their Wedding rings off. Willing to risk everything they had for a piece of young black pussy.

He had no idea how Money Mike met all these different men but one hustle that he had been clued into by Ashley was the internet hustle. She had showed him her profile on a popular site called edslist.com and D had been shocked. Prostitution on the web? And it was legal?

His admiration for Money Mike never stopped growing. But it definitely made him wonder what was in it for these girls besides a cut of the money. Some of these dudes looked less than healthy and D couldn't imagine having to continually have sex with an unattractive girl.

A sudden commotion coming from the front of the house brought his head whipping around as he peered down the hallway to see what was happening. There in the front of the hallway, Chris was scuffing with a middle aged looking black man while Jamie was yelling at him with only panties on and no top. Her breasts bounced in the air as she yelled and hopped around the fighting men.

D watched the fight for a couple seconds in amusement then pulled out his gun and began jogging down the hall. Up ahead the older man got the better of Chris and tripped him to the floor.

"Aww hell naw nigga not in this house!" D called out. The man looked around in surprise but D was already bringing the hand gripping his pistol down through the air.

CRACK!!!

The butt of D's pistol collided with the side of the man's jaw with terrifying force!

"Ahhhhh," Ashley screamed!

The man hit the wall and collapsed on the ground next to Chris. Chris immediately jumped up and began kicking and stomping on the man's head. But he was already out cold. Shoving his gun back into his pants D pulled Chris off the man's unmoving body. Once Chris stopped struggling they turned and looked down at the man.

"That's what you get for fucking with my girls you punk ass beyotch!" D spit on the man's face. He was black middle aged and dressed in a cheap suit. Ashley ran up and spit on him too.

"That motherfucker tried to jam it in my ass with no warning and no lube!" She yelled!

D looked over at her in mock pity.

"Oh what that wasn't part of the deal?"

"No!" Said Ashley looking offended, "he didn't pay for all that."

"So why didn't you let him?"

He looked back down at the prone body.

"Now instead of more money we gotta drag his ass out of here. Go clean yourself up."

Looking extremely offended at his lack of empathy, Ashley walked past him and stormed up the stairs heading for her private bedroom. Shaking his , D featured for Chris to grab the man's feet. Picking him up the two boys awkwardly maneuvers him out the front door down the porch steps and across the yard to where his car was parked. Bundling him into the back seat, they tied his hands with his shoe laces and rolled him onto the floor. Chris hopped in the front seat and started the car with the man's keys.

"I'm gonna drive it up to like 140th and ditch it in an alley or something." He told D.

"Aight cool," responded D, "I'm thinking we close down for today just to be on the safe side. The girls don't work well after shit like that. They spend the rest of the night paranoid someone else is going to start tripping." Chris nodded in agreement.

"Aight cool. Be back in a second."

"Hold up," D passed Chris a few bills through the window. "You should stop by the liquor store when you're walking back. Get a bottle of Tequila and some Swishers. I'm almost out."

Chris took the money.

"Yup!" Shifting the gears into drive, he sped off down the block. D watched him go for a second then turned and walked back towards the house.

Thirty minutes later…

"Hey D. You got a second?"

Looking up from where he sat hunched over the kitchen table counting the days earnings, D saw Ashley standing in the hallway entrance. She was dressed in a wife beater and sweats with a pair of puffy pink slippers on her feet. When he had first come to the house, D had tried to stop himself from looking to hard at the girl's curvy bodies. His embarrassment had long ago vanished and now, he openly eyed her up and down before responding.

"Yeah I got a second. Just let me finish counting this money." He nodded to the chair on the opposite side of the table. Ashley took a seat, watching silently as d wrapped rubber bands around rolls of money and tossed them into a drawer.

"Good day?" She asked. D looked down at her as he leaned against the counter.

"Yeah it was cool. Money was right when he said "Mufuckaz" love these damn pills up here. I'm almost out of the Oxy's and he just brought a new pack in a couple of days ago!" Taking out a hefty sized bag of weed and a swisher from a bottom drawer d joined Ashley back at the table.

She watched silently as D began his rolling process and was impressed with the concentration he showed this task.

"You're pretty good at rolling up," she said less than five minutes later as D lit the blunt and leaned back in his chair. "That was hella fast. How long you been smoking for?" D took

207

another hit then held the blunt out to Ashley. She took it after a moment with a small smile. D paused. He'd never seen Ashley smile before.

"Since like eighth grade. I used to be a loner back then. Mary was my only real friend. Shit, it's still the same way now. What about you?"

Ashley blew out a long thick cloud of smoke.

"Sixth grade. My mom was never home and I used to go in her room and take joints out of the ashtray. My older cousin showed me how to roll my own blunts but they never look as good as yours."

"I'm just a no good lazy pot head ain't no other reason." D explained. Ashley passed the blunt back to D.

"Thanks," she said quietly. D looked at her in surprise then waved his hand dismissively.

"You ain't got to thank me it's just weed," he told Ashley. "I smoke blunts all day long you ain't intruding."

"No not for the weed. I was saying thank you for earlier."

"For what?"

"You know for helping take care of that man earlier. If you and Chris hadn't been here he might have kept going. I can take care of myself but I'm not as strong as most men out here. I ain't even gonna play myself into thinking that."

"You ain't gotta thank me girl. It's my job to look after you and Jamie. If I let somebody hurt either of you then I'd be failing in that job. This while shit is like a family. We live and work together so we gotta look out for each other. Were like a family that ain't related to each other. Besides, this is all I got right now and I'm not trying to part ways with this shit. We got money, shelter, food, everything we need.

"All we gotta do is play our positions and we won't have any problems. So don't trip. Long as I'm around ain't nothing about to happen to you guys. That's on everything." D passed the blunt back to Ashley spilling the ash on his shirt in the process. Cursing, he wiped his shirt off then glanced up. Ashley was looking at him with a strange expression on her face. Like someone who had just found something they'd been looking for but suddenly didn't know what do to with it.

"Can I ask you a question?"

Her words caught him by surprise. D looked Ashley straight in the eyes, searching for signs of a motive. But she seemed genuine. He decided it couldn't hurt to tell her.

"Honestly, I don't really know. I just kind of ended up here. I didn't mean for anything that's happened this year to take place. But it did. Now I've been here for hella long and since I'm not dead yet I figure I'm doing something right."

"So you weren't trying to be here?"

D sighed. He was getting slightly annoyed with Ashley's questioning.

"I don't where I want to be. All I know is I can't be at home and I can't be at school so why not be here. Shit while were being so honest with each other why don't you tell me why your here doing what you do? No offense but if rather be doing what I'm doing then what you're doing."

Ashley looked down at the floor for a moment before answering.

"My step dad raped me when I was 11. I know it ain't no excuse but I wasn't the same after that. Before you know it I was on the street. I met Money Mike after I got out of Juvie and spent the longest time trying to get with him. But he always made me do things to get money for him.

"He said I was his ride or die. When he said he needed girls to work a new spot I immediately told him I'd do it. I even told him I could get a friend to work with me. I thought he'd eventually make me his girl so I wouldn't have to do this anymore. But he never did. Now he spends more time looking at Jamie then he does even talking to me. Sometimes I feel like... never mind. At least I'm still getting money out this shit."

Ashley stopped talking and silence filled the kitchen. D was surprised to hear how Ashley felt about money mike. She was so cold and unforgiving most of the time he'd figured she'd forgotten what love felt like. There were times when D felt he didn't even know the meaning of the word. But with Money Mike? D could have told her she'd have better luck marrying R.

Kelly. But somehow he thought she'd already realized that. Shaking her head, Ashley looked back up at him.

"Well thanks again," she offered. "I've never really felt safe anywhere before. Or respected. But here with you, I feel safer than I've ever felt before. Even safer then when I was at home."

D nodded. The irony that this girl felt safe around two shady gang banging drug dealers wasn't lost on him but he chose not to comment on it.

"My pleasure. Besides knocking these fools out when they get tough is kind of fun." D looked at his cell phone. "Chris should almost be back now. He's bringing a bottle with him. I'm closing down the house for the day we've had enough excitement for right now. Time to relax. You should go get Jamie."

Ashley was momentarily speechless. This was not the same boy she had first met all those months ago!

She stood up and walked over to D holding out the blunt to him. As he took it she gently touched his wrist with her fingers. D looked sharply up at her. She stared back, their brown eyes drilling holes into each other's heads attempting to see the thoughts swimming just behind the thin layer of skin and bone protecting it from the outside world.

The sound of the front door opening shattered the spell of the moment.

"WHERE THE FUCK Y'ALL AT" Chris called out. "DRANKS ON DECK PLASTIC CUPS AND SWISHERS FOR DAYS COME GET YOU ONE! I GOT MAD PARTY FAVORS YO!"

The moment was ruined. Ashley winked at D then turned and walked down the hallway.

"Nigga you are not from New York so quite that noise!"

"Aww shit B! Shorty is tripping mad hard son! Eh yo word is bond son I'll body you B! Back up yo!

Ignoring the sounds of Chris and Ashley playfully bickering, D puffed on the last of the blunt and stubbed it put in the ashtray. Money Mike had told him that shit like this would happen and that the girl's minds might get fed up with their occupations from time to time. When that happened he had told

D it was all about catering to their needs while keeping them pointed in the right direction.

Talk with them. Appear to connect with them. Even sympathize with them. "Take their minds off the fact that they ain't shit but some hoes. Give em a purpose. Remind em we all in this together. Just remember that you're the one in charge ," Money Mike had advised. It was all to keep them in the house and making money. That was all that really mattered at the end of the day.

Just then Chris cell phone rang. He answered it then quickly gestured for someone to turn the music down. Jamie ran to the stereo and hit mute.

"Hold up money you said what? Yeah we here what's going down? Umm, aight peace." Chris hung up the phone. D and the girls looked at him for an explanation.

"Sup nigga?" asked D.

"Money Mike is outside. And he got somebody with him."

Thirty minutes later...

Standing slightly behind Money Mike as he explained what was going on to the two boys and two girls that were sitting on a couch in front of him, Chanelle, a recent runaway and Money Mikes newest recruit, could feel several different vibes radiating out towards her.

The two girls were giving her extremely hostile glares whenever they weren't looking at Money Mike. Arms crossed and feet tapping on the floor, they looked extremely pissed off about the whole situation. The dark skinned boy had barely looked at her and didn't seem to give a damn about what was going on. The other boy however the light skinned one had been staring at her with a mild curiosity ever since she had come through the door.

His eyes were cold and his face expressionless as he sat unmoving on the couch. Mostly he was looking at Money Mike but every now and then he looked over at her with that steady unnerving gaze. Like he was carefully extracting all of your life's secrets and considering what to do with the information.

"Mike this is some bullshit," said Jaime.

Money Mike exploded.

"BITCH I'M GETTING REAL TIRED OF TELLING YOU GIRLS WHAT THE FUCKING DEAL IS! This is something beyond your control! And if you would use your heads you would see this only benefits us!"

"How the fuck does bringing another girl in here benefit us?" Asked Ashley. The look on money mikes faces was one of pure fury. His hands were trembling as his eyes found D and he pointed at him.

"D take Chanelle upstairs and show her room. I'ma be up shortly since these two obviously need reminding of who the fuck calls the shots around this mufucka!" Money Mike looked at every person in the room daring anybody to defy his orders.

Knowing what he was supposed to do, D got up and motioned for the girl to follow him up the stairs.

They hadn't even reached the top before they heard Money Mike's voice explode in rage as he yelled at Ashley and Jamie. Reaching the top of the stairs D was glad to be out of the living room. He honestly didn't care whether a new girl came in or not. And he already forgotten her name. He sneaked a glance at the girl behind him as they walked down the hallway.

She looked dirty. Dressed in a hoody and baggy jeans, she looked more like a boy then a girl. But he could see the hint of a sexy figure beneath. Her face wasn't too bad either. She was cute. And there was something about the energy radiating off of her. D immediately sensed that his girl was a survivor. Her eyes were cold just like Ashley and Jamie's but unlike them there was still life sparkling in her pupils. But D wasn't a fool. If she associated with Money Mike then she was far from innocent.

They reached the door to the bedroom and he opened the door for her. She stepped past him and D noticed that despite her look her hair still smelled freshly washed. He breathed in the scent softly as she walked by him.

She entered the room which was D and Chris old room and looked around at the bare furnishings. Placing her backpack on the bed she turned to look at D.

212

"Well this is yours now so be happy," D said, "Me and Chris will be crashing on the couches from now on." For a moment the girl looked nervous but D put her at ease by quickly explaining.

"Naw don't trip girl it's all right. You deserve it anyways. So check it out, the bathroom is the door to your left when you come out of the room. There's some extra towels in there and some soap bars and shit. What's your name again?"

Chanelle looked up.

"Chanelle. What was yours?" Her voice was soft and a little raspy but it sounded sexy to D.

"Damien. Everybody calls me D though. So you can too I guess." She nodded then slowly sat down on the bed.

"Thanks D."

"It's nothing. You need something just let me know and I'll take care of it." She nodded again and fell silent. D was about to walk out of the room but something stopped him. He looked at Chanelle again. Despite the shabbiness of her clothes, her nails were done or at least cut and manicured. He'd never seen her before at any of the Deuce Trey parties and he was sure she didn't go to Central High. Where the hell had Money Mike gotten her from? Did she really know what went on in this house?

"Where you from?" He asked. Chanelle looked up at him.

"Tacoma."

"Tacoma? What the hell you doing up here?"

Chanelle shrugged.

"Home sucked so I ran away. Came up on some cash so I came here. Tried to come up again and got caught trying steal from the wrong nigga."

"Yeah. Who?"

Chanelle nodded at the floor and suddenly it all made sense.

"So you tried to get over on Money Mike huh? And now your here. He didn't beat yo ass for trying that slick shit?"

Chanelle laughed bitterly.

"Oh don't get it twisted he slapped the shit out of me! Told me I would've got way worse if I actually got away with it. We talked for a bit afterwards. He was being really nice. Took me to get some food. Then he said he had a job for me if was ready and willing to do it. Said I'd have a safe place to stay and food to eat and people to look out for me. Was he talking about you?"

Before D could answer, he heard footsteps in the hallway and Money Mike's shadow fell across the doorway. He put a hand on D's shoulder.

"Sup lil nigga good looking on taking care of business for me." D felt Money Mike take his hand and a wad of bills was forced into it. "Loyalty like yours is hard to come by D." he said into the teen's ear. "Just know I appreciate it from the bottom of my heart. Now go on back downstairs and keep on with the party." He patted D's shoulder and forcefully moved him back into the hallway.

"Excuse me while I explain to Chanelle what her new responsibilities are gonna be. A wise business man always samples his products before placing them on the market!"

He smiled ruthlessly and closed the door in D's face.

D stood there for a few seconds with a frown on his face. Then he turned and walked away.

Chapter 27

It had been so simple. D was furious with himself for not having thought of it earlier. No one would know. Money Mike would still get the money from his pills and powder. D would get a little more motivation to work harder and longer. Chris didn't need to know shit about shit and could stay oblivious for all D cared. None of the girls were anywhere near involved in the drug operation so he didn't need to worry about them.

D had started selling weed out of the back of the house in addition to moving Money Mikes products. He had gotten the idea when his regular customer Nate had asked if he could buy the blunt tucked behind D's ear. D had turned down the offer but sold him some out of his personal stash instead. The rest was history.

He didn't know why he hadn't told Money Mike or Chris. They had ignored him when he first brought the subject up. Money Mike said weed wasn't a money maker but D had to disagree. Weed was a big seller if you had the good quality shit. And D always had quality shit. So far his operation had avoided detection due to the fact that money mike was never there and D was always in the back of the house alone free to operate as he pleased.

The question if what to do if his operation was discovered remained unanswered. D wasn't too worried. For the moment there was a bigger issue to work out that had everybody's full attention. Right after he smoked this blunt!

Several weeks later…
"Bitch, you lucky Jamie was willing to take care of your customer and do him for free. Don't you know some of these

fucking low life crackers got connections with people who could have all our black asses locked the fuck up! The last thing we want to do is have them felling like we got robbed and bring unwanted bad attention on this house. That's why we're not in the CD the south end or anywhere else that's super-hot in the first place! Who would want to pay to have sex with a bitch that just lies there anyways?!"

Throwing up his hands in frustration, Chris walked back across the room and sat down in one of the armchairs. D was leaning against the wall watching the proceedings with an amused expression on his face. Ashley was sitting on the foot of the staircase frowning at Chris weak attempt to get control of the situation.

"I don't know what they want me do," Chanelle argued back. "These fat sloppy and ugly dudes just climb on up and start humping! What else am I supposed to do?"

"Whatever the fuck it is you're not doing that's making em get all angry with yo dumb ass! Suck his balls, lick his ass, and kiss his fucking big toe nail! C'mon now do I have to tell you how to be a hoe?"

Chanelle eyes got cold.

"Well you could show me how it's done that might make me learn faster," she snapped back at Chris. Quick as flash, Chris jumped across the room and backhanded Chanelle hard across the face.

SMACK!!!

The force of the blow sent Chanelle sprawling across the couch. Chanelle's arms flew up to protect her face and Chris, spotting an opening, sent a hard cruel punch thudding into her stomach. The wind was knocked out of her and she immediately curled up coughing and gasping for air.

"Chris no!" screamed Ashley. But he ignored her. Chris cocked back his arm to throw another punch but immediately found his target blocked by D. D quickly lashed out with a quick jab that caught Chris square in the nose!

"Aww what the fuck nigga?" cried Chris hands flying to cover his nose just as the blood began flowing. D was staring at him breathing evenly not scared at all. The adrenaline of

216

impending combat was boiling through his veins but he appeared calm on the outside when he spoke.

"Don't damage the merchandise Chris. We're gonna miss way more money with her out of commission then working. C'mon nigga what the fucks wrong with you? You think Money Mike would be happy?"

Chris mouth dropped open in disbelief,

"But this fucking bitch is running her mouth and talking shit! We supposed to just let her get away with that? Fuck naw nigga!"

"So? That's what bitches do this ain't no new phenomenon. But this is a place of business. If you wanna gorilla pimp hoes take yo ass to Aurora Avenue or PAC highway and find some street walkers to work for you! We tryna do some next level shit here nigga train your mind! She's fucking it up for nobody but herself right now bro we don't need her! But we could sure use the money she could bring in if she can learn how to act right!"

Looking back down at Chanelle for a moment, Chris stared at her holding her face and glaring up at him. The rage smoldering in her eyes almost made him take a step backwards. He looked back at D who was staring right back at him without blinking or averting his eyes. For the first time since they'd met, Chris experienced a weird sobering sensation in the pit of his stomach.

He'd always had sort of seniority over D because the only thing separating them was the fact d hadn't actually been a part of deuce Trey. Now that could Chris could no longer use that card, he had noticed subtle changes taking place that didn't sit well with him and he could no longer ignore. Between him and D, Chris was no longer the alpha male. They were now equals.

Shaking his head in disgust, Chris turned away from d and Chanelle and stormed across the living room to sit on the couch against the far wall.

"So how the fuck do we make her do what she's supposed to then since you know everything?" asked Chris.

"I'm right here! You ain't gotta talk about me like I'm not in the room!" said Chanelle angrily. Immediately, D turned

217

around and leaned down in front of her grabbed her jaw roughly with one hand while smacking her upside the head with the other.

"Oh my god bitch do yourself a favor and shut the fuck up! If you didn't wanna do none of this shit you should have never came here in the first gotdamn place. Now your either gonna quit being difficult and get with the fucking program or get the fuck out of here and go find another place where you can eat sleep and shit all without paying a dime or worrying about getting raped!

"You wanna stay here then earn your fucking keep like the rest of us and quit acting like u got somewhere better to be cuz you don't. That's why you came here and that's why you ain't left already. So what's it gonna be? Decide now cuz if you can't make up your mind I ain't got no problem putting my foot in yo ass and kicking you off the front porch!"

D's words completely silenced Chanelle. She was staring up at D and he could see the truth reflected in her eyes. Street level operations were always more dangerous. The people were more unhinged the deals less organized and the places of transactions were basically murder scenes with nobody. And young girls always got it the worst in the street. He knew she didn't want be in the street and now he had called her bluff. Chanelle hung her head in defeat.

Chris, observing the scene from the other side of the room felt an unnatural chill settle over him. Ever since Anthony had died, he had basically been trying to replace him with D. There had been times when he had thought that d just wasn't cut out for this kind of life but now he had no doubts in his mind. His friend had turned Cutthroat

He'd already punched him in front of two hoes and hadn't thought twice about it. No matter who they were the one thing Chris did not tolerate was disrespect. He was gonna have to start keeping an eye on his friends progression.

D looked down at Chanelle through hazy eyes. He couldn't help but notice that even though she was clearly at a disadvantage with everything going on, her eyes still shone fierce and determined. He liked her spirit but was annoyed but her actions. He definitely wasn't going to kick her out. That was mostly a scare tactic. But He also knew that she didn't really want to be here. She just didn't have many options that were better. She was like him in a way. But she was having trouble adapting. D came up with a solution that would at least get him somewhere they could talk without extra ears listening in. His curiosity was aroused.

One week later...

"So the bags with the powder are $50 and the pills are $20 each?"

"Yup. It's simple. Just put the money in the different drawers so we can count it at the end of the day. Helps keep track of sales."

"Shit. You guys really do operate like a real legitimate business."

D looked over at Chanelle with narrowed eyes.

"Of course we do. That's what you seem to have a problem realizing. The only way to survive out here is to operate like a real business. And real employees do their mother fucking job without complaining or you know what happens? The boss fires yo ass. Is that what you want to happen Chanelle? Cuz that's damn sure how you acting. So my question to you is this? If this ain't what you're trying or willing to do in this world to have a place to sleep and things to eat then what are you trying to do?"

"I don't fucking know ok?" Chanelle responded cupping her forehead in her hand. Tears were welling up in her eyes and her breath was coming in quick short gasps. She looked like someone on the edge of a breakdown.

"I don't even know how I ended up here. I mean I do but I don't. I didn't ask for any of this shit! I just wanna be at home with my mom but I can't and every friend I thought I had keep turning their backs on me! I don't know to how fucking deal with this shit. It's not fair that all this shit happens to me I haven't done anything to anyone!"

D was staring hard at Chanelle while she shifted around in her seat uncomfortably. Despite the tears that fierce light never went out of her eyes. And even as he asked her the question mostly in an attempt to feel surer of himself, D found his own mind pushed into unfamiliar territory. Was this what he was trying to do with his own life? Drugs and prostitutes? D had barely spent any time in the Lake City neighborhood before this and now he couldn't remember the last time he'd left. He hadn't seen or spoken to his dad in months. The graduation packet that Ms. Richards had given him was still in his backpack untouched.

He could almost feel his life blurring into one long ever repeating cycle. Wake up sell drugs get fucked up at night and pass out then wake up and do it again. He'd almost forgotten how it felt to be around "normal people" as his only regular human contacts were drug addicts, alcoholics and sleazy sex craving businessmen. D sighed heavily.

"Why can't you stay with your mom's?" He asked Chanelle. He was genuinely curious. She looked up into D's eyes. The expression on her face told him her next words would be nothing but truth.

"My mom's boyfriend raped me. She didn't believe me so I ran away to my best friend house. But he only let me stay as long as I had sex with him. Eventually I went back to my mom's house but her boyfriend came home drunk one night and tried to tape me again. So I stabbed him with a screwdriver and left for good. I been on the streets ever since. I was getting by I guess till this drug dealer caught me stealing from him and beat the shit out of me. I had nowhere to stay till I met Money Mike and he brought me here."

She stopped talking suddenly and was silent looking surprised that she had said as much as she had. D looked at her for a long silent moment. He'd heard this story before. What was the deal with older men raping little girls? This girl had not had an easy time. But her spirit was strong. The streets hadn't broken her. Could he say the same for himself?

A knock at the door interrupted his train of thought. Glancing over at the door, he looked back down at Chanelle. Grabbing a couple paper towels, he gently touched her shoulder and handed them to her.

"Well here dry your eyes. Don't think you got out of working though. You're going to be my helper today. Your first mission is to answer the door and see what the hell this person wants. And when you ain't doing deals maybe we can figure out a way to either get you out of here or get your head right so you can do what you supposed to do.

Several hours later…
D sat alone at the kitchen table after he had sold the last of the pills. He had sent Chanelle back upstairs to clean up and rest. They had had a very interesting conversation that was actually bothering him more then he would have liked to admit. He shook his head.

"Emotions…" He muttered. Chanelle had had it pretty fucking rough up to this point and it was clear she was no stranger to violence. It was also clear that she wanted no part of any of it. Apparently her dream was to be a news reporter. She just had no idea how she was going to make it happen. Talking with her had also raised questions D's mind that he had tried to previously ignore about his own future. But the more he thought about it the more he realized he didn't have a clue.

He shook his head, trying to clear his head to make way for the business at hand. Laid out on the table in front of him were three large stacks of money, his pistol, an ashtray, a pint bottle of whiskey and his camera.

"I'm not a bad person," he said out loud to himself. It felt like a lie even as it came out of his mouth.

"Oh yes the fuck you are!"

D jumped slightly and looked around. Chris was leaning against the wall arms folded staring at D with one eye cocked.

"What you doing down here all by yourself nigga? Philosophizing about life?" He pushed himself off the wall and came and sat at the table opposite D. Picking up the piles of money he felt their weight.

"You been down here moving shit like u haul huh? How much is all this?"

D hesitated before answering. He hadn't had a chance to pocket his weed money yet. In all there was around $3000

221

dollars on the table but $900 of that was from D's side operation. He couldn't tell Chris the real number because he wasn't handing all of it over to money mike. How had Chris snuck up on him? D tried to appear casual.

"No I'm not down here philosophizing. I was just thinking. And that's about $2000 there so don't mess with it I just got done counting." Chris looked at

D for a moment then put the money back down. Opening the whiskey bottle he took a pull from it. His face screwed up as the flavor hit his tongue.

"Aaah, that some good shit. Well I hate to break the news to you d but you are a bad person."

He laughed loudly at the look on D's face.

"Don't look so surprised nigga! It's true! You've beat the shit out of plenty of niggaz, you've shot at people, I just saw you pistol whip a fool last week. You sell drugs, and I know for a fact you've stolen hella cars from right in front of people's houses and let's not forget the whole reason you joined is because you want to murder that nigga who killed Anthony! You're a fully-fledged gang banger D! How the fuck are you not a bad person? You sure' ain't doing shit that's good! And don't say it's my fault either cuz you was keying with disaster way before you met me."

"Shit it might as well be your fault!" D said slightly annoyed. He couldn't argue with anything Chris had just said. No matter how he tried to look at it he always came up with the same answer. He was a bad man. A contributor to the monstrous cycle of violence death and imprisonment that that plagued most inner city neighborhoods. He'd tried to avoid it. But Anthony's killing had changed that. D had thought he was helping avenge Anthony's death. But all he had done was sink waist deep into a pile of shit that Anthony had been warning him not to step into.

Reaching across the table D snatched the whiskey bottle out of Chris hands and took a swig himself. Sticking the blunt in his mouth he lit it and sucked the smoke greedily down into his lungs.

"Speaking of Anthony god rest his soul, why the fuck are we not out trying to find Devontay? Why are we still up here in fucking Lake City like we don't have something better to be doing?"

"Huh? What you mean? What's better than making money my nigga? You just doing what you always been doing this shit ain't no stress on your mind. Besides the CD is a war zone right now. Just riding around looking for someone ain't really a good idea. "

D passed the blunt to Chris.

"Nigga that's where you wrong. All the shits that's happened was all because I wanted to find Devontay. That's the whole reason I got down with this shit. It ain't about the money I'll always get money regardless i ain't worried about that. What does bother me is the fact that Anthony is up there looking down on all this shit and shaking his head cuz he tried to keep me out this life and now I'm deeper than ever. And I still ain't taken care of Devontay like I promised I would! I know he's up there hella pissed off."

Chris passed the blunt back to D. He was silent for a few moments. What D was saying was true. If they were ever going to avenge their friend's death, they were going to have to return to the central district.

"All right D. If you're dead ass about this then I'll talk to money mike about it. I wanna find that bitch ass nigga too. But until then concentrate on keeping this shit running smooth."

D snorted.

"Man a fucking kid could keep this shit running smooth. Anyone could run this house and Money Mike knows that shit. Some other niggaz can watch this dump while we go handle some real business!"

Chris smiled. It looked more like a wide sneer. D's new way of talking was starting to sound like music to his ears. It was about time he showed some imitative. He stood up and shook D's hand.

"Good to see the savage in you coming out my nigga. Just remember though. What you gonna do after we take care of Devontay? This house is bringing in more money than I ever made down in Pioneer Square. Shit might look easy but not everybody built for this. You're good at this shit though nigga don't beat yourself up about it. Look at all that money on the table! The fuck else you gonna do anyways?" With that, Chris turned and left the kitchen leaving D alone with his thoughts and a pretty decent buzz.

"The fuck else you gonna do anyways?"

The phrase kept repeating itself over and over in his head. He took another swig from the whiskey bottle. He puffed on the blunt to get the whiskey taste out of his mouth as he felt the liquor warming his insides on its way down to his stomach. His thoughts strayed back to the talk he and Chanelle had had earlier that day. A fucking Anchorwoman? He thought that was a strange thing to want to be but at least she had aspirations beyond this house. So where did his aspirations lie? And what was he going to do with the money he was making besides put in the empty shoebox he was using as a bank?

Tapping his fingers on the table, D's eyes strayed to the video camera that Breanna had given him. The black lens was pointed right at him like a giant lidless black eye.

He went still then relaxed and sank back into his chair with a thoughtful look crossing his features.

D had an idea.

Chapter 28

The waiting room was quiet, a sharp contrast to the bustling hallway on the other side of the office door. Pictures of young men and women receiving various academic awards lined the walls. Brochures for the numerous programs offered and many careers that they led too were placed on tables for anyone to take. D was sitting in a chair alternately going from looking at one of the brochures to the clock on the wall while nervously bouncing on his heels.

Today felt unreal. After being struck with a life changing idea the other night after talking with Chris, D had stayed awake all night planning his next move. The next morning he had told Chris he was leaving for the day. Money Mike was in Portland at the moment and D wasn't sure he would approve if D asked him for the day off to look at options outside of working for him. So D decided not to tell him.

Hopping the bus, D had travelled all the way downtown then walked up to Capitol Hill through old familiar streets to arrive at Seattle Central Community College!

A door on the far side of the room opened and a plump middle aged white woman opened the door.

"Damien Gram?"

D quickly raised his hand. The woman smiled and waved at him.

"Nice to see you young man c'mon in!"

D entered the office and sat in one of the chairs facing the desk. The woman closed the door behind them and gracefully slid into the chair on the other side of the desk. D noticed she carried her weight well. Taking out a brochure she placed it on the table in front him then clasped her hands together.

"So Damien so nice to meet you and welcome to the Seattle
 Central Community College department of film. My name is Wendy and I'm the adviser for this department here to answer any and all questions you might have about out program." Wendy was energetic and jovial and some of the nervousness d was feeling slipped away. Maybe this wasn't going to be as difficult he had imagined. He cleared his throat.

"Hey Wendy how are you doing?"

"I'm very good young sir and how are you?"

"I'm all right, I'm all right I guess."

"Well what can I help you with? I'm assuming you want some information about the program. Are you a registered student yet?"

D shifted uncomfortably in his seat.

"Uhh no not exactly."

He leaving out the part about being kicked out of school, D explained the situation he was in involving the graduation packet. When he was done be waited nervously for Wendy's response. She nodded her head when D had finished speaking.

"I am actually aware of the situation regarding central high and I am delighted to see you taking advantage of the program. It beats another year in high school right?"

D eagerly agreed pleasantly surprised at Wendy's attitude toward his circumstance.

"Well in that case you would be graduating this spring. So get that packet finished up and turned in so you can come and register with us. You've only got about two months."

D cringed on the inside. He hadn't even looked at the packet since he'd first gotten several months ago. Wendy however seemed to assume he was almost done with his packet and was already moving past the issue.

"Now something I like to always do with incoming students is ask them this; what is your vision? What made you want to pick film as your area of study and what do you hope to do with it?"

It was a good question. And a hard one. D chose his words carefully, not knowing if Wendy would approve of his last minute decision making.

"Well, uhh honestly I've been having some trouble with the packet but I'll get it done in time for graduation. Just nervousness ya know?" He paused.

"It's nothing to worry about Mr. Gram," said Wendy, "this is a big change coming up and plenty more young people then just you will be feeling the pressure in the coming months. It's very important however that you stay in control and focused and don't become a victim of your greatest enemy; your own self-doubt! Most people are their own biggest obstacles."

D thought for a moment. Wendy probably had no idea how much that statement had hit home with him. But would she still be this cordial with him if she knew the type of things he did on a day to day basis? Instinct told him to keep quiet. Instead He decided to give Wendy a mix of fact and fiction.

"Well I guess my interest in film started late last year when I got a video camera as a back to school present from my aunt Beatrice!"

For ten minutes, D told Wendy various made up stories about his love for film while Wendy related the finer details of the film production and the schedule he would follow.

"The really wonderful thing about our film program is that it covers all the aspects of film making. Directing, editing, script writing and so on. That way when you complete the program you will be eligible for a multitude of jobs in the film industry. You would be able to pursue the one of your choosing instead of settling for less. Of course it all depends on job availability but the film industry in Seattle as well as up and down the west coast is a strong one. You might even find yourself in Hollywood one day."

D liked the idea of one day ending up in Hollywood at one of the big studios. Maybe even make a movie about his life with himself playing himself!

Just as he was beginning to really get excited about something he'd only thought of a couple days ago a sobering

227

reality began to sink in. That damn packet! He only had a couple months to complete it!

Wendy saw his change in expression and leaned across the table to gently pat his hand.

"Don't worry young man. Change can sometimes be a scary thing but it's also a good thing. Don't worry about that packet it's very straight forward. You still have a couple months to finish up any spots that you've missed so take your time and do it to your best ability on?"

D nodded his head slowly. Wendy didn't know how far behind he was and D wasn't going to tell her. What he needed to do was get back to the house immediately so he could find out exactly what he had to do in the packet.

Thanking Wendy for her time, D rose and left the office. Walking back slowly through the hallways, he found himself slipping into a state of depression.

His entire life consisted of a broken down house with two young prostitutes an army of drug addicts and a friend whom D was liking less and less with every passing day. His only way out seemed to be in completing the graduation packet. But could he possibly get a whole year's worth of work done in less than two months?

D suddenly stopped walking. Something had caught his attention a couple of doors back but he was moving so fast he had passed it without stopping. Returning to the spot he gazed at a large colorful poster on one of the classroom doors.

"College fair," he read out loud. "Come and get acquainted with over 50 colleges from around the country! Your future awaits you in the auditorium! 11am until 3pm."

It was two-thirty right now according to the clock on his cell phone. D frowned thinking hard. The packet was enough to get him into a community college but it had been made clear that it would be next to impossible to apply to a four year university with.

"Fuck it," he said. It couldn't hurt to just look. Turning around, he headed off quickly back the way he had come.

Now this was something D had not been prepared for. There were almost a hundred different tables crammed into the auditorium from wall to wall and it seemed like every high school senior in Seattle and their parents were here looking at colleges. Not that it mattered but he noticed that the majority of people in here were white. Or maybe that was precisely why he was feeling a certain type of way.

As he walked down the rows of tables gazing at the poster boards filled with pictures of smiling students, statistics about their high achievements and graduation rates and listened to the college reps talk animatedly about the finer points of their Institutions D found himself drifting into a daydream. He pictured himself walking across some giant lawn with hundreds of other college freshman on some campus laughing and joking far away from his troubles in Seattle. He imagined seeing all the fine college women and going to class in his sweatpants like he's seen in all the movies. And the parties! The campus wouldn't know what hit it when D came marching through the gates.

At that thought, D stopped walking and his smile quickly vanished. All that sounded good except for the fact that it would never come true. He was forgetting the predicament he was in. He wouldn't be attending any college much less one that could take him away from all the nonsense that was going on. Shit he'd be lucky to get out of high school at this point. The hell was he still doing here?

As he turned towards the exit, D heard a loud deep voice call out over the general sound of voices.

"Hey you there! Young brother!"

D paused. That had to be a black man shouting. He hadn't heard any white man that could out that much base in their voice. Turning around d immediately spotted the owner of the voice. A large bald black man in a crisp navy blue suit stood in front of a large maroon and white colored poster board waving in his direction.

"Yeah you son! Come here let me holla at you for a quick second!" D hesitated. He really should be leaving seeing as how he had no real business being in this room. But the man's familiar way of speaking appealed to D's ears and he automatically headed over. He was curious. Nobody else was in front of his table. Did that mean his school sucked? The large man stuck his hand out as D approached.

"Hey how you doing there young man?"

D shook his hand, glad the man didn't try to crush his fingers.

"I'm good. Could complain but I won't."

The man chuckled.

"Could complain but I won't huh? I like that. My name is Robert Brown assistant dean of admissions at Morehouse College in Atlanta Georgia. Ever heard of it?"

D had. But not in the way the man probably expected.

"Yeah I heard that name before. Cuba Gooding Jr. goes there at the end of that movie "Boyz n da Hood!"

The man shook his head.

"Yes that's right but were known for way more than that. Did you know Martin Luther king attended and graduated from Morehouse?"

"Naw," said D impressed. "That's dope!"

"Oh he's not the only one to have walked through our halls. Thousands of black men that have walked out halls have gone on to do amazing things! Morehouse college can trace its roots back over a hundred years and is one of the few historically black all male colleges in the unites states today! African American students from all over the world come to study at our institution. And did I mention Atlanta is the hip hop capitol of the nation right now?"

All of this information caught D's attention. He looked at the pictures tacked up on the presentation board. Each one showed groups of well-dressed young men not much older than him smiling and waving at the camera! Other pictures showed young men in class or just walking through what looked like an extraordinary campus.

D was entranced. Usually when he saw groups of black men in pictures they were all scowling or throwing up gang signs or just making other crude gestures. Or at least his friends did. This was a world entirely different from the one in which he now existed! And it looked damn appealing. He imagined

230

himself out there on the college campus with his video camera making amateur movies starring some girl who wanted to be an actress.

But wait...

"Look, Mr. Brown..." he started.

"Please young sir, call me Robert."

"Ok Robert. Well the thing is how come it's all male? I don't see any girls in these pictures. How's a man supposed to concentrate with no women around."

Robert laughed.

"Son you will do exactly that. Concentrate! The reason Morehouse is an all boy school is to take away the distractions of having girls everywhere taking your mind off your studies. Now this is where the deal gets sweet. Directly across the street from our campus is Spelman College for girls. It's called Morehouse's sister school and we are closely related in everything we do. Trust me girls will not be hard to find. But while you're in the classroom we want you to give your full attention to the professors and their lessons.

"There are hundreds of social activities that take place between the two schools every year so believe me when I say this you'll get ample opportunity to meet plenty of girls."

D nodded his head.

"Do y'all have a film program? That's kind of what I think my focus is gonna be once I get out of high school."

"Well it's good to know what you want to do young man. Knowing is half the damn battle. I'm sorry to say Morehouse doesn't offer a film major at this time but it's something we are planning on incorporating. You could however enroll in film classes in another one of the many well-known and respected schools around Atlanta that we have relationships with.

"If you can, I'd encourage you to come down to Atlanta to visit our Campus in person so that you could really get a feel for the environment and get an up close look at the facilities."

At this, D felt his spirits begin to drop. It was time to end this charade. Imaging a life outside of Seattle had been good while it lasted. He stuck out his hand to the promoter who took it and shook it firmly.

"Well all right then Robert it's been real. I gotta get back to reality now though."

"Well good talking to you son. Hear let me give one of packets so you can give this for your parents to read. Are they here with you?"

This was definitely getting old now. D could feel himself becoming irritated and annoyed at the fact that he'd blown his chance at going to a school he had never known anything about. But it wasn't like anybody in his circle was worried about getting into college and discussing school options.

"No they ain't," said D. "Honestly man I'm here alone. I just walked in here cuz I was curious. I've been wasting your time here Robert cuz I can't even go to college. I just thought it would be nice to imagine I could. Take care though. If I see some smart black men I'll send em your way."

As he was turning to leave, he felt a gentle hand on his shoulder.

"Hold on now son don't leave like that. Tell me what's going on?"

Turning around, D looked up into Robert Brown's eyes and saw real concern. D stared up at him and Brown stared back never breaking eye contact and told him the short edited version of what had happened to him since the start of the year. Not everything but enough so that Brown got the point that D was positive he had a snowballs chance in hell of ever getting out of the state.

Robert listened to him talk the entire time with his face screwed up in concentration and his right hand rubbing his chin. When D had finished talking he waited for Brown to tell him that he wasn't college material and should've gave up on hope a long time ago. Robert cleared his throat loudly but the words that came next were not what D had expected."

"Young man, I have to be honest when I tell you that if what you've just told me is true then all I can do is say that your story is one of great inspiration. All that stuff from your friend being killed to your mom leaving and this mess with gangs, it reminds me believe it or not of me when I was younger and how ridiculously hard it can be for young black men growing up.

232

"I'm from Jackson, Mississippi young man and it goes down in Jack town! Also believe it or not many of the students are from places where according to statistics they should have been dead or in jail years ago. But they didn't give up hope and neither should you. I wish I could help you out more but it sounds like the school district kind of screwed you guys with this mediocre packet. I don't know why they didn't make an alternate one that would actually qualify students to apply to a four year university."

D shrugged.

"Politics I guess who knows. Thanks for the nice words."

Robert stared at D for a few seconds.

"What's your name again son?"

"Damien. Damien Gram!"

Robert froze.

"Gram?"

"Yeah. As in 'hey lemme get a gram of that sticky'!"

Robert shook his head chuckling.

"I can tell you're a character Mr. Gram. The reason your name stands out to me is because you happen to have the same last name as my wife."

"Oh that's what's up," said D not really thinking too much of the matter.

"What's her name?"

"Cynthia. Cynthia Gram,"

Now it was D's turn to freeze. He hadn't heard that name in a while but it was impossible to forget.

"That's my auntie man. My dad's sister matter of fact. He never really talked about her though."

Robert shook his head slowly stroking his chin.

"Yeah, Cynthia don't day too much either. I think there's some bad blood their but I don't pry to deep you know what I'm saying?"

He stuck his fist out and D pounded it no hesitation.

"Ya I feel ya mane." D felt comfortable around Robert. He had a big brother type of vibe about him. D figured it aided him greatly in his job as a college promoter. The fact that they were almost related was crazy! Fucking small world!

"How is your pops by the way?" Robert asked innocently. He could tell by the sudden shift in D's mood that he had hit a nerve. D looked him straight in the eye.

"Honestly I haven't seen or spoken to him in months. I didn't tell you this earlier but he kicked me out of the crib and I been staying with some associates."

Robert looked shocked. Looking around him, he quickly closed up his presentation and picked up is brief case. Before D knew what was happening, Robert had ushered him out of the building and into the faculty parking lot. They stopped next to a shiny black new Lincoln town car and after putting his goods in the trunk, Robert beckoned D to get in.

"Ok son I want you to tell me the whole truth and no bullshit this time. Tell me what's going on with you and where you trying to get to!"

This time it took D an hour to tell his whole story with no filters. Robert sat quiet the entire time attentive and never interrupting him. D was surprised he didn't make any faces or cringe when he told him about the basketball court rumble. Finally, he finished with his current predicament at Money Mikes trap house. After a few moments of staring off into space, Robert spoke up.

"Young man, your story is horrible but magnificent. I can't believe you've been through all of this and you're not even out of high school yet. A place like Morehouse would really benefit from the experience you could bring to the rest of the students. Most of them have never known struggle like yours. And it sounds like you know what you want to do."

He fell quiet for a moment face screwed up like he was thinking hard. D watched him as a sort of adrenaline was running through his body after all that truth telling. It had felt good. But what the hell was brown talking about? Him? At a place like Morehouse? Not only did he not have money or the grades but he found it hard to picture himself smiling in a maroon turtle neck. Robert spoke up again.

"Now listen, I don't want you to get excited or anything but I have a certain amount of influence at the school. My heart has gone out to you Damien and I know I just met you but feel like I've known you for years. How would you like to come to Atlanta?"

D's eyes popped open. He wasn't sure he had heard right. "What?"

Robert smiled.

"Yeah you heard right. I have to go back and see what the incoming freshman numbers are and then shift some things around but it might be possible. I'll need to get some personal information from you. Here, take this card. That's the direct line to my office. I'll be back in Atlanta in about a week I want you to call me so we can get this process started."

D took the card feeling like he was in a dream. Was he really being handed a way out just like that? There had to be a catch. Would he really pick up the phone?"

"Don't fuck about either Damien in complete serious about this. If I'd have known what was going on I would have told Cynthia to come with me."

"Bet you she wouldn't have," said D.

"Yeah you ain't never lie," agreed Robert. Then his tone turned serious.

"Now D, I want you to listen to me very carefully. The only reason I am doing his is because you're my wife's nephew and I would do anything for family. That and the fact that for some reason you stroke me as a very genuine person. All this nonsense that you're mixed up in has to stop now. I know there's some extraordinary circumstances going on with you but the road your on will only lead to bad things happening.

"I want you to be able to take what you know about this and help others escape the troubles that plaice our people in this country. But you can't get caught up like so many have around you. I need you to distance yourself from all the activities you just told me about and those people if you can. You can't go to college for free I might add if your locked up or six feet beneath the ground. And get that packet done! I can't pass your classes for you!"

D almost believed him. It sounded too good to be true! It had to be true! He looked coolly over at the black man beside him.

"Look Robert, I promise whatever I have to do I will do it. I need to get out here I don't have anybody up here and no reason to stay. You got my word I'll be a model student down in Atlanta!"

Robert was looking at D with a deadly serious expression and D felt a will begin to grow inside him to prove to his man he was worthy of his kind actions. This was a once in a lifetime opportunity. Robert cracked a smile and stuck his hand out!

"That's what I want to hear young sir. That's what I want to hear!"

Chapter 29

"What do you mean would I leave here if I could? Where the hell would i go? The whole reason I'm here in the first place is cuz I don't have anywhere else to go."

D sighed in exasperation. What about this concept was so difficult to understand?

"It's just a damn question Chanelle relax. Shit you act like this is some invasion of personal space. All I'm saying is that if you had the chance get out of here would you take it?. Out of Lake City or even out of Seattle. Leave Washington State and start fresh somewhere else, Would you?"

D and Chanelle were once again sitting in the kitchen. Chanelle was busy breaking down and bagging up a fresh quarter pound of purple Kush that D had brought back from Seattle. D was sitting opposite her puffing a blunt and keeping a watchful eye on Chanelle's progress.

"What kind of question is that D? I mean obviously id get the fuck out of here if I could. But whose gonna make that happen? I don't know anybody or anyplace outside of Seattle. I have nowhere to go so please stop fucking asking me!"

Chanelle's hands were shaking so bad that she dropped the bag she was currently working on crossed her arms and sat back in her chair staring anywhere but at D. D started to say something but then fell quiet. He passed her the blunt. A large part of him wanted to ask her to come with him with to Atlanta. But his rational side was keeping his mouth closed. He didn't even know if Robert Brown would be able to get him in. He had said he would try but that was far from an answer to rely on. And yet that's exactly what D was doing. It had to work.

D had begun to have a strange feeling that a shadow of doom was growing over the house. It was time to get out of here but no matter what he said to Money Mike all his words went ignored. Even though he had tried to keep up his usual relaxed non caring vibe, inside his was almost bursting with excitement, hope and fear. He was excited about the prospect of actually having a future hopeful that it would indeed actually happen but also a little scared at the prospect of leaving behind everything he knew for a place he'd only seen in rap videos. But what was here that so good?

A knock at the back door interrupted his thought process. Wearily, D forced his feet to make the short walk across the kitchen to see what whoever was on the other side of the door wanted. *Pills most likely*, he thought. That's all anybody seemed to want these days. D figured they should start listing "crack-like addiction" as a side effect along with the thirty or so other accidental symptoms they always listed in the commercials.

One hour later…
"Oh daddy you know just how to treat a girl I can't wait to order me a big old steak and some of those big old French fries."

"You mean steak fries girl?"

"Whatever they called Ashley I don't give a fuck. A bitch gotta eat that's all I know!"

Tuning out Jamie and Ashley's pointless conversation, D looked over at Chris who was lounging on the couch beside him flipping through TV stations and taking sips from a pint bottle of whiskey. He was dressed in a large sized white polo black jeans and white Nikes. His form of a tuxedo. D held out his hand and Chris passed him the bottle.

"Make sure you bring me back a bacon cheese burger bro. With the fries! I haven't been to Red Robins in hella long."

"So why don't you just come on then? Money Mike already said it's all good to close down for the night. I don't know why you want to stay here and miss out. We bout to go act a fool!"

D took a quick sip of the cheap whiskey.

"Oh boy that shit is harsh. Here take this thing back I'm gonna stick to this weed smoke." He tossed the bottle back. Just then Money Mike came walking down the stairs looking fresh in a dress shirt slacks and a nice pair of Kenneth Cole shoes on his feet. He had a pair of dark sunglasses on his face and his hair was cut into an immaculate low top fade. Ashley and Jamie stopped arguing and each ran up to him to put their as around him.

"All right y'all ready to go? The car is parked out front. D, you still tryna stay here?"

D nodded from where he sat on the couch.

"Yeah it's all good Money. I'm just not in the mood to be around a bunch of people. I'd rather stay here and get this money anyways. It's not gonna make or count itself."

"I'm gonna to have to think about giving you a promotion," said Money Mike. "The way you sticking to this shit is like white on motherfucking rice! Well we can still bring you some food back!"

D nodded at Chris.

"I told Chris. A bacon cheese burger is all I need. Plus some fries!"

Money Mike nodded and beckoned Chris.

"All right well keep it going then. We shouldn't be too long. A few hours at least."

"We getting drinks right Mike? I'm trying to get on my level!!" said Ashley swinging her hips from side to side.

"Yeah I know the waitress. Aight y'all come on. D, Chanelle upstairs in the shower right now says she got some customers coming in a little bit. You know what to do. I love your hustle young g keep it up! Hit me if anything comes up."

With that, Money Mike walked out behind Ashley, Jamie and Chris and closed the front door, locking it behind them. Silence fell in the house. Except for the distant sound of water running in the bathroom upstairs D's breathing was the only other noise to be heard. He sighed in relief as complete calm washed over him. He liked being alone these days. Besides now he could get some work done on that packet.

He usually worked at night when everyone else was asleep. It was slow going and the fact he didn't have a computer was really starting to hinder his progress. Sparking a blunt that he had ticked behind his ear, D leaned back in the couch and puffed contentedly away at the best thing that had never been invented. Mother earths own personally remedy for the stress that life caused. There was nothing in the world like weed!

"D?"

Looking up from where he had laid his head down in the kitchen table, D saw a familiar profile standing in the doorway. Rubbing his eyes, D yawned loudly and stretched.

"They gone already?"

Chanelle nodded.

"Was that the last one?"

She nodded again. Walking over she handed D a wad of bills.

"One hundred bucks! Damn you must really..." He fell quiet suddenly and shot a quick look in Chanelle's direction.

She was always the same afterwards. Never looking anyone on the face. Staring at the floor and holding herself tightly with her arms. D stared at her for a second longer. Standing up, he went over to her and touched her gently on the shoulder.

"Look go upstairs and wash up. What's that like three times you've showered today? You've got to be the cleanest female in the city!"

Chanelle smiled softly at his words but it quickly disappeared. There was honestly nothing D could think of to say to lessen the grief that her job gave her so he didn't say anything. Chanelle looked up at D and for a moment their eyes remained locked on each other as if speaking in a language that only their pupils understood.

Despite knowing exactly what she had just done, D couldn't help but to notice the perfect shape of her petite body and the beautiful perfectly imperfect face that looked out on the world with eyes too old for the body they inhabited. She nodded her head and walked away back down the hall towards the stairs. D watched her go, her hips swaying from side to side a slim round backside that seemed to be screaming at him to grab a hold of. But he kept himself in check. Now wasn't the time to start slipping.

Still, he became aware of a thought growing in the back of his head. If he would have been more advanced in the art of love or even just more emotionally aware, he would have realized that the feeling he had was that he wanted to show Chanelle some form of, appreciation. He just didn't have a clue about what to do.

As he heard the water turn on again upstairs, D was reminded of what exactly Chanelle was washing off of her body. But he didn't cringe or make a face. In fact, the obvious imperfection that was Chanelle was the entire reason he was drawn to her in the first place. He just didn't know the proper way to go about showing it. He was sure Money Mike wouldn't approve. But then again, Money Mike wasn't here.

A growling stomach let D know he was hungry and he would bet money that Chanelle would too. But what? Pizza? Chinese? There was nothing in the fridge as usual. And what about refreshments?

D put his brain to work. It would have to be pizza. He only had a limited time to prepare. The Safeway down the street would have that. As well as some other items he was thinking about purchasing to help brighten the occasion. As far as refreshments there were always bums outside the liquor store willing to help a soul in need in exchange for a tip! D checked his pocket. More than enough money! Fifteen seconds later, he was halfway up the block heading toward the illuminated street lanes that signaled lake city way.

Thirty minutes later…
"What in the hell is all this?" exclaimed Chanelle. D looked up from where he was busy pouring sprite into two plastic red cups.

"Oh wassup girl damn you took long enough! Look just grab a seat aight? The fucking cheesy bread should be warmed up in like thirty seconds."

Standing by the entrance to the kitchen, Chanelle wasn't sure she knew what was going on. The table had been cleared of its usual mess of baggies scales beer bottles and over stuffed ashtrays and was covered with a nice black table cloth. There were a stack of white paper plates and napkins arranged nicely around a fifth bottle of Hennessey and a sparkling clean ashtray lined with five pre rolled blunts. A single small candle was burning.

"D what the...?"

Standing up straight, D cut her off. He couldn't explain what had come over him but there was no going back now.

"Damn woman quit arguing and just take a seat. This is for you genius! Just cuz we ain't out at some dumb ass red robin don't mean we can't have a lil celebration ourselves. Now sit ya ass down!"

Walking away from the table, D pulled out the chair closest to Chanelle and made a sweeping gesture.

"C'mon now get ya fine ass in this chair goddammit of you make me burn the cheesy bread then I'm calling the whole thing off!"

Chanelle didn't know what to say or do. Except exactly what D told her.

Before she knew it a pizza and a side plate of cheesy bread were placed on the table along with their cups. D hit play on the stereo on the counter and immediately began rapping along with a familiar slick voiced rapper.

"Yeeeeeeeaaaaahhhhh, nigga what you about this? Rollers on D but they can't catch me slippin! He's mobbin down that Deuce Trey gas break dipping! Shaking the feds making the bread! ChingChing!"

"Nigga you ain't got no car," Chanelle said jokingly.

"Nope and who gives a fuck! I'm out here nigga!"

"C'mon D really? Dre is filthy and all but honestly right now? You had me thinking you was going somewhere completely different!"

D stopped bobbing his head. It was then he realized what was happing. What he should have done was be a player like

Money Mike and put on some slow jams to help set the mood. Instead here he was bumping gangster rap.

"Oops my bad. I just fuck with Mac Dre that's all. Lemme lighten the mood a little."

Chanelle reached across the table and grabbed one of the blunts out of the ashtray. Crossing her legs she sat back in the chair.

"I mean man my nigga The Bay is cool but take it down the coast a little bit and let's listen to a different Dre. You got the Chronic 2001!"

D looked at Chanelle like she had three eyes and two foreheads!

"Do I? Pass me that CD folder!"

One hour later…

D couldn't remember having this much fun. He couldn't explain what had come over him. After Chanelle had gone upstairs to shower, he had found himself running out of the house and headings towards Lake City Way. He and Chanelle had spent a relaxed hour eating talking and listing to music. D hadn't brought up the subject of Atlanta again. He told himself he'd wait until something actually happened. Meanwhile, he would just continue to save as much money as possible and keep stashing it in the house until it was time to go.

The bottle was now half empty and there were only two more blunts left. D and Chanelle had just finished rapping the song "housewife" together and now leaned side by side against the kitchen counter.

"   You rap a lot D? Like for real in studios?"

D looked over.

"Naw it ain't nothing like that. I just like rap. It's just fun to come up with stuff off top of your head and tell stories and make them rhyme. Why?"

"No reason. I heard Chris telling Jamie and Ashley that you guys were a rap group or something."

"Yeah or something," said D. "Don't listen to that fool if he says something involving me."

Chanelle sensed a shift in D's mood and immediately changed topic.

"Can you rap something for me? I've never heard you before. I mean like other than you just rapping the words to someone else's song."

D looked over. He didn't really want to but the liquor and weed in his system plus the fact that Chanelle was looking particular sexy right now helped him get over his nervousness.

"What you wanna hear?"

Chanelle took a sip from her cup.

"I don't know. You got anything for the ladies?"

D laughed softly and took a sip for himself.

"Naw not really. Well, I do got this one song I've been working on." He took a huge gulp of Hennysse and pointed at the ashtray.

"Light that blunt during the third verse so I can hit that shit when I'm done." D wiped his lips.

"I call this piece 'Never'. It's about a guy meeting a girl," he coughed once turned the radio down and began;

What's happening girl? You wanna ride with a G
Would you stay if I told you what these eyes have seen
If I picked you up would you switch sides with me
And show me how you work the wheel in these Sea town
streets
But first, I just need to get a taste of your mental
A feel for your attitude and look at your dentals
Nice waist, cute face, straight teeth and hair
You could've been walked by, I still smell you in the air
A pair? Yeah we different but the matchmaker closed
I'm hoping I can get a chance to tell you what I know
I aint asking you for much, just one chance
I aint asking you for love just some romance
Take a chance, I aint plotting on the ways to get in you
I'm telling you the truth I wanna know what you into
For too long I've fought the long arm of the law
Now I'm thinking with my head I'd never think of doing
you wrong

Cuz I aint never met a girl like you
One to teach and show me things I never thought true
Already set in my ways you made em brand new
I thought change was something to get used to
I never thought you could like a guy like ne
It seems like trouble and drama are all I ever meet
2 swishers some liquor no room for three
I got my eyes on you, you got your eyes on me

I'm liking the things you do, liking the way you move
Sexy with the strut cuz you know what that body do
Sneaky lil grin like you knew I was peeping you
Slowed when you passed like you knew I would speak to you
Dark brown eyes same color as Hershey bars
Caught me with your smile, you know how appealing you are
Early in the game I already noticed your frame
Curvaceous outline almost got me going insane
I see you seeing me too imagine the things we could do
The thoughts saying "what if?" but what if the feelings were true
Walked up and told you I was digging your style
You told me back, you liked the way I'm puffin the 'mild
You feeling wild? I'm feelin it too lets head back to my place
Like 2003, let's make use of my space
Whispers in my ear got seeing inside of your mind
I know how you want it, you wanna know how I want mines

Cuz I aint never met a girl like you
One to teach and show me things I never thought true
Already set in my ways you made em brand new
I thought change was something to get used to
I never thought you could like a guy like ne
It seems like trouble and drama are all I ever meet
2 swishers some liquor no room for three

245

I got my eyes on you, you got your eyes on me

Shit, I'm used to fights used to suspicions
Used to bad endings but you, you seem different
Smiling when you see me, chill when I come around
Throwing up the block, you she from the hometown
Grown and sexy cuz she oh so west
She likes me for me, she aint caring how I dress
Shit life is rugged I aint out here for nothing
Surrounded by chaos somehow she keeps me above it
No place I'd rather be, an eighth and some sweets
A fifth of that Hennessey in a whip it's just you and me
No title to this outing we just driving and getting lit
No time for the drama I'm surviving and getting rich
Street reflexes quick so you know you safe
Got a couple knucks for the punk tryna gain face
Let's ride out together all through the streets
We can get high together I got some good weed believe

Cuz I aint never met a girl like you
One to teach and show me things I never thought true
Already set in my ways you made em brand new
I thought change was something to get used to
I never thought you could like a guy like ne
It seems like trouble and drama are all I ever meet
2 swishers some liquor no room for three
I got my eyes on you, you got your eyes on me

"BUK BUK BUK!!!" D shouted as he ended his
rambunctious rap. Channel had been nodding her head even
though there had been no beat and looked thoroughly impressed.
     "You're kind of nice though I have to admit."
     D sat back down and waived away her comment.
     "Thanks but there ain't any future in rap for me. I just do
it for the people! I'm thinking about something else."
     Chanelle nodded her head and leaning down resting on
crossed arms. She stared at D with a mixture of wonder and

regret. He looked back at her, her hazel eyes trapping him in her stare. He could almost feel the room filling up with everything they weren't saying to each other. *Damn she's beautiful*, D thought to himself. What if he did get to go to Atlanta? And what if she did happen to come with him? What if he could just rewind time and go down to Tacoma and meet Chanelle before she ran away from home? She seemed to be thinking along the same lines as he was.

"What do you think would have happened if we'd have met under different circumstances?" she asked him softly.

D could only imagine.

Chapter 30

High on top of a bluff overlooking the still dark blue waters of Puget Sound, D and Breanna were relaxing with their backs against a log and a case of beers sitting on the ground between them. They were in Discovery Park, one of the biggest parks within Seattle's city limits. It had once been an active military base and several old buildings were still scattered throughout the grounds complete with an immense cemetery off to one side.

Despite the lack of military activity there were still some buildings that remained in use and there was still a section of the park that was closed off to the general public. The rest was free for anybody to come and enjoy. There were people walking their dogs, playing with their children and some just strolling by themselves admiring the beauty that nature provided. Even though it was in the middle of a city the high trees and dense forests blocked the sight of the tall downtown buildings in the distance and could make a person feel like they were miles from civilization.

Currently, D had gotten up and was standing several feet away from Breanna. He was almost at the edge of the cliff staring out at the view in front of him. Behind the dark swirling waters and islands directly across the sound the Cascade Mountains rose up into the sky silhouetted by the sun sinking low in the sky behind them.

The chill of the crisp breeze made D pull the hood of his sweatshirt tighter around his neck. The bite of the cold wind was tempered a little bit by the sun rays that occasionally peeked out from behind small clouds haphazardly dotting the afternoon sky.

Shaking the beer can he was holding, D turned and looked at Breanna.

"Excuse me bartender!? I'm all out and you over there getting way to friendly with the whiskey bottle! Can a young black man drink with ya or you gone keep me on this cheap ass beer?"

Taking one more swig, Breanna wiped her gorgeous lips and passed the bottle over to D along with a full can of beer. D tossed his empty can into a bag they were using for trash and opened up the bottle in a swift fluid motion. The whiskey felt good going down and D welcomed the warmth he felt flooding through his veins. He took one more sip and passed it back to Breanna looking up into her face at the same time.

He knew something was wrong. Breanna had called him that morning sounding shaken and had asked d to meet her ASAP with an ounce of weed! After telling Chanelle to take over operations while he was gone, D had practically ran out of the house. Breanna had picked him up at North Gate Mall with an open bottle of whisky in her hand and a cigarette in her mouth looking like she had just gotten into a fight. And knowing her husband, she probably had. They had sat in silence in the mall parking lot until D had suggested that they go somewhere to avoid funny questions from mall security.

He didn't remember who had suggested Discovery Park but now they were here deep along a secluded trail on a cliff top and he had never felt more at peace.

Breanna looked the exact opposite. Taking another sip of beer, D went back and sat beside her. He took a blunt from behind his ear and lit up.

"So, you want to tell me what happened?" he asked as gently as he could.

Breanna looked over at him and took a swig from her beer without saying anything. D shrugged and turned back to admire the view. He knew Breanna would tell him what was going on when she was ready. The sun was beginning to creep low in the sky outlining the cascades mountains majestic heights. Beside him, he heard Breanna move.

"I think he's cheating," she said simply. D didn't have to ask who she was talking about. It was obviously her husband Todd.

"Oh. Do you know who she is?"

"Some floozy at the office or a hooker but I'm positive he's cheating! He stays out all night and comes home smelling like alcohol and cheap perfume and doesn't even try to tell a good lie! I know he doesn't love me. So why do I still feel some type of way about him!"

D looked over at her out of the corner of his eyes. Breanna was staring at the ground drawing lines in the sand with a short stick. Her shoulders were slumped as if the very air around them was weighing down on her. She looked defeated. D frowned. He would have expected her to be jumping for joy.

"Umm Breanna?"

"Yes?"

"Well, I guess my question is if you're sure he doesn't love you or you him then wouldn't this be the instance where you make up your mind to finally leave him? He's basically giving you a get out of jail free card right now!"

Breanna was staring at the ground.

"I know, I know. Believe me dammit I know. It's all out there now. I just can't believe that after all this time and the effort I've put in and things I've put up with this is what it comes too. I've tried to be the best wife I could be! I cook for him I wash his fucking clothes I look fucking great and I work out all the time to stay this way. I try to give him his space and not bother him when he's tired. I do everything he wants me too in bed. So why the fuck does he treat me like this?"

D awkwardly took a big sip of whisky at these words and stayed quiet. Turning to look back out at the view in front of them, he waited a couple minutes while Breanna sniffed quietly to herself.

"I need to get out of Seattle," she said.

"Who you telling? Lately I feel as if I'm getting suffocated," D agreed.

"No I'm serious D. I need to get out of here like yesterday!"

"Me too Breanna. Serious as case of mouth herpes! And I need it just as bad as you do."

The two friends fell silent. D was bouncing a thought around his head and arrived at a conclusion. After a moment, he spoke.

"You know, I got a chance to go to a college down in Atlanta this fall."

Breanna stopped in her sniffing to look over at him in surprise.

"Really? That's wonderful D I'm so happy for you! But the last time we spoke it sounded like you were giving up on school. What changed your mind?"

She listened closely as D related what had happened during his visit to Seattle Central Community College.

"So if I can finish the packet on time and Mr. Brown can work his magic at the school then I should get accepted even though i don't have the grades."

"How much do you have left on the packet?"

D shook his head and took another sip of beer.

"Too much. It's basically a huge take home test but I don't have a computer so progress had been hella slow."

Beside him, Breanna blew out a long thin stream of smoke.

"I'd love to help you finish it D! If you'd like my help that is."

"I would love it if you did Breanna thanks!"

Breanna smiled sadly.

"Words I've never heard from my husband."

She passed the blunt to D and looked out over the water thinking to herself. Beside her, D puffed away on the blunt while admiring the still quiet beauty that only nature provided. He was excited about the prospect of getting out of Seattle and with Breanna's help he was sure he could get the packet done in time. So why was a piece of his mind still keeping him from calling Mr. Brown back?

Out of the jumble of thoughts running through his head an image immerged; Chanelle's perfect figure walking towards him with that sexy smile spreading across her lips. Rubbing his temples with his middle fingers, D began praying for solution to get Chanelle to come with him.

Looking at the tortured look on D's face, Breanna was worried about her young friend. She had never known a young person so mature and adult like before in her life. But it clearly came at a price. She didn't know the full details of what D did in his everyday life but from the hints he had dropped she figures it was anything but positive. They both needed a break from life. And that's when she had a sudden idea.

"Hey D, you ever been to San Francisco?"

D looked over slowly and passed her the blunt.

"The city with the Golden Gate Bridge and all the gay people? Nope. Haven't been anywhere outside of Seattle really. Why have you?"

Breanna nodded.

"My mom lives down there. She's a florist at this little flower shop in the Outer Sunset district right across from golden gate park. She lives right around the corner from her job and the ocean is just a couple blocks away! You should come with me!"

D looked around in surprise.

"Huh? You want me to come with you to San Francisco!"

Breanna blushed and looked away briefly hiding her face behind her long flowing blond hair. Tucking her hair behind her ears, she took a pull of the whisky then sipped her beer to wash down the bitter aftertaste. She eyed D closely for a few seconds before speaking.

"I'm only going for a couple of days. I just need to clear my head and San Francisco is the most wonderful and most beautiful place I've ever been to. It's just so colorful down there from the food to the people. You just can't help but feel, happy. Besides my mom who I'm always happy to see there's the real nice beach I just like to sit on and watch the waves come in and think. Or not think. But I think it would do you some good and anyways you're not exactly a stranger. I trust and respect you D. If you don't want to come that's done I just thought I would ask. It could be fun."

D scooped up the whisky bottle and took a quick gulp while his mental gears were grinding inside his head.

"Your mom wouldn't feel weird about me staying at her house?"

Breanna laughed loudly.

"Boy I'm getting a god damn hotel! My mom's good for a conversation but her partying days are way behind her. No wine bottles for me please I need fifths of bourbon and some swisher sweets!"

"I hear that," said D.

He rested his arms on his knees and stared at the calm swaying of Puget Sound far below. He really could use a couple days away from that damn suffocating house!

"When are you going?" asked D.

"The week after next."

"Damn thanks for the short notice!"

Breanna blew out a thick cloud of smoke.

"I know I'm sorry. But I need to go ASAP! Not even Todd can stop me! I understand if you can't make it."

D frowned thinking hard. And just like that his mind was made up.

"You know what, fuck it! It's not every day a nigga gets to see a new city! Give me a couple days I just gotta work some things out."

Breanna smiled. A small sad smile that didn't do her beautiful face justice. Reaching out, D gently and awkwardly patted her shoulder. Still looking out over the water, Breanna's hand grasped D's in a tight grip and kept if there on her left shoulder. The two friends stayed like that for another hour until D realized it was time to get back to reality. But if he could just hold out a little longer maybe soon the paranoia, anger, violence and Seattle in general would soon be just a distant memory.

Back in Lake City...

"Man don't worry about where I was just hurry up and go to the store!"

"Nigga hold up! You the one that's been gone all day doing whatever the fuck you be doing out there. All the business is here bro you ain't even got a reason to be leaving for hours and hours!"

253

D spread his arms wide.

"Umm excuse me! Are we in jail? Look around Chris, I don't see no fucking steel doors or no gotdamn police! We stay up in here all week long you telling me getting out every now and then is against the rules? I ain't nobody's slave!"

Chris shook his head.

"Oh so you a shot caller now huh? We here to a job D don't forget that shit! You ain't superman nigga so stop acting like it. If you got a problem then tell Money Mike and quit arguing with me fool! You been here damn near half a year! Don't start acting brand new now! If you don't like making money then bounce!"

D stopped himself from responding. He couldn't let Chris in on his plan to leave all of this behind. The two boys glared at each other for a few seconds longer neither wanting to be the first to back down. Finally, Chris snorted in disgust and turned around heading for the front door.

"Where you going nigga?" D called out as Chris opened the door.

"Out nigga I ain't a slave! It's your turn to watch the fucking crib!" The door slammed and D listened to the sound of Chris footsteps marching down the front porch stairs.

Sucking his teeth, D turned and walked up the stairs to the girl's room. He knocked once and then opened the door.

Ashley and Jamie were sitting on Ashley's bed with several different colored wigs laid out between them.

"Girl I think this one makes me look like Beyoncé what you think?"

"Yeah it's ok. You really want all that red in there though? And those bangs is almost covering your eyes they're so long."

"Ugh your right! Pass me those scissors!"

D poked his head into the room.

"Man don't neither one of you bitches look like Beyoncé! Ain't no video cameras up in here! What you think? Hova aint bout to come walking through that door!" He cracked up laughing at his own joke. Ashley made a face and Jamie just flipped him off.

"Whateva nigga please these tricks pay top dollar for this pussy!" said Jamie.

"Yeah well hurry up and make the money so you can give it to me then! Chris just bounced so it's just me right now. Where's Chanelle at?"

"Yeah we heard him slam the door," replied Jamie, "Chanelle's in the bathroom taking a shower. You staying in tonight?"

D nodded.

"Yeah I'm here. Been trying to take care of some shit that's why I've been making all these runs. Y'all got any business I need to know about or something y'all need?"

Jamie shook her head but Ashley spoke up.

"I got a customer coming in about an hour but it's looking slow the rest of the evening."

D nodded to himself and glanced down the hallway towards the bathroom. He thought of going to say hi to Chanelle but decided against it. He's see her when she was done washing up. He turned back to Ashley and Jamie.

"All right then y'all, I'll be in the kitchen if you need me. Lemme know when that guy is supposed to arrive so I can let him in aight?"

Ashley nodded. D waved at the two girls then headed back downstairs.

When he reached the kitchen, he set about checking that each drawer had its designated amount of drugs or money. Then he checked his own stash that he had hidden behind the oven. In the almost six months that he had been in Lake City, D had been able to stack up over fifteen thousand dollars. The pay he received from Money Mike added with the money he got from skimming off the drugs Money Mike provided him and the profits he received from the weed he was selling were bringing in hundreds every few days.

For a moment, he sat gazing at the small pile of money. Fifteen thousand dollars was a lot of money to make in just six months. Nowhere near what any corporate white collar worker would make in the same amount of time. But D had no job experience no references degrees or certificates of any kind. To him fifteen thousand dollars was a hell of a lot of money. More than he'd ever had in his life. Was he really going to leave this kind of money behind?

Footsteps coming down the staircase jerked D out of his thoughts. Stashing his money back behind the oven, he sat back down and began acting nonchalant, taking a swisher out of his pocket and beginning to break it down the middle.

There were footsteps in the hallway and Ashley entered the kitchen looking stunning and ready for work in matching black bra and panties with delicate black shawl draped around her shoulders.

"My guys almost here" she said quickly before disappearing back down the hallway and entering one of the bedrooms. D quickly broke down a couple nuggets of weed and rolled up his blunt super-fast.

"Aww man that shits hella ugly," he scolded himself when he had finished rolling and held the crooked blunt up to his eyes. "That's why you take your fucking time D, you fucking asshole."

Suddenly the doorbell rang. Getting up, D stuck the blunt behind his ear and walked to the door. Opening it, he was confronted by an older black man in a very shabby suit who looked as if he'd been up for a couple days and was actually familiar to D. He'd sold him crack on occasion and it was strange to now see him at the other end of the house about to make a deal with a prostitute.

"Hey, brother where's that other Youngblood at?"
D sniffed. The man stank and something about him was making D frown. Not only were the man's clothes dirty and shabby but something in the man's eyes didn't sit right with D. He was constantly shifting about and couldn't seem to keep still for more than two seconds. He seemed on the verge of collapsing or blowing up.

"Don't worry 'bout that, I'm here and that's all that matters. You got money bro?"

From inside his pocket the man withdrew a wad of bills.

"I'm just down on my luck brother i didn't mean no harm. Chris is my man baby I was just checking. You know me man I'm all right!"

D relaxed a little at the sight of the money. Behind him he heard Ashley coming down the hallway.

"Aight mane come on."

D let the man in.

"Oh hey Ronald baby how you doing?" said Ashley. So that was his name! Walking up and putting a hand around his waist, she steered him down the hallway towards the room she was using tonight.

"It's bad tonight Ash, I'm in a bad place," the man named Ronald babbled out. Ashley kissed him on the cheek.

"Well come on inside here and let's talk about it." She whispered. The door closed. D watched them go. Sitting down on the couch, he picked up one of the note books that were scattered across the coffee table and a pen. He flipped the book open and began working on a rap he had started a couple days ago.

Sometime later…

THUMP! THUMP!

Jerking awake, D looked around trying to catch his bearings. He was in the living room of the trap house with the note book spread open across his chest. At first nothing seemed wrong until he became aware of a dull pounding that was coming from the room Ashley and the man had gone into. D frowned. Why the hell were they being so loud?

Rubbing his eyes he stretched and then froze as an ear splitting scream erupted out of the bedroom.

"Aaaaahhhhhhhhhh!!!"

Instantly, D came awake. Looking around wildly, he realized the sounds were coming from the bedroom Ashley had taken her customer too. Jumping up off the couch he ran to the bedroom door.

"Hey open the fuck up!" He yelled out pounding on the door with his fist.

"What the fuck y'all doing in there?"

Then came the sound of a struggle and breaking glass from inside the room.

"GET OFF OF ME!" Ashley screamed out! Immediately D knew that something bad was happening. Backing up against the wall, D ran forward and kicked the door right beside the handle with all his might!

BAM!!!

The door flew back on its hinges and bounced against the wall. Barging into the room, D saw Ashley and the old black man engaged in a violent struggle. He had one hand around her neck and the other was trying to stop Ashley's swinging fists from doing too much damage to his face.

Without stopping to think, D threw himself into the fray! Grabbing Ronald from behind in a bear hug d pulled him off Ashley and threw him into the corner. As he was struggling to get up D kicked him viciously in the face! Thinking Ronald was down, D turned back to Ashley. She was on the bed with her hands around her throat struggling to catch her breath and shaking. D was panting hard.

"You ok?" Ashley's eyes were bugging out of her head and she was shaking he made to move towards her when she suddenly screamed and her arm pointed at something directly behind D. He was caught completely unaware as Ronald got up and came in low and fast.

Whump!

D was football tackled into the far wall banging the side of his head on the hard wood! Gripping D around the waist with freighting strength in his arms, Ronald propelled d around and into the hallway slamming the D against the wall again. Struggling to get around D began swinging desperately at Ronald's unprotected head. Immediately, Ronald let go of D's waist and came up swinging hard and fast!

WHAP WHAP WHAP!

D took three hard connecting punches to the head and face! And it hurt! D was scared by the hardness of Ronald's hits. His ears immediately started ringing! He was shaken by the ferocity of the old man and just got his hands up as Ronald came in again.

"ASHLEY RUN!!!!" D screamed out before throwing up his arms to protect himself anyway he could. Ronald eyes were wide red veined and seemed to be on the verge of popping out of his head. He had to be on some hard drugs. Ronald's blows came in hard and furious. D's mouth was full of blood and his face was quickly swelling up from the beating he was taking.

In attempt to gain the upper hand, D wrapped an arm around Ronald's throat and attempted to choke him while punching him hard in the kidneys. It was like Ronald's didn't feel it. D was thrown to the floor and Ronald was immediately on top of him. He felt two big hands grab the back of his head.

CRACK!

Pain exploded in D's brain as Ronald slammed his head face first into the hardwood floor with terrifying force. D scrambled to dislodge Ronald from his back but his strength was no match. He saw the floor towards him again.

CRACK!

This time a horrible gash opened up on his temple and blood immediately began to flow down his face and onto the floor. His left eye was closing and D was growing disoriented from the pain. He thought he heard footsteps above him. The girls! Where the fuck was Chris and Money Mike? He struggle to turn over but Ronald grabbed his head again and slammed it down on the floor a third time.

CRACK!

This time D went limp. Ronald let go of D's head and punched him hard in the side. D groaned but didn't move. He was still on the floor his face in a pool of blood with one eye completely swollen shut and while face bruised and cut. He was dimly aware of Ronald looking down at him as if thinking about the best way to finish the job.

Suddenly a scream rang out!

"Oh my god! Damien!"

Ronald and D both looked towards the sound of the voice. D squinted through one battered eye. It was Chanelle! D tried to yell out a warming but Ronald punched him hard in the face splitting his lips.

Chanelle was frozen in her footsteps until she saw the man called Ronald look up and stare at her with his crazy bugged out eyes. Chanelle had seen that same look in many men's faces before.

With a lurch, Ronald was up and running down the hall towards her. Panicking, Chanelle ran back up the stairs with Ronald right behind her.

Lying on the floor coughing and spitting blood, D struggled to fight his way past the fog of pain clouding his system. He could hear horrible loud noises coming from upstairs as if an exorcism was taking place. He had to help Chanelle. Struggling with all his might, D lifted himself up and limped down the hallway to the living room. Going to the couch with the guns, he lifted up the cushion and picked up the pump action Mossberg.

Pumping a shell into the chamber, D headed slowly up the stairs banging into the wall as his vision went in and out of focus and he struggled to keep from passing out. Reaching the top of the stairs, he stopped for a minute to catch his breath. There was an animal like growling coming from the room at the end of the hallway coupled with the high pitched screams that were obviously coming from a female. It was Chanelle's room! And the door was still open! The screams suddenly stopped but there were still loud grunts and the sound of the bed posts scraping against the floor.

Limping quickly down the hallway and still trying to block out the horrible pain his body was in, D shouldered his was into the room. He froze as he eyes adjusted to the scene in front of him.

Ronald had his back to d and his pants down around his ankle. Chanelle was lying on the bed with her face towards the door not making a sound or offering any resistance as Ronald stood over her. The bed was shaking and moving around as Ronald viciously thrust himself in and out of her! Blood was dripping onto the sheets from between channels legs but as D stared completely unprepared and horrified by what he was seeing he realized why Chanelle didn't appear to be struggling.

Her unblinking eyes stared sightlessly back at D as he stood in the doorway. Her tongue was hanging out of her mouth and she wasn't breathing. That's when D saw her neck. It was twisted almost impossibly far over and he suddenly became aware a foul smell in the room. Her bowels had released. Piss and shit dripped across the sheets and still Ronald continued his assault. She was dead. D staggered back against the door as the realization hit him. The sound caused Ronald to turn his head and look around him.

"HEY BOY YOU BACK FOR SOME MORE?" Ronald shouted out as he stared at D with that maniacal look in his eyes as he continued to fuck Chanelle's dead body. D could only stare. His mouth refused to open. His mind was blank and there was a loud roaring in his ears that prevented him from hearing anything Ronald had just said. He just stared as Ronald' continued to plunge his erect penis into Chanelle's ass even though it was now covered in blood and shit. D could almost feel his insides crumbling within him and his heart had jumped so much it felt like he was gripping it between his teeth. Ronald turned around and looked at D again. He pulled out and turned to face D, his dick still dripping with Chanelle's bodily fluids.

"Well if all you gonna do is stare how bout you come join in the fun?" said Ronald. His mouth was foaming and he looked almost like a rabid dog. D tightened his grip on the shot gun in his hands. Ronald looked from the gun in D's hand to his face.

"Don't do it." D finally found enough strength to gasp out. Ronald only laughed loudly stepped out of the pants crumpled around his ankles and rushed at D suddenly and without warning. But D was ready. Up came the Mossberg barrel!

BOOM!

Sometime later…

Money Mike and Chris arrived back at the house at the same time. Money Mike was in the middle of severely cussing Chris out for leaving when Ashley and Jamie came running out of the house screaming. Unable to calm them down, Money

Mike left then in the car and he and Chris ran inside. The scene they discovered upstairs chilled both of then to the bone. Ronald's body was stretched out across the doorway. His head was a mess of blood bone and muscle tissue, most of it having been plastered across the wall behind him. D, looking like he just been beaten half to death was sitting on the floor next to Ronald's body with the shotgun still in his hands and a blank expression on his face as he stared at Chanelle's lifeless body draped across the bed.

They couldn't get D out of his trance. Money Mike instructed Chris to take him outside to the waiting car. Once D was leaning against the car with Ashley and Jamie looking after him, Chris ran back into the house to help Money Mike. Together they gathered the guns and cleaned out the kitchen drawers of all the drugs and money. They missed D's stash behind the oven.

Next they doused the entire interior of the house in gasoline. Making a trail out to the front yard, Money Mike lit a match and dropped it on the ground.

Whoosh!

Instantly the gasoline ignited and a trail of fire quickly raced away into the house following the path of flammable liquid.

"Ok we gotta get the fuck outta here right now everybody in the car!" Money Mike ordered. The girls helped D into the passenger seat then everyone else hopped in. As they sped away down the block, D looked in the rear view morrow at the reflection of the flaming house.

Chanelle and Ronald weren't the only things turning to ash in the cool fall night. D's cheat was on fire. And he thought he knew exactly why. His soul was burning.

Chapter 31

Knock knock knock!!!

Looking though the peephole, Latoya scowled deeply upon seeing who it was but opened the door none the less.

"Wassup Latoya where's..."

"Shhhh!"

Latoya silenced Chris immediately and ushered him inside the house. Closing and locking the door, Latoya pointed Chris towards the kitchen.

"So how he's doing?" Chris asked. Latoya nodded her head at the ceiling.

"He's as good as he can be! It's only been a week! Why the fuck did you leave him alone in the house in the first fucking place!"

"Man he had left me alone in their plenty of times before this. That could be up there just as much as him!"

"But it's not you so shut up and lower your voice! He took a pretty bad beating trying to protect whatever you had him up there doing. But was it fucking worth it? Ask yourself that!"

Chris fell silent.

"So how is he really?" he asked after several quiet moments. Latoya leaned against the counter.

"He still hasn't said a word even after a week. I got him cleaned up as much as I could. That old dude really messed him up."

"Yeah we found a funky smelling pipe in his pocket. Meth or something else foul. D took care of him though! Blew his fucking brains all over the room! He made that dude pay for killing that girl."

Latoya sneered at Chris.

"What about the girl, Chris? You see what happens when you get innocent people wrapped up in this bullshit lifestyle you and money mike love so much? They die or get fucking scarred for life from the things you make them do! Anthony's dead! Whop is in prison! D is lying fucked up in my spare bedroom upstairs and almost looks dead! That poor girl got killed and burned to a crisp in a fucking bullshit trap house! Even you almost got killed in front of your own crib! When will the shit fucking stop already!"

In the heat of the moment, Latoya's voice had risen about five octaves and the sound of a lil boy crying crept into the room from upstairs.

"Great you woke up my lil prince! What the fuck do you want Chris?"

Chris, usually cocky and self-assured found himself for the first time at a loss for words.

"Well?" Latoya looked at him expectantly.

"I...I just wanted to say wassup to D right quick. Tomorrow's his birthday and shit you know?"

"Yes I do know and you come back and say wassup then. Now leave. He needs his sleep!"

Upstairs in the spare bedroom Latoya had, D was lying awake listening to the raised voices below. He heard the door slam then Latoya coming up the stairs and going into her son's room. He listened as she gently soothed him back into a state of calm serenity. Safe from the problems if the world in his mother's arms, Anthony Jr's cries soon subsided.

D was grateful Latoya had gotten rid of Chris. Lying still under heavy covers, he had stayed like that for eight days straight not speaking and barely eating. His mind was a tornado of dark thoughts and emotions. Images were replaying in his head like a horror movie that he couldn't stop watching.

Ronald pounding away at Chanelle's dead body. The explosion of blood, brains and bone as the shotgun shells tore Ronald's face off. The sight of Chanelle's broken neck. It was too much to handle. His brain had shut down.

D gently touched his face. Under Latoya's care the swelling had gone down and his cuts were healing nicely. But he still felt dead inside.

Chanelle was gone. He wasn't sure how to describe his feelings for her but it was painfully apparent that without her his life didn't feel the same. Or maybe it was everything he'd been through.

What was he? Who was he?

He'd committed unthinkable acts of violence all in the name of a group of people he honestly barely knew and what did he have to show for it?

Chris and Money Mike hadn't known about D's secret stash and as such hadn't removed it from behind the oven. It was gone now. Burned to ashes. Over fifteen thousand dollars!

He had had several futures snatched tonight out of his hands in a matter of minutes. Now even thoughts of Atlanta couldn't even make him feel better at this moment. Breanna's San Francisco trip was a couple days away as he still hadn't called her. He didn't deserve to get away.

He hadn't cried throughout his ordeal. He didn't know if he had enough emotion inside him to do such a thing anymore. He turned his head and stared at the wall. He knew now he's made the biggest mistake of his life ever getting involved in the inner workings of Deuce Trey. But it was too late to be anything else. He closed his eyes and found himself wishing karma would catch up with him quickly. Or a bullet to the head.

The next morning...

"D! Yo D! Wake up nigga happy motherfucking birthday!"

D's eyes slowly opened. As his pupils adjusted to the dark gloom he could make out Chris sitting on the foot of the bed. Rubbing sleep out of his eyes, D sat up and scooted back until his back was against the wall. He stared silently at Chris with no emotion in his eyes. After a moment, Chris held up a fat pre rolled blunt and a lighter.

"I brought you your favorite weed mane! Purple Kush and there's like a dub inside here! I bet you ain't smoked since you know...never mind that nigga here spark up!"

He held the blunt and a lighter out towards D. After a still few seconds, he took them. Without looking at Chris, D held the blunt up to his nose and took a sniff. It was definitely some Purple Kush. Sticking the blunt in his mouth he lit it and took a deep pull while closing his eyes.

"Sooo, what's up D? You looking like your healing good."

D remained silent.

"C'mon nigga don't do this silent treatment shit! I'm sorry I left but I was hella hot! You'd been leaving me alone in that damn house and you wasn't even saying where you were going. We supposed to be closer than that!"

D took another long hit then held the blunt out to Chris. Chris took it gazing for a second at D's battered face then looked away the floor.

"Damn D. I honestly didn't mean for you to get fucked up like that. You just been walking round like you were the shit and I got pissed off. I guess though it's cuz you used to be kind off timid. I'm glad to see you hardening up. I guess you just shocked me with how far you came."

D was still gazing at him with the same expressionless look not saying a word. Chris passed him back the blunt and looked d straight in the eyes.

"I'm sorry D. I'm sorry bout Ronald's bitch ass and Chanelle and for leaving like that. But at least you killed that nigga! He won't do any crazy shit like that again. You blew a niggaz head off for the set! That's the biggest thing you can do you bout to get hella respect! "

Still, D gave no indication that'd he heard anything that Chris was saying. Just inhaled and exhaled the strong grey smoke then held it out for Chris. Chris sighed heavily.

"Look homie I know you're pissed at me! I've been thinking about what you were saying about us not doing anything about Anthony's killer. So I've been in the streets doing hella research and I got something that maybe will make you feel better."

D's face stayed completely emotionless and he made no movement. So Chris continued.

"I found out where Devontay lives."

At this D's eyes narrowed but other than that he still made no movement.

"He stays over by Judkins Park on Irving Street. It's him and his grandma and a couple uncles or something. Took a whole bunch of sneaking around playing street detective but I did it. And I saw him too so I know he's there."

"Now I already talked to Money Mike about this. You know what he told me?"

D said nothing.

"He told me that if we can take out Devontay then both you and me will be promoted to lieutenants! That means no more errand running cause we'd be the ones telling others what to do! No more standing on the front lines taking all the risks! And Anthony can rest in peace finally knowing we got the nigga who killed him!"

By this time the blunt had gone out. D and Chris sat in silence for a few moments. Then, Chris stood up and turned to face D.

"I know you didn't want all This to happen. Shit I know you wasn't even really tryna get down with Deuce Trey. But shit happened the way it did and now were here. No one made you fight that nigga at that party. You did that all by yourself. We saved you from getting jumped that night so don't blame me for everything. The shit happened at the Lake City house was fucked up too but it happened and it's done. This life air pretty and shit like that happens. True we should have looked for Devontay way before this but shit we got him now. You started this D. It's time to take responsibility for your actions and finish what you started.

"You won't have to do shit after that anyways. We'll be sitting pretty giving orders and collecting dues. I'll let you think about what you wanna do. Me and Money Mike will be by later. We got a bottle and an ounce of Kush and a big ass chocolate cake for you that Latoya made. Damn, I shouldn't have said that!" Chris laughed awkwardly. D stared back at him still unmoving.

"Well aight D I'll holla later. Maybe then you can tell me what you tryna do. Happy Birthday nigga!"

Then he was gone. D listened to him descending the stairs and the front door open and close. The strong weed was making him sleepy. Lying back down in the bed, D closed his eyes, his mind racing! It was true what Chris had said. D had started all this. And everything that had happened was his punishment. He opened his eyes and stared at the dark ceiling.

After all the bad things he'd done, maybe it was time to a bad thing for a greater good. It was obvious to D that he might never escape this life of violence and danger. Since he was already waist deep why not end it by actually doing what he set out to do in the first place?

Devontay would finally get what was coming to him. But not because of the rewards promised. But because it was the only thing that made sense to him anymore. An eye for an eye. A death for a death!

D wasn't stupid. If they killed Devontay then that meant FEB would be out for blood as well. Someone from deuce Trey would die and then someone from FEB would have to go. A never ending cycle.

D sighed painfully aware that his own death could be waiting just around the corner. The strange thing was though, he almost welcomed it.

He laid awake the rest of the night thinking.

Chapter 32

"There it is my nigga. It's that blue house right In the middle of the block. The one with the big bush in the yard!"

Sitting inside an old grey Chevrolet Caprice, D looked down the street at the house Chris was pointing at.

"Yeah I see it."

"Who would have thought he stayed here on Irving Street? I been over here hella times fucking around at this park and I've never seen him out here."

"Maybe he just got over here."

"Well whatever the reason he's here now. So what you think? Should we wait to catch him outside and blast him? Or should we sneak in the house and catch him slipping in his bed on some assassination shit?"

D quietly gazed down the street at the house. Killing Ronald had been different. D had been scared for his life. Now he was here calculating the best way to kill another teen in cold blood. On the outside he was resolved and unemotional as he looked out the window at what was supposed to be Devontay's house.

"You're positive he stays here?" D asked, looking over at Chris. "I'm not tryna run up into some innocent family's home"

"Positive," replied Chris immediately. "The info is good."

D looked back down at the house thinking hard.

"Ok look! If we wait to catch him outside there's no telling when he's gonna leave the house. We could be here for days if he's being careful about what he does. There is a fucking war going on. We should come back at night, sneak in the house and see if we can get inside and find his bedroom. One shot to the head and we get the fuck outta there fast! Do you know where he sleeps?"

"Naw didn't get that far but this is definitely the right house! Your plan sounds solid anyways. Who's going in?"

"I am," said D with no hesitation, "I started this shit so I'ma finish it. Just keep the fucking engine running cuz I'm bout to dip out there fast!"

Chris nodded silently.

"Aight man let's get out of here before we start looking suspicious. We'll come back later tonight and finish this shit!"

Pulling away from the curb, Chris made a U-turn and headed back towards his house.

"Eh look I'ma stop at the red apple right quick I need some shit for the house."

D was skeptical.

"Bro are you sure you wanna go to the promenade? We might run into some niggaz up there man I'm tryna stay low so tonight goes smooth."

"Then stay in the car nigga," said Chris. "The burners under your seat so if something do go down that's where you reach."

D just looked out the window. Subtlety was not something Chris was very good at. He didn't even see the benefit of avoiding problems now to handle a bigger problem later. D didn't bother praying to The Lord that they made it safely through the day. He knew his wishes would go unheard.

Pulling into the red apple parking lot, Chris left the keys in so D could play the radio and hopped out. Pulling his sagging pants up, he ran inside the store. Not hearing anything he liked on the radio, D turned it off. Sitting back in the wide comfy seat, D looked out the window at the various people moving throughout the parking lot. Old ladies. Mothers, young and old followed by their children. It was the teenagers that D was looking at but so far he hadn't seen any hostile faces. He began to relax a little.

270

A few rows over a mini van parked and two older women got out then helped a large boy with a droopy face get out of the back seat. They handed him two crutches and then began slowly making their way towards the Red Apple's front door. Something about the boy's big physique made D stop and look at him more closely. Then he realized who he was looking at. D was in shock! It was Sumo!

Except why did he have that droopy expression on his face and why was he walking with crutches? Then In a shocking moment Sumo turned and looked directly at D. They locked eyes through the window. But there was no recognition behind Sumo's pupils. Even as D tensed up, Sumo looked away and off at something else one of the women was pointing at. He stopped to stare off into the distance at something but then the women gently began pointing him back in the direction of the store. They walked off slowly. D was dumbfounded.

Shortly after, Chris came walking out of the store holding a small bag of groceries. After he got inside the car, D told him what he had just witnessed. Chris nodded his head and shrugged.

"That's why Whop got locked up you don't remember? Socked that big ass nigga in the head a few good times with the brass knuckles. He was saving your ass if I remember the story right!

"Yeah Sumo had me up against the wall punching the hell out of me. What's up with the crutches and blank stare?"

"Well, word is he left the hospital with brain damage. Can't walk or talk the same anymore. Think his memory got wiped clean too. Anyways he's nothing to trip about now so don't worry about him. Fucker probably can't even wipe his own ass."

As Chris started the engine and pulled out of the Red Apple parking lot, D sat in silence, staring out of the window. He could see it clear as day now. Violence solved nothing. Just got people hurt beyond the point of no return. It had to stop. He had to do something. But what? It was already too late to stop what had already been set in motion.

That night…

"You lil niggaz ready!" asked Money Mike.

Chris was almost bouncing on his heels he looked so excited. D looked up at Money Mike. His face was deadly serious. There was no mercy in his eyes.

"Hell yeah bro this niggaz gone! We should dip right now though it's been past time."

Money Mike nodded then looked back at D.

"You ready young gunner?"

D peered into Money Mikes ruthless stare. Even Money Mike didn't scare him now.

"Yeah." He knew what he had to do.

"Then lets fucking be out nigga!" hollered Chris

Leaving the house like shadows in the night, D and Chris circled the block to find the stolen car money mike had described to them. It had been stolen by some younger Deuce Trey members earlier that day. Getting inside, they found the pistols under their seats and checked them. Chris had a 40. Caliber high point while D's gun was a 9mm black Beretta.

Starting the engine, Chris pulled out and headed towards Judkin's Park. The drive was a quiet one. With no loud music to draw attention to them, the two teens sat side by side each with their own thoughts. It was almost midnight. The dark streets of the Central District were absent of people and they only passed a few other cars. Between now and morning all activity on the street would stop. These were the killing hours.

As they reached Irving Street and Chris pulled over hitting the lights.

'You ready D?" Chris asked. His voice was low and menacing. D took a giant sip from a whiskey bottle they had picked up earlier that day for this very purpose. D didn't even fling at the bitter taste. He picked up his gun and put his hand on the door handle. Chris grabbed his shoulder as he was about to leave. D looked over at him with narrowed eyes.

"Look D, this is for Anthony. It got nothing to do with anything else. Just do it and get the fuck outta there aight! He killed the homie man, he don't deserve to take another breath! I'll be right here."

272

D looked at Chris for a second longer nodded silently and pulled a ski mask over his head then exited the car gently closing the door behind him, D looked up and down the dark quiet street looking at house windows and Inside cars to make sure there were no people around. Curtains were drawn and cars were empty.

Creeping low across the street, D didn't stop moving until he was hiding behind a bush growing on the side of Devontay's house. He stopped to catch his breath and evaluate his progress. He had made it so far without being detected. Now he just had to get inside.

Suddenly there was the sound of a door opening and closing. D froze. Someone had just exited the house and was now standing on the front yard. There came the rustling of clothes and then the distinct sound of a lighter being flicked. Then came the smell of tobacco.

Whoever it was they were smoking a cigarette and therefore probably in a moment of relaxation. D brought his gun up holding it tightly in his hands. His palms were sweating with anticipation and he realized it was now or never. If it wasn't Devontay then he would knock them out with the gun and enter on the house through the front door. If there was anyone else on the house, they'd figure it was just the cigarette smoker coming back inside.

D counted silently to three then stood up and quickly ran around the bush into the front yard with his pistol up in front of him. And came face to face with Devontay himself!

Devontay's face was a mask of surprise as he suddenly found himself staring down the barrel of a gun. One moment he had been calmly enjoying his last cigarette of the night and he next he had a pistol in his face. The cigarette slipped between his fingers and dropped to the ground. Devontay looked past the barrel into the cold eyes of the masked man who had suddenly appeared in his front yard and knew he would find no mercy. The eyes behind that mask were cold and lifeless. He swallowed hard. He only had one chance.

"Eh look man i don't know who you are but I'm pretty sure I know what this is about. You're from Deuce Trey right? I was wondering how long it was going to take y'all to find me."

Devontay held is hands out to either side to show he had nothing else in them. His eyes flickered from left to right searching for a passing car or some sort of salvation approaching that would save him from this deadly situation. None came. Quickly he realized his past actions had finally caught up with him. There was nothing left to do but come clean. He had been waiting a long time to tell somebody his truth. He stared at the masked man in front of him.

"Ok look, I know your here to kill me for what I did to Anthony."

WHAP!

As soon as is friends name had left Devontay's mouth D had cocked his arm back and brought his pistol crashing down on Devontay's face! The force of the blow broke his nose and knocked Devontay to the ground. Rolling over on his back holding his face, Devontay let the pain wash over him like a refreshing morning shower. D stood over him pressing the gun to the side of his head. But Devontay was surprisingly calm.

"Do it," he whispered out of the corner of his mouth. D only stared back at him. His finger didn't move.

"I know you probably don't believe me bit I didn't mean to kill Anthony that night. I was trying to get the guy he stood in front of. That fucker had raped my sister and I was going to make him pay. I know Anthony was just trying to stop the fight. But I had already pulled the trigger. I would take it back if I could. I didn't know he had a kid. Believe me, I haven't slept good since that night. I always see his face when I close my eyes.

"I would've turned myself over to you guys but you know my cousin Trouble, he likes violence. He told me never to be sorry or he'd cut my fingers off so I could never do something like that again and never feel sorry again. But I don't care anymore. I hate this life and everything that comes with it. So do me a favor and just kill me nigga. Get this shit over with. Maybe then these demons will stop bothering me," finishing his statement, Devontay laid his head on the ground and closed his eyes.

D was still. Devontay's last words had eerily echoed his own feelings. He wanted to die. To curl up and rid himself of the feelings and faces that haunted his sleep at night. But how many others were like him? Innocent boys caught up in wars and rivalries they had absolutely no control over. Losing friends to death before losing their first girlfriend to a breakup was no way to live. It was vicious cycle that he saw now would never stop. A life for a life. No matter how Devontay felt about his death someone would be out tomorrow trying to avenge it. Killing Devontay, while maybe justified would bring no peace. D lowered his weapon. Devontay opened one eye and looked up, surprised he was still alive. D knelt down beside him and spoke quickly into his ear.

"Look you muthafucka, Anthony was my best friend. Killing him was the worst thing that ever happened to me. I joined Deuce Trey because of that and now my life has practically been ruined because of my decisions. But I did it to myself. The hate this life makes you feel is more powerful than anything I've ever known. But I got a chance to get the duck out and I'm gonna take it. I'm not gonna kill you. I should but I won't. I don't need your face creeping in my head like my friend does to you. Live with your fucking filthy act."

Devontay kept deathly still. He couldn't believe what he was hearing but he didn't want to do anything to change the masked man's mind.

"So what do we do from here?" he asked.

D looked around quickly. He was out of sight of the car but he knew Chris was waiting to hear the sound of gunshots. He looked back down at Devontay.

"Look nigga we came here to kill you and everybody in that house tonight. I got a Patna waiting down the block that wants to personally out holes in you himself. This is what's gonna happen, I'm going to stand up and shoot into the ground right next to you. Lie absolutely fucking still do not move for anything. Once you hear a call pull off and the block is silent get up and run! Get the fuck out of Seattle man run as far as you can! I'm getting outta here too cuz once they find out I didn't kill you there gonna be after your head and mines."

"Thank you! I don't know what to say man!" Devontay gasped out. D looked down at him pressing the barrel of the gun into Devontay's cheek.

"This ain't for you bitch nigga. It's for me. Killing you ain't gonna bring my friend back. Anthony wouldn't have wanted this either. Now don't fucking move."

D stood up quickly and pointed the gun at Devontay's head. Devontay closed his eyes and for a brief second d almost shot him right through the temple. Instead, he moved his gun several inches to the right and pulled the trigger.

BANG BANG!

D quickly fired into the ground and ran as fast as he could back to the waiting car. Hopping inside he slammed the door.

"I got him nigga two bullets to the head let's get the fuck outta here!"

Chris nodded and peeled out of the parking spot. Lights were flickering on inside houses but no one had yet came outside to see what happened. Suddenly the car slowed down and came to a stop. D who had been looking all around them to make sure no one saw them looked around at Chris. They had stopped right in front of Devontay's house and Chris was staring at the still body lying on the ground.

"Nigga, he's dead let's go!" shouted D. Chris just turned to look at d and smiled.

"Not until I get my two cents in!" Turning around the hand gripping his gun came up and Chris extended it out the window pointing right at Devontay's still form. D instantly realized what was going to happen but the time to do anything about it had already passed.

"NO!" D yelled out! But it was too late. He saw Devontay's head lift slightly off the ground apparently trying to see what was going on at the exact moment that Chris yanked the trigger back!

BANG BANG BANG BANG BANG BANG BANG!!!!

D could only watch in horrified wide eyed silence as Chris sent bullet after bullet slamming into Devontay's body jerking it and making it jump with each impact. One well aimed bullet tore off a piece of his skull as it hit Devontay just above the ear. Chris was jumping in his seat and yelling out the window!

"CLOSED CASKET BITCH THAT'S FOR ANTHONY! DEUCE TREY!"

With that, Chris slammed his foot on the gas and tore off up the street.

"Yeah nigga we got that motherfucker!! Fuck FEB! Retaliation is law! Shit that was some shit nigga in over here perking! We gotta ditch this shit quick! Oh man did you see his head blow up? Goddamn!" So hyped up about the murder he had just committed, Chris didn't even see the expression on D's face as he raced through the dark streets. It was a look of pure unfiltered fury.

Chapter 33

The sand felt good between D's toes. It had been so long since he'd set foot on a real beach he had forgotten what it was like. Looking out over the never ending expanse of blue water in front of him, D watched the glowing yellow sun sinking lower in the sky. The waves regularly breaking on the beach pushed the water up the sand and around D's ankles. The cold water felt good on his skin. Turning to look behind him back towards the dry sand, D saw Breanna relaxing on large beach towel. She out her hand over her eyes to shield them from the sum and waved. D nodded and waved back. Turning back around to face the incoming waves, D once more stared out at the ocean.

He was glad he's been able to catch Breanna before she left. As soon as he had gotten out of the car with Chris, D had taken off running and hadn't stopped until he was almost downtown. He had walked the rest of the way to Queen Anne and arrived outside Breanna's house where he stashed his gun in a bush then went and hid in the garage. Luckily, Breanna had come down just a couple hours later to load up her truck and almost screamed when D popped out of the shadows.

He'd quickly calmed her down and explained that he'd changed his mind and asked if her offer to come to San Francisco was still open. Breanna had smiled and ten minutes later they were flying down I-5 heading for the airport.

D liked everything about San Francisco. There were people of color everywhere; Black's, Latinos, Asians and of course plenty of white people. After picking up Breanna's rental car they had driven into the city to the Sheraton they would be staying at down by the waterfront. D had fallen out exhausted on the bed almost immediately. He was stressed out and tired.

The next day had been spent cruising the city. They stopped in neighborhoods like The Mission, The Tenderloin, and Chinatown and spent over two hours cruising up and down Market Street looking at all the stores and people watching.

D fell in love with Market Street. There were groups of black people hanging out in front of various stores laughing, cracking jokes with each other and smoking blunts of some good smelling weed like there were no worries in the world. He had even bought a quarter ounce off someone for only 50 bucks! Deals!

Later, they had driven through the predominantly white neighborhood of Sunset and stopped by Breanna's mom's flower shop. She was a nice old lady with a great smile and extremely talkative. She had taken an instant liking to D and had eagerly shown him around her little store.

Promising to come by again, Breanna pulled D from her mom's clutches and hopped back in the car. Then they had driven to the beach. It was a nice beach. To his left the beach continued down to a large outcropping of rocks with the Golden Gate Bridge just on the other side. To his right the sand stretched on for another couple miles. Looking back down at his feet, D watched the water wash over them and play around his ankles before heading back out to the ocean.

A noise behind him made him turn. Breanna was walking towards him with a bottle in one hand a two glasses in the other. She looked amazing in a blue and white sundress. All her curves could be seen and D noticed more than a few men looking after her with list filled expressions on her face.

Breanna came up beside him smiling from ear to ear. D didn't feel the least bit like celebrating but he could tell Breanna was in a good mood and didn't want to spoil it.

"What you got there?" he asked pointing at the bottle.

"Champagne," said Breanna, "enough slumming it with cheap beer and booze. Tonight were kicking it suburban style!"

"Uh oh, go white girl, go white girl!" said D waving his hands in the air, "when did you get that? We haven't stopped at a liquor store all day?"

"Just now! You looked so peaceful down there looking at the waves I didn't want to disturb you. There's a grocery store a few blocks away so I just walked up there."

"You're sneaky."

"A little."

Breanna tore off the foil covering the top and pointed the bottle out to the ocean.

POP!

The cork went flying out over the water as she popped it out with a single smooth motion.

"What are we celebrating?" asked D taking one of the glasses Breanna handed him.

"To not being in fucking Seattle right now!" she said filling both of their glasses.

"Man I second that," muttered D. The two bumped glasses and fell silent.

Standing side by side they gazed quietly at the magnificent sparking Ocean laid out in front of them like a giant endless blue quilt covering Mother Nature's body as she slept. The last of the setting sun's rays danced across the surface of the water and flocks of birds tumbled and dove through the air filled with some sort of magical pre sunset energy as if they knew they only had a little bit of play time left before it was time to settle down for the night.

Despite the beauty of their current surroundings both D and Breanna's minds were consumed with thoughts of what they would face when they returned home.

D heard a sniffing sound next to him and looked over. A single year was making its way down the side of Breanna's cheek. Reaching out with his thumb, he gently rubbed the tear away. Breanna looked over at him eyes wide and scared looking like a child on the verge of a breakdown.

"Don't worry Bre,, Todd can't get you down here," said D. "Anyways remember what you said? You know what you gotta do. You're too good for that asshole and he probably knows it. But since he ain't even trying to do what he should do, you need to chuck up the deuces and leave while you still got legs."

"But what if Todd changes?" said Breanna. But her argument held no weight. She already knew the answer deep down inside. That's why she had come to California in the first place. To clear her head form the jumble of emotions it had become and finally decide what she was going to do about her abusive husband. In all honesty she knew exactly what she had to do. She just had to work up the courage to do it.

"Breanna, he's not going to change." said D. "I know people like him. Fools set in their ways and oblivious to the pain and hurt they cause others. People like that are why this world is so fucked up. They suck honest people into their webs and deceit and spit out more versions of themselves. The only thing that will come out of you staying with Todd is more blood from your body. You're beautiful Breanna! And cool as shit! Trust me you've got options even if you don't see them!"

Breanna smiled softly at D's words.

"Thanks' D. How come you don't have a woman? You sure know how make a girl feel important."

D fell silent as Chanelle's face floated into his mind. Her fierce eyes and her delicate cheeks and her wide happy smile.

"Never found the right one is all. Thought i did. But someone took her from me."

"Well can you get her back?" asked Breanna. D took a giant sip of champagne which drained his glass as he struggled to keep himself from picturing Chanelle's dead and ruined body.

"No," he said simply staring blankly out at the ocean.

Breanna reached out and gently rubbed her hand across D's back.

"I'm sorry D," she said. D shrugged.

"I'll be all right. Just give me a second."

Breanna nodded. Wiping a few strands of her hair out of her face, Breanna refilled D's glass then turned and walked back towards their blanket.

D stayed by the water looking at but not really seeing the sunset before him. He was thinking hard.

His one chance at making a difference and finding redemption had failed. He'd recognized Devontay as just another form of himself. One that fell a little deeper than he did but still they were one in the same. Affiliations and family ties had dictated Devontay's fate long before he had a choice in the matter. But had he really had a choice? Now he was dead just like Anthony. Another victim of Chris blatant disregard for human life and the feelings of others.

Of course Chris had thought Devontay was already dead. But regardless what kind of person would pump a body full of bullets after they had already died!

Chris was a real menace to society. A danger to anyone that might cross his path. Friend or enemy! D still remembered the day Chris had pointed a gun at him while sitting in the back seat of a car and threatened to shoot him in the leg.

His friend was a danger to both friend and enemy alike and to D the world wasn't meant for people like that. A nudge in the ribs from Breanna's elbow snapped d out of his trance.

"What?" D asked sharply looking all around him. Breanna grabbed his arm to calm him down.

"Whoa easy mister, I didn't mean to scare you! I was just trying to get your attention."

D felt guilty.

"My bad Breanna I didn't mean to snap at you. I just got some things on my mind."

"I can tell," said Breanna, "you had really mean look on your face like...like you want to hurt somebody or something."

D gazed over at Breanna. An adult in more ways than he was and not a novice to hard times. But her hard times were different from his. He had never really known how to talk to her about the kind of things he'd been involved in.

Gangs. Drugs. Hoes. He'd robbed houses and stolen cars in the same neighborhood Breanna lived in! But she was convinced he was a good person.

He laughed inside. How could he ever be a good person? Influenced by greed and destroyed by evil. But what was the evil? He looked over at Breanna who had been standing looking at d like a concerned mother.

"What would you do if you knew where the root of all evil was?"

Breanna looked surprised then thoughtful.

"Is it an actual root? Like in a garden?" she asked. D though about it and shrugged it away.

"Yeah sure why not. Do ya thing."

Breanna refilled their glasses.

"Hmmm…if I knew where the root to all evil was. I think is find it and destroy it! I don't even think that's a hard question to answer. What else would you do?"

D watched a seagull hovering above him on a draft of rising wind.

"What if it's not a root? What if it's a person?"

Breanna, who was about to sip her champagne, went very still. D was busy watching the seagull above him and didn't notice.

"What do you mean a person? Like Hitler or Castro?"

"No like someone we know. Good choices though."

Breanna was silent. She didn't know where d was going with this. But she thought she had an idea.

"I'm just saying. How long do you allow bad fucked up things to happen in the world simply because someone you know or love is the one doing the deed? How can you ever justify yourself as a good person while this is going on? How can you even justify yourself as a person?"

Breanna was looking down at the sand.

"I guess you can't. But what can you do except remove yourself from the situation?"

"True but what if you know they'll just continue to do the same to someone else whether you're around or not?"

Breanna looked over at D. You would never know just how caring and sensitive D really was just by looking at him. He was a constant source of amazement and inspiration to her. She didn't know what was making D talk like this but it was making her reflect on her situation with her husband. It was obvious he was struggling with some internal moral battle.

"I don't know D. The root of all evil? It sounds like the only course of action would be to do the world a favor and get rid of it."

"Even if it meant doing something evil yourself?"

Breanna thought about all the times that Todd had threatened, slapped, pushed and verbally abused her. He was every woman's nightmare and she had allowed herself to be his punching bag. Well no more. She now knew her idea of being able to change him and finally creating a happy home would not come true.

It had kept her from going to the police all these years but now she had no more scruples. D was right. She was just as much to blame as Todd for even allowing him to treat her the way he'd been doing.

"I think that your right about everything you've said T. The person who allows evil to exist is just as bad as the person committing the evil. I realize I've been guilty of that myself. As soon as I get home I'm putting a stop to it. I've been scared shitless to do it but I can't keep living like this. I might not be able to change the past but I can change the future. I won't let Todd hurt me or any other woman ever again! As soon as I get home I'm going to the police!"

D finally looked over at Breanna. Her words about not being able to change the past but still changing the future resonated around his head. He was impressed by Breanna. He knew it took considerable strength to be able to stand your ground against a close friend or lover. But it had to happen. Especially if it meant saving a life. D stared back at the water and clenched his jaw.

Suddenly, D felt a hand circle around his waist. Breanna had moved closer to him while he'd been staring silently at the water. The feel of her touch sent electric jolts zipping through his body. D turned to look at Breanna. She was staring up at him gazing into his eyes with a searching look. She pressed her other hand against his stomach and began tracing the outlines of his abdominal muscles.

D was completely still. He wasn't sure what he was supposed to be doing. He knew what he wanted to do and had imagined doing it countless times to her when he was alone in his room at night. But now that the moment was here, he was frozen and nervous. Slowly he dropped his left hand down to rest on the hump of her booty. He could feel her soft smooth skin through the light fabric of her skirt.

Breanna smiled. The hand that was rubbing D's stomach moved slowly down his torso and slipped down inside his basketball shorts. D's breathing sped up as he felt her fingers wrap around his member. She began to slowly massage and squeeze it gently. As he came to life in her hand, Breanna was thrilled and excited at the size D's penis. She looked up at him with lust heavy in her eyes and glanced around them. The beach was almost empty now as the chill of evening began creeping in off the water. She turned back to face D and before he knew what was happening Breanna had grabbed his right hand and pulled it up under her dress and pressed it against her pussy.

D was shocked! It was so wet down there he could feel her juices dripping down his hand and onto the sand. As he parted her lips with his fingers and slipped one inside her womanhood, Breanna let out a long deep groan of pleasure. Grabbing D's elbow she walked his back to the blanket still rubbing and squeezing him. They fell back onto the blanket and Breanna wasted no time in hiking up her skirt and pulling D's shorts down.

D looked around nervously but Breanna grabbed his neck and forced him to look back at her. Slowly, she guided him inside her, gasping as D's length and thickness filled her up completely. They stared into each other's eyes.

"It's ok. I want this," Breanna said, her voice thick with lust.

"Me too," said D.

He began his strokes long, slow and smooth. Breanna was instantly overcome with pleasure. Wave after wave swept over her body as D directed himself in and out of her with an almost mathematical precision. It was the same for D. Each time Breanna's tight warmth enveloped him he thought he would lose his mind at how good she felt. Pulling the top of her dress down, D watched hungrily as Brenna's heavy breasts were exposed and instantly began to massage and suckle them as gently as a feeding baby. Breanna threw back her head moaning loudly as waves of ecstasy washed over her body.

The sun's last rays turned the sky orange and yellow as it left behind San Francisco, Baker's Beach and two people locked in a lovers embrace as they attempted to find a brief moment of escape and pleasure from their respective worlds of fear and violence!

Chapter 34

It was all over too soon. After saying goodbye to Breanna's mom, she and D headed to the airport dropped the rental car off and took the shuttle straight the Alaska Airline terminal. Breanna hadn't said much the rest of the trip. She always seemed to be deep in thought and D hadn't wanted to disturb her.

At first, D had thought that she was regretting what had happened between them on the beach. But eventually that thought was pushed from his mind. Breanna would occasionally look at him with a warm loving expression and reach out to hold his hand. She would never say anything. But the small smile on her face told him everything he needed to know. If anything the feeling that D felt radiating from Breanna was gratitude.

Their plane departed San Francisco at 9:45pm and touched down in Seattle shortly after midnight. Breanna slept the whole flight her head resting on D's shoulder as he gazed out the window at the dark world outside thinking.

Breanna woke as the plane landed. Yawning and stretching her arms out, she looked around.

"Damn babe are we back already? That was fast!"

"Maybe for you sleeping Beauty but not me. My ear's been full of your snores for bout two and a half hours straight!"

Breanna gasped and playfully slapped his arm.

"I do not snore mister you take that back!"

D shrugged and tilted his head to the side.

"I mean man, I'm not tryna lie to you Bre, but it sounds like someone else might have! Your mom is a nice lady how do you know she hasn't just been sparing your feelings all these years?"

Brenna's eyes widened in mock outrage.

"You talking about my mama you little shit! I'm gonna kick your ass for that!"

The two play fought as the plane arrived at its designated gate. At the signal from the captain everybody got up grabbed their bags and disembarked. The walk through the quiet airport was calm and peaceful. The shops and gates were closed except for a few people waiting on a red eye or overnight.

D felt good about him and Breanna's little exchange on the plane. It had been the most they'd spoken since the beach. Breanna hadn't checked a bag and D had no luggage so they bypassed baggage claim and headed straight for her car parked in the overnight lot.

Breanna let D drive back. She said she was still tired from the flight. D piloted the big truck out of the airport and on to I-5 heading north to Seattle.

Breanna was silent again. Gazing out of the window her eyes were distant, oblivious to what was passing by outside. D finally decided to approach the subject he knew she was preoccupied with.

"Look Bre, I know what happened was unplanned and unexpected. I honestly didn't mean for that to happen…I just…I mean you just… and then…you feel me? It was just so quick I couldn't stop myself!"

Breanna looked over at D and smiled. This smile was different though. It was a smile filled with joy, lust, wonderment, anger, sorrow and acceptance. It was the most beautiful thing D had ever seen in his life.

Breanna reached out and grasped D's right hand which had been resting lazily on the shiny metal gearshift. She looked at D directly on the face and he turned to meet her gaze as often he could without taking his eyes off the road for too long.

"D never ever in your life regret what happened back there at Bakers Beach! I know I won't. You have been more than a friend to me these past few years. And it's not just that you hook me up with good weed for good prices."

D laughed.

"I'm serious D! All our conversations about everything under the sun really kept me going. I don't really have any friends. The ones I did have I neglected and lost because Brian didn't want me hanging out with them. You've been the only person I could talk to. Plus all those smoking sessions we've had! Oh my god those were some of the best times I've ever had. You kept me alive whether you know it or not. Believe me, you are the last thing that's bothering me. "

D had never known appreciation like the kind he was feeling for Breanna. It was like a confirmation that hope, while hanging by a thread was not entirely lost to him. But she didn't know what he was about to do. He might be a good person to Breanna but that's where it stopped.

"I hope you didn't do that because you think you owed me something. Because you don't. Your company was enough for me. And this trip is something I could never possibly repay you for! I owe you if anything."

Breanna just shook her head.

"Just keep being you sweetie that's enough for me."

They drove the rest of the way back to Breanna's house in silence. As the Seattle downtown skyline finally came into view, D felt the seriousness of his situation come back in full force. He'd turned his phone off the entire weekend so he had no idea if Chris or Money Mike had been looking for him. He figured he would find out soon enough.

Pulling into Breanna's garage, D killed the engine and both he and Breanna exited the vehicle. D grabbed Breanna's bag and they both headed upstairs. Breanna went straight to the kitchen and opened up one of the cupboards.

"Whew," she said, rubbing her eyes "I need a drink before I go lay down. Do you want anything D?"

D placed her bag in the hallway and joined her in the kitchen.

"Damn Bre, all these years we've been kicking it and I just realized I've never been up here before! Nice crib! Yeah I guess so. I gotta be out in a second. What you sipping on?"

"I got this Makers Mark I know you're fond of. I'll pour us both a glass?"

"And how about one for me too?"

Breanna screamed and D whirled around on his heels as Breanna's husband appeared out of the dark living room and came striding into the kitchen. His clothes were rumpled and his eyes were bloodshot. He looked like he'd been drinking for a while. His narrowed eyes traveled back and forth between Breanna and D. His hands were clenched in fists.

"And where the fuck have you been? Coming in here with a fucking suitcase and a fucking black kid who looks like he's some kind of wanna be gangster! Pouring out MY whisky! Where have you been all weekend? What the fuck is this shit? What are you some kind of hoe?"

Breanna looked too shocked to say anything. D was strongly reminded of the way Money Mike, Chris and even he had talked down to the young girls that had been working for them. But Breanna was no hoe!

"Eh man don't talk to her like she ain't a hoe!" D spoke up, anger overtaking his nervousness. But Todd instantly rounded on D holding up his cell phone and yelling at the top of his lungs!

"YOU SHUT THE FUCK UP YOU LITTLE NIGGER! WALKING UP IN MY HOUSE WITH MY WIFE LIKE YOU OWN THE PLACE! I'M CALLING THE POLICE RIGHT NOW TO COME LOCK YOUR BLACK ASS UP!"

"Todd no we were just..."

SMACK!!!

Todd backhanded Breanna swiftly across the mouth and she was knocked against the counter. Her hands flew to her mouth as she leaned against the counter breathing hard and looking at Brian with fear in her eyes. D made a move towards brain but Todd whirled on D and held the phone up again.

"Whoa there cowboy I thought I told you get the fuck out of my house! You know what fuck this! I'm calling the cops." Todd pressed two buttons and looked up at D.

"Just one more button," he growled fiercely.

D looked slowly from Todd to Breanna. She was wiping blood from her lip and trembling but there was also a look in her eye that D had never seen before.

"It's ok D just go. I'll be all right."

D highly doubted that but one look at Todd and D was convinced he would call the cops if he didn't leave. But he was reluctant to leave Breanna here alone. He was positive the beating would be begin as soon as left the house. But what else was there do?

That's when D remembered the pistol he had stashed in a bush just a few feet from the garage entrance! All he had to do was act like he was leaving. He looked at Breanna again.

"Just go D," she said pointing to the front door. "No need for you to get in trouble. Go on. Everything will be fine."

D nodded. Everything would be all right. He would leave. But he'd be right back!

"You have no idea how right you are Breanna." D said. Turning to Todd, he looked him dead in the eyes for a couple seconds then walked quickly past him and out the front door. Todd followed him slamming the door shut as soon as D had stepped onto the front porch. D stayed put for a second as he listened to the sound of Todd yelling and the occasional whimper from Breanna as he slapped her across the face again and again.

D felt his mind break as all his restraint left his body. Quickly leaving the porch, he ran to the bush where he had stashed his gun before leaving with Breanna for San Francisco. His eyes narrowed and his resolve deepened as his fingers closed around the cold steel handle.

He was making a decision right now that could possibly end in disaster for him but he didn't care. He was sick of evil people calling the shots and dictating the way others lived their lives. He couldn't be just a witness anymore.

Running back up to porch of Brenna's house, D stood in front of the door took two deep breaths and charged!

SMASH!

Running forward, D dealt the door a ferocious kick to the side of the handle and the door crashed open! D came striding across the threshold like a conquering warlord who knew victory was near. He was in the kitchen in an instant. Todd was standing over Breanna who was curled up on the floor attempting to shield herself from his punches. Todd whirled around.

"What the fu..." was as far as he got before D was on him.

CRACK!

Raising his arm, D whipped the butt of the pistol across Todd's face! Todd was knocked against the counter but D quickly grabbed the collar of his shirt and pulled him back to a standing position!

CRACK! CRACK! CRACK!

Three more times D hit Todd in the face with the butt of his pistol. Todd tried to fight back but his weak and feeble effort were no match for the youthful rage that had taken hold of D. Blood flew through the air and bits of broken tooth, spit and more blood were dribbling out of Todd's mouth and down his shirt front. He was sobbing and Twin Rivers of snot and blood were flowing from his nose.

He looked a complete mess. Nothing like the loud yelling macho man he'd been when he'd first found Breanna and D in the kitchen. D hit him one more time for good measure and Todd went limp. All the fight was literally knocked out of him.

D let go of his shirt and Todd fell to the floor. He was unconscious. D spit on his body then hurried over to Breanna. She was still on the ground in the fetal position. He fell to his knees on the ground and gently lifted her into a sitting position. She was breathing hard and she was spitting up blood but she didn't look as bad as D had first thought.

"Shit Breanna, are you all right? I wasn't really gonna leave you here I just had to run and get something. Are you hurt badly?" Breanna looked as if she couldn't believe her eyes. She wrapped her arms around D and he returned the hug.

"Oh my god thank you D! I'm okay. My stomach really hurts though. He knocked me down and kicked me but just kept yelling."

"Stay here I'll get some bandages. Let me handle this chump first."

Standing up, D went back over to Todd and kicked him hard in the side. He was still out cold. Binding his hands with duct tape he found in a drawer, D sat Todd up against the stove he wrapped his belt around his throat and tied it to the stove handle.

Returning to Breanna, D helped her up and over to the kitchen table. He fetched bandages from the hallway bathroom and fixed her up as best he could. Then he waited.

Twenty minutes later…

Todd woke with a splitting headache and a throbbing pain coming from his mouth. He tried to move but it became apparent his legs and hands were tied up. He couldn't move his head either without choking himself.

As his vision swam slowly into focus, he almost jumped with fright. Crouching directly In front of him inches from his face was the young black boy. His eyes were filled with an angry fire and Todd soon became aware of the pistol barrel that was being forced into his hurting mouth. He whimpered in pain but the angry eyes showed no mercy.

Sitting in a chair behind the boy was Breanna. Todd looked at her with his wide scared eyes but the emotionless stare he recovers from her told him she would not be helping him tonight.

"Naw don't look at her yet you fucking scumbag honky bitch look at me!" the boys deep voice growled.

Todd eyes slowly travelled back to the boy's wild and dangerous looking eyes and immediately pissed his pants. D's nostrils flared as the scent of urine suddenly flooded into his brain.

"Whoa wassup you bitch ass cracker did you just fucking pee? You did just fucking pee! Ah hell mane, you is one pathetic pussy bitch ain't ya? Breanna is this really the type of men you like?"

Breanna stayed quiet but the look in her eyes perfectly expressed the feelings she had about Todd's manhood.

D laughed and turned back to Todd. He took the gun out of Todd's mouth and wiped the bloody barrel on his pants.

"She's cold ain't she? Now listen up you sick fuck cuz I'm only going to say this once. You're a fucking piece of shit! You're a spineless, worthless, no ball having, not even half a man acting, no good woman deserving fuck boy looking, bitch made ass white boy!"

D punched Todd in the face twice to drive to point home.

"Please, please no more," Todd begged. The blood was flowing pretty thick out of his mouth by now and both his eyes were black and swollen. He looked a mess but D's sympathy was nonexistent.

"Yeah right no more. How many times did your wife tell you that when you were beating her ass bitch?"

SLAP!

"Owww!"

"Shut up!"

SLAP!

D grabbed Todd's chin and forced his face up looking him straight in the face.

"You are the definition of a coward. Beating up on a beautiful woman who dedicated her life to you. Moved for you. Bends over backwards to do everything she thinks you want and you treat her like she's less than a dog! What is it Todd? Dick to small? Job fucking you over? Andy got the promotion over you? So what? That's life Todd. What gives you THE MOTHERFUCKING RIGHT TO PUT YOUR HANDS ON THIS WOMAN!!"

D moved so Todd had a clear view of Breanna and the damage he had done.

"Look at her!" commanded D. "Look at her! You see what you have done! That woman right there is a woman the type of which few guys would ever get the chance to experience. I've known her for some years now and she always be talking about how she wishes it could be with y'all! Fool don't you know she's never plotted a thing on you! Never thought about cheating or even leaving yo bitch ass! She loves you to death even though it might be hers and what does she get from you! Nothing but punches and verbal abuse!

"Do you see how beautiful this woman is? And you wanna destroy it! For what? What could you possibly gain? You had a ride or die bitch something everyman dreams of and instead of play your position you went and fucked it all up! Would you do this shit to your mom's? Your grandma? I know your bitch ass had one! Think of them! Is this what they would want from you! Beating your wife like she stole something from you! A woman abuser! Wake the fuck up Todd! Look at what you did to an innocent woman!"

Todd was overwhelmed. The young man was unrelenting in his onslaught and refused to let Todd look anywhere but at Breanna and the bloody towel she had against her mouth. He couldn't close his ears and if he tried to shut his eyes the young man dug his fingernails into the skin covering his eyeballs blinding him and causing excruciating pain.

Breanna said nothing throughout the whole ordeal. Just sat and watched D deal out his violent brand of justice. Finally, Brian could take it no more. The liquor had left his system and his was now faced with the result of his demons and their consequences. With a shock, Todd had a flashback to a childhood memory of a scared boy hiding in a broom closer shaking with fear while his drunken father destroyed the house and terrorized his mother.

Todd was beginning to realize that the young black boy might kill him. Why else did he have the gun? Todd also realized that if he died tonight it would be on the same night that he realized the only real accomplishment he had been able to achieve in life besides cheat his way through college was to become exactly like the man he had most hated and loathed. All the fight left him and he broke out Ito horrible sobs of anguish and guilt.

D stood up. The gun in his hand felt refreshingly heavy and he was reminded that most of the bullets were still in the clip. He stared down at the whimpering mess of a man beneath him. Scum. Complete filth. A waste of space, air and every other life sustaining source that he was, Todd wasn't worth killing. When D realized he wasn't going to shoot Todd, he began to relax. Slowly the adrenaline left D's body and his breathing returned to normal. He looked over at Breanna.

"Is it all right if I leave you with this fuckboy? I might kill him if I stay here plus I really got some business I have to go take care of."

Breanna nodded. D went over to her and gave her a gentle hug. Getting up from her stool, she walked with D to the front door.

"So you gonna call the police or what?" D asked as he stood on the front porch.

"I don't know. I have some things I want him to hear me say first. Then I will. I decided in San Francisco it was time for me to leave and tonight showed me I decided right."

She was quiet for a moment then threw herself into D's arms. Caught off guard, D wobbled for a second before catching himself.

"Breanna what..."

"I love you D."

Her words silenced him. So genuine and from the heart they sounded that he was in shock for a second at feeling this burst of true emotion that another person had for him. He stood awkwardly for a second then slowly wrapped his arms back around her.

"I don't know what made you come back but I thank god that you did. I thought he was gonna kill me. Thank you D, I owe you so much! Everything you've done all the times you listened to me. I can't believe this you deserve a Medal of Honor!"

D laughed softly as he gently patted Breanna on the back.

"I ain't in nobody's military so that'll be the day. As far as that other stuff, you don't owe me anything Breanna. You've done as much for me as I've done for you. You just didn't know you were doing it. You sure you're gonna be all right? I'd give you this gun but I need it!"

Breanna looked down at his gun but didn't say anything. She just hugged D close and kissed him on the cheek.

"You've never told me what you do when you leave me but i won't bother you now. Just be careful ok?"

"I promise."

Slowly, Breanna turned around and reentered her house. She looked over her shoulder as she closed the door. D was already gone.

One hour later…

Two knocks brought Chris shuffling lazily to the door in sweatpants and a basketball jersey. He had got the call earlier today and had stayed awake all night to see what the fuck was so urgent. Opening the door with a blunt smoking between his fingers, he stared down at the person waiting on his porch.

"Waddup?"

"Waddup," the person on the porch replied.

"So what the fuck you want nigga? It's late o'clock out here man I'm tryna go back to sleep."

"You."

"What nigga?"

BANG!

Chapter 35

"...in other news tonight violence has erupted in the Central District of Seattle following the deaths of two teenagers over this past weekend. One was shot outside his house late Friday night on Irving Street and the other youth was killed in a similar fashion outside his house Sunday night on 23rd avenue and Marion Street.

Early reports from police indicate the aggression is centered between two rival central district gangs. So far this week there have been multiple reported shootings centered mainly in the areas around 23rd and Madison and 23rd and Yesler. Harbor view medical center had seen a steady flow of young gunshot victims coming through its doors. although no other fatalities have yet occurred the question on everyone's minds is with all these bullets flying through the air, how long before someone is fatally injured Gang member or not? Residents are worried and detectives have promised swift justice for those responsible for the deaths. This is Tricia Chapman reporting live for Komo 4 news."

"These niggaz don't understand D, they just don't understand."

D understood. All was lost. There was no other way to put it.

"I'm telling you D. These niggaz started a war they ain't ready for. I'm bout to tear this whole neighborhood apart until Trouble got nowhere to hide! He should've let us deal with Devontay from jump and this whole shit could've been avoided. But now, fuck it!"

The storm had broken. D was almost certain that he wouldn't make it out alive. It was a miracle he hadn't been shot dead already. Weed smoked wafted into his eyes as money mike passed him a half smoked blunt. They were riding around in a maroon SUV that money mike was borrowing from one of his women who happened to have an office job. His face was like that of an angry wolf and he even alternated between vicious snarls and a sound that seemed like it was half growl half bark! DMX would have been proud. Silent tears were streaming down his face but he constantly wiped them away.

"Mufuckas wanna kill my cousin! Fuck no! These lil niggaz been out shooting all week and ain't killed shit! I need to teach these niggas how to aim D there's supposed to be ten dead niggaz lying in the street by now! I need more niggaz like you D. I need you out here fam. You're the last one left out your squad lil homie these niggaz is killing us! It's time to take these niggaz out the picture entirely!"

D remained silent. He just hit the blunt and looked out the window. Money Mike took D's silence as a sign of the grief he was feeling. He patted D on the back.

"Don't trip lil homie. You took care of Devontay so Anthony god rest his soul is avenged. Now as soon I get word about who killed Chris we gonna get him too. But we ain't stopping there!"

D finally decided to speak up. He addressed Money Mike by his first name only.

"Look Mike, I know this shit sucks. But I mean, you ever thought of calling a truce?"

Money Mike just stared silently. D continued making his point.

"I mean what I'm saying, we killed Devontay. They killed Chris. It's even. Nobody else has died yet and nobody else has to. It's like an eye for an eye type of thing right?"

Money mike looked as if he'd been slapped with a two by four.

"D, you sound soft in the head! Ain't no meetings getting called to squash this shit! This is a fight to the death! Don't forget you're the one who started this shit so don't get cold feet now. You wanted to live the life well here it is nigga!"

D said no more. It was his fault after all. Devontay, Chris, all those kids who'd been shot this week, he was the one responsible for everyone suffering. What had he honestly expected to happen? A sort of "ok I got you and you got me ok we can all go home now" type of deal? He'd lost that gamble. Minutes later Money Mike came to a stop in a 7-11 parking lot.

"Aight then D be safe. I don't know what you doing over here in this bullshit ass white ass neighborhood but hurry up and handle this urgent business you talking bout. Call me soon as it's done!"

"It's just a customer man no worries. I'll hit u up soon."

"Hold up," came Money Mike's voice.

D looked around. Money Mike reached under his seat and held out a black pistol.

"This is the Glock I gave Chris. I'm giving it to you now since you lost yours. Keep it close and watch yourself out here. If they knew Chris was there when Devontay died that means they coming for you next. You understand that right?"

Tucking the gun in the waist of his jeans and pulling his shirt down to conceal it, D looked over at Money Mike and nodded.

"Aight then go on."

D nodded and exited the vehicle.

He waited until Money Mike had drove off before heading off down the block. Fifteen minutes later he was staring up a Breanna's porch. He hadn't been back here since he saved her from possibly getting beat to death by her husband Todd. D had almost never expected to hear from Breanna ever again. But she had called him today offer almost a week of silence and she had actually sounded like she was in a good mood considering all that had happened.

She had fist asked how he was. D had lied his ass off. Then she had told him to come to her house as soon as could. She had something for him. Since D hadn't bothered to obtain more weed to sell he was pretty much sitting on his ass all day listening to Money Mike throwing tantrums. Steeling his nerves,

300

he walked up the porch and rang the doorbell. What if Todd was home? D unconsciously fingered the pistol in his belt. It made him relax a little.

Breanna came to the door and opened it. The giant hug she gave D eliminated any thoughts he had of her being angry. She ushered him inside and into the living room. She offered him a drink and D asked for a beer. Bringing out two ice cold bottles they say down at the dining room table. An envelope and a thin suitcase lay between them. Todd was nowhere in sight. D looked down at the envelope then up at Breanna. She looked happy.

"Sooo what's up? You said come as quick as I can so here I am. I don't see Todd anywhere and you look like a million bucks! What's going on?"

Breanna set aside her beer and grabbed a hold of D's hand.

"Damien, I'm sorry if I interrupted something you had going on but this is very important. Major accomplishments have been made this week and I wanted to share the good news with you since without you they would have never become a reality."

D leaned back and took a sip of his beer. He felt happy for Breanna but his mind was clouded from the stress his current situation. He also felt slightly uncómfortable. He had beaten her husband up pretty bad. What if he walked in on them again?

"Bre, I already told you it's nothing. I owe you if anything. So what's so urgent? You acting like there's not a chance that Todd could walk up in here at any moment and start tripping again! And he might really call the police this time since he knows now not to fuck with me! Can we go somewhere else please?"

Breanna shook her head. She frowned slightly at first but then smiled.

"Don't worry D it will be fine. Todd won't be coming back here anytime soon so you don't need to worry about that."

D cocked an eyebrow.

"And why is that? He locked up? Did you call the cops on him?"

Breanna took a sip and shook her head.

"No. He left on his own. It was his idea and there wasn't any argument from me!"

At that, D stretched his arms out and leaned back in his chair.

"Well shit when's the party? You got a nice floor plan up in here we could design a crazy layout with DJ booth, lights and everything."

Breanna laughed and even D cracked a smile. Then he got serious again.

"So where's he really gone Breanna? And what are you bout to do in this big ass house all by yourself?"

Breanna looked down at the envelope for a moment then back up at D.

"That envelopes for you D. So is that suitcase. Both are from Todd. He wrote it to you before he left. I never told him your name. He told me he that the best thing that ever happened to him was that ass whooping you gave him. He said he'd never had anyone talk to him like you did. You humbled him D. And he was very grateful. Go ahead and read it. He wanted to show his appreciation."

D was curious. He stared at the letter for a second before reaching out and picking up the envelope. It was thick and slightly grey rather than white.

"Nice paper," he commented before unfolding the letter.

Dear Stranger,

I don't know who you are Breanna refuses to tell me your name or anything else about you. All I know is that apparently you've been the truest friend that she's ever known. For that and more I am eternally in your debt. It's too bad we had to meet the way we did. Everything you said that night was true. I've been a horrible excuse for a man and an even worse husband. Alcoholism runs in my family but I thought I could beat it. I couldn't. My job doesn't help either. I've been stressed and over worked so long i don't remember what a weekend even is. You helped me see what I had allowed myself to become. I've since chosen to do what I should have done years ago. I've divorced

Breanna and checked myself into a rehab clinic in New York.
I've left everything in her name. The house and everything in it,
the cars and all my bank accounts. It's still far short of what she
deserves but it will at least give her a comfortable life. As for
you, look inside the suitcase. It's all yours no strings attached.
It's far less them you deserve but it's all that was left over. I wish
the both of you success and happiness. Take care young sir.
You're a better man then I could ever hope to be.

Todd Wychamp

D looked over the top of the letter at the suitcase a few inches away. His eyes went to Breanna. She pointed at the suitcase.

"Go ahead it's not for me!"

D was suspicious. Putting down the letter, he pulled the suitcase towards him. It wasn't heavy but it wasn't light either. D was picturing something like a dead rat! He was sure this was some kind of set up. He unlatched the brass clasps that held the suitcase shit and lifted the top compartment up. His entire body went still.

"Uuhhh...wait." D was confused. He looked up at Breanna. She was smiling from ear to ear her beautiful white teeth on display for the world to see.

"Take it D trust me! He's not going to miss or need it where he's going. He wants you to have it there's no gimmick involved."

D raised his eyebrow but said nothing. He was looking down on stacks of twenties fifties and hundreds all lined up crispy and new. It looked like a lot of money.

"How much is in here?" D asked.

"$50,000," said Breanna proudly. "And there's this also." She got up and walked into the kitchen. She returned with a large manila folder. Come over to stand by D she held it out to him. "It's all filled out and completed. I hope they don't check to close because your writing voice isn't anything like mine."

D took the envelope with shaking hands and tipped out the contents on the table.

303

"Oh my god no you didn't!" D exclaimed. It was the Take Home graduation test Ms. Weathers had given him what seemed like an eternity ago. He picked it up and thumbed through the pages. It was all filled out! Every question, every short paragraph even the receipts from the museums that Breanna had gone too. Doing a quick mental check, D realized it was only May 16th! There was still a week left on the deadline!

Realization that he would now be able to get out of high school and be eligible for a job hit him like a thunderbolt followed by another equally hard jolt to the brain! Atlanta! With the money in the suitcase he had more than enough to pay off the tuition costs for at least a couple years! Robert Brown had assured him if he could come up with at least the first year he would find a way to finance the rest depending on his grades at the end of the first year.

D looked up at Breanna and before she knew what was happening he had leapt out of his seat and gripped her in a giant bear hug.

"Whoa shit D you scared the hell out of me!" said Breanna laughing loudly. D was so overwhelmed with emotion he couldn't respond. He just hugged her tighter. The weight of despair, hopelessness and barley contained rage seemed to lift from his shoulders as easily as throwing off a blanket. He had thought himself a slave to the horror that his life had become but with one act his entire life opened up before him in a way he had never thought possible.

D suddenly felt very strange sensation on his face. He had been shaking so much as he hugged Breanna and thinking hard about his newly acquired future that he hadn't paid attention to it earlier. It felt like something crawling down either cheek. Peering over Breanna's shoulder at a mirror hanging on the wall, D realized with a shock that he was doing something he had almost forgotten he was capable of. Something that perfectly explained the feelings of regret, shame and happiness flooding through his veins.

He was crying!

Chapter 36

Walking up the steps of Woodruff Library, D paused for a moment to gaze in wonder at his new surroundings. Everywhere around him were young black people on their way to becoming professionals in their chosen career paths. Aspiring doctors, lawyers, actors, scientists and countless other occupations he hadn't even heard of before.

Young men in suits strutted up and down the sidewalks and paths of the campus and women in everything from business attire to club outfits were walking around in the hot Atlanta weather! It was like a paradise no one had ever bothered to tell him about. An oasis where black people were co-existing without the threat of violence. So why did he feel so awkward?

D knew they were not the same kind of people he had grown up with and it made him feel nervous about approaching people and trying to establish new relationships. But he was determined to adjust. Every now and then D had spotted small groups of young men who looked like they belonged on a street corner somewhere.

A familiar comfortable feeling always settled over him when he saw them but all they ever did was stare and try to look mean. D wasn't concerned. He had learned long ago that either shit was going down or it wasn't. Simply looking mean wasn't enough to scare him. He stuck to himself mostly.

Adjusting his backpack straps, D was almost at the door when the familiar sound of a heavy bass system reached his ears. Automatically nodding his head to the beat, he looked over his shoulder. A dark blue Chevrolet box caprice was making its way slowly down the street known as the Promenade by all the college students and James P. Brawly by the city. Passing in front of the library and several dorms the street was a popular place for youngsters to come and congregate in an attempt to be seen.

Looking out of the window of the car was a mean faced young man with brown skin and cornrows. He and D locked eyes. For a moment the hostility that emanated from the other boys eyes almost made D throw up the Deuce Trey hand sign and about out some profane curse in the boy's direction. But he caught himself. He wasn't in Seattle and this boy wasn't his enemy. Choosing instead to sneer insolently at the passing car, D turned his back on the angry looking young man and walked into the library.

In the car, Kevin Smith flipped up his middle finger at the kid who had been staring at him. The kid only stared back completely unafraid and sneered at him. Then he turned around and went inside the library.

"Who the fuck are you flipping off cuz?" asked the tall man with an Afro who was driving.

"I don't know," responded Kevin, "some nigga that was looking at me like he wanted to do something! Stop the car Mac let me go see what's up!"

Mac glanced over at his little cousin and grinned.

"Calm down cuzzo you ain't in South Central no more. This is Atlanta! Greatest black city in the south! All the ass you could ask for and still there's more to be had! You best get out of that gutter mentality right now lil cousin. Focus on these niggaz and you gonna miss all these fine women out here!"

Chris looked unconvinced and briefly considered jumping out of the car. Mac must have sensed it because he quickly locked the car doors.

"Cuzzo, this is not the place to start banging on random fools. We have an opportunity here. A golden ticket to get with as many women as we want! Believe me this city ain't seen no west coast niggaz like us so we got to play this real smooth. Do it right and we could leave out of here with our hands in more pockets then just our own. But you gotta be smart! All these dumb ass school girls out here just waiting to spend daddy's money and guess who they gone spend it on?"

"Us?"

Mac grinned.

"You ain't as dumb as you look lil' Kev that's a fact. Now come on. It's about time I see this mall all them rappers be talking bout in their songs. Lenox mall is the name or something? Fuck it whatever let's just go get some broads!"

"Hell yeah cuz I'm down! Fuck that nigga let's go! He's probably a lame ass nobody anyways."

"Right!"

As Mac pressed the gas and the big car accelerated down the block, Kevin turned on the radio and twisted up the volume! He and cousin roared off down the street doing the shoulder lean dance in their seats and rapping as loud as they could along with Young Dro as the popular song blasted out of the speakers!

Epilogue

In the aftermath of the killings of Devontay and Chris, Money Mike launched an all-out war on Trouble and everybody involved or affiliated with FEB. The central district became a neighborhood under siege as the two gangs battled it out with each other and the police on a regular basis. It ended with trouble fleeing the state and Money Mike getting sentenced to fifteen years to a federal prison on charges of drug trafficking, conspiracy to commit murder and illegally carrying concealed weapons.

Latoya woke one morning to find a backpack with $10,000 in it and a note saying "I will never forget you or Anthony Jr.! Thank you and good luck in Texas!"

D's father Marcus returned home one day to an envelope that had been slipped under his door. It was a letter from D apologizing for everything he'd done and telling his dad that he wouldn't have to worry about him anymore. He left him $5000.

Breanna sold the house and everything in it and moved to San Francisco to live with her mom and help run her flower shop. Business is literally blooming and she is happier than she's ever been!

Todd is clear across the country attempting to rid himself of his demons at a clinic in upstate New York.

Ms. Weathers retired from her long career as a principal and started a nonprofit organization called " The Loving Corner." It is a place that At-Risk youth go to learn reading writing and math skills to help them achieve in school. She loves her job!

D went to Atlanta and with the help of Robert Brown was accepted into Morehouse College for the 2006 fall semester.

He chose to study psychology hoping it would help him learn how people's minds work and enable him to better understand why people make the choices they do. His specific question of "what drives a person to do evil deeds" is a repeated topic of interest in class.

Author's Note

Lost in Transition is my second novel and is the Prequel to my first book *Everybody's got a dream, right?.* They are all a part of a series of books I have decided to call the "Damien Trilogy". Each book takes place during different stages of Damien's life, specifically the ages of 17, 21 and 29. I chose to focus on these stages because they are where I believe critical evolution in the brain happens the most. I know very few people who have stayed the same throughout these years and it's fascinating to me to see how and why people grown and change over the course of the years. All of this change is due to outside influences and different people all have different experiences which in turn create the varying influences we all come in contact with. I chose to follow Damien's journey because his is so much like mine. A young African American man growing up in the age of a Black President, mass incarceration, debt, joblessness, soaring homicide rates, natural disasters, spikes in the divorce rate, cyber bullying and above it all, the contused praise and rush to achieve the so called "American Dream" that takes so many of us off of our chosen paths and into lives of greed, destitution, misery, and death. It's hard out there. For everybody. But we are the world we live in and the only ones that can change it is us. The people that walk the face of the earth today. Maybe by reading Damien's stories and seeing the results of his decisions will help clue people in on the seriousness of the lost state of mind we as a people are currently in. This is my way of trying to help. What's yours?

facebook.com/talesfromthatown

TALESFROMTHATOWN

@takeit2thamax

THANKS FOR YOUR
SUPPORT!!!

www.ingramcontent.com/pod-product-compliance
Lightning Source LLC
Chambersburg PA
CBHW031158020726
47499CB00002B/415